IMMORTAL CURSE SERIES ORDER

Book One: Blood Laws
Book Two: Forbidden Bonds
Book Three: Blood Heart
Book Four: Blood Bonds
Book Five: Angel Bonds
Book Six: Blood Seeker
Book Seven: Wicked Bonds
Book Eight: Blood King

Immortal Curse World - Short Stories &
Bonus Fun
Elder Bonds
Blood Burden
Assassin Bonds

Join the Immortal Curse Discussion Group for more
Immortal Curse fun!

A WARM TINGLING SENSATION TICKLED Leela's senses, drawing her to awareness.

Lips caressed her skin.

Her neck.

Her shoulder.

Her collarbone.

A moan teased the edges of her mind as heat shot down her spine. *When did I fall asleep?* she wondered, noting her revitalized senses. She felt rejuvenated. Alive. *On fire.*

"Shh," a deep voice hushed in her ear. "Just relax."

Balthazar.

Oh, how many times she'd dreamt of having him in her bed again...

Mmm, but now he was here, with one thigh resting on top of hers and a heavy palm claiming her abdomen.

She'd lost her shirt.

And her jeans.

Last night while kissing B, she recalled dreamily. He'd remained true to his word, taking her mouth until she'd fallen asleep.

There had been some light petting. A few knowing touches. But nothing over the top. Just a sensual embrace filled with unspoken memories and wicked intentions.

It'd been exactly what they'd both needed.

And yet it hadn't been nearly enough.

Which had been entirely the point.

"B..." The nickname left her mouth on an unexpected plea. She wanted to taste him. To kiss him. To devour him.

To make him reenact every detail.

Part of her realized this weakness stemmed from still being on the cusp of sleep, lost to that pleasant hour where fantasies thrived. She wanted to fall back into a dream.

Indulge the cravings of her soul. Revel in Balthazar's talented touch.

"You stole my memories, Lee," he whispered. "I want them back."

"We can re-create them."

"We're going to do more than that," he vowed, his palm a brand against her skin.

WICKED BONDS

USA TODAY BESTSELLING AUTHOR

LEXI C. FOSS

Wicked Bonds

Copyright © 2021 Lexi C. Foss

Editing by: Outthink Editing, LLC

Proofreading by: Katie Schmahl & Jean Bachen

Cover Design: Covers by Julie

Cover Photographer: CJC Photography

Cover Models: Dan Rengering & Lauren Summers

Title Page Photography: Xram Ragde/Marx Edgar Chavez

Title Page Model: Vlad

Interior Art: Phatpuppyart Studios

Interior Art Photography: RLS Images Photography

Published by: Ninja Newt Publishing, LLC

Paperback Edition

ISBN: 978-1-68530-048-7

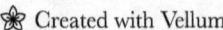 Created with Vellum

To Bella and Lola, I hope you're chasing balls and playing with the angels. Until we meet again over the Rainbow Bridge…
And to my readers, for your love and support. Thank you for making my dreams come true. <3

WICKED BONDS

IMMORTAL CURSE SERIES
BOOK SEVEN

WICKED BONDS

Welcome to the Immortal Curse world where angels and vampires exist in secret... for now.

A passionate affair of sizzling heat.
Forgotten and buried.
Because what happens in Brazil stays in Brazil.

That was the plan, anyway. Until Balthazar started to remember everything. Now he's forcing Leela to pay the ultimate price—by making her beg.

Every hot touch ignites her soul. Every smoldering glance makes her thighs clench. And worse, there's no escaping him.

They're on the run from a horde of warrior angels, protecting an innocent from a fate worse than death.

The High Council of Seraph has issued an edict.
Comply or die.
Only the faithful will survive.

GLOSSARY

PRETERNATURAL BEINGS

Fledgling (noun): The child of a male Ichorian and a human female, who has not yet been reborn as a Hydraian; they do not typically possess supernatural or psychic gifts until their immortal rebirth.

Hydraian (noun): An immortal offspring of a male Ichorian and a human female, who possesses two supernatural or psychic gifts and does not require human blood to survive.

Ichorian (noun): An immortal being of unknown descent who possesses one supernatural or psychic gift and requires human blood to survive.

Immortal (noun): A general noun designating a being who does not age and is immune to natural human death.

Progeny (noun): The term Ichorians use to refer to those they created through the Ichorian turning process.

Seraphim (noun): A being who belongs to the highest order of angelic hierarchy.

GLOSSARY

KEY TERMS

Arcadia: Notorious Ichorian club in New York City that also serves as the primary meeting location for the Ichorian government.

Blood Laws: A series of ordinances created by the Ichorian governing board in response to the Treaty of 1747.

Catastrophic Relief Foundation (CRF): A global humanitarian aid organization headquartered in New York City with a secret paramilitary unit designed to destroy rogue supernaturals.

Conclave: The Ichorian governing board.

Edict: A law or rule issued by the High Council of Seraph.

Elders: The original Hydraians who also serve as the Hydraian governing board.

Fated Line: Seraphim who can foresee the future.

High Council of Seraph: Seraphim governing board.

Nizari: Ancient Ichorian assassins who hunt and kill fledglings.

Nizari Poison: A green substance notorious for killing fledglings and preventing their rebirth.

Sentinel: A soldier in the CRF unit designed to slaughter rogue immortal beings.

Treaty of 1747: An armistice between Hydraians and Ichorians to cease fire and live in their designated areas. Those who opt to cross these boundaries do so at their own risk.

WICKED BONDS

INTRODUCTION

The Immortal Curse series is best read in order, starting with *Blood Laws*. However, I try to write these stories in a way that catches up readers—new and old—with current events, and I also feature one primary romance per book. So, in theory, it can be read as a standalone. It's just not recommended.

The recommended reading order for Immortal Curse is as follows:

Blood Laws
Forbidden Bonds
Blood Heart
Elder Bonds (Immortal Curse World Collection of Stories)
Blood Bonds
Angel Bonds
Blood Seeker
Blood Burden (Immortal Curse World Short Story)
Wicked Bonds

There will be appearances and chapters from previous characters in this story. Also, *Wicked Bonds* slightly overlaps with *Blood Seeker* at the beginning. You can blame B for that; he wanted his shower scene.

And speaking of showers, I'll leave you with one final cautionary note: this book is hotter than the others. Again, you can blame B for that. Andddd maybe Leela, too.

Happy reading!

Hugs,
Lexi

PROLOGUE

LEELA

WAR IS COMING.

I can feel the violence buzzing down my spine, the savage need to slay a tangible tickle against my ethereal feathers.

We've reached a point of no return. The prophecy will soon be realized. And all of us will be forced to choose a side.

I'm a Seraphim. My allegiance should be clear. But everything I've seen throughout my very long existence has left me conflicted.

My kind do not feel. They're stoic beings who make practical decisions, not emotional ones. Humanity means little to them. Humans are a burden more than a gift. Toys that die too easily. Beings far beneath their superiors.

As the daughter of the fertility line, I often find myself immersed in mortal nature. Sex fascinates me. Love, too. And I love watching humans fulfill their dreams.

That's partly how I've ended up in this mess, choosing a side no one would have expected. However, the Seraphim Council's penchant for destruction terrifies me.

They want to exterminate all of Hydraian and Ichorian kind. The immortal beings are seen as abominations because Osiris, the Seraphim of Resurrection, made them through his powers to re-create life.

And Osiris is an outlaw.

He was banished from the Seraphim nation, sent to live among the humans, as a punishment for something not even I understand.

So he built an army. An army he intends to use against the Seraphim. It's why he's spent the last three or four thousand years ensuring his creations have the best combination of powers.

Human life comes from Seraphim existence.

Which means every mortal is born with a natural skill —a skill that is enhanced upon rebirth into an Ichorian existence.

And when an Ichorian mates with a human, they create a Hydraian, thus giving the child two gifts.

Plus immortality.

Of course, Ichorians need human blood to survive, therefore marking them as slightly less resilient than their Hydraian offspring. Hydraian blood is also toxic to Ichorians, which is another fault in their programming. But Ichorians prevail in strength, age, knowledge, and the mere fact that they're the parents of the Hydraians.

For years, Osiris has pitted the two kinds against each other, ensuring only the strongest of both lines survived.

The Treaty of 1747 put an end to the battles.

But the angry feelings remain.

Which means we're in for the fight of our lives. Because neither side is going to want to work with the other, but the Hydraians and Ichorians are about to face a common enemy—the Seraphim—who want to kill them all.

Hence, I'm on the wrong side.

I should be fighting with the council, trying to take down all of Osiris's abominations.

Except, some of those abominations have become my friends. Family, even.

I've spent the last two decades protecting a prophecy. Guarding Sethios and Caro's child—*Astasiya*. Or Stas, as she prefers to be called.

Stas is our salvation. Our hope. Our future. She's power reincarnated, the daughter of two very powerful Seraphim lines, and her entire life has been molded by humanity.

She won't bow to the council.

She also won't bow to Osiris.

Our whole lives are about decisions, each one dictating our future path.

I've chosen to walk down mine, side by side with the very abominations I should hate.

But that doesn't mean I'll survive this fate. It would be so easy to be taken by the Seraphim Council and subjected to the infamous reformation. Without a true bond to tie me to these abominations, I would no doubt be reprogrammed, just as many Seraphim before me have been.

So this path is not without risk. It's terrifying. It's dangerous. It's deadly.

And it's officially intertwined with a male I have no business loving.

He's a Hydraian. Powerful. An Elder of his kind.

We played once on a beach. Engaged in a sensual dance. Spent hours in bed. Tasting. Licking. Fucking. I gave him a piece of my heart then. Perhaps all of my heart.

But I took away his memories.

My best friend, Vera, a Seraphim renowned for her ability to manipulate recollections within the mind, removed all thoughts of me from his memory.

It was fine. *We* were fine.

Until that same friend created a rune that weakened my natural resistance to Hydraian gifts. She did it to allow me to be healed after an attack.

And the alteration opened my mind to the very male I've been hiding from.

Balthazar.

He claims to know everything now.

All my deepest, darkest secrets.

I'm not sure if he wants to murder me, fuck me, or both.

However, there's one thing I know for sure now—our fates will forever be intertwined. The question is, will we survive it?

We're not meant for each other. We're not meant to love. We're not meant for anything other than destruction.

Yet a part of me hopes that we'll find a way to make this work.

To have and to hold.

In sickness and in health.

For as long as we both shall live...

CHAPTER 1

BALTHAZAR

CHAOS ERUPTED IN THE BEDROOM.

Screams.

Cries.

And a silence that was deafening to Balthazar's ears.

No heartbeat. No breath. No sign of life.

The infant… was dead.

Agony ripped through the air, the emotional wave so intoxicating that it nearly brought Balthazar to his knees. His ability to sense and control emotion, plus hear the minds of those around him, was debilitating in moments such as this. It hurt to inhale, to attempt to think, to fucking focus.

But a voice reached his ears.

One higher than the rest.

Filled with hope, life, and knowledge.

Leela.

He latched onto her thoughts, sucked in the underlying sensation of expectation, and clung to her existence like a lifeline.

Over three thousand years of experience had taught

him how to tune in and out of people's minds, how to ignore some emotions over others, how to exist in a world of perpetual chaos brought on by his supernatural abilities.

He stole a deep breath.

Exhaled.

Inhaled again.

And closed his eyes.

Lizzie's anguish and Jayson's concern created a harsh ripple of energy that Balthazar fought to contain and soothe. He'd assisted his best friend, Jayson, through the birth, helping him to remain calm as he held his wife, Lizzie. But when the baby finally arrived without any sign of life, the overwhelming despair from the parents had drowned Balthazar's intentions beneath an avalanche of uncontrollable emotions.

Leela's mind anchored him, her thoughts the only ones holding promise in the room.

She tried to calm the others, to tell them to let her focus, but they were too consumed with grief to listen. The frenzy worsened as Stas returned to find Lizzie in hysterics. Issac followed.

Sethios and Caro were behind them.

Too many voices. Too much pain.

But Leela's certainty overwhelmed the others, providing Balthazar with the leverage he needed to regain control.

His power lashed out, harnessing those around him and sending a wave of coolness through their auras, demanding calm.

Breathe. Pay attention. Think.

Because Leela needed them to quiet down in order to save the child in her arms.

She held the baby to her chest, her blue-green irises

swirling with power as she met Balthazar's gaze. He nodded once, telling her without words that he understood.

She frowned in response.

He knows, she thought, her words crystal clear in his mind. *But how is that possible?*

A flash of a recollection swirled in her psyche, one he'd been trying to understand for what felt like an eternity, but was truthfully only days.

From the second she'd misted into his life, he'd known that they'd met before. He just couldn't place the memory. However, trickles of information had bled into his mind since that pivotal moment, reminding him of Brazil.

It was a trip from only a few months ago.

One that had resulted from a dare between Balthazar and Luc. They were constantly at war over breakfast foods, a humorous nuance to the group, but a very serious debate between him and his fellow Hydraian Elder.

Waffles or pancakes?

Balthazar always chose pancakes because they were superior in every way, and he'd designed a game with Luc to test their little wager.

It had involved women, a beach in Brazil, maple-flavored shots, and the Seraphim standing before him now.

He was certain of it. *She was there.*

Yet his mind refused to provide the details he craved. All he could pick up on were glimpses in his mind, a recollection that had clearly been altered to paint the female of his dreams in a different image.

When he'd found out that Vera, another Seraphim, could alter memories, he'd known immediately that she'd fucked with his own mind.

Rather than press the issue, he'd waited as that same Seraphim had drawn a new rune on Leela's arm—one that made her susceptible to Hydraian powers. She'd needed a healer to help bring her back to life after being shot in the head. Lara had done her job, helping Leela back to full health just in time for Lizzie to go into labor.

And ever since, Balthazar had been toying on the edge of her thoughts, searching for that strand he knew existed.

He caught sight of it now as Leela fought to focus on the child instead of the startling realization that he understood her better than she should.

Sweet vixen, you have no idea how well I understand you, he thought, his gaze tracing over every exquisite inch of her stunning form. *I've absolutely tasted you before.*

And it killed him not to know when or how.

He didn't push too hard into her mind, not wanting to impact her current responsibilities. But he lurked inside her thoughts, listening intently for more information.

She thought about how he called her Lee in Rio de Janeiro—confirming what he already knew about having met her in Brazil. And the drink he'd made for her, the one he'd somehow known she'd favor, also linked back to that memory.

However, before she could tell him more, she shook herself and concentrated on the child.

You and I are going to have a conversation, little one, she thought at the tiny bundle in her arms.

As are we, Balthazar mused, aware that she couldn't hear him.

He folded his arms, waiting for more.

Starting with how not to freak out your parents, she concluded.

Balthazar listened as she reasoned through a typical Seraphim birth process. While Lizzie was technically a lab experiment—a being created to resemble a Seraphim in every way, including immortality—she wasn't a pureblood. But Leela appeared certain her child would follow the norm, which included not crying as an infant, possessing an insurmountable amount of intelligence at birth, and having a strong will to live.

Her mind explained to him that the baby wasn't dead at all; her soul had just wandered off into the abyss, avoiding the agony of a rather painful birth. The poor sweetheart had broken a few bones on her way out, the immortal birth faster and more excruciating than a standard mortal one.

All Balthazar's experience was founded in human biology, not Seraphim or immortal means. Hydraians couldn't procreate.

Except, apparently, with a genetically engineered Seraphim, as Jayson had just proved with Lizzie.

Still, the birth had been unlike any Balthazar had ever witnessed, leaving the infant in dire straits. Which had caused her soul to flee while her body mended itself back together.

Fascinating, Balthazar thought, his attention divided between keeping everyone calm and watching Leela work.

"She's going to be okay," Balthazar said, his emotional control tightening over Lizzie and Jayson as he attempted to placate them with words. "Leela's confident, which makes me confident."

Not a lie.

His faith in Leela was paramount, her mind granting him the confidence to voice his opinion out loud.

Which troubled the Seraphim a bit because it further proved he could read her.

And *that* scared her, confirming to him that his sweet vixen had something to hide.

Brazil, he knew. *You know what really happened in Brazil.*

He'd always felt uneasy after that trip, like something wasn't quite right.

Now he knew why.

You played with my—

Lizzie's rambling distracted him from finishing the thought, her fear spiking and forcing him to push another wave of calmness over her. She inhaled sharply, tears rolling down her cheeks. But her heart rate slowed once more, helping to keep her from going into complete hysterics.

"Did this happen to me?" Stas asked her parents.

"No," her father, Sethios, murmured. "But your situation was different."

"Seraphim souls can't perish," Caro said, echoing what Balthazar had already discovered in Leela's mind. "The body can die, but it'll regenerate."

Something Balthazar saw happening right now in Leela's arms.

He cast a swirl of reassurance over his best friend, urging him to comfort his wife, and Jayson started whispering soft words to Lizzie as a result. Jayson likely knew this was Balthazar's doing, an act he might comment on later, but he was helpless to obey Balthazar's emotional control.

It was what made him so deadly—he could read minds and manipulate the feelings of others. A combination of gifts that could yield lethal results, but Balthazar rarely engaged in his secondary skill. Reading minds was natural and not easy to turn off, whereas toying in others' emotions required thought and intent.

Stop exploring, little one. It's time for you to meet your parents in a corporeal state.

Balthazar fought the urge to smile at Leela's mental tones. She sounded so motherly, which he supposed was appropriate, considering her Seraphim lineage.

A fertility goddess, he mused. *I wonder what else you can do.*

They'd discuss it once she finished saving the child.

They would also have a long conversation about what had actually happened in Brazil. He wanted to know how many times he'd made her come.

What she'd tasted like.

What positions she'd favored.

How she'd sounded in the throes of passion.

What her eyes had looked like during orgasm.

How tight she'd felt wrapped around his shaft.

There were so many unknowns, both exciting and infuriating him. Because she'd messed with his mind, something he might never forgive her for.

Unless she apologized and explained why.

He also might be persuaded by her plump mouth wrapped around—

Come on, sweetheart, she cooed, distracting his sensual mind. *I feel you nearby. Find yourself and show me those pretty brown eyes.*

Apparently, Leela had seen those brown eyes prior to the soul departing the body. Balthazar took that as a healthy sign that the child would return.

He threaded that reassurance through his gifts, touching Lizzie and Jayson with a soothing caress. They hugged each other on the bed, Lizzie's dark red hair matching the bloodstains throughout the room.

Balthazar almost asked the others to help clean up, but he sensed in Jayson's and Lizzie's thoughts that they didn't care about the mess. All they wanted was their child.

There you are, Leela whispered a few minutes later. *Show me those eyes, sweet girl.*

It seemed the child couldn't exactly hear Leela, just feel her comfort and the warmth of her fertility essence. He picked up that fact in Leela's mind, followed by her intimate thoughts regarding her specialization in birth and fertilization… and *sex*.

Mmm, tell me more, he nearly said. But she was already thinking about satisfaction and how she didn't require it for survival—which would have likened her to a succubus—so much as she merely liked to fuck.

Which made him snort.

Because who didn't enjoy a good fuck?

Well, Seraphim, apparently. They were notoriously stoic and known not to feel a damn thing.

But Leela clearly defied those expectations.

He stepped closer to her, his palm finding her hip as he pressed his lips to her ear. "You and I are going to have a long conversation after this, Lee," he told her softly, the words meant for her alone. Then, louder for everyone else to hear, he asked, "How's she doing?"

Leela shivered as she debated whether or not to acknowledge his previous statement. He nibbled on her ear, deciding for her.

Because he'd meant it.

They *would* be discussing this later.

In great detail.

Whilst naked.

In bed.

Her mind flashed with memories of straddling him on a stool, her body heating against him in response. But it was there and gone too fast for him to detail the embrace.

However, it was enough to know that he'd been inside her.

And she'd thoroughly enjoyed it, too.

She shook her head, turning to face him and knocking his hand off of her hip. He merely met her gaze, allowing her to see that he knew. But he wouldn't tell her how much.

No, that wasn't how they would play this game at all.

If she wanted to fuck with his head, then he'd repay the favor in kind.

However, there were other, more pressing priorities at the moment, including the bundle of energy in her arms. *Beautiful darling*, Balthazar thought as he met a pair of stunning brown eyes. They were exactly as Leela had described.

"Well, hello there, little LJ," he murmured to her. "I see you have your mother's eyes."

The baby blinked at him, the intelligence in her depths confirming what Leela had whispered into his mind about Seraphim births.

He pressed a finger to the little darling's nose. "That's all Jay," he decided out loud, admiring the mix of her mother's and father's traits. "But the cheekbones are definitely Lizzie."

He couldn't help his smile, the sight of the little one warming his heart.

Her short fuzz of auburn hair seemed a little darker than Lizzie's, likely a result of her father's darker features blending with Lizzie's genetics.

"You're stunning, little beauty," he told the child. *Positively breathtaking.*

Little LJ—a nickname Balthazar had decided on prior to the baby's birth—studied him for a moment before puckering her lips.

Leela giggled. "Yes, yes. You need to bond." Her blue-green eyes met his once more before turning toward Lizzie and Jayson on the bed.

"Oh, she's alive!" Lizzie said after taking the child from Leela. Her surprise reminded Balthazar to pull back on the emotional control because the mother should have recognized that several minutes ago.

"I told you, she just needed to heal a little," Leela replied. "But yes, she's very much alive, and quite a survivor, if you ask me. She's also impatient. You exchanged power during the birth, but she needs a little more."

Balthazar recalled that power exchange, the act also differing significantly from a mortal birth. Truly, nothing about this experience could have been considered human at all.

Which made sense with everyone in the room being of immortal heritage.

"How do I do that?" Lizzie asked.

Leela guided her and told Jayson to help the mother sit up. Balthazar continued unraveling his emotional control while they worked, and he noted that Lizzie was already mostly healed as well.

There'd been concerns prior to the baby's birth about what to expect since Lizzie wasn't a pureblood Seraphim, but it seemed she had enough in her to guarantee her survival.

Jayson would be pleased by that.

Because it meant his daughter would be the same way.

Lizzie and Jayson murmured a few words about their child's beauty, working as a cue for Leela to slowly inch away.

Balthazar slid casually into her path, ensuring Leela moved right into his chest. He caught her hips, holding her back to his chest.

Another shiver traversed her skin, the ease with which their bodies seemed to move together suggesting an intimate history existed between them.

Because it did.

One he wanted to know every detail about.

I'm in so much trouble, she thought, making him grin against her ear.

"Yes, you are," he agreed, ensuring she knew he could read her mind. She hadn't seemed to put that together yet, as she'd been so caught up in healing. But that rune Vera had etched onto her arm allowed *all* Hydraian gifts to work on Leela.

Did I say that out loud? Or did he just read my mind? Leela wondered.

Balthazar waited, enjoying the pieces coming together.

Then she started, her entire body jolting as she realized what he already knew about the rune.

"I know everything," he confirmed softly, his arms sliding around her waist as he rested his head on her shoulder. It served to confirm that he would not be letting her go easily. "We'll talk later, Lee. For now, let's admire the life we helped bring into the world."

Balthazar had assisted with most of the initial preparation for the birth, his medical training marking him as a reasonable aide. Then Leela had taken over once the child had arrived.

Together, they'd made one hell of a team.

Leela didn't fight him, her eyes wandering over the party and thinking about how she'd gone through something similar to this twenty-five years ago when she'd brought Stas into the world.

Caro appeared to be considering the same memory, but Balthazar couldn't read her thoughts. He caught the misty gleam of her blue eyes as she glanced at her mate, Sethios, and back at their daughter.

Issac stood nearby, his own expression more emotional than usual.

Balthazar couldn't hear the former Ichorian like he used to, thanks to his recent bonding with Seraphim Stas. Now the other man's thoughts were all fuzzy and incoherent—a fact that delighted Issac to no end.

However, Balthazar was able to pick up enough

emotion in Issac's aura to know that while the male might not want a child now, he would one day.

Balthazar could see that truth in his sapphire gaze as he glanced adoringly at Stas.

Those eyes grew softer as Stas asked her best friend about the child's name—something Balthazar had already heard whispers of between Jayson's and Lizzie's minds.

"Aidyn Lee," Lizzie replied. "Aidan saved us both. It's only fitting she carry his name in memory of his sacrifice. And Lee after Leela, for ensuring we all survived."

Balthazar remained quiet but felt the overwhelming love in the room.

Luc would appreciate having his father honored in such a way.

And Leela… she was stunned by the gesture.

However, Balthazar wasn't. He'd felt her bond to the child during birth, then sensed her deepening that connection when she'd coaxed the little spirit back into Aidyn's body.

An unspoken vow remained between the child and Leela, one grounded in protection.

Balthazar understood because he felt similarly about the little beauty. He would forever watch over her, just as he'd spent millennia guarding her father and his fellow immortal brothers.

The Elders of his kind had an unspoken bond that included all those they loved.

Which meant little LJ was Balthazar's to protect, too.

"A fitting name," Balthazar said after Leela commented that no one had ever named a child after her before. It was appropriate, not just for Leela but also for the man who'd saved the tiny child's life while growing in her mother's womb. "Aidan would be honored."

"He would," Issac agreed, emotion thickening his voice. "Thank you for honoring his memory."

"We wouldn't be here without him," Lizzie replied softly. "It's the best way for us to remember him. It's also a strong name befitting our miracle. Our baby Aidyn."

Another heavy silence fell, everyone relaxing now that the crisis had been averted.

All because of Leela and her seraphic ability to connect to the child's soul.

Balthazar continued to hold her, thinking about her power, what it meant, and how she might have used it on him before. But in a sensual manner. *A fertility Seraphim.* His lips nearly curled. *A pleasure indeed.* One he would be exploring at length, just as soon as he had his answers.

If any of the others noticed that he stood with his arms around Leela, holding her captive, they didn't comment. Instead, Issac and Stas left with smiles for Lizzie, Jayson, and their newest addition. Sethios and Caro soon followed suit, leaving Leela and Balthazar as the last two standing.

"Call if you need anything," Leela said.

"We will," Lizzie hummed, all her attention on the baby cradled in her arms. Whatever power exchange was happening between them appeared to be soul-deep and intangible.

Jay glanced up at Balthazar, gratitude showing in his features. *Thank you.*

Balthazar nodded. He would do anything for his best friend and his new family. Jayson knew that.

Leela attempted to move, but Balthazar didn't allow it. He'd let her lead during the recovery, but now he'd asserted his position on top—a position they could negotiate once she provided him with the details he desired.

"We won't be far," he promised. "You know how to grab my attention."

"Thanks for calming me down," Jay said, surprising Balthazar. *Don't ever do it again, though.*

Balthazar almost smiled but nodded again in understanding, not agreement. Because he refused to commit to such a promise, not when they had no idea what the future held in store for them.

He straightened and dropped his hold of Leela's waist. He didn't quite trust her not to mist away, so he grabbed her hand and tugged her from the room.

The moment they reached the hallway, she considered misting, just as he'd expected her to.

He told her with his eyes that he wouldn't recommend it before dragging her down the hall to a room with an open balcony at the back.

It'll do, he decided, shutting the door and ignoring the blue-silk bed at the center of the large open space. Instead, he led her to the bathroom and took in the giant marble shower. *Yes, it'll do indeed.*

"Strip," he told her, deciding to get straight to the point.

"You can't intimidate me," she told him softly as she followed his command to the letter. No hesitation. No concern. Just a confident, beautiful woman ripping off her bloody clothes as though they burned her skin.

"I don't want to intimidate you. I want to take care of you and demonstrate my gratitude for what you've done for my best friend. Then I'm going to consider fucking you. And after that, we're going to talk. Unless you want Vera to alter my mind again?" It was voiced as a taunt, a way of confirming he knew everything.

Which he didn't.

But he wanted her to believe that he did so she'd be more likely to think and speak freely around him.

She stared at him. "I don't need you to take care of me."

"I know you don't, but I'm going to do it anyway." Because she'd earned his brand of comfort after everything she'd just done for his friends. He also suspected she was long overdue for some pampering, given that she'd been shot in the head shortly before helping Lizzie give birth.

"And there's no considering anything when it comes to fucking me," she added, ignoring his reply. "If I want to fuck, we'll fuck."

His lips curled. "I can make you beg."

"You can try."

"Oh, Leela," he said, stepping into her personal space and kicking her bloody clothes aside. "I'm going to make you crawl, baby." It would make for a nice apology after taking his memories away.

"That'll never happen." The words she spoke out loud didn't match the ones in her head, which were along the lines of, *Yes, please.*

She went on a mental tangent about Vera not doing a thorough enough job, further confirming that Leela had asked Vera to wipe his mind.

"You think what happened in Brazil was the best I can do?" he asked, hoping to trigger another glimpse of a memory. "That was just an introduction. By the time we're through, you won't even know how to move without feeling me between your thighs."

Her mind conjured up a memory of dancing and fucking in front of a crowd, rivaling a recollection that taunted the edge of his thoughts. He'd dreamt of that scene, the one where a female rode him on a stool and went down on him after making him come.

Fuck, that made him hard.

And the way her mind melted into a follow-up thought about him taking her for hours in a bedroom only made him that much more desperate for her.

The warmth trickling off her body, coupled with her stiffening nipples, told him she felt similarly.

Then her mouth confirmed it as she breathed, "Show me," in response to his promise to slay her ability to move.

"I will," he vowed. "After I make you crawl."

She snorted. "Then it's all talk, baby, because I'll never crawl for you."

His groin tightened, his anticipation mounting by the second. He brushed a soft, teasing kiss against her mouth, the electricity between them a hum of expectation. "Thank you, Leela."

She frowned. "For what?"

"For providing me with a new challenge," he informed her in a low murmur. *One I intend to win in record time.* "Now get your fine ass in the shower. I'll join you momentarily. And we'll see how long your resolve lasts."

CHAPTER 2

BALTHAZAR

NAKED. WET. FEMALE.

Three of Balthazar's favorite things.

Too bad he couldn't indulge in the stunning display before him now. He needed answers first. And he very much wanted to make this woman crawl before he took her.

She'd played a dangerous game in his mind.

She'd stolen his memories. Twisted the facts. Toyed with his sensual experience. Made him forget one of the most mind-blowing weekends of his life.

He didn't have all the details yet but understood enough from her hidden thoughts to know she'd altered one hell of a memory.

It unnerved him, the sense of someone else having played in his head. He was a mind reader, a being of immense emotional power, and couldn't stand the notion that his own psyche had been altered via seraphic magic.

"Hmm," he hummed, his gaze sliding over her perfect form. She was exquisite in every way—aside from her mental trickery, of course. But Balthazar could work with the gorgeous body standing beneath the showerhead.

The water darkened her long blonde hair to a light brown, the droplets teasing the ends before dripping down to her pretty breasts and lower to the flat planes of her stomach. Balthazar wanted to follow the tempting path with his tongue, kneel before her, and worship the goddess between her dancer-like thighs.

Her blue-green irises flickered with heated flames, telling him she knew her allure and power over men. She was a Seraphim with fertility powers—a fact she'd admitted out loud and also confirmed with her thoughts.

Oh, he definitely remembered her.

He couldn't say how or why, but there had been this inkling of familiarity the moment she'd returned to his life. One that had told him he knew her. Intimately, too. He just hadn't been able to determine when they'd met. Several thousand years of existence made it far too easy to forget acquaintances, but his soul had recognized her immediately.

And now he knew why.

"I'm tempted to make you re-create those memories with me," he informed her, his voice low yet carrying through the water raining down around them. He stepped forward, his palm circling her throat as he forced her to hold his gaze. "Down to every last detail."

It wouldn't be the same, she thought. *He knows who I am now.*

Balthazar canted his head, curious. "If anything, that would only intensify our connection."

"Stay out of my head."

"Not a chance, Lee," he murmured. "It's only fair that I read your mind and recover what you stole from me."

She considered misting—something she kept thinking

24

about doing—yet remained as though ensnared by his presence.

Balthazar told her with a look similar to the one he'd just given her in the hallway that he didn't recommend her following through with that idea. She might be able to teleport herself out of here, but he'd find her, and he would make her talk. Better to face the truth now than to prolong the inevitable.

"Why?" he asked. "Why did you take my memories of you?"

"Because it wasn't time for you to know me yet. I shouldn't... *we* shouldn't..." She trailed off and cleared her throat. "I'm here to protect Stas. Nothing else."

Her mind immediately contradicted her words.

He studied her as the memory peeked at him, reminding him of a day he wouldn't soon forget.

Lizzie and Jayson's wedding reception on the beach. Attacked by Jonathan's men. An enigma dancing between Balthazar and the lethal bullets destined to kill him.

He arched a brow. "I see." That certainly wasn't a memory he desired to replicate, but it told him a great deal about her intentions. She might be here for Stas, but it'd been his life Leela had saved that day. His ability to manipulate emotions told him how she felt about it, too.

Protective.

Like he belonged to her.

And it was duty to keep him alive.

For Stas, she added. *He's a good guardian for Stas.*

Balthazar's lips curled. "And that's the only reason, hmm?"

"Stas is what matters," she reiterated. "Her legacy trumps everything else."

The whispers of a prophecy hummed through her thoughts, grabbing his attention. *An unknown power is surfacing. She will possess the strength and will to destroy us all unless certain measures are put in place to curb her inclinations.*

Balthazar hadn't heard the exact wording of Prophetess Skye's premonition before, but he committed it to memory now.

Being a mind reader definitely had its perks, such as being able to interrogate someone whilst naked in a shower and capture all the answers he required without drawing a speck of blood. It was why he believed in making love over harming others.

There was a time and a place for violence.

But all that pent-up aggression could be used for other means entirely.

And he certainly preferred those latter methods.

He drew his fingers through her damp hair and walked her into the tiled wall at her back. She grabbed his hips, her nails biting into his skin as he pressed his groin to her flat belly.

"I promised to take care of you," he reminded her softly.

She'd just finished delivering and saving his best friend's child. It was one of the primary reasons Balthazar had chosen this method of interrogation. Not only did she need a shower to remove the blood from the birth, but she also deserved his gratitude after everything she'd sacrificed.

Not just in protecting Stas or saving Balthazar's life at the beach that day.

But in what she'd just gone through to coax Jayson and Lizzie's child back into existence.

Balthazar had heard every word, every whisper of a thought, and then he'd felt her fertility energy drawing the seraphic soul back to its corporeal infant form. It'd been magnificent, heartbreaking, and beautiful all at the same time.

However, she'd left her mind vulnerable throughout the experience.

And he'd taken full advantage.

That might make him an asshole, but she was the one who had stolen his memories. It only seemed fair for him to retrieve them in kind.

He just hadn't expected to find that many recollections involving his name.

They weren't clear by any means, just high-level details that she stored in the outer layers of her mind, thus suggesting she thought of him often.

He rather liked that development. It helped put him at ease in a way because she'd captivated his focus when she'd arrived shortly after Stas's death.

Leela shivered as he shifted to retrieve a bottle of shampoo, her irises spinning with a flurry of emotion.

Lust. Fear. Acceptance. Desire.

It was an intoxicating blend that taunted his own senses, stoking a flame within him that burned entirely for her. He couldn't remember the last time a female had done this to him. He loved women, men, sex, living life. It was all natural to him.

But something about Leela enthralled him in a manner many others hadn't.

An impressive feat, considering his several thousands of years of existence.

Perhaps there's more she's hiding, he marveled as he combed the shampoo through her hair. He'd uncovered Brazil from her thoughts, but maybe they'd met prior to that, which could explain the bizarre connection he felt to her.

"When did we first meet?" he asked her, carefully listening to the answer in her mind rather than the one that graced her lips.

"The first time I ever spoke to you was in Brazil," she said.

Her mind confirmed that to be true. However, it also clued him in to another secret. "But that's not the first time you saw me."

"No. I've been aware of you for… a while."

"Oh?" He cocked a brow, amused. "Are you a fan of my work, Leela? Is that why you sought me out?"

She snorted. "I didn't search for you," she told him. Her thoughts immediately verified the statement as true. "And being a fan suggests I envy something about you. Which I don't."

"Being a fan doesn't equate to envy. It suggests excitement. Intrigue. A desire to learn more, perhaps." He pulled her back beneath the water while he spoke, waiting for her thoughts to confirm his suspicion.

But they didn't.

Yes, there was some interest—enough that she'd indulged him in Brazil. But not because she'd longed to experience his prowess.

No.

She'd allowed their playtime purely because she'd wanted to see if he could keep up.

Fascinating.

He'd never met a woman who considered herself his equal, let alone his better.

"I really am going to make you re-create those memories with me," he decided out loud.

"Maybe I don't want to re-create them."

He merely looked at her. Her thoughts told him it was a lie before she even finished speaking, and the pretty blush on her cheeks told him she knew it, too.

Rather than push for more, he focused on rinsing her hair, then repeated his actions with the conditioner before grabbing a bar of soap. She might have betrayed his mind, but she still deserved this show of affection.

He could hear her confusion.

Because she knew he wasn't happy with her.

Balthazar didn't really embrace anger. Although, he could admit, he wanted to punish this female for the violation inside his mind. She'd stolen his memories, manipulated his recollections, and hadn't told him the truth after meeting again.

"Were you ever planning to tell me?" he wondered out loud.

But her eyes told him the answer before her mouth did. *No.* "Why would I?" she asked.

"Because it's wrong to take someone's memories from them, Leela."

"I did it to protect you."

"Lie. You did it to protect yourself." She could at least admit that to him. He'd heard it in her mind.

"I did it to protect *us*," she amended. "You couldn't know about me. Not yet."

"What would it have changed?"

"Potentially everything."

Balthazar considered that as he began soaping up every inch of her. Most females would be hot and bothered by the mere stroke of his caress, but Leela proved more challenging. Oh, she was aroused. He could practically taste it as he knelt to work on her legs.

But she wasn't begging.

Nor did she appear to be all that expectant.

She knew he wanted her to grovel, and he could hear in her mind that she had no intention of even apologizing for what she'd done.

Her lack of remorse bothered him immensely. She'd fucked with his mind, distorted his memories, and couldn't even be bothered to provide him with an apology. He could hear it in her thoughts how much she didn't regret it, how she knew it was the right thing to do, but not once did she consider talking to him or letting him decide his own path.

She'd chosen *for* him.

Because she clearly didn't trust him.

Which was an effective way to kill the lust burning between them because Balthazar didn't play with females who held him in such low regard.

Maybe they wouldn't re-create those memories after all.

He stood and set the soap to the side before working on his own hair.

Most conquests in this situation would fantasize about him openly.

Not Leela.

Her mind shifted between the past and the future, mingling a bit with the present, and what would come next.

There were undertones of interest, her eyes naturally following his hands when he picked up the soap again to lather himself, but she didn't fantasize about taking over or licking him clean. Instead, she merely admired the view while considering how best to protect Lizzie and Jayson's child.

The High Council of Seraph will be coming now, she was thinking. *We can't hide here forever.*

"Where do you want to go?" Balthazar asked, not bothering to hide his ability to read her thoughts. It often bothered those around him, typically inspiring snarky remarks or thoughts. But Balthazar wouldn't apologize for his talents. Nor would he hide them.

"I don't know," she replied, her voice and thoughts

void of irritation. If anything, she seemed to accept his ability as a norm. Perhaps because she'd been raised among powerful beings, thus making his mind reading a natural experience.

And if that's the case, then she's likely adopted some tricks to hide as well, he mused, allowing his gaze to run over her gorgeous body once more.

So far, I'm unimpressed, he heard her say, the twinkle in her gaze as he returned his eyes to hers suggesting she'd meant for him to hear it. *Brazil seems to have been the best you can do.*

He hummed in amusement, stepping toward her and backing her into the wall once more. She shivered, her nipples stiff little peaks that taunted his chest as he aligned their bodies in an intimate kiss. "You can't distract me with sex, Lee."

Her fingernails trailed up the sides of his thighs, her touch knowing. "We both know that's not true." Her touch slipped to his lower back and down to his ass, where she brazenly squeezed. "You wanted to re-create the memories, right? We're going to need a dance floor and a stool for that."

She started describing the scene in her head, painting a picture of the first time they'd met on the beach. Balthazar listened, the conversation one he remembered. But it hadn't been with Leela. He'd spoken to another female, an enigma he'd dreamt of for months.

A woman without a face.

A fantasy he'd merely enjoyed without considering too heavily.

But as Leela recounted more of their conversation, telling him how it had led to them joining Luc to observe his maple shot challenge. "I remember that…" But it hadn't been quite the same way she described it now. "I took one of those brunettes back to my room for the afternoon."

Leela shook her head. "No. You didn't." She almost sounded sad. However, he heard the conviction in her mind, the one that told her she'd removed these memories for a reason.

To protect him.

To protect us.

To protect Stas.

Balthazar cupped her cheek, his thumb drawing a sensual line across her bottom lip. "You're wrong, Lee," he whispered.

"I'm not."

"You are," he countered. "You could have trusted me."

She shook her head, her lips parting on an argument he didn't want to hear. *I barely knew you. We were never meant to meet. It was a mistake.*

All those thoughts fought for purchase in her mind, each statement true to an extent.

And yet... "You didn't even give us a chance, Lee."

"A chance?" she repeated incredulously. "Don't insult my intelligence. Neither of us is the relationship type, Balthazar."

"I meant us, as in the Elders," he corrected her, his lips curling. "But good to know where your head is at."

She rolled her eyes. "You already know, *mind reader*."

"Mmm, I do," he agreed, leaning even more into her and ensuring she could feel every inch of his interest pressed up against her. "And you know where mine is, too."

Blue flames licked a dangerous path around her pupils, overtaking the green in her irises. "I expected you to be angry."

"I am angry," he admitted softly. "Very, very angry."

She'd fucked with his mind. He didn't take kindly to that.

However, having access to her thoughts helped him understand why she'd done it.

That didn't mean he was okay with her actions. No, he intended to make her pay for them in a way that gratified them both.

But he still wanted her to admit that she was wrong to erase the memory of their time together.

Then he wanted her to beg for more.

To implore him to make new memories.

To apologize with her pretty lips wrapped around his cock.

He angled her face upward, his mouth hovering a scant inch from hers. "You're going to crawl for me, Lee," he vowed, repeating the words he'd said to her before dragging her into this shower. "You're going to crawl and beg me to fuck you. But I won't give in. Not until you truly want it. And even then, we'll see."

"I won't crawl for you," she countered, her voice holding a conviction that escalated the stakes between them. "I don't crawl for anyone."

"You will for me," he promised her.

"I won't apologize, Balthazar."

"I wasn't asking for an apology, Leela," he countered, his lips skimming hers. "I was merely promising to make you beg for another night in my bed."

She smiled. "What makes you think I want another one?" she asked. "I remember every minute of our last session."

His own lips curled in response. "Which is how I know you'll be begging me for more." Because while he couldn't recall the details, he heard the overwhelming satisfaction in her mind. Those memories had kept her up late at night, her body aching to be sated by another as skilled as him.

"Only in your dreams," she replied sweetly.

"You would know," he returned.

He captured her mouth before she could reply, his tongue slipping with ease between her beautiful lips to dip inside and provide her with a sensual reminder of his prowess.

Her nails bit into his ass, holding him to her as he devoured her in a manner that felt all too familiar to him. He'd *definitely* kissed her before. He could feel it in his very soul. Just like he'd known her from the moment she'd reappeared in his life.

Little snippets had fallen into place.

A smile he'd seen in a dream.

A voice that had made him hard without any foreplay.

A body built for sin.

His instincts took over, driving his actions, dominating her senses, and consuming his own at the same time. Heat sizzled through his veins, his desire mounting with each passing second.

Only it wasn't just *his* need he sensed, but hers.

His ability to sense and manipulate emotions went up in flames as Leela's lust hit him square in the groin.

But he could hear her intent.

She wanted to break his conviction before this game even started.

Sweet vixen, he thought, amused by her antics.

The Seraphim was built for this match, more than prepared to fight his sensuality with a healthy dose of her own.

He groaned, the pure intoxication of it all drowning him in a sea of yearning unlike any he'd ever experienced before.

This female oozed sex.

A master of sensuality and grace.

She knew exactly how to play him, too.

Her nails proved it as she drew a sensuous line across his backside to his hip, her intent evident in the trajectory of her path. But he caught her wrist before she could reach her goal. He allowed her a graze of a finger against his shaft, then pulled her hand over her head to pin it to the wall.

Balthazar repeated the action with her opposite wrist, successfully capturing her in front of him, their wet bodies slick and ready against each other.

"I'm not that easy, baby," he said against her mouth. "I take my challenges very seriously." Something she should know after having met him in Brazil.

"What makes you think I want to play?"

"Oh, little vixen," he murmured, his lips grazing hers. "You started this game when you altered my memories, and then you upped the ante when you didn't come clean the moment we met again. So don't feign innocence with me, Lee. We both know that's not your role in this game."

She swallowed, her pupils dilating.

"I won't crawl," she repeated.

"You will," he promised, grinning against her mouth before releasing her and taking a step back. "Now tell me about the High Council of Seraph. What do you think they're going to do next?"

Chapter 3

Leela

Balthazar's swift topic change made Leela's head spin.

One minute, he had her pinned to the shower wall with a hot promise pressed up against her lower belly, and the next, he observed her with a clinical expression. She blinked, startled. Then glanced down to find him still hard and very ready for more.

Which meant this was a demonstration of restraint.

Because he wanted her to beg.

Fine.

She would just have to show him what he was missing.

Except his comment hung heavy in her mind. "*What do you think they're going to do next?*"

"The Fates would have predicted Aidyn's birth," Leela said, thinking out loud. "The council is probably meeting now to determine her fate. It may…" She trailed off, swallowing. "It may be enough to finally push them over the edge."

"Over the edge?" he repeated.

"Into war," she whispered, her desire wilting with each

passing second. "Hydraians and Ichorians are abominations—beings that were created through an abuse of power by the Seraphim of Resurrection. The council wants all of you dead."

They just hadn't acted on it yet, waiting for the right time to intervene.

The High Council of Seraph never moved quickly with their decisions. They were practical to a fault, waiting for the precise moment in history that they should insert themselves into a situation.

And they relied on the Fates to tell them when.

"Everything they do is driven by the seers of my kind," Leela continued. "If the Fates predict anything nefarious where Aidyn is concerned—such as the ability to make more Seraphim in a lab, similar to Lizzie—the council may decide it's finally time to clean up Osiris's mess."

Clean up, meaning *kill them all.* Because the High Council of Seraph wouldn't attempt to reform anyone; they'd just slaughter the abominations and move on.

The only reason they hadn't intervened yet was because of the Fates.

It's not time yet.

To involve ourselves now is premature.

There is still hope that Osiris will reform.

Leela had overheard the whispers of those prophecies outside the chamber walls. She and Vera took turns spying on the council meetings, hiding in a nook on the outskirts of the coliseum where voices carried and no one ever looked.

Seraphim would never see spying on a council meeting as practical.

Because the notion that a Seraphim would go against her own kind was inconceivable.

Why would anyone question the council? They were

founded in logic and purpose. Of course, they put the best interest of the Seraphim first and foremost in their decisions. To do otherwise would be unreasonable and serve no greater purpose.

But that was precisely the sort of ingrained logic that caused her kind to turn a blind eye to the truth.

The High Council of Seraph is corrupt.

She could still remember the first time she'd had that realization. It'd been after spending several centuries around humans, learning about their proclivities for war, sex, and violence. But as she'd watched the politics unfold throughout the years, she'd realized how it applied to her homeland. How the Seraphim Council used logic and practicality as a way to keep the angels in line.

It was strategic. Beautiful. Cunning. And dangerous.

The more Leela understood, the more she feared for her existence.

She was already heavily monitored for signs of humanity due to her ties to the fertility line of Seraphim. Her entire purpose for existing revolved around caring for others, marking her as at risk for experiencing emotions.

The council had programs in place to curb those sensitive inclinations.

Reformation.

Which Caro had just escaped from.

Leela didn't know much about the requirements or what went into the process because she'd never experienced it herself. However, she'd seen what it had done to others.

And yeah, no, thanks, she thought.

It was part of the reason she kept her emotional side a secret. But she suspected the council already knew. They had a team of seers—*the Fates*—and Leela notoriously preferred to live among the mortals. The latter served as a dead giveaway regarding her emotional state.

Fortunately, they hadn't chosen to pursue correction in the matter.

Perhaps because the Fates hadn't foreseen any threat related to Leela.

Or, more likely, because the council couldn't track her.

"Why can't they track you?" Balthazar asked, his gaze unapologetic. He'd clearly been listening to everything she'd been thinking, including her knowledge of the council and how she preferred humans over Seraphim company.

Rather than respond out loud, she turned to show him the rune on her backside. It was a heart, just like the one Caro had given her daughter. It helped hide Leela's whereabouts, allowing her to be a proper guardian for the daughter in question—Stas.

I received the mark when I pledged fealty to Stas, Leela explained, not bothering to shy away from Balthazar's natural ability to read minds. She'd fix that as soon as she removed the charm Vera had etched into her skin.

"Or you could keep it," Balthazar suggested, grabbing her hips to stop her from rotating toward him again. "I rather like your mind," he whispered, his lips against her ear now. "It's fascinating, Lee."

His warmth wrapped around her as he pressed his chest to her back and his groin to her ass.

Mmm, she hummed to herself, indulging in the way they naturally fit together. His strength married her curves in a sensuous harmony that set her blood on fire.

His lips skimmed her neck, pausing at her pulse. She knew what he would feel, the escalation of her need, the desire thrumming through her veins, the craving to finish what they'd started all those months ago.

That experience had been memorable in more ways than he could imagine.

"Tell me about it," he murmured, his breath a sensual kiss to her senses. "How many times did I make you come, Lee?"

She shivered in response, her thighs clenching as she recalled what he'd felt like inside her. Hot. Thick. *Perfection*.

A moan caught in her throat, the memory of their first kiss assaulting her mind. He'd tugged her into his arms with a confidence that had called to her very soul.

"No, sweetheart," he'd said, responding to her teasing about his typical approach to courtship. "I don't have an approach."

"Yeah?" Leela had replied, grabbing his bare shoulders and meeting his gaze directly. "And why is that?"

He'd palmed her ass and cradled the back of her neck before replying, "Because I don't require one."

Then he'd taken her mouth with a boldness that she felt in his touch now, his self-assurance one of her favorite traits about him.

Balthazar knew how to tease, how to fuck, how to ensure gratification for all parties involved over and over again. She'd watched him perform several times over the last few months.

And each time, she'd indulged in the memory of their shared experience, bringing herself pleasure at the mere thought of his touch and tongue.

He grinned against her neck, his tone soft as he said, "Voyeur."

But she felt the evidence of what that admission did to him. Sensed the hardness against her backside and knew he *liked* that she'd watched him.

She'd suspected he would, had fantasized about what he'd do when he found out. Those fantasies had led to ecstasy and enhanced need. However, there hadn't been time to properly sate herself.

These last few months had been a whirlwind of protecting Stas.

"Yet you found time to spy on me." Balthazar uttered the words in a voice that promised sex, his grip on her hips tight. "Fascinating."

She really wanted to shove him out of her head, to keep him from hearing these secrets.

"Liar," he accused, his tongue tracing the shell of her ear. "I think you wish I would have heard your thoughts while you watched."

She swallowed, refusing to admit that out loud.

However, it wasn't needed.

He could hear the truth in her mind.

"Would you have wanted to join?" he asked softly. "Or was the fantasy for me to finish, find you, and indulge in a new round?"

Both, she thought, squirming. She'd pictured both avenues of that fantasy, preferring the latter more than the former. Because his prowess always won out, giving her the best of him after warming up with the others.

His teeth skimmed her throat, his hardness a beacon at her back that she longed to touch. But he held her effortlessly in place, forcing her to keep her focus on the wall.

Men frequently tried to dominate her, to take control, to prove their sexual worth over her own. She usually laughed, allowed them to try, and then taught them a lesson in bed.

Except Balthazar was different. His confidence came from a place of worth, cemented in experience and bolstered by his compassion.

He meant his sensual threats.

He always followed through.

He also possessed the ability to play this game just as well as she did.

Which only made it that much more fun. And dangerous, too.

"Put your palms on the wall," he instructed. "Above your head."

She considered denying him, just to see what he would do next. However, she complied because it was exactly what he desired. How he would toy with her. Persuade her. Subdue her instincts.

Leela knew everything about Balthazar—his likes, his methods, his seductive technique, his *stamina*—which provided her with the ultimate advantage in this situation.

Her knowledge allowed her to play him just as thoroughly as he played her. Because she could anticipate his every move.

"How long have you been watching me?" he asked, a hint of wonder in his tone.

"Long enough," she admitted. She'd known of his existence for millennia. But it wasn't until Brazil that she'd allowed herself to truly meet him.

He hummed against her neck, his palms sliding up her sides in a slow movement. "When did you become my personal voyeur, Leela? Before or after Brazil?"

After.

But technically before, too.

She'd watched him before, been impressed by his game, and then moved on.

However, the last few months, she'd done more than watch. She'd... *indulged* herself afterward.

"Indulged yourself how?" Sensuality caressed his tone, eliciting goose bumps down her arms. His fingers brushed the swells of her breasts, causing her to inhale sharply, the need inside her singing for more.

He touched her with the knowledge of their past, making her wonder what he remembered.

Or maybe it was all in her head. Some answer to an endless wish, a hope, a *want*, that she'd denied for too many months.

Because he wasn't hers to desire.

Her job was to protect Stas, not play with Balthazar.

His hand slid downward, skimming her flat abdomen on the way to the smooth skin between her thighs.

Except he didn't touch her where she wanted him to. He went back to her hip instead, his thumb drawing hypnotic circles against her skin.

"If you've only really been watching me for the past few months, then you have no idea what I can do. Not yet." He grazed her neck with his teeth, his hot arousal a promise and a threat against her back. "But you will, Lee. Soon. Very, very soon."

He nipped her thundering pulse and took a step back with his hands still on her hips and pulling her with him.

She went because she was too tired to fight him. Too exhausted to decline. Too emotionally drained to do anything other than follow his lead.

"I have you," Balthazar promised, his voice low as he rinsed them both off one final time.

She heard the double meaning in his words. He had her, as in he would keep her safe. But he also had her in a manner that implied sensual intent.

Leela accepted both definitions of the phrase.

But I still won't crawl, she vowed.

Balthazar chuckled. "You will," he replied as he reached around her to turn off the shower. "And you'll love every minute that follows."

She let her thoughts answer his statement, the ones that told him she'd never crawled for anyone and wouldn't start with him.

But as he turned her to face him, she caught the challenge in his gaze, the one that said he liked her fight.

He allowed that to be his response, similar to how she'd given him her mind.

Rather than comment, she merely smiled. He still had no idea whom he was up against. And once she fixed the rune, he'd lose the ability to read her mind.

His eyes narrowed. "Seems only fair to keep an open line of communication, considering your self-expressed advantages."

"Open line of communication?" she repeated. "Is that what you call it?"

He opened the shower door to tug a towel from the rack. Rather than wrap it around his waist—and alter her view of his more-than-impressive form—he used it to dry her off thoroughly. Then he swathed her in the cotton and tugged her forward into an unexpected kiss.

No tongue.

Just the pressure of his lips.

The whisper of a wicked promise.

Leela shivered despite the warmth, her desire returning with a vengeance just as he pulled back to stare down at her. "Communication, Leela. It's how relationships work."

"Relationships?" she repeated, breathless. That wasn't how Balthazar worked. Hell, it wasn't how *she* worked. "Define *relationship*."

He didn't reply. Instead, he grabbed his own towel and wrapped it around his hips without drying off. Then he held out his hand for her, his expression daring her to deny him.

She almost did on principle.

But she was too intrigued to say no—a fact that earned her a knowing grin.

That doesn't mean I want a relationship, she told him.

"It's too late to change that, sweetheart," he said as he led her out of the bathroom. "Our story is just beginning." He glanced at her, his chocolate irises swirling with intent. "Now get on that bed and spread your legs. I want to hear you scream my name."

"I thought you wanted me to crawl first?"

"Oh, you will," he replied, devious intent radiating from his expression. "And when—"

A shimmer of seraphic power caused the hairs along her arms to dance, cutting off Balthazar's words.

Because he heard the reaction in her mind, a problem she desperately needed to fix.

Navy feathers appeared, followed by Vera's familiar energy. She immediately turned corporeal, causing Balthazar to grin. "Just the Seraphim I wanted to see. You and I need to have a chat about my memories."

She blinked at him. Then she shook her head as though to clear it and shifted her attention to Leela. "Leek and Kital are on their way here. We need to move. *Now.*"

CHAPTER 4

LEELA

LEELA GAPED AT HER BEST FRIEND. "WHAT? HOW?"

Leek and Kital were warrior Seraphim, just like Gabe. Except, unlike Gabe, the other two warriors were not on Team Stas. They were on Team Council.

Fortunately, Gabe was the strongest of the three warriors, despite being the youngest by several centuries. He'd actually bested his half brother, Leek, a few decades ago, thus proving that age didn't matter when it came to power and skill.

But that didn't mean Leek or Kital was weak.

No, they were absolutely a threat.

Except protection wards surrounded the property—something Gabe had mentioned prior to Leela and Balthazar arriving. She'd checked a few of them herself, noting their ties to Lizzie's essence.

"There's a cloaking rune outside," she added, recalling the magical marker that made the land invisible to anyone seeking to harm Lizzie. "They can't find us here."

"Patreel and Arvane are with them," Vera replied, the two names darkly familiar to Leela. *Trackers.* "They've been

46

ordered to try to take Elizabeth and her child alive. But they've been given permission to exterminate as well."

Of course they have, Leela thought. The council wouldn't want to give Lizzie a trial; they'd just want to experiment on her and kill her afterward.

"Have you informed Gabe?" He would want to know, given it was likely his father, Adriel, who had issued the order.

"I haven't spoken to him since I altered his memories," she replied. "I thought he would be here."

"He's not." Leela frowned. "Where is Gabe?" She hadn't thought to ask with everything else going on, but she could understand why Vera had assumed he would be here. It was the logical place for him to be.

"Is he still at Ezekiel's place?" Vera guessed.

"No, last place I saw him was in Hydria. But I thought he meant to meet us here." Unless he couldn't find the island.

Which seemed unlikely, considering how easily Leela had found it.

Vera clearly had as well.

Because they all knew where to look. *However...* "How did the council find us?" she wondered out loud. "We're in the middle of the Caribbean Sea. Nowhere near Hydria."

Balthazar's gaze narrowed, his expression suggesting he had a thought, but he didn't express it out loud.

All Vera did was shrug. "I don't know, but we need to move. I suggest Iceland. Ezekiel and Skye have wards in place. We can regroup at his place and decide where to go from there."

Leela nodded. "All right. I'll need dir—"

Vera reached for her wrist, her power flaring to life as she shoved a false memory into Leela's head. She shuddered in response, the wrongness of the thought

47

slicing through her mind with rapid speed. Then it settled, blending with her other recollections, making her blink.

It felt so real that she almost questioned the fakeness of it.

Have I been there before? she asked herself. *Or is this just one of Vera's mental tricks?* It was so hard to know what Vera had altered in her past, how much of it was real versus fabrication.

When Vera reached for Balthazar, he took a step back. "Do not touch me unless you're planning to fix the memories you've already altered."

She sighed and shook her head. "It's not like I enjoy it."

"Could have fooled me," he retorted, the anger in his voice surprising Leela. She'd not heard him use that tone before. Although, she normally only observed him in intimate situations. And while they were both clad only in towels, the burning sensuality between them had dialed back several notches upon Vera's arrival.

Which also fascinated Leela.

Balthazar almost always took on a role of allowing anyone and everyone into his bedroom.

His brown eyes swirled with darkness as he met Leela's gaze.

She swallowed, the intensity radiating off him suffocating yet enthralling at the same time.

"I want my memories back," he said. "Until that happens, Leela's mind remains open."

Her lips parted. "That's not—"

"Fine," Vera agreed. "Whatever it'll take to make you both *move*. We're running out of time." With that pronouncement, she disappeared.

Balthazar stared at the space she'd just vacated, eyes

narrowed. "How do you think they found us?" he asked, his voice low.

"I don't know," Leela admitted. "That's why I asked that question."

He fell silent for a moment, then nodded as though he accepted that explanation. But his expression as he glanced at her in the next second suggested he had a theory.

She frowned at him. *How do you think they found us?* she thought at him, arching a brow.

He shook his head in response before saying, "Get dressed."

Part of her wanted to protest the command, but a prickling of unease skated up her spine. It radiated from her rune—the one that whispered danger when it approached.

Trackers.

She swallowed, her fear of being found an icy prick to her senses. She'd hidden herself for centuries, escaping the most profound of the tracker line with an ease she prided herself on.

But they'd found them now.

How? she wondered again.

A pair of jeans and a tank top appeared in her vision, both of which were held by Balthazar. They weren't her clothes but an outfit he'd retrieved from the dresser beside them.

"These appear to be your size. Almost as though someone knew we would be in this room, at this precise moment." He handed her a sweater next. "Also your size."

She peeked around him to find another outfit in the drawer, one that appeared to be for him.

Skye, she thought.

He grunted, whether in agreement or not, she wasn't

sure. She'd never seen this side of him—the part that made him a leader of his kind.

Hydraian politics were much more laid-back in nature in comparison to those of the Seraphim, and even the Ichorians.

The Hydraians valued power and age, naming the oldest of their race as Elders. Balthazar was among that group, his several thousand years of existence marking him as revered and well respected. Yet he always maintained an easygoing air, delicately handling disputes with a loving touch rather than one of reproach.

Balthazar snorted, interrupting Leela's mental assessment. "There are all manner of discipline, Lee. Not all of them are violent."

He stepped into her personal space, making her acutely aware that she hadn't put on her clothes yet, while he'd spent the last minute pulling on a pair of jeans.

"Certain punishments require a sensual approach," he informed her softly. "And not everyone wants to be led. Some need to be coaxed into behaving." Heat radiated from his bare chest, his chocolate gaze swirling with hot intent. "Get. Dressed."

The dominance underlying his tone made her want to rebel. Not because she minded his demonstration of power, but because she wanted to find out what he'd do if she refused.

However, the tingling against her spine reminded her of the lingering threat outside. And that forced her to comply.

Balthazar slipped on a pair of thick socks and black boots from the closet before bringing her a matching pair. She didn't need to ask to know these also fit them perfectly. Just like the jeans, tank top, and blue sweater he'd handed her.

A glance over his now-clothed torso told her that his clothes were the right size as well. Although, his black, long-sleeved turtleneck shirt appeared to be painted on, thus accentuating his flawless physique.

Leela suspected that had been done for her benefit.

Thank you, Skye, she thought when Balthazar turned to show off his fine ass in those fitted jeans.

He found two coats in the closet, handing a white puffy one to her before slipping the black leather jacket over his shoulders.

Someone had obviously expected their need to travel to Iceland because this was not appropriate attire for the Bahamas.

And there was only one person who could have predicted who would need the clothes in this exact room.

Which meant Iceland was their next stop for a multitude of reasons.

"Let's go meet with the others," she said. Vera had either already told them about their necessary trip, or she'd expected Leela and Balthazar to pass on the message.

Stas would also probably sense the lingering threat outside. Sethios and Caro, too.

Leela started toward the door, only to find her wrist caught in Balthazar's grip. "Take us to Iceland."

"What?" She blinked back at him. "We need to tell the others."

"No. We need to make sure we're not misting into a trap, then we will return for the others," he corrected.

She gaped at him. "I can sense the danger."

"From a rune created by Vera, right?"

"No, Caro…" She trailed off, frowning. "Sort of."

Runes were complicated. All Seraphim knew how to create them. But it was somewhat taboo to mark oneself.

Mostly because there were certain risks involved with

drawing the wrong edge or angle.

So Seraphim always helped each other.

However, that assistance came with a catch—only the rune's maker could alter it once etched into flesh.

Wards and runes on inanimate objects could be changed by anyone. But anything on a live creature required the original Seraphim.

Or, in Leela's case, multiple *Seraphim.*

Because Vera and Caro had worked together to connect Leela's rune to Stas during the fealty pledge.

"I don't see what that has to do with anything," Leela finally said. "We need to tell the others."

But Balthazar shook his head. "We need to check the location first to make sure it's safe before everyone mists there. I won't put little LJ or her parents in danger."

Protective energy swarmed around him, cloaking him in a cape of assurance and necessary control. He meant what he'd said—he needed to ensure the safety of the situation for his best friend and his family.

Because they were Balthazar's family, too.

Leela swallowed, then nodded. "All right. But at least let me tell Caro. That way they can react appropriately to whatever is happening here if we don't return."

They would be returning. Of that she was certain. Vera had no reason to betray them.

But Balthazar didn't know the memory-manipulating Seraphim like Leela did.

"I've already shared the visual with Issac," Balthazar told her. "He's aware."

"I thought you couldn't hear him," she replied, her brow furrowing.

Issac's blood bond to Stas had set the Ichorian on a path to become a Seraphim. Which made him mostly immune to Ichorian and Hydraian gifts as a result.

In twenty-five years, he'd have his wings. And a healthy dose of indestructible immortality to go with it.

"His mind's unclear, like an untuned radio," Balthazar confirmed. "But he sent me a visual response. He knows what we plan to do and is informing the others."

An image flashed in her mind of Issac and Stas finding outfits meant for them in a fashion similar to how Balthazar had discovered their clothes.

Leela shook her head, trying to clear the visual as it morphed into Issac and Stas walking down the hall to find Caro and Sethios.

Then Issac looked directly at Leela and mouthed, *Go.*

Her eyes widened when the image dissolved into Balthazar's amused expression. "Did you tell him to do that?"

"No, but I imagine he sensed you stalling and decided to take matters into his own hands. He's not one to waste time."

"Neither am I."

"Then why are we still standing here?" He squeezed her wrist for emphasis, causing her to narrow her eyes.

All right. You want to go to Iceland? We'll go to Iceland. She triggered her misting ability with a flick of a thought, grabbed the back of his neck, and whisked them through time and space.

To Balthazar, it probably felt like riding full speed through a tunnel. But it didn't feel that way to Leela.

To her, misting resembled freedom.

It was a state of being where no one could touch her, allowing her to move gracefully away from the Bahamas and more or less teleport them directly north to the much colder climate.

Without anyone suspecting her presence.

Because of her rune.

They might sense Balthazar, but only for a split second. It wouldn't be long enough for Patreel or Arvane to latch on and follow, a fact that helped quell the twisting in her gut.

She hated the notion of anyone tailing her. Just the mere thought suffocated her.

If anyone discovered the fractures in her conditioning, she'd be subjected to emotional reform.

She would never survive it.

She wasn't bonded like Caro. She had no anchor to keep her sane. Only a deep love for humanity—which was the very weakness the High Council of Seraph sought to destroy.

The chill that swept over her had nothing to do with the frigid air that kissed her feathers upon their arrival.

However, it wasn't just the concept of reformation that sent ice through her veins.

No. It was the reminder of *him* and what he would do when he found her. He hadn't bothered to chase her. But if Patreel or Arvane reported her presence to him, he might change his mind and pursue her.

The mere notion of being caught sent a violent shiver down her spine, one she would usually attribute to the change in temperature outside and say nothing more about. Because this was her secret, the fear she harbored inside that no one knew existed.

Until now, she realized, glancing at the mind reader beside her. She might be invisible to him, but he could *hear* her.

Balthazar scrutinized her as she returned to her corporeal state, his eyes unerringly finding her own despite his inability to see her when she went ethereal.

His mind knew hers, could picture every detail without seeing her.

And that truly terrified her.

Because he knew exactly what she feared now more than anything else in existence. *Being caught and the acts that would follow her capture.*

Reformation would destroy her mind and crush her soul.

The fact that it scared her said everything there was to know about her current condition. A stoic Seraphim would never fear the mind-numbing pod because they had nothing to lose.

No joy. No fond memories. No *life*.

Leela would rather die than be subjected to that torment.

Which was precisely the problem.

Seraphim didn't die.

Thus, if she was ever caught, she'd reside there in torturous limbo for eternity. And *he* would merely watch her suffer. Uncaring. Unfeeling. Waiting for her to be corrected so he could complete what the Fates had told him to do with her.

Breed.

Which wouldn't be for at least another century.

One benefit of her fertility line—she knew her own cycle.

Something that had allowed her to escape her fate more than once. But it also meant if she were caught, she might suffer for a hundred years while they attempted to fix her.

All while *he* observed the "correction."

Balthazar didn't comment. Didn't ask questions. Just studied her for another beat before glancing around at the abundance of snow.

January in Iceland meant it was cold and dark. *Just like a reformation chamber.*

She swallowed, shoving the concept from her mind, and noted the home about twenty yards in front of them. The shimmer of energy outside confirmed it was warded. But the fact that they could see it meant they were allowed to enter.

Balthazar didn't appear as convinced.

"I haven't lived this long by trusting everything I see," he said, his focus returning to Leela. "How did Vera know about the home in the Bahamas? She misted inside with the ease of someone who has been there before. Yet she wasn't there for the birth."

"Gabe must have told her." Except Vera had said that the last time they'd spoken was after she'd altered his memories. Or had she said *seen*?

"She said *spoken*," Balthazar confirmed. "So how did she know about Osiris's home?" he asked again.

"I…" Leela trailed off. "Honestly, I have no idea how Vera's learned half the things she knows." She was always several steps ahead and one hundred percent prepared. "She's a genius."

"Who can manipulate memories at will."

"She's on our side," Leela insisted.

"We'll see."

"We will," she agreed, certain. Vera was her best friend. She trusted her implicitly.

Balthazar hummed something unintelligible under his breath and started toward the house.

"We need to go back for the others."

"Not until we find out who is here and you check the wards," Balthazar replied. "Then, once we've agreed it's safe, we can go back for them."

She stayed in the snow as he continued toward the house, his steps sure.

This protector side of Balthazar rather appealed to

Leela.

As did his backside in those jeans.

"Keep your fantasies for later, sweetheart," he called back to her. "We have work to do."

"And you're not one to work and play?" she taunted, misting to his side.

He grabbed her by the back of the neck before she finished turning corporeal, his reflexes impressive.

"I'm always playing," he said, his voice deceptively low as he pulled her into a kiss. It was fast and unexpected, leaving her immediately winded as he released her in the next breath.

No tongue.

Again.

Just his lips.

How…?

"I told you a few months of observation is nothing," he whispered darkly. "You'll crawl."

The confidence in his tone rivaled his steps as he continued toward the house.

She stared after him, helplessly inhaling in his wake.

This version of Balthazar was nothing like the one she'd met in Brazil. Yet he was exactly the same in that he continued to blow her mind with each move he made.

Her lips curled.

Suave men were common. Sexy ones, too. But Balthazar took those adjectives to a whole new playing field and underlined them with intelligence and strategy and sprinkled a healthy dose of protectiveness on top.

We'll see, she decided, using his words from earlier as she followed him once more.

Leela finally understood the point of his challenge. It wasn't about being difficult or denying him. It was about making her *want* to crawl.

For him.

To him.

With her own pleasure in mind.

He wanted to be worth her version of a sensual apology. And he intended to indulge them both in a series of erotic games along the way.

His expression gave nothing away as they reached the front door, but she knew he was actively listening to her mind as she deduced his true intentions for her.

"Oh?" Ezekiel's voice graced the midnight air, his amusement palpable even through the thick wood of the door.

Leela shared a look with Balthazar, her eyebrows lifting. He appeared equally as intrigued by whatever was happening inside. It wasn't necessarily uncommon for Ezekiel to find amusement in situations, but it helped to know what had him intrigued now.

Ezekiel's penchant for volatility and violence marked him as a worthy adversary. Leela trusted him to an extent. However, the "retired" assassin would always put his own interests before the rest of them.

"And what else has he borrowed?" Ezekiel asked.

"You'll have to ask him about that," a female replied in a softer tone.

Balthazar's eyes widened as he reached for the door handle, his expression and actions confirming he recognized the woman's voice.

"Hmm," Ezekiel hummed in response. "I'll wait and see where this goes."

"See where what goes?" Balthazar demanded, stepping inside without knocking or announcing himself. He took in the sight of Ezekiel speaking with a blonde woman and arched a brow. "What are you doing here?"

CHAPTER 5

ISSAC

SEVERAL MINUTES EARLIER

ISSAC'S PALM RESTED ON ASTASIYA'S FLAT ABDOMEN, HER skin warm beneath his touch. They both lounged in a lazy silence filled with a myriad of unspoken words that they naturally understood without needing to utter them aloud.

Of course, it helped that they could speak via their bond.

But they both remained intrinsically silent, merely existing in the pleasure of their coexistence.

A beautiful moment of bliss and harmony.

They'd just witnessed the creation of a life, something Issac had never desired to see before. However, the experience had changed him in an irrevocable way.

He wondered what his future son or daughter would look like if he and Astasiya chose that path. It wouldn't be now or even soon. And three hours ago, he would have added *never* to that thought.

Yet seeing the joy in Jayson's and Elizabeth's features had left him… curious.

Aya tilted her head back to meet his gaze, her green irises sparkling with understanding. He could sense her agreement in the shift of fate, the intrigue in her mind at what they could create together.

A baby Seraphim.

Would she have her mother's elven chin? Those beautiful, long blonde strands? Or would it be a boy with sapphire eyes and a thick mane of dark hair? Maybe some stunning combination of them both.

He chuckled a little to himself, thinking about what his sister would say if she could hear these thoughts right now. Amelia would be overjoyed by the prospect and maybe a little starstruck that he would even consider such an avenue of exploration.

Aya lifted onto her elbow beside him, her soft hair falling over her bare shoulders as she gazed down at him.

She didn't speak.

Because she didn't have to.

He understood her on every level, which was how he knew exactly what she intended to do now.

His hand slipped to her hip, his body automatically reacting to her every move. Her thigh slid between his as she bent to kiss him, her lips whispering tender words of forever against his mouth.

So intuitive and perfect.

His sweet Seraphim.

His mate.

His Aya.

He drew his fingers up her side, skimming the swell of her breasts on his way up to her throat. She smiled as he palmed the back of her neck, then moaned as he took control and deepened their kiss.

Every touch and lick and stroke felt like the first time between them. All hot, consuming passion. A promise of intensity. A foundation of forever. She belonged to him in every way, just as he belonged to her. It fulfilled him on a level of incomprehension. Nothing else compared. Their relationship severed every boundary, broke every rule, and defied all expectations.

He adored her.

Loved her.

Worshipped her.

And he told her that with his tongue now, vowing to always be there for her, no matter what the future held in store for them. He'd die for this female. Give her his soul if it meant one more breath.

She responded in kind, the same pledge hummed back at him through the sensual skill of her lips.

He smiled, his grip tightening as she slid onto him, straddling his hips and placing him right where he needed to be.

Until she shivered from some unexpected intrusion.

Her gaze immediately lifted to the ceiling, then went to the door.

He didn't need to ask to understand that she'd sensed a disturbance, her skin practically vibrating beneath his touch. She frowned. *My rune is tingling.*

Issac considered her statement, his affinity for visual manipulation triggering to life without a thought. He searched the compound, taking in everyone's visions at once. It was akin to perusing multiple television channels at the same time, only there were fewer frequencies here because they were in the middle of nowhere.

Which made it easy to find the one he sought. "Vera's here," he said, seeing her through Balthazar's gaze.

Astasiya relaxed.

But Issac didn't.

Because he saw the way Leela tensed in response to whatever Vera had just told them.

Issac captured Balthazar's vision, manipulating it to show himself on the edges in a ghostlike form. It was his subtle way of saying, *I see you. What's going on?*

The mind reader used to be able to hear those thoughts, making this a little trickier than usual. But the Hydraian Elder didn't miss a beat, his mind already dipping into his imagination as he pictured angels dressed as warriors swarming in from above.

"Balthazar says we have company," Issac translated out loud.

That explains the tingling, Aya muttered, her hand going to her lower back to touch the heart-shaped rune near her spine. *It doesn't usually do that around Vera.*

Issac didn't reply, his focus on Balthazar as he continued to draw up fantasy images in his mind. He was picturing a field of ice and snow now.

"I think Vera's telling him and Leela to travel to Iceland." It was a guess based on the fact that Sethios and Caro had been there before misting to the Bahamas.

Balthazar pictured Ezekiel in the next minute, then flicked his gaze upward toward the sky.

Issac sent an image back of Seraphim Skye's face, wondering if that was who he'd met. Then it dawned on him that the Elders hadn't met her before. She'd always been tucked away in Osiris's grip until he'd allowed her to be recently taken by Ezekiel.

Or that was the way Osiris had recounted the actions, anyway.

He'd described the entire event of saving Sethios and Skye as a training exercise for Astasiya.

The ancient Seraphim of Resurrection had a twisted view on how to properly teach someone their powers.

Balthazar's mental image changed again, this time as he knelt to draw words into the snow on the ground. *Going to Iceland to check wards. Don't trust Vera.*

Issac's eyebrows lifted at that last part. He wanted to ask why but suspected there wasn't a lot of time, as Balthazar was already looking for clothes—something he saw through the mind reader's gaze.

Vera had disappeared.

And Leela appeared unconvinced.

Issac relayed the details as Astasiya went to check the dresser beside the bed. "We have two outfits as well."

"Definitely Skye's doing," Issac said, noting the winter jackets Balthazar pictured in the closet.

Aya checked their own as soon as Issac mentioned it, and sure enough, they also had similar outdoor gear.

"So she's been here before," Issac murmured. "But when?"

"Or she shared these details with Osiris," Aya replied, her expression saying she wasn't thrilled with either possibility.

Balthazar's vision snagged Issac's attention again as he wrote another message in the snow. *Going now. Tell the others.*

"Right," Issac said, rolling off the bed to begin pulling on clothes. He sent Balthazar an escalated visual of them already dressed as a way of saying he'd handle things here. They would inform the others and prepare for next steps while Leela and Balthazar checked out the Iceland route.

Knowing Balthazar, he would refuse to move Jayson, Elizabeth, and baby Aidyn until he knew for sure the location was safe.

The mind reader could be counted on for many things, such as turning any potential situation into a sexual encounter, intruding on everyone's thoughts without invitation, and ensuring the safety of those he cared about.

His mental connection disappeared, confirming the Hydraian Elder had left with Leela.

The other Hydraian Elder, Jayson, appeared to be lost in a blissful family moment with Elizabeth, as she and the baby were all he pictured.

Issac left his visual behind as he searched for Caro and Sethios. He'd skimmed over them before, avoiding whatever intimate act they were experiencing. But he found them both dressing now in the wardrobe Skye had left for them.

"Either Vera visited your parents, or they felt the disturbance in the atmosphere," Issac stated.

Aya scratched her lower back again, her lips flattening. "Definitely the latter, but maybe also the former. Why didn't she come talk to us?"

"Because I was busy talking to Osiris outside," a feminine voice replied as a flurry of navy feathers appeared in Issac's peripheral vision.

Vera ruffled them out in annoyance before settling into her corporeal state.

"He's providing a distraction so we can escape," she continued. "But I need to check Caro for a tracking mark first. It's the only explanation for how they found you all so quickly."

Balthazar said he didn't trust Vera, Issac thought at Aya. *However, I don't know why.*

Perhaps because she'd shown up without any explanation? Gabriel had likely given her the directions. But her chatting with Osiris seemed a bit suspect as well.

Astasiya didn't reply, instead saying, "We should go find my parents."

Issac agreed. "They're waiting for us in the hall."

They'd either heard them speaking or had sensed Issac somehow as he'd checked their vision.

He wasn't sure how the runes worked to block power, but thought they might allow access based on trust. Or maybe it only deterred Ichorian and Hydraian supernatural energy.

As Issac was no longer an Ichorian, his gifts now worked on a Seraphim.

At least the ones he'd met, anyway.

Except for Sethios. His mind appeared dark. It'd been Caro's eyes he'd looked through minutes ago. And even that had been a bit blurry.

Perhaps he just hadn't finished coming into his powers yet because Sethios appeared susceptible to other seraphic powers. Such as his father's compulsion and Vera's memory manipulation.

Issac made a mental note to ask about runes later and how his own seraphic abilities would develop over the next twenty-five years—otherwise known as the length of time it took a Seraphim to finally grow wings after birth or the creation of a blood bond.

Hence the reason Astasiya, a born Seraphim, hadn't been able to mist until after her twenty-fifth birthday.

She pressed her palm to his, drawing him from his thoughts as she linked their fingers together to pull him toward the door.

Vera led the way, her steps certain.

She wasn't acting guilty of anything.

Perhaps Balthazar was—

The foundation of the house vibrated beneath them, sending Aya sideways into his chest. He caught her, his knees nearly buckling from the impact. She misted on instinct, her fingers digging into his brown suede jacket.

"That would be the wards," Vera gritted out, misting to the doorway to throw open the door.

Caro and Sethios were on the other side. "What's

happening?" Sethios demanded as Aya turned corporeal once more. She didn't release Issac, something her father noticed with a slight narrowing of his gaze.

"The council sent two warriors and two trackers. Orders are to take alive, but they were given permission to kill on sight," Vera summarized. "I told Leela, but she and Balthazar already misted to Iceland."

Caro's brow furrowed. "Without us?"

"Balthazar wanted to check the property to ensure it's safe for Jayson, Elizabeth, and Aidyn first," Issac explained.

"Why wouldn't it be safe?" Caro asked, her flat tone reminding him of Gabriel's trademark stoicism.

Issac shrugged. He couldn't exactly say that the mind reader didn't trust Vera. That would just raise more questions he couldn't answer.

Instead, he replied, "That's a question for Balthazar."

Sethios gave him a look, one that seemed to say, *You're not telling us everything.* Followed immediately by, *I imagine there's a good reason for it.*

"I'll go with Astasiya and Issac to talk to Jayson, as I'm sure that little quake has put him on guard. You two determine our exit." He locked gazes with Caro.

She nodded, agreeing to the plan and probably whatever he'd just said via their bond.

"I need to check you for a tracker first," Vera said, her focus on Caro.

"A tracker?" Sethios repeated. "Why?"

"Because it's the only explanation I can think of for how the council found you all so quickly."

"If that's true, then they would already know about Iceland," Sethios interjected. "And that's where you just sent Balthazar and Leela."

Vera frowned. "True."

Which meant they might be in danger there. Issac walked over to his discarded clothes to find his phone. "No service."

"Likely from the war—"

"Could someone tell me why the ground is shaking?" Jayson called from down the hall, interrupting Vera.

"Warrior Seraphim are attacking the boundaries," Sethios replied without missing a beat. "Fucking with cellular service too, apparently."

"Osiris is distracting them," Vera added. "He's working on a diversion so we can flee."

"To a place they're potentially already aware of," Sethios deadpanned. "Fantastic plan."

"Do you have a better one?" Vera snapped.

"I do."

She arched a brow. "And it is?"

"We go disable the assholes up there to buy us some time to find a new place to hide," he said, pointing at the ceiling. "I have new wings and I could use the exercise."

"You don't even know how to use them yet," Vera pointed out.

"Sometimes the best way to learn is trial by fire," he replied.

Vera groaned. "Gods, you really are your father's son."

"Unfortunately," Sethios replied, his gaze on Caro. "Want to play with your new knives?"

"Against the warrior Seraphim?" Her lips twisted as she seriously pondered the question, her seraphic-like practicality on full display. "My knives won't be very useful against them. They prefer swords."

Sethios's eyebrows lifted. "Swords? Why not guns?"

"Guns are mortal toys," Vera interjected. "We are wasting time. Osiris said to go to Iceland. Skye and Ezekiel will know what to do."

Caro and Sethios gaped at her. "Since when do you take advice from my father?" Sethios demanded.

"Since I witnessed the cause of his exile," she retorted.

Silence fell as Caro and Sethios exchanged a glance.

Maybe this is why Balthazar doesn't trust Vera? Aya guessed.

Maybe, he agreed, thinking through everything Vera had just said. *Do you think she's been working with Osiris?*

Her commentary about Osiris telling them to go to Iceland to meet with Ezekiel and Skye suggested Vera was taking directives from him. But was that a new development, as in he'd just told her that plan upon her arrival? Or was it a command she'd accepted among others?

Do you think she could be the mole instead of Mateo? Issac wondered, hopeful. He really didn't want to think his progeny was capable of betraying them all, even though the technology involved painted him as more than guilty.

Maybe, Aya replied, doubt underscoring that single word.

"You weren't alive when he was exiled," Caro finally said. "You didn't witness it."

"Not in person, no. But I saw it in his memories." Her multicolored gaze landed on Issac. "I'll share the memory once we're safe. Issac can distribute it for me."

Issac wasn't sure he appreciated the crude description of his powers, but he didn't comment. Just nodded. Because he sensed his Aya's curiosity. And he wanted to know more about the exile as well.

"Iceland," Vera reiterated. "That's where we need to go."

"No." Sethios's tone thrived with power, his decline vibrating through the air with a finality everyone had to feel. "I will not go where my father suggested. Especially since you seem to think Caro is the reason we were found here. That means they already know about Iceland."

"It also doesn't bode well that Balthazar and Leela have yet to return," Issac added, meeting Sethios's gaze head-on. "Balthazar isn't the type to waste time when his loved ones are in danger. He should already be back."

Which meant he'd found something or had become distracted by an uncertain development.

Sethios nodded. "New plan. Subdue the attacking Seraphim. Then regroup to decide where to go next." He looked at Vera. "Search Caro for a tracker. I'm going to go learn more about these swords. And, you"—he looked at Jayson—"keep your wife and child calm."

Sethios's black wings appeared, the edges tipped in a dark blue that flickered in the moonlight streaming through the windows. He disappeared in the next moment, causing Vera to sigh. "He probably just went to Iceland by accident."

Caro blinked, her gaze unsteady. Then her lips curled. "No. Montana."

Vera rolled her eyes. "Fool."

"Lizzie needs clothes before we can travel," Jayson said, ignoring them. He wore a pair of jeans and no shirt. Issac couldn't remember what he'd been wearing when Jacque had teleported him here, but imagined it hadn't been much more than what he already had on.

"Check your dresser and closet," Issac told him. "Skye left us all some gifts." Or that was the theory, anyway.

Jayson nodded and disappeared back into his room as the ground shook again.

Should I go help Osiris? Aya wondered.

Maybe wait, Issac suggested.

He didn't doubt Astasiya's ability to fight—although, neither of them had experience with Seraphim other than

Osiris—but merely wanted her to remain with him to help observe Vera.

She grabbed Caro's arm without warning, but she didn't appear disturbed or shocked by it. She simply watched as Vera worked.

How is she checking her? Aya asked, the question more of an internal musing than anything else.

Perhaps she's checking her memories? Issac suggested.

Maybe, Aya murmured, then flinched before reaching around to scratch her lower back.

Still tingling? he guessed.

Yeah. Her tone expressed irritation.

He slid his hand beneath her jacket to rest his palm near her spine and began massaging the area with his thumb. *Any better?*

She melted into his side in a nonverbal response, her head naturally finding his shoulder.

Caro glanced at them before frowning down at Vera. "I'm not enjoying these memories."

"Neither am I," Vera gritted out. "But if they put a tracker on you, it was during reformation."

Some of the images filtered through Issac's mind, the isolation pod one that made him feel immediately claustrophobic. He shivered in response, not enjoying the sensation that had evoked at all.

Understanding the concept of reformation vastly differed from *seeing* it. Caro had been trapped in that small, sterile space for years. It was almost worse than drowning —a state they all had originally thought she'd been in for nearly two decades.

Alas, no.

She'd been inside a pod.

Your mother is quite strong, Issac decided, his words for Aya. *Admirably so.*

What memories are you seeing?

Some from her reform—

Another jolt struck the compound, this one harsher than before. Vera cursed, her wings flaring to life as she disappeared.

"What just happened?" Aya asked, her own feathers appearing as a loud snap sounded through the air.

"They've just breached the initial wards," Caro explained, her tone flat. However, her expression turned grave as she met her daughter's gaze. "The Seraphim are coming."

CHAPTER 6

BALTHAZAR

"STARK BROUGHT HER," EZEKIEL SAID, ANSWERING Balthazar's question about why Clara was in Northern Iceland.

To say her presence here had shocked him would be an understatement. The last he'd heard, she was still locked up in a Hydraian prison cell.

"Then he disappeared to work on the wards," Ezekiel continued, referring to Stark, otherwise known as Gabriel. "Or perhaps he had another *engagement*." The final word held a wealth of knowledge that Balthazar could only begin to understand.

What have you two been up to? he wondered, his focus on an oddly muted Clara. She typically exuded powerful emotions, as she possessed a natural affinity for reading the feelings of others. As an Ichorian, she only had the one ability, but it was a strong one.

Yet she seemed mysteriously stoic now. Unfeeling. As though she weren't even *here*. Even her mind was vacant.

His clear scrutiny drew her gaze to his, her blue eyes rimmed with a plea he couldn't hear.

Which was troubling indeed.

"Why did Stark bring her here?" Balthazar asked slowly, his question for Ezekiel while he continued to assess Clara's silent mind. *Why can't I hear you?*

"He didn't explain himself," Ezekiel drawled.

"He rarely does," Leela added.

Balthazar barely heard them, his attention entirely on Clara and the fuzziness of her thoughts. It reminded him of Issac, a realization that made his eyebrows shoot upward.

Her eyes widened in response, that plea radiating through her depths once more. *Please... anything...* The two words were muffled as though she were speaking through a thick glass or whispering something from several yards away.

But it was enough for him to understand.

Please don't say anything, she meant.

Balthazar cleared his throat after a beat, his eyes narrowing slightly. "Does Luc know you're here?"

"Gabriel said he's aware, yes," she replied.

Gabriel, Balthazar repeated. *Not Stark*.

That was telling indeed.

He glanced at Leela, curious as to if she'd noticed anything off about Clara. But she didn't think or say anything at all, just met his gaze and said, "I'm going to go check with Gabriel about the wards, then head back for Jay and Liz."

Because obviously it's safe here, she added mentally. *As I knew it would be.*

Looks can be deceiving, he nearly said. But she disappeared before he could reply.

Clara's eyes widened at the display of Leela's departure, capturing his focus once more. Teleporting wasn't new to her, which suggested she'd seen something unique about this disappearing act.

The wings? he wondered. *Did you see Leela's wings?* Because Balthazar couldn't. But Stas would have been able to. Issac, too.

So if Clara had witnessed the misting, then that could only mean one thing—she'd bonded with Stark.

How? he wanted to demand. *How the fuck did you bond with Stark?*

Yet her gaze had pleaded with him, suggesting she didn't want him to acknowledge the truth out loud. While he wanted to demand answers, he chose to respect her unspoken request.

It was the least he could do after the way he and the others had treated her this past week.

She'd been framed as an informant, leading the Elders to believe she'd been feeding information to Jonathan— information that had led to several deaths. However, the Elders had recently realized Clara wasn't the real mole. But they'd kept her locked up in order to placate the real mole so they could gather more intelligence on what he was telling Osiris.

However, it appeared that Stark had not only sprung Clara from her prison cell, but he'd also *mated* her.

What in the actual fuck is happening here?

"What else was Luc told?" Balthazar wondered out loud. *Is he aware you and the Seraphim have bonded one another?* was what he really wanted to know.

"Uh." Clara cleared her throat, his question clearly leaving her uneasy. "I, um, don't know."

You don't know? Or you don't want to tell me? he wanted to ask.

But there were easier ways to find out what Luc knew.

"I see," he told her, taking out his phone to dial the male in question.

The Hydraian King picked up on the first ring. "B."

Balthazar didn't bother with formalities, jumping straight to the point. "Have you heard from Stark lately?"

"No. But Ezekiel told me Stark has Clara in New York City." Luc's tone indicated he wasn't pleased about that development.

Which meant he'd be furious when he learned Stark had taken Clara to Iceland.

Rather than inform him, Balthazar merely nodded to himself. Because it was as he'd suspected—Stark and Clara were definitely hiding something.

Something buzzed through the phone, followed by Luc saying, "Jacque just texted to say you're in Iceland now."

Balthazar searched for the teleporter's mind, curious as to his whereabouts, and heard him upstairs with Owen. His lips threatened to curl at that development. Those two Hydraians had been dancing around each other for decades. Apparently, it took Owen dying and coming back from the grave to convince Jacque to act on his instincts.

About time, Balthazar thought. He'd have to congratulate the teleporter later.

"Are you on your way here?" he asked Luc, curious about whether he intended to join them here.

His question also served as a warning for Clara, as Luc would likely not be pleased by whatever development had occurred between her and Stark. Not that it was really any of Luc's business, but he'd been different since Aidan's passing. Angrier. Crueler. And a bit… unpredictable.

"Yeah, Jacque's on his way," Luc replied.

Balthazar met Clara's gaze, ensuring she understood the meaning beneath his words as he replied, "See you soon."

She swallowed, the message received.

"In three minutes," Luc clarified. Then he promptly ended the call.

Balthazar slipped his phone back into his pocket, held Clara's gaze for another beat, saying, *This conversation isn't over*, with his eyes. Then he switched focus to Ezekiel.

"We need to talk," Balthazar said.

"We always need to talk," Ezekiel drawled back before wandering over to collapse onto a couch. A svelte female with pale features and a submissive demeanor moved alongside him as though tethered to him via some invisible string.

This must be Skye.

She clasped her small hands in her lap and blinked a few times, her blue eyes oddly out of focus.

Yes, definitely Skye.

He'd ask questions about her later.

Right now, he had a different concern he wanted to address—one he needed Ezekiel to elaborate upon.

"Osiris," Balthazar said slowly. "Specifically, his history with the council. And what his intentions are now."

"You assume I know?" Ezekiel asked, arching a pierced black brow. He resembled a laid-back rocker with his tight jeans, black T-shirt, inked arms, and long, dark hair. Meanwhile, Skye depicted the image of innocence beside him with her raven-colored hair, light blue eyes, porcelain-like features, and lacy white dress.

Balthazar refocused on Ezekiel, not in the mood for word games. It was late. He was tired. And he wanted answers. Right fucking now.

"I know you do," he told the infamous assassin as he crossed his arms. "Start talking."

Ezekiel smirked. "Well, once upon a time…"

Balthazar narrowed his gaze, unamused with the story time antics. "Ezekiel."

The assassin sighed dramatically. "You're usually the fun one."

"It's been a long day, and I'm tired of being played by Osiris at every turn. Now tell me why Osiris created a safe house for Lizzie and why he's currently protecting that safe house by battling a pair of warrior Seraphim. I also want to know what you can tell me about Vera."

"Warrior Seraphim?" a deep voice repeated as a male with blond hair and sea-green eyes appeared. "You didn't tell me there were warrior Seraphim."

"Because you misted back here before I could finish my sentence," Leela said, appearing beside the other Seraphim with an irritated expression. "Your father sent them." She disappeared again without elaborating.

Gabriel glared at the vacant space, surprising the hell out of Balthazar. The Seraphim never displayed emotion, but he clearly did not appreciate her misting away after dropping that statement.

Clara moved closer to him, an action not lost on anyone in the room, just as Jacque appeared in the hallway with Luc.

His emerald irises flared upon seeing Clara in the living area. "What the hell are you doing here?"

"Oh, good. A game of repetition," Ezekiel muttered, drawing his fingers through his hair before flopping his head back on the couch. "Wake me when they're done, love."

Skye merely blinked in response, her head canting a bit to the side at whatever vision she appeared to be following.

Balthazar had never actually met the prophetess in person. However, he'd overheard a bit about her from the minds of others, helping him to know what to anticipate from the female.

So far, she was living up to his expectations.

"Clara goes where I go," Stark declared, standing in front of the female in question and folding his arms while staring directly at Luc. "There will be no questions. No elaborations. No discussions."

Balthazar arched a brow.

What the fuck? Luc thought. *Is he protecting her?*

Balthazar gave a slight nod, answering the question.

Since when? Why? How? Luc's questions rattled off in sequence, his complex mind puzzling through the situation at rapid speed.

He analyzed their mannerisms, noting Clara's hand as she touched Stark's lower back and the way she peeked out around him with guileless blue eyes. Then he took in the manner by which Stark moved just enough to continue blocking her in a shielding motion.

All of it ran through his thoughts, coupled with his omniscient ability to know and remember every detail. Luc almost immediately concluded that the two were engaged in some sort of romantic affair.

Unexpected. Odd. Perhaps related to the blood Stark imbibed earlier. Similar to Issac with Stas... He trailed off, his emerald irises flashing as he took in the Seraphim's neck. *Did she bite him back?* He tried to search for evidence and found none.

He switched focus to Balthazar. *Are they bonded?*

The mind reader paused for a moment, uncertain of how to reply. He wasn't entirely sure, and yet, it seemed relatively clear that they'd engaged in some sort of connection. So he gave the Hydraian King another nod.

Fascinating, Luc thought. "Where are Jay and Lizzie?"

The shift in conversation was normal for Luc. His mind constantly contemplated five thousand avenues at once, making it impossible to know what route he would pick next until he voiced it out loud.

Although, several millennia of knowing each other allowed Balthazar to guess better than most.

And, of course, it helped that he could read the other man's mind.

"Leela went to retrieve them," Stark replied, his brow furrowing. "She should be back by now." He pulled his phone from his pocket and dialed, his expression darkening. "Something's wrong."

Balthazar couldn't hear how he'd come to that conclusion—thanks to his inability to read the other man's mind—but he guessed it was a result of the call not going through.

"War," Skye whispered, her gaze still far away. "There will be war. It's certain now." She canted her head again into an angle she seemed to favor. "Death. Destruction. *Reformation*." She shivered.

Ezekiel immediately wrapped his arm around her, his opposite palm going to her chin as he tilted her face toward his. "What do you see, my love?"

It was the gentlest tone Balthazar had ever heard from the man.

Just as he'd never seen him handle someone with such care.

The assassin preferred knives and pain, not sweet words and soft caresses. But he clearly used them with this female.

Luc's mind rivaled Balthazar's thoughts, his surprise drowned out in understanding. They both knew Ezekiel had worked with Osiris for a reason—his love for Skye. But it was a concept neither of them had understood.

Until now.

Until seeing it with their own eyes.

Unfortunately, the seer appeared to be oblivious to his

affection. Her expression remained vacant as he attempted to connect with her gaze.

"It's coming," she whispered. "The power is coming. Awakened. Destructive. *Reformation*." She blinked, startled, and focused on Ezekiel. "We're no longer safe here."

"Where do you want to go?" he asked without missing a beat.

She shook her head. "We need to split up."

He narrowed his eyes, causing the gold flecks of his ebony irises to glitter in the low lighting. "Not happening."

"They're not ready," she pressed. "The Seraphim need a distraction, or they will attack too soon."

Balthazar wished that he could read the female's mind to better understand what she meant, but she remained as blocked to him as Ezekiel, Gabriel, and now Clara.

It was irritating. His natural abilities were ingrained in him. They helped him thrive on a daily basis. To not be able to use them felt as though he'd lost one of his senses.

"Hydria needs better boundaries. Runes. Protection." She blinked again before focusing on Luc. "Your wards will fail."

"What wards?" Luc asked.

"The ones Osiris created," she replied. "They're old. Too old. Too fragile. He must—*you must*—bolster them to survive."

Luc and Balthazar shared a glance. This was the first they'd heard about wards around the island.

"Were you aware of this?" Luc demanded, his attention having shifted to Stark.

"Yes." A flat response, one that suggested Stark didn't intend to elaborate. But then Clara pressed her palm to his lower back again, her nails digging into his shirt, and the Seraphim continued speaking. "I didn't know Osiris created them, as the wards lacked an energy signature. But

Skye is right. They've been deteriorating with age and need to be fortified."

"Why would Osiris place wards around Hydria?" Clara asked softly.

"To protect the Hydraians," Skye hummed, her eyes falling closed. "Prized creations. Worthy. He values them."

Luc didn't reply, but he intently considered her comments and started running a thousand scenarios through his mind at once.

Balthazar didn't even try to track his thoughts. When Luc reached a conclusion, he'd share it.

Skye jolted upright, her eyes widening. "We can't stay here," she reiterated, her wild gaze landing on Jacque. "Teleport your king home. *Now*."

A crack thundered through the air outside, punctuating her words.

"Go," Balthazar said, giving the teleporter the command he needed to react.

Luc's lips parted to protest, but Jacque already had a viselike grip around the Hydraian King's wrist. The two vanished as Ezekiel jumped off the couch, a gun in each hand.

Stark drew a sword out of thin air, causing Balthazar's eyebrows to lift. *That's impressive.*

But it was a quick thought that died as the ground began to shake beneath them.

"*Leek*," Stark said, disappearing.

Lightning lit the sky outside, illuminating the windows of the home. Owen came flying down the stairs in a pair of jeans and a T-shirt that he'd only partially pulled over his freshly shaved dark head. "Where's Jacque?"

"Hydria," Balthazar answered. "With Luc."

Owen nodded, seemingly relieved until another flash

of light startled the night. "What the fuck is going on out there?"

"They brought the fight here," Skye said, slipping off the couch and to the side. "Incoming."

Bodies began to materialize as she uttered the word. First Jay with Caro. Then Lizzie and Aidyn with Leela. Followed by Stas and Issac.

More lights flickered, thunder reverberating behind them.

Balthazar picked up what had happened from Leela's mind as she thought about her arrival in the Bahamas and the war that had exploded in her wake. The name *Patreel* echoed through her mind, followed by a whisper of terror.

Leela feared the tracker and what he represented.

But Balthazar couldn't exactly see why or what their history entailed.

She was already thinking about the fight, how Sethios had appeared and demanded Kital hand over his sword, and how chaos had ensued.

Seraphim didn't fight with their inherent powers. They fought with *runes*. An error Sethios had quickly realized.

However, it was already too late.

The wards fractured and disintegrated beneath a wave of strength from Patreel that forced the others to flee.

Iceland was an immediate solution, the protective markings here fresh and able to keep out those wishing to do harm. Except leaving in the middle of a fight had allowed the others to follow.

And now the real battle had begun.

In the sky.

CHAPTER 7

SETHIOS

GABRIEL APPEARED IN A BLAZE OF RED FEATHERS, HIS swords glowing in the moonlight as he slammed his blade against the Seraphim asshole trying to slice Sethios into pieces.

Sethios had almost taken the sword from the fucker, but then Osiris had unleashed a compulsion spell that had forced Sethios to mist back to Iceland.

And this warrior Seraphim had followed right along with him.

Allowing him to gain the upper hand.

Thanks, Dad, Sethios thought, irritated as hell.

He'd finally figured out how to return to the Bahamas in time to play, and his persuasion-loving father had sent them all to Iceland to freeze. It was probably meant to be some sort of elaborate training exercise. Or maybe he thought he was helping.

With Osiris, it was hard to say.

The warrior with the wicked sword and short, dark hair paused to blink at the blade clashing against his own. Then he looked up at the red-winged angel holding the hilt of the offending weapon. It happened in slow motion, as though he was struggling to comprehend what had just occured.

"Gabriel." His voice didn't convey any surprise or emotion at all. Just a flat comment accompanied by a vacant expression.

"Leek," Gabriel returned. "Your presence here is unnecessary."

"Adriel sent us," Leek replied. "Our presence here is mandatory. We've come for the abomination and her child."

"They're under my protection," Gabriel replied. "Leave."

Leek stared at him for a beat. "Your conditioning is flawed."

"My conditioning is refined."

"I will report this to Adriel," Leek continued as though Gabriel hadn't spoken. "You will be scheduled for reform."

Gabriel snorted, the noise highly uncharacteristic of the Seraphim. Then he took his other sword and sliced it through Leek's neck.

No hesitation.

No second thought.

Just beheaded the angel in a swish of metal that had Sethios's brows flying upward to meet his hairline. "Well, that's one—"

A blistering light sailed through the air, interrupting his response. Gabriel caught the light with his sword, the power vibrating in a ripple of thunderous sound. "*Go*," Gabriel grated out. "*Now*."

He volleyed the energy back into the night, resulting in a wave of static electricity that fizzled along Sethios's new wings.

Caro appeared in the next breath, her hand finding

Sethios's as she whispered, *Let Gabriel handle this*, into his mind.

Like hell, Sethios retorted, too intrigued by the bizarre weaponry to move. *I want to see him slice off another head.*

Caro grumbled something in his mind about being a sadist, which only made him smile.

Because she wasn't wrong.

He flew downward in the direction of Leek's fallen body, determined to find his sword. Only all he found was a pile of dead flesh waiting in the snow below. He frowned. *Fuck.*

The weapons are part of a warrior Seraphim's power, Caro explained, landing beside him. "They manifest at will." She glanced around then, her expression wary. "It won't take him long to regenerate. Maybe thirty minutes. We need to come up with a plan."

"Thirty minutes? From a decapitation?" Sethios was begrudgingly impressed.

"Seraphim are resilient. Warriors even more so." Her gaze flew upward as another light shot through the sky. "They're fighting with runes from their swords. That's why you can't compel them. It's a defensive marking similar to the one I etched into our daughter's skin as a child."

Her brow pinched, suggesting she was contemplating what she'd just said.

He waited, aware that his angel wasn't finished.

"Well, except Stas's was a ruse meant to conceal her bloodline, too. So not exactly the same. Regardless, had the rune been designed to deflect Seraphim powers, it would have needed to be rewritten regularly to maintain the block because Seraphim are constantly evolving and working around wards."

Sethios vaguely remembered Caro discussing this—the

way Seraphim fought—with him before, but he hadn't been given the opportunity to witness it until now.

"Can a rune stop a bullet?" he wondered out loud. Vera had referred to guns as mortal toys, but perhaps her narrow-minded view stemmed from being a Seraphim and fighting with supernatural magic. After all, there was something to be said about mortals and their penchants for war and lethal weapons.

Caro shook her head. "Sort of. Warrior Seraphim use runes to create shields. And those shields would repel the bullets." She spoke matter-of-factly, her Seraphim nature shining through.

"Why have you never taught me about these runes?" Sure, they'd been busy raising a daughter and hiding from Osiris. But this information could have proved beneficial against a Seraphim attack.

"Seraphim are practical and divide information by power lineage. As a daughter of the messenger line, I grew up learning about concealment markings, not defensive or offensive runes."

"You mean your council divided the information equally among the masses, ensuring not one area knew too much," Sethios translated. "Sounds about right."

It was strategic. A way to maintain order through inconspicuous means.

And since the Seraphim were programmed to rely on logic, they didn't question the protocol. It would be seen as practical to only learn runes that paired well with their lineage.

Why would a messenger angel need to learn defensive markings?

To fight the system, Sethios thought.

But an average Seraphim would never consider that option. It would serve no reasonable purpose because they saw their existing government as flawless and founded on their prized principle of practicality.

"The Seraphim are victims of their government's brainwashing, carrying out orders like glorified puppets," Sethios murmured, his gaze falling to the beheaded Seraphim on the ground. "That almost makes him innocent."

Except for the fact that he should be questioning everything.

A lack of intelligence had earned him that punishment. He'd come here hoping to kidnap or kill an infant and her mother.

That wasn't fucking honorable at all.

"How many more Seraphim will they send?" There were only four here now. Three of whom were still battling somewhere up in the sky.

"They won't send more unless Leek requests it."

"Why Leek?" Sethios asked, studying the dead remains. He hadn't seemed all that impressive, apart from his sharp swords. Had Sethios's ability to compel worked, those blades would have been dust. And then where would he be?

Dead. On the ground. Like he is right now.

Yet he was in charge… why?

"He's the highest ranked of this group," Caro explained. "But Gabriel is technically ranked higher since he defeated his half brother a few decades ago." She glanced at him. "In my world, power has nothing to do with age."

He arched a brow. "What are you implying, angel?" He stepped into her personal space, his palm finding her hip. "Is my old age and experience not enough for you?"

"I'm saying the hierarchy in my world is different from that of your world."

"It's not different," he said, his voice low as he brought his lips to her ear. "Because you're my world, Caro."

She snorted. "Are you seducing me? Here? In the snow? Next to a decapitated Seraphim?" *Sadist.*

He grinned, his lips skimming her neck to find her throbbing pulse.

"Blood turns me on," he reminded her. "And I'm always seductive, angel. It's part of my charm." He nipped her tender skin before pulling back to stare down into her pretty blue eyes. "Doesn't make what I said any less true, angel."

Her lips twitched. "I missed you."

His arms circled her waist as he pressed his forehead to hers. "I missed you, too." A soft admission. But not exactly a secret.

His mate had been locked away in a reformation chamber for nearly two decades. Of course he'd missed her. And their reunion hadn't necessarily been thorough, given everything happening around them.

"Did Osiris compel everyone to mist here?" he asked. "Or just us?"

Her brow furrowed. "He didn't compel us. We chose to come here when we heard the wards fall. But the trackers anticipated it and followed."

Sethios met her frown with one of his own. "No. Osiris compelled us here. I felt it."

"I compelled *you* to counter your untrained misting ability," a deep voice corrected as his father landed near the dead body in the snow.

The olive tone of his bald head glistened beneath the moonlight as he glanced down at the Seraphim remains. He analyzed it for a moment, his expression giving nothing away.

"Hmm. Gabriel is far more useful than I ever realized."

He lifted his green gaze to Sethios. "It's most fortunate that I didn't destroy him as I'd originally intended to when I thought he was a council spy."

His statement lacked emotion, as usual.

"Did you compel the Seraphim to follow?" Sethios asked, glancing up at the sky. The lights had stopped flashing, suggesting the battle was temporarily over. "Seems like it would have been easier to leave them in the Bahamas."

"My compulsion wasn't required, as they followed Caro." Osiris's gaze ran over the female in question. "They must have taken your blood while in reformation. Now the trackers are using it to follow you."

"Perhaps, but how did they know I would be with Lizzie?"

"Educated guess based on you being the only Seraphim who could help her deliver the child," Osiris said. "Or they're aware of your daughter's loyalty complex. In which case, she's either being watched or informed upon."

Sethios didn't care for either option.

"How do the trackers work?" he asked. "Similar to Ezekiel?"

Osiris dipped his chin. "Yes. Once blood is imbibed, they can forever trace to the source. Unless the link is altered in some way." He glanced upward as Vera joined them with her navy wings slowing her descent from above. "Which is where you come in."

She sighed as her boots met the ground. "Yes, I can shift their memories toward a new objective. But we need to give them something to chase, or they'll just return to the council, where my faltering allegiance will be discovered."

Gabriel joined them next, his swords nowhere to be found. *That's a very useful ability.*

As is the power to compel, Caro returned.

Yes, but apparently, I can't compel swords to appear. And I find that disappointing. He wasn't exactly pouting, but he certainly felt a bit petulant about this development.

I'll buy you some swords, she replied, her tone underlined with realistic intent.

To go with your knives? he suggested, thinking about how he could use the longer blades during sex. They would certainly prove challenging.

No sword play in the bedroom. She sounded so stern that he almost laughed out loud.

Oh, angel. There will always be sword play in the bedroom.

She frowned, looking at him. The innuendo in his statement was clearly lost on her. A fact she confirmed when she replied, *But I prefer knives.*

Yes, I know. I'm talking about my *sword, darling,* he informed her, aware of her penchant for taking everything literally.

But you just pointed out that you don't have… She trailed off. *Oh.*

He smiled. *Yes.* That *sword.*

Color touched her cheeks as she cleared her throat to give Vera her focus once more.

She and Osiris had been discussing different ideas, their easy candor confusing Sethios a bit. The last time these two saw each other, Vera had more or less bested Osiris in a fight. It seemed strange that they were conversing freely now.

"We need to consult with the others," Vera concluded, her wings unfurling as she took off toward the house in the distance.

Osiris watched her for a beat before facing Sethios and

Caro. "I'll remain here, as we can't afford to waste time with reactions to my presence."

"Well, maybe if you were more likable, this wouldn't be a problem," Sethios drawled.

"Leaders are not meant to be likable," his father returned. "Leaders make the decisions no one else can. Which is why you need me to help train Astasiya. I'm the only one capable of doing what needs to be done."

"Not all training methods need to involve heartless cruelty," Sethios replied, folding his arms.

"No. But the most effective ones do."

"You wouldn't know that for sure, though, would you?" Sethios countered, arching a brow.

"I've lived far longer than you," he reminded him. "My techniques have been perfected for tens of thousands of years. And they work."

"They won't work on Stas. She's not like your usual subjects." Meaning she wasn't like Sethios.

He'd grown up beneath Osiris's cruel tutelage. His father might be able to argue that Stas was still a child, given her young Seraphim age, but Sethios had witnessed her stubbornness.

Osiris's version of training would infuriate her more than teach her. Because she possessed the ounce of humanity that the rest of them lacked.

"You have no idea what Stas needs to grow," Sethios continued. "Forcing her to learn from you will only make her hate you more than she already does."

"She doesn't hate me; she fears me," Osiris corrected.

"And you think that's better," Sethios replied. "Which is precisely why your methods will fail her." Not that this was even up for debate. She'd already turned down his offer to train her.

"Gabriel will train her," Caro interjected. "He's a

warrior Seraphim and second in line behind Adriel. You've now seen him fight, and you remarked that he was useful. Let him train Stas."

A practical suggestion that could only have been given by his angel. She'd also obviously struck a chord with Osiris because he'd fallen silent to assess her words.

After a beat, he dipped his chin. "All right. He can provide her with a proper introduction. Then, when she finishes her elementary training and realizes she needs more, send Ezekiel for me. I'll be waiting."

Sethios nearly told him he would be waiting for a very long time, but Caro agreed with a soft "All right."

It'll keep him away from her for now, she added into Sethios's mind. *Buys us time to determine how best to handle this situation going forward.*

He's not going to give up. It wasn't in his father's blood to do so. Sethios understood that because he was built the same way. And it seemed his daughter was similar, too.

No, he's not, she murmured. *But at least he's not using compulsion to force the issue.*

True. When his father wanted something, he took it. So this was almost a gift of sorts to let them try their way first.

Rather than belabor the point, he nodded, agreeing to the terms, and glanced at the house. "We should join the others in determining the new plan." Particularly as it involved Caro and the ability of the Seraphim to track her.

Osiris nodded, slipping his hands into the pockets of his gray trouser pants. He'd paired the gray with a white button-down shirt that was unfastened at the neck and rolled to the elbows, giving him a businesslike appeal. Yet the air around him remained deadly, confirming he'd more than held his own with the Seraphim in the sky.

"Why didn't you teach me about runes?" Sethios asked him, genuinely curious.

"Because you've never been able to access ethereal energy," his father replied. "I thought you might be able to after your twenty-fifth mortal year, but your wings never sprouted. So I didn't waste my time teaching you something you couldn't use."

"Why didn't I fully change?" Sethios pressed. "According to Leela, Seraphim genetics override the mortal half. So I should have become a full-blooded Seraphim."

His father's expression remained stoic. "Divine intervention, I imagine. Perhaps from that of a fertility Seraphim." His attention returned to the body on the ground. "The regeneration process is well under way. If you're going to determine a plan, I suggest doing so now."

Caro grabbed Sethios's wrist. "He's right. We need a plan. Now."

The midnight air swirled around him as she misted them to the house.

Where it appeared Jayson and Balthazar were engaged in some sort of argument.

"No," the new father was saying. "That's not happening."

Balthazar grabbed the other male by the shoulder, giving it a squeeze. "It's a solid plan."

"Did you miss the part where Seraphim are immune to our powers?"

"I'll have Leela with me."

"She's a fertility Seraphim," Jayson snapped. "What's she going to do? Impregnate them?"

Leela snorted.

Balthazar ignored the comment, his focus intent. "She delivered your child and brought her back to life. That *bonded* her to Aidyn, making her the perfect person to impersonate Lizzie. I will go with her and pretend to be you while you protect Lizzie and Aidyn. End of discussion."

"Don't *end of disc*—"

Balthazar pulled Jayson into a hug, cutting off his comment. "I hear your concerns, brother. But this is the best plan."

"And what plan is that?" Sethios asked as he casually leaned against the wall near the door. "Leela and Balthazar pretend to be Lizzie and Jayson and take the Seraphim on a wild-goose chase across the globe?" The guess was based on what Balthazar had said about Leela impersonating Lizzie.

"Something like that," Ezekiel drawled. "Meanwhile, the others will work on improving the wards around Hydria."

"And where will the real Lizzie, Jayson, and Aidyn be?" Sethios pressed.

"In Hydria," Balthazar replied, his gaze still on Jayson as he released him from their embrace.

"Also known as the first place the Seraphim will look," Ezekiel muttered, taking the comment right from Sethios's thoughts. Not literally. But it was exactly what Sethios was about to say.

"Which is why we're going to give them a false lead to chase around," Balthazar said. "Jayson knows it's a good plan. He's just worried about losing his favorite wingman. But who better to impersonate you than the man who knows you best, yeah?" He added that last part with a pat against the other man's cheek.

Jayson wasn't amused, his hand snagging Balthazar by the back of the neck. "If you get yourself killed for me, I'm going to bring you back just to kill you again."

The mind-reading Hydraian grinned. "Noted."

"I mean it, B. I will fucking rip you apart."

That only made Balthazar's smile grow. "Sounds like a promise I would enjoy."

Jayson growled. "Balthazar."

"I'll be all right," the mind reader promised. "Leela's been playing hide-and-seek with trackers for millennia. Isn't that right, sweetheart?"

She ignored him in favor of Vera. "I need you to remove this rune. Now."

"I'll barely have enough time to make this plan work, Lee," she replied, a note of exhaustion in her tone. "The warriors have regeneration powers and the trackers have healing runes to expedite their recoveries. Not even a beheading will keep them down for long. So the rest will have to wait."

Sethios straightened, his gaze finding the memory-manipulating Seraphim. "And what is it, exactly, that you're planning to do?"

Chapter 8

Leela

Vera explained the high-level plan to Sethios—alter this evening's events in the minds of the Seraphim pursuing them and give them a new target.

Leela and Balthazar.

Only, they would think the manufactured trace belonged to Lizzie and Jayson. Because that was what the memory would tell them.

They would also still remember Caro and be able to track her, but a rune paired with a barrier ward would fix that problem. Which meant they could mist in Caro's general direction, but the rune would make it difficult to pinpoint her exact location within a certain-mile radius and the ward would keep them from setting foot on the island.

Assuming everything was set up before Patreel and Arvane realized they'd been tricked.

Leela and Balthazar just needed to mist around the globe long enough to keep the Seraphim occupied while the others built up the security around Hydria.

Caro, Gabe, and Vera were in charge of revitalizing

the wards. They would teach Sethios and Stas as well and would hopefully have plenty of time to create enough defensive markings to keep the Seraphim out.

It was a temporary plan, but a worthwhile one to pursue.

Even over the phone, Luc's stance had been clear: "Splitting up weakens all of us. We need to provide a fortified front, and the only place to do that is in Hydria."

Balthazar had immediately agreed, as had Jayson. "We've been anticipating an invasion since 1747," the latter had said.

"By Ichorians," Issac had pointed out. "Not Seraphim."

"Yes. Which is where the wards come in," Luc had replied. "We just need some time to 'bolster' them, as Skye recommended earlier."

Which had led to the diversion discussion and Leela volunteering to play the role of the *mouse* in this renewed game of cat and mouse.

She'd spent millennia avoiding tracker Seraphim.

Why not benefit from all that experience now? Vera wasn't giving the Seraphim a vial of Leela's blood—that would make hiding nearly impossible.

Instead, she'd suggested they leave behind a few specks of blood on a cloth. It would be something that the trackers could use to initiate a chase, but not enough for them to establish a firm connection. They required at least a swallow of another's essence to fully track them.

Thus, Leela would only leave behind a few meager drops—enough to tease without engaging in the full seduction.

However, she hadn't anticipated that Balthazar would insist on accompanying her.

He'd claimed it would provide a more believable

distraction because he could pretend to be Jayson. Vera had agreed that it would work better because Leela had the bond to the child that the Seraphim might be able to scent in her blood, and Balthazar would have the essence of an abomination.

Together, they would make for intriguing prey.

At least, that was what the group had said.

Now it seemed she had no choice but to go along with the plan. Not that she disagreed with it. She just… didn't want to give anything else away.

He already knew too much.

And this would just make things more complicated.

"On the contrary, Lee," he murmured, his lips suddenly at her ear. "I think this is going to make everything more interesting instead."

The warmth of his body pressed into her back as he gently took hold of her hips. It wasn't forceful or even uncomfortable. Merely natural. Like their bodies were meant to relax with one another.

Yet she suspected that if anyone else had entered her personal space in this manner, she would have had a few comments.

But Balthazar wasn't anyone else.

He was… *hers*.

A risky realization. A false one, too. However, it felt like an accurate proclamation.

She'd claimed him in a way she'd never claimed anyone else. She didn't quite understand it. But such was life.

His lips met her temple. A tender brush of a kiss. Yet it was underlined in so much mutual understanding that her heart skipped a beat.

You shouldn't come with me, she told him. *It's dangerous.*

"It's already done," he whispered, drawing her attention to the energy in the room.

Everyone was preparing to depart.

Even Ezekiel and Skye.

Does she agree with this path? Leela wondered. *Did anyone even ask?*

She opened her mouth to do just that, when Skye turned toward her as though Leela had called the seer by name.

She met Leela's gaze in the next breath, her startling blue eyes rimmed with uncertainties and unfathomable sights. "Don't go to Morocco. He will know, and your true allegiance will be revealed."

Ezekiel frowned. "True allegiance?"

"To the council," Leela said, her voice barely audible. *To the Fates. To* him.

Because she knew what Skye meant. *Whom* she referred to. And what would happen when *he* found her.

There was a reason Leela excelled at avoiding tracker Seraphim.

"It's not worth the risk, Leela. Nothing is worth that risk," Skye stressed. "He's one of *them*. Not true in form. A mask. All of them are *masks*."

"Who?" Ezekiel pressed, his palm cupping her jaw and shifting her focus to him. "Who are the masks, Skye?"

She blinked at him, then canted her head to the side. "Can I go swimming in the Aegean Sea now? I would enjoy that much more than this frigid snow."

He sighed, his lips curling up fondly as he studied her features. "Of course, love."

"Thank you," she whispered, brushing a kiss against his jaw before curling into him. "Take me to the sea."

His ebony irises glistened with golden flecks as he lifted his gaze apologetically to Leela. She nodded in response, understanding. Skye's prophecies were fleeting, her warnings typically cryptic and only occurring when lost in a trance. Once lucid, she focused on the present, and as those moments were short-lived, Ezekiel preferred to honor them by doing exactly what she desired.

Such as tracing to Hydria now and letting her play in the water despite the wintry temperatures.

The pair disappeared, leaving Leela and Balthazar in the home with Gabriel, Clara, Sethios, Issac, and Stas.

Caro had left with Jayson, Lizzie, and Aidyn shortly after Vera had explained the plan again. Jacque had returned to take Owen back to Hydria as well. The phone Luc had spoken through was also nowhere to be seen. And Vera was outside manipulating memories.

Which meant the chase was about to begin.

"Where's Osiris?" Balthazar asked, his chest vibrating her back.

"Outside," Sethios replied. "At least, he claimed he intended to wait outside until the plans were decided. Vera might have already conveyed the intentions to him."

"Do you find that odd?" Balthazar pressed. "That she's conversing so freely with Osiris?"

Sethios shrugged. "Better her than me."

"What's your concern?" Issac interjected, his sapphire gaze astute as he assessed the male standing behind Leela.

She had always liked Issac Wakefield's no-nonsense approach. It differed greatly from Balthazar's fun-loving one, causing the two to bicker often. However, they were both fiercely loyal. Therefore, while they might argue frequently, they always valued each other's input during serious conversations.

Sort of like brothers.

Except Balthazar often tried to seduce Issac into bed—

something Leela fully appreciated and understood—making it a little less familial.

Still, their relationship was one she enjoyed observing.

And she would not mind being in the middle of them in bed. She'd even invite Stas to join. The more the merrier.

Balthazar's arms tightened around her waist, indicating he'd heard that little tangent in her mind. However, his words and tone didn't give anything away as he said, "She misted into the Bahamas compound without any hesitation, suggesting she'd been there before. Did you give her directions?"

The question appeared to be for Gabriel, though she couldn't see the trajectory of Balthazar's gaze since he stood behind her.

"No, I didn't," Gabriel replied.

"Then how did she know where to go?" Balthazar asked. "And why isn't she hesitating where Osiris is concerned?"

"Because she understands my intentions," a deep voice informed them all as a flurry of black feathers appeared around Osiris. He materialized half a beat later, his wings disappearing as he took on a corporeal state. "Stas needs to understand runes, wards, and defensive maneuvering. I expect you to provide her introduction since she's not yet ready to train with me."

"Not yet *willing* to train with you," Stas corrected without missing a beat.

Issac wrapped his arm around her as though to hold her back, or perhaps to caution her from speaking again. Osiris might be aiding them all today, but that didn't make him an ally or someone who would tolerate that tone.

"Her manners need improvement as well," he added as though plucking the thought from Leela's mind. "You'll handle that." That comment was for Sethios. "This strategy you've all decided on might buy you a few days, which is nothing in the grand scheme of time."

"Do you have a better suggestion?" Issac asked, his tone politely curious, not sarcastic.

"I do," Osiris replied. "But that requires Astasiya to agree to my tutelage, which I've been told she isn't ready to accept yet. Therefore, I'll indulge her wishes. For now."

"How kind of you," Stas deadpanned.

Sethios casually stepped in front of her, the movement not lost on anyone in the crowd. He knew her attitude would upset Osiris, and he was saying, bluntly, that his father would have to go through him to touch her.

Fortunately, Osiris didn't appear to be in a punishing mood.

Instead, he just shook his head and looked at Leela. "Good luck, Seraphim. You're going to need it." His gaze went over her shoulder to the mind reader at her back. "I'll be sorely disappointed if you get yourself killed, Balthazar. Try not to die."

With a rustling of feathers, he disappeared without another word.

"Vera's working with him," Balthazar said a second later. "That's why she understands his motives. She's our mole."

"In addition to Mateo or in lieu of him?" Issac asked.

"That remains to be seen," Balthazar replied. "Keep Tristan on him."

Issac nodded. "Consider it done."

"Good." Balthazar's lips met her ear. "We should leave soon, Lee. I have a place in Stockholm we can hide in."

She shook her head. "We're not going to Stockholm." She had warded homes all over the globe. They would mist to one of those locations instead. "Vera needs my blood before we go."

Not enough to swallow.

Not enough to truly trace.

Just a few drops.

A tease.

A… a *taunt*.

Leela swallowed. *I can do this. I can do this. I can do this.*

It went against her instincts, but this was only temporary. And it would hide the child.

Aidyn. She's the reason I'm doing this. That poor little soul had done nothing wrong. She didn't deserve to be hunted. Neither did Lizzie or Jayson. Leela knew what she was getting into with the Seraphim; they didn't. That made this the logical route. A sound plan.

Temporary.

Except Balthazar was going with her. And that complicated things. "You should—"

She yelped as he spun her in his arms. "It's done," he reiterated. "Tell me where to cut you."

Leela's thighs squeezed in response to the dominance underlying that statement. *Fuck, I'm in trouble.*

"You are," he agreed, his voice a low murmur.

It wasn't the first time she'd had that thought, nor was it the first time he'd responded to it. The dark promise in his gaze told her he was going to collect on her punishment soon, too.

By making her crawl.

She shook her head, denying the inclination. He would have to work a lot harder than this to earn such an act from her.

She only knelt for men when they deserved it.

His eyebrow cocked upward.

She arched hers in kind, holding his gaze.

This felt normal. Natural. Thus calming her immensely. Because squaring off with this male grounded her in the moment, in this reality, dispelling her fears and allowing her to breathe.

He cupped her cheek, his thumb skimming her bottom lip, his gaze following the path.

So bold. So intense. So *Balthazar*.

He didn't ask; he took. Because some part of him knew she would always give him permission. Perhaps because he could read her mind to know her intent. Maybe because it was just the way they worked together.

Regardless, she loved that he didn't waste time with questions or permissions. He just knew where the lines were and did his best to skate along them without crossing into forbidden territory.

Except, she wasn't sure a forbidden territory existed with him.

She might just let him take everything instead.

His brown irises glittered with intrigue, his mouth curling into a sensual grin.

He'd heard every thought. Every consideration. Every desire.

And his expression promised he would deliver on each one in time.

The glint of a blade caught her eye as his palm went to her nape. "Tell me where to cut you, Lee," he repeated.

She suddenly understood Sethios and Caro's penchant for playing with knives in the bedroom. It had never been her kink. Ropes, blindfolds, dominance, yes. Drawing blood or leaving marks, not so much.

But there was something undeniably intimate about trusting one's partner enough to play with a deadly weapon in the bedroom.

"Your choice," she whispered to him.

He smiled as he lifted the blade to gently stroke her throat. She swallowed as the cool metal touched her skin, her lips parting when she realized it wasn't the sharp end but the handle.

"Give me your hand, Lee," he told her.

She held it up between them as though pulled by a string. It almost felt as if she were compelled to obey him, something she typically fought. But with him, it was more fun to submit.

Although, seeing him on his knees would be an enticing sight indeed.

"Only if you earn it," he murmured, playing on her earlier thoughts.

Sounds like a challenge, she thought.

His lips curled, but he didn't otherwise acknowledge her comment. Instead, he focused on her hand. "Palm up."

She did as he requested, causing his grip to tighten against her nape as his opposite hand brought the knife to the fleshy part of her palm.

The tip bit into her skin, eliciting a hiss from her lips.

He pressed the metal siding against the small laceration, saturating the end of the blade in her red blood. Then he released her and walked over to grab a towel from Issac's hand. Leela hadn't even seen the other male move to the kitchen to find it, nor did she know where Balthazar had found the knife.

Because she'd been too distracted by everything else to pay attention.

That didn't bode well for their chase.

She needed to have her head in the game to survive.

Balthazar had grounded her, drawing her back from the brink of fear, leaving her to wonder if anyone else had noticed. But their expressions now gave nothing away. Everyone appeared determined.

This is going to work, Leela told herself as Balthazar wiped the blade clean on the towel. *This has to work.*

She curled her hand into a fist, the stinging sensation trailing up her arm. It would go away in a minute, her Seraphim genetics helping her heal at inhuman rates. But Balthazar returned in the next breath with a damp paper towel that he used to soothe the cut along her palm, causing her to frown.

Where did that come from? she wondered.

He winked in response. "Preparation is vital to success, Lee." The innuendo in his tone was not lost on her. "Ensures pleasure for all involved, too."

Only Balthazar could turn a dangerous situation into a seductive opportunity.

Well, Leela could, too.

Usually.

Just not today. Not right now. Not with what lay ahead of them.

Balthazar pressed the damp paper towel against her wound, just enough to apply pressure to stop the bleeding, but also in a manner that grabbed her attention. Taking her away from her fears and forcing her to focus. *Again.*

She met his knowing gaze and gave him a little nod of gratitude because she recognized what he was doing.

He removed the paper towel and added it to the cloth one. "I'm not sure where Vera wants to put this," he said, handing it to Issac. "It'll depend on whatever memory she just created. Assuming she was telling us the truth about that."

"She wouldn't lie," Leela interjected, certain. "And if she's working with Osiris, she has a good reason, too." She hadn't stuck up for her friend earlier, mostly because she didn't see the need to. Vera had more than proved her loyalty to Leela over the years. She was her best friend and confidant.

And she'd helped her on countless occasions.

Balthazar studied Leela for a long moment, his curiosity clearly piqued. But he gave her a dip of his chin, conceding to her point. At least, she hoped that was what he meant.

Perhaps he was referring to how Vera had manipulated his memories for Leela and was nodding in understanding of one of those occasions where Vera had helped Leela.

It was hard to say what he meant.

For as obvious as Balthazar seemed to be, Leela found him actually quite difficult to read. Sex was a clear motivator for him. But his desires went so much deeper than a mere roll in the sheets.

He was quite complicated beneath the seductive veneer.

It made her want to be able to read his mind.

Which would surely lead them straight to the bedroom.

"I'm ready when you are," Balthazar said, holding out his hand.

She narrowed her eyes at him. "That wasn't an invitation."

"It was," he countered. "But I meant misting, sweetheart. Vera has what she needs. It's time for us to lead the Seraphim away from Hydria."

"We'll be awaiting your call in twenty-four hours," Issac said, his arm around Stas.

Balthazar's head tilted once in confirmation. "You'll hear from us."

Issac returned the gesture with a nod of his own before he and Stas vanished.

Gabriel met Leela's gaze, the warrior Seraphim oddly

quiet after beheading two of his brethren. He didn't seem upset so much as resigned to his fate.

However, if Vera had done her job correctly, the Seraphim outside wouldn't remember his involvement at all. They also shouldn't recall Leela or Vera being here. Only Osiris, as it was his power that had subdued the two warriors long enough for him to gain the upper hand.

That had been the plan, anyway.

Assuming Vera had been able to complete the full revision of history.

She'd prioritized Leela first, wanting her presence here a secret to allow for the distraction to work.

"Leela," Balthazar murmured, capturing her attention once more. "Ready?"

No, she thought. But she grabbed his hand anyway and said, "Hang on." Because they were about to go for a ride neither of them would soon forget.

CHAPTER 9

BALTHAZAR

"MELBOURNE," BALTHAZAR MUSED, TAKING IN THE familiar sights. It was summertime on this side of the world. "Beautiful."

He much preferred the sun to the moon. Not to mention the warmer weather. His jacket would not be needed here, but he kept it on, waiting for Leela's next move.

Her lips curled down, her brow furrowed. *How....?* Her thought trailed off, piquing his curiosity. He waited for her to elaborate, then caught the strand causing her confusion. She'd meant to mist them to Sydney, not to Melbourne.

He glanced around again, the area one he'd visited many times before. "The Elders have a flat about two blocks that way."

The four-bedroom condo technically belonged to Alik, but they all shared it. Just as they did their properties throughout the world. It made for easy visits and comfortable stays.

"One of my favorite Italian restaurants is right over there," he added, gesturing to the street across from them.

"Their pizza is better than some of the most famous places in Rome."

It was part of what he loved about Melbourne. So much culture all fused together in one place. Too bad they weren't on vacation. Otherwise, he'd take Leela for a little stroll, feed her, then fuck her for dessert.

The concern radiating from her mind suggested a good time wasn't on the menu for tonight. Or maybe it merely meant he needed to work a little harder. "Talk to me, Lee," he said, his hand giving her a squeeze. "Do we need to mist to Sydney?"

She shook her head. "No. I have another place here. I'm… I'm just trying to figure out why we ended up here and not in Sydney." *And why it feels so familiar to be in this exact place next to him*, she added to herself.

He considered that for a moment, searching his memories for times he'd walked this street. But there were too many for him to bring up at once. He wasn't omniscient like Luc.

"Perhaps we've passed each other on this street before," he suggested. "If you have a place here, too, it's certainly possible we've been here before."

Particularly as they both appeared to enjoy casual sex. Perhaps it hadn't been together but with others around the same time. Or even a group experience. Balthazar was never opposed to those. The more the merrier, as far as he was concerned.

"It's just…" She frowned, her brow pinching as she fought some sort of block in her mind. A thought that was there and then gone in the next instant, too fast for even him to catch. Like she was trying to remember something that should exist yet didn't.

A sense of déjà vu, he realized. That occasionally happened to him when he'd frequented an area often.

He'd lived so long that it seemed only natural. However, something about this instance bothered her. Like she should be able to remember exactly why it felt familiar but couldn't.

Balthazar released Leela's hand to draw his fingers up her arm. She was still wearing that adorable puffy coat. He wanted to remove it to admire the sweater beneath and her lack of a bra.

Alas, he needed to free her mind first.

"Maybe we can take a stroll and see if something jogs the memory." He kept his tone soft, coaxing, but the glimmer in her blue-green irises told him she saw right through his words.

She wrapped her hand around his wrist and engaged her misting ability again, whirling them through time and space for a flash of a second.

Walls replaced the open air around him. Carpet cushioned his shoes, removing the concrete. And a sea of windows overlooking the water graced his vision.

They were still in Melbourne.

He knew this because Alik's flat boasted a similar view.

But this wasn't Alik's home.

The furniture was too white, the balcony too bare, and the rooms were smaller. A living area bled into the kitchen. No dining room. And the hallway beside him suggested it led to only a single bedroom.

Not a problem with him. He'd happily share a bed with Leela.

She released him, but he caught her by the nape, tugging her forward. "You can mist all you want, sweetheart. That won't distract me from wanting to know the truth."

"About what?"

"Everything," he said slowly. "Brazil. How many times

you've seen me. What it felt like inside you. What you look like when you come." He wanted to know it all.

Almost as badly as he wanted to understand more about her fears of reformation and the allusive *him* that she kept thinking about.

Who are you afraid of, sweet vixen? he wanted to ask. But he knew better than to push. Revealing secrets required a delicate touch. One he excelled at more than most.

Being able to read minds helped.

As did his ability to manipulate emotion.

But it really came down to bedside manners.

He brushed his lips against hers, tasting her with the age of experience behind his touch. Having access to her mind gave him the permission he sought, telling him that his kiss was very much approved and appreciated.

She would never say no.

It wasn't in her nature to deny him.

He knew this because he felt the same about her. There was an odd sense of intimacy between them, one he'd felt from the moment she'd arrived in Hydria. His body knew hers. His mind did, too. And his mouth… his mouth had kissed hers many, many times before.

"How many days did we spend in bed together?" he whispered.

Because it felt like hundreds, maybe even thousands. There was so much history here. Yet they'd only been together in Brazil. Part of his mind wondered if that was true. Maybe she'd taken his memories before then.

If Vera were here, he'd demand answers.

But it was just him and Leela.

"Only two," she replied against his mouth.

"Impossible," he breathed, his free hand unzipping her coat while the other remained clasped around her nape. "I *know* you, Lee."

"Because we're similar, B," she murmured. "I'm a goddess of sex. Seduction. Fertility. *Lust.*"

He pushed the jacket from her shoulders.

She let it fall to the floor before wrapping her arms around him.

"I'm the woman destined to destroy everything you think you know about fucking," she promised him, her voice a low caress that went straight to his dick. "Which is why I won't crawl."

His lips curled against hers. "Oh, sweetheart, this game just gets more and more interesting every time you speak."

He slid his tongue into her mouth, silencing her reply. But it didn't quiet her mind.

Her thoughts rioted, recalling his skill and prowess. The rightness and knowledge of his touch. Their fiery passion. The heat that had burned in her veins for weeks after Brazil.

Yet on the edge of her mind, he sensed *more*. Some vague recollection that pulsated within her psyche without being fully tangible. He prodded at it, curious as to what she kept hidden there. However, her nails bit into his neck, drawing him back to their embrace.

Her opposite hand wandered down his jacket to the bottom before sliding beneath the fabric to caress his flat abdomen.

Bold. Knowing. Intoxicating.

He hummed in approval, liking a woman who knew how to take charge. However, he squeezed her nape in the next moment, reminding her that he wasn't that easy.

Challenge thrived between them, her teeth skimming his lower lip as she threatened to bite him. He opened his eyes to find her irises flaring bright blue with no sign of green, reminding him of a succubus.

Fucking stunning. He wanted to see what intense ecstasy did to her gaze. How fiercely could he make her glow?

You won't win this battle, she thought at him.

He smiled, intrigued. Except those words struck a chord. Some memory he didn't quite understand. Whether in her mind or his own, he couldn't say.

There was some sort of strange connection between them, one he couldn't define.

Her brow furrowed as though she felt it, too. "Did you say that to me in Brazil?" he wondered out loud.

"I…" She swallowed. "I don't know." Her nails left his neck, and he released her nape. She took a stumbling step back. He caught her hip just to stabilize her. "My head feels fuzzy, maybe from being shot?"

His brow furrowed. "You should be fully healed from that."

"Then maybe the rune?" She glanced at her arm, but the marking was hidden beneath her sweater. "It could be conflicting with my other one." She shook her head as though to clear it. "Maybe I just need sleep."

"Or food," he suggested. "When was the last time you ate?"

"I have no idea," she admitted, blowing out a breath as she glanced around. "I need to secure the wards, too. It's been a long time since I was here."

"Then why don't you do that while I cook something."

"That would require groceries," she muttered. "Or something to cook."

"I could go pick something up," he offered.

But she shook her head again. "You have to stay nearby in case I need to mist."

"We can order something and have it delivered, then," he said.

"You really like food, don't you?" He sensed she was

drawing on a memory of Brazil because she started thinking about pancakes.

"I like anything that gives the body pleasure," he informed her, deadly serious.

Her eyes brightened in response. "A man after my own heart." The way she said it suggested she was just as serious.

However, rather than elaborate, she merely continued their previous topic by saying, "There are a few places nearby that have decent food. You'll have to pay cash."

She walked over to open a cabinet in the kitchen that revealed a safe. Her nimble fingers quickly keyed in a code, granting her access.

"Take whatever you need but don't leave the apartment. I'll be in the air." She disappeared in the next breath, leaving him to play.

And play he would.

———

"Your lingerie collection is impressive," Balthazar said when Leela finally returned.

He'd arranged their dinner—Italian from the place he'd thought about earlier—on the coffee table in her living room because she didn't have a proper dining table anywhere. And while he'd waited for it to arrive, he'd made himself at home in her personal space.

"Portovinos," she murmured, ignoring his lingerie comment and focusing on the food. "I approve." She collapsed onto the couch beside him. "Which phone did you use to order?"

"The burner I left on the counter," he replied. "You have quite the stash of supplies." Including several passports and a shit ton of cash. It rivaled Jay's vault of similar items for the Elders. He had an entire room devoted to foreign currency alone.

Right next to his armory—something he didn't find in Leela's one-bedroom flat.

In fact, she appeared to be completely weaponless. The only sharp objects were her steak knives. No guns. Nothing modern.

Although, one could argue that the black negligee in the top drawer of her dresser was a weapon.

Because she would absolutely slay in it.

"Are you going to open that?" she asked, gesturing at the wine. It was a dry white to go with the seafood pasta dish he'd ordered for them.

He reached for the bottle and the opener beside it, then started working on the cork. "Tell me about the wards." He wanted to understand how they worked. "Will they alert us of incoming Seraphim?"

"They'll alert *me*," she told him. "You can't sense ethereal energy, so you can't see or feel the wards."

He finished uncorking the bottle and started pouring her a small amount to taste. "Ethereal energy, similar to what happens when you mist, right?" he asked while handing her the glass.

Leela inhaled the fruity aromas of the wine, swirled it a little, then took a sip. "It's good."

He tipped the bottle over her glass to give her a proper fill.

"And yes, that's right," Leela continued. "Seraphim souls are ethereal in nature. It's where our powers come from. Blood is what carries that energy in a corporeal state, which is why Osiris's Ichorian lines require it as a sustenance."

"But Hydraians don't."

"Right, because you're children of a Seraphim-like

116

creature. Or that's the theory, anyway. Your bloodlines are somehow purer and closer to that of my kind as a result. Which is why Seraphim have always considered Hydraians to be the bigger threat."

That was an interesting detail, one Balthazar would need to share with Luc later. He poured himself his own glass while he considered what she'd said about ethereal energy. "Wakefield can see Stas's wings now. Does that mean he can create a rune or a ward?"

Leela shook her head and set her wine glass down to fuss with her salad plate. Balthazar had purposely left the lettuce naked, as he wasn't sure of her preferences. "Seeing ethereal energy is the first phase. Being able to access and manipulate it is the final one. He has about twenty-five years before he'll be able to draw on the essence. But he can at least see the markings now to learn them."

Balthazar observed Leela's assembly of tomatoes, onions, greens, and a light application of olive oil and vinegar. They were details he might need again later, as he enjoyed cooking for his lovers. It was an important step in the overall relationship. That, and listening when his partners spoke. Words were powerful and conveyed far more than most people realized.

Such as now—Leela's tone suggested openness.

Which meant she was in a sharing mood.

Thus allowing him to continue asking questions while they ate.

He asked about the Seraphim growth process first, curious as to how that would impact Wakefield. That led to questions about teaching Seraphim wards, where he discovered that the various lines learned their own versions of the markings.

"It's all about practicality," she continued, having switched to her pasta dish of tomatoes, onions, scallops, and spaghetti noodles. Balthazar had noted that preference for later, picking up the pesto dish that she'd ignored in favor of the other. "Seraphim don't bother learning unnecessary information."

"Something your council defines, not the Seraphim in question," Balthazar said, deducing the detail from everything she'd told him.

"Exactly. They tell each bloodline what to learn, and no one questions it."

"Yet you did." It wasn't a question so much as a statement because he'd heard the inner workings of her mind while she'd misted around nearby, fixing the ethereal markings. "All the runes you just altered were protective in nature, which I can't imagine is something most fertility Seraphim would consider necessary to know."

"Yeah, most of what I learned growing up was focused on establishing the perfect environment for mating and ensuring health and prosperity at birth. I know a few helpful tricks for keeping younglings in line as well."

He considered that while twirling some pasta around his fork. "So what prompted you to learn the protective wards?" He knew the answer revolved around *him*—some unknown entity from her past—and the tracker Seraphim. But what was the history there? What had prompted her to learn outside her requisite line?

She clearly saw through the council's partitioning of knowledge—that much was evident in her mind. But her thoughts didn't clarify how she'd become the woman she was today or why. What events had brought her to that point in her life that forced her to grow beyond the societal norms of her kind?

That was the true heart of the woman beside him.

The mystery.

The allure.

The fascination that he couldn't deny.

He wanted to know everything, craved the pieces of her that she kept locked away and the memories she'd stolen from his mind.

Who are you, sweet Leela? Tell me every detail. Let me know the real you.

"The High Council of Seraph rely on the Fates to dictate our futures, our uses, what we do in this life," Leela started, her voice low and thoughtful as she stared down at her half-eaten meal. "My mother is the Seraphim of Fertility, meaning she's the strongest of our line." She glanced up at him. "All Seraphim bloodlines have someone at the top. They sit on the council."

"And that's decided by age?" he guessed, then frowned, recalling something he'd heard in her head about Stark. "No, power."

"Power," she echoed, nodding. "Age can play into it in terms of living and learning, but power... power cannot be defined by age. Stas is proof of that. Gabe, too."

Balthazar reached over to steal a scallop from her plate.

She responded by taking one of his shrimp, the mannerisms between them natural and underlined with familiarity.

But he didn't comment on it.

Instead, he waited for her to elaborate.

"So, my mother is the strongest of our kind and issues commands down through our line—commands that come from the council based on feedback from the Fates. They can be as simple as detailing living assignments, jobs and tasks on the islands, or..." She trailed off, her gaze narrowing. "Or ideal *partnerships*."

Balthazar swallowed his current bite and arched a brow. "For procreating? Or...?"

"Procreating," she confirmed. "They tell us who to

fuck and when." Her dark tone told him how she felt about that. "Seraphim children are rare and difficult to create. Our cycles are unpredictable at best, but that's part of my job as a fertility Seraphim—I can sense when a female is most viable to receive a seed."

"How beautiful sex must be for your kind," Balthazar deadpanned.

She snorted. "Pleasure is a human emotion. Seraphim don't enjoy it."

"And yet a male has to feel something to be able to empty his seed into the heart of a woman," Balthazar replied.

"Exactly what I've been saying my entire life." Leela set her bowl down and pulled her knee up onto the couch to face him. "Male Seraphim proclaim not to feel anything. They don't even grunt when they come. However, I'm a fertility Seraphim. I can sense their pleasure. They can hide it all they want, but it's there."

"Of course it is. It's only natural."

"But not to a Seraphim. We're not allowed to feel." Her tone held a sardonic note to it. "That's the problem. I know it's a lie. I've always known it was a lie. They state it's a biological response. Yet my abilities prove that's a lie. So why hide it?"

He waited, aware from her thoughts and tone that she meant it as a rhetorical question.

"That's where my deviation started. I didn't understand the point of lying about a clear emotion just for the sake of hiding. And my curiosity spiraled from there. But the problem was, I still had to help orchestrate procreation activities between Seraphim. It was my job. Except it never felt right. Which is why I started seeking out human touch." Her lips curled a little at that, her blue-green eyes alight with mischief and desire.

He smiled in response, very much enjoying that look on her.

Like a little sex nymph, he decided, amused. He'd met her type before. Yet Leela took it to a whole new level. One he very much wanted to explore.

"Mortals don't shy away from what they feel. They embrace it. Their lives are so short that it's the only way for them to live. And I found that to be intoxicating. So different from my kind. But the problem is, that leads to deviations in the thought process, which the council frowns upon."

He nodded, following what she meant. "Seraphim are stoic by programming, not by nature."

"To an extent, yes. We're born without emotion. I see it in newborns all the time. Souls need time to grow and breathe and learn. My kind choose to embrace stoicism as a result. But I've often wondered if that's a result of societal pressure or a desire to live without feeling."

"Seems like a boring existence to me," Balthazar admitted. "But it also makes a powerful species easy to control if they only think in terms of logic and not emotion." As someone who could manipulate the emotions of others, he could definitely see the benefits of turning off those feelings.

"Yes," Leela whispered. "Which is why reformation happens. They call it a fatal flaw that needs to be fixed, or sometimes refer to it as immortal insanity. But I think there's more to it than that. Which, to answer your original question, is why I taught myself about protective runes."

Hmm, that didn't explain her thoughts about the trackers or the allusive *him*. However, Balthazar suspected the two were related in some way.

He wouldn't press it tonight, as his instincts told him she would shut down if he asked her about her fear of

LEXI C. FOSS

being caught by the trackers. Those were thoughts she hadn't wanted him to hear. So he'd respect her by not mentioning them.

But that didn't mean he would stop trying to understand them.

Whatever she feared was obviously important.

"So how do the alerts work?" he asked, bringing them back full circle. "How much time will it give us to escape?"

"Maybe ten minutes," she replied. "They'll have to disable the ward to enter, assuming they mean to cause harm, and that'll buy us enough time to mist elsewhere."

"All right. How long until they find us again?"

She shrugged. "It depends how much of my energy signature they pulled from the blood sample. It could take a few days, or a week, maybe? If we're lucky, anyway. With a straight connection, they can mist to a source within hours. But they don't have enough blood for that."

"And this is just because they're a tracker line, right?"

Her chin dipped in confirmation. "It's their natural skill, similar to Ezekiel's tracing."

Right. He'd suspected as much. "Do Seraphim have dual lines of power, like Hydraians?"

"Yes and no. We're born with a stronger side, such as my link to fertility. But many of us have dormant skills, such as Caro's ability to heal."

"What's yours?"

She considered him for a moment and smiled. "Maybe I don't have one."

"That sounds like a discovery challenge." One he would enjoy because it served as an invitation to delve even deeper into her mind.

Which intrigued him indeed.

Particularly as she had a lot of unexplored areas littered with blocks.

122

He wanted to know the stories there, why she hid herself away, what memories she refused to access. "I'm going to learn everything about you, Lee."

Her eyes sparkled. "We'll see." She held out her hand, her eyebrow raised. Hearing the desire from her mind, he handed her his bowl, then leaned over to pick up hers. She took his fork and twirled a bite of pasta, completely unfazed by the intimacy of their shared meal.

Because it felt normal.

Like they'd done it before.

Yet he couldn't find a thought of it in her mind to confirm that.

He couldn't outwardly state what he wanted to know because he didn't want her to realize how little he'd pulled from her mind. This game worked much better by leaving her under the assumption that he knew everything. It kept her from guarding her thoughts about him.

Instead, he indulged her in a round of silence while they ate.

Her mind was quiet, too.

Comfortable. Tired. Complacent.

When they finished their meal, he cleaned up the dishes and waited for the invitation he knew was coming. The one that would lead them straight to the bedroom.

The invitation he intended to deny.

Not outright. Not rudely. Just subtly.

Trust meant a great deal to him, and she'd fractured that with her memory tampering.

Which meant they had to start all over again.

That was a blessing and a curse.

A blessing in that *new* was always exciting. A curse because of the how and why of their situation. Balthazar didn't hold grudges—not for the long term, anyway—but he didn't appreciate duplicity.

It would take a lot more than Leela asking him to bed to foster his forgiveness.

"Normally, this is the part where I offer dessert," she said, her gaze running over him as she pushed herself up off the couch. "But we're not ready to play yet."

"No, we're not ready to play yet," he agreed.

"That doesn't mean we can't share a bed."

"And sleep?" he offered.

"Rest," she replied. "Dream. Fantasize. Draw out the gratification under the guise of me needing you nearby in case we need to mist."

Amusement warmed his chest. This female truly was his equal in almost every way. "You invite me into that bed and I'll kiss you until you fall asleep." He wouldn't do more. He wouldn't do less. This was a battle of wills, one he intended to win.

Preferably with her on her knees.

"And then you'll follow me into my dreams," she mused.

"I'm already there," he murmured, stepping into her personal space to take hold of her hip. "I've been there since Brazil."

Her gaze went to his mouth before traveling upward to meet his eyes. She didn't deny it.

"Take me to bed, B, and kiss me all night. Make the challenge worthwhile. Show me what I'm missing and see if you can convince me to crawl."

His original goal to say *no* died because the intent he required was absent from her thoughts and emotions.

She really just wanted comfort.

To chase away her fears.

To feel a sense of safety.

To think.

To kiss.

But not to fuck.

A shame, really. He'd wanted to teach her a lesson. However, it seemed she didn't require one because she already knew they weren't ready.

The past still lurked heavily between them.

A problem to resolve once they'd both caught their breath and slept a bit.

After all, Leela had just recovered from being shot, helping Lizzie give birth, and misting them all over the globe.

She'd earned a temporary reprieve from this game.

For tonight, Balthazar decided.

He pressed his lips to hers, his hand remaining on her hip while his opposite palm went to her nape. Then he walked her backward into her room and guided her to the bed.

Tonight, they would rest.

Tomorrow, the real challenge would begin.

CHAPTER 10

STAS

STAS STARED UP AT THE DARK SKY, HER LIPS PURSED TO THE side. "I don't see anything other than the moon and the stars."

Perhaps it was the exhaustion of the last few days, but she couldn't find anything that resembled ethereal energy above her.

Yet her mother was adamant that it existed.

Issac stood with them, a mug of coffee in his hand. Stas had finished two of those before leaving B's house thirty minutes ago.

After returning from Iceland, she and Issac had decided to rest despite the morning hour. And they hadn't woken up until nearly six in the evening, thus impacting their entire sleep schedule.

Fortunately, according to her mother, the wards were easier to work on at night.

Because they were supposedly easier to see.

A fact Stas was currently proving to be a lie, as she couldn't see a damn thing.

It was a beautiful night.

Just not sparkling with ethereal energy like she'd anticipated.

I don't see it either, Issac murmured into her mind. *But that doesn't mean much.* He took another sip of his coffee, his opposite hand tucked into the pocket of his black jeans. Stas rather liked the casual clothes he chose to wear in Hydria. They were still expensive and of a designer variety, but they gave him a sort of soft appeal that made him more approachable.

His sapphire irises left the sky to meet her roaming gaze, his dark eyebrow inching upward. *Searching for signs of my ethereal energy, darling?*

No. Just admiring the view, she replied.

He took in her jeans and thin sweater, his lips curling in appreciation. *It is rather ravishing, yes.*

Ravishing? She nearly snorted at the term. *Your age is showing.*

Alluring. Beautiful. Stunning.

Her cheeks warmed as he stepped closer with each word. His hand left his pocket to reach up and brush his knuckles against her blush.

Delectable, he added.

You don't need blood anymore, she reminded him.

Doesn't make me desire it any less.

The soft clearing of a throat returned their attention to the reason they were here. Stas's face grew even hotter at the realization of her mother having witnessed their flirtation, making Issac chuckle into her mind.

However, out loud, he sounded entirely normal. Cultured, even. "I can't see the ethereal markings either. All I see is my Aya."

Stas's mother smiled. "You'll do." The approval in her tone warmed Stas's heart. It was a bit overwhelming having her parents back after nearly two decades without them, but she preferred that to the alternative of them really being dead. "I also don't see any wards from this vantage point. We should try another beach."

Soft blue feathers appeared as Stas's mom shifted into her ethereal state. Then she disappeared as she misted to another beach.

Stas wrapped her arms around Issac's torso. "Don't spill your coffee on my wings."

He chuckled again, his free arm encircling her lower back. "I wouldn't dream of soiling such beauty, love."

This time she did snort.

There was nothing beautiful about pink wings.

Opal, he whispered into her mind. He didn't even need to hear her thought to know what she was thinking. Her opinion of her pinkish feathers was very well known between them.

Rather than respond, she misted them to the next beach, where she found her father waiting for them. He had a sword in his hand, something her mother appeared to be commenting on as Stas and Issac appeared.

"…from Gabriel," her father was saying.

"And does he know you have it?"

Her father shrugged. "I'm sure he'll figure it out eventually."

Stas's mother sighed and shook her head. "You're incorrigible."

"So you've said before," he drawled, his green eyes flicking up to Stas. "How is the ward lesson going?"

"Considering we haven't found one yet, I'd say not well," Stas replied as Issac moved to her side. His coffee mug remained steady in his hand as he took another sip.

Her misting skills had definitely improved.

Or maybe that was all him.

Perhaps a mixture of both.

Regardless, she was pleased and returned to her corporeal state with a smile as she turned her gaze upward into the night.

Same thing.

No sign of ethereal energy. "We're sure these wards exist?" Stas asked, frowning. She didn't trust anything involving Osiris, and he was the one who had supposedly made them. Which could mean nothing or everything, really.

"They might not be in the sky," her mother murmured, her gaze turning to the black sand and the nearby rocks. "He would have wanted to disguise them—not to hide them from Hydraians, as they can't see the runes, but from other Seraphim."

"They're all over the island," a new voice informed them as Stas's half brother appeared in a pair of jeans and a black T-shirt. No shoes. Very unkempt and not at all like the male she'd come to know over the last few months.

He casually held out his hand, causing the sword to disappear from her father's grasp and reappear in Stark's hand.

"Don't play with weapons you don't understand," he said as the wicked blade disappeared into thin air. "You never know who will use them against you, Sethios."

Her father smirked. "I've always enjoyed learning via trial and error."

"Then it's amazing you're still alive," Stark deadpanned.

"Isn't it?"

Stark ignored him, his focus shifting to his and Stas's mother instead. "Osiris disguised the wards with camouflaging markers. There's one about fifty yards up. I'll show you." He misted, followed by their mother.

Stas glanced at Issac. *Want a lift?*

You go. I'll see it through your eyes, love. His ability to manipulate vision was very useful, especially in a situation like this.

She nodded and took off after her mother and half brother.

They were both floating in the sky, their wings easily keeping them steady. Stas was newer to the notion of flying, making it difficult for her to remain aloft beside them. She studied their feathers, noting the angle they used to stay in one place. But when she tried to mimic it, she started to fall.

"There's an art to it," her mother said softly as she caught Stas by the elbow. "It's a lot like standing. Once you learn, it'll come naturally. But it takes practice."

Stas swallowed, nodding.

"Similar to misting," her mother added. "Which you seem to have already mastered."

"Only with locations I've seen or know," Stas admitted. "I have to be guided otherwise."

"That's normal. A lot of it comes with experience and age." She gestured at the darkness before her. "Or magic, as is the case with your brother. Because I can't see the ward at all."

Stas studied the vapid space and shook her head. "I can't either."

"It's in the edges," Stark explained, pointing to a subtle line in the air that shouldn't be there. It gave off a dull glimmer, similar to the moon casting a glow on a snowflake. "He hid these very well, but once you understand the energy signature, they're easy to find. By my review earlier, there are over four dozen of these on this side of the island alone. Most of them are deteriorated, just like Skye prophesied."

"Did you notice them before she said this?" Stas asked, curious.

"Yes, but I didn't realize they were drawn by Osiris. I thought Vera or Leela made them. I've also created a few of my own over the last year, but they were designed to protect you more than the others."

He spun his hand through the air, stirring a streak of mist-like magic with his fingertips. Then he drew a symbol that reminded her of an upside-down horseshoe with a diagonal line across it.

"Osiris masks his energy signature," Stark said as he drew another slash through his mark, this one horizontal in nature. "So it requires a rune to reveal the true ward, and even then, it's only temporary." He traced a final vertical line through the charm, allowing the energy to glimmer behind it.

Wow, Stas marveled, noting the cloudlike air forming an intricate dance in the night. It glimmered softly, similar to a moon reflecting off the water. A trick of light.

"I see why you said we needed to wait for dark," she whispered, talking to her mother. They would struggle to see this during the day, the marking easily blending into the sun's rays streaming down upon the earth.

"All these need is a little extra energy," Stark continued, his fingers traveling over the markings. "They're old, which is why they're fading. But even at full power, they're not that much brighter." He demonstrated what he meant by unleashing a strand of energy from his index finger, the ethereal magic glowing in the night with a red tint to it.

His essence, she realized, frowning. *Does that mean mine will be pink?*

Issac's chuckle warmed her mind.

It's not funny.

It is, love. It really is.

I hope your wings are fuchsia, she told him. *Neon pink. So bright they blind you.*

He was full-on laughing now inside her head, making her scowl. But then Stark began to weave his enchantment through the ward, seizing all her focus.

So beautiful, she mused, watching the strands fuse together to form a hum of magic she felt tickling the night air. It was unlike anything she'd ever witnessed. The ward twinkled like a thousand stars strung together in some faraway galaxy.

It's like… like a constellation…

Except far less bright.

Can you see anything down there? she wondered at Issac.

Only your brilliant wings, love, he replied. *But I can see the visual through your eyes.*

"There." Stark dropped his hand. "It's done."

The layer of his red mist twined with the black, forming a rope of solid power that slowly began to dissolve into the sky as the concealment rune took over once more.

"How do you create the ethereal strand?" she asked, glancing down at her fingertips. They appeared normal, just a bit translucent in her misting state. Her hands were also shaking a little from the exertion of trying to stay steady in the sky.

The wings at her back weren't exactly heavy, just awkward. She supposed her mother's comments about standing were right—she felt unsteady, like a toddler who had just discovered her legs.

Even the mere process of calling upon her wings had taken her a bit to master. However, it came naturally to her now, just like moving through time and space. But actually flying with her wings… that was another matter entirely.

"Try drawing a letter in the air," Stark told her.

She arched a brow but did as he requested.

Nothing happened.

He grunted. "No, Stas. Try *drawing* a letter in the air. Like, move the air around your hand to make the letter appear in the night."

"You're a terrible teacher." Stas didn't mean it as a whine, just a comment. Because her brother's no-nonsense approach left a lot to be desired.

"And yet I'm the best one available. Now draw a fucking letter."

"Gabriel," their mother cautioned softly.

He ignored her and folded his arms, his focus entirely on Stas.

She blew out a breath, aware that he would stare her down all night until she tried to do what he wanted. Or he'd just mist back to wherever he'd just been and ignore her until she decided to follow his directive.

As much as she disliked his mannerisms, she had to admit he was right about being the best trainer available.

So she tried again.

And received the same result.

Her brow furrowed as she considered the air around her. She glanced again at the gentle glow near the edges of the rune beside them, noting the energy pattern around it.

Like a cloud, she thought again. *No, like* mist.

Except it wasn't wet.

It was *power*.

An element only Seraphim could see.

And it existed all around her.

Drawing on that detail, she attempted another letter.

Her lips twisted to the side when the air remained untouched. But she could feel the energy humming against her skin. It needed to be unleashed somehow. Perhaps similarly to how she called upon her wings to appear.

Hmm.

She drew a Z in the air.

Then a T.

Then an A.

Try visualizing, Issac suggested, hearing the frustration in her mind as she recited each letter.

She tried a W next. Then an A. K. E. F. I. E. L. D.

A sigh escaped her mouth as she shook her head.

Stark flicked his fingers at her in response, sending a burst of energy through the air. It sizzled in front of her, dissipating in the air. "You'll need to master this before I can teach you how to fight a warrior Seraphim. The swords are made of energy, not metal. Which is why your father can't keep my weapon. It's part of me."

"He wants you to teach him how to make them," her mother said, her tone flat and very Seraphim-like. "It would be a useful skill, considering what's coming. You should train all of us."

Stark nodded. "Yes."

Stas arched a brow. "Oh? You can be reasonable and share information? Who knew that was possible?"

He merely looked at her in response, the word *brat* floating between them unsaid.

Because yeah, she was being a bit of an annoying kid to him.

But the bastard had withheld a myriad of useful information that could have saved Stas and Issac a lot of pain. She wasn't anywhere near forgiving Stark for it, even if he was being helpful at the moment.

He flicked his fingers again, sending more energy at her, this time enough to reach her wings. She flinched at the heat, the ember-like magic fizzling against her feathers. "Ow."

"That's nothing compared to what Leek and Kital can do," he replied. "Defensive markers will be important for you to master. Which requires you to call upon ethereal energy."

He hit her with more of that dustlike energy, making her growl.

"Sounds are impractical," he stated bluntly. "Deflect my energy. Or better yet, *absorb* it." He sent a larger ball toward her this time, one that slammed into her shoulder with the force of a baseball being thrown at full speed.

She narrowed her gaze. "Stark—"

He threw another one, forcing her to duck.

Except a third sphere came barreling at her half a second later. Her hand flew up on instinct to catch it, and the sparks collided with her own.

"Better," Stark praised.

But he didn't give her a chance to reply.

He shot several more fiery balls her way, each one faster than the next.

She caught four of the five and hissed when the fifth hit her wing. "Ow!"

"Then *absorb* it, Stas. It's not like I'm hitting you with seraphic fire."

Stas almost asked what seraphic fire was, but the incoming onslaught of magical spheres derailed her thoughts and forced her to focus on dodging the incoming orbs.

Apparently, her evening of reviewing wards with her mother had quickly transformed into a game of dodgeball.

She growled as one brushed her feathers. Then she caught another and threw it back at Stark with a strength that surprised her.

He caught it and volleyed it back.

She repeated the action.

And their bout of dodgeball turned into baseball.

Or football.

Or whatever the fuck it was called for Seraphim.

"Try adding your energy to it," he said as he tossed it back to her.

"Right now, I'm focused on not letting you burn me."

"I wasn't burning you. That tingling sensation is your ethereal energy reacting to the familiarity of mine. We're blood kin, not enemies."

"Could have fooled me," she muttered as she caught his sphere for the tenth or eleventh time. She attempted to infuse her own essence into it.

And cursed as the ball diffused to nothing but air.

Stark didn't give her a moment to complain. He merely volleyed another orb at her head.

She ducked, then twisted to avoid the second one, and cried out as the third one met her shoulder blades. He was throwing them harder and faster now, pushing her as he always did.

I'm—

She misted behind him.

Going—

She shot upward to avoid his too-accurate throw. The bastard knew exactly how to anticipate her now.

To—

She misted again, attempting to throw him off his game.

Kill—

Fuck! The fiery energy he unleashed tangled in her feathers, dislodging her balance and sending her downward.

Her mother snapped something in her wake, but the wind rushing in her ears drowned out the noise.

Stas misted in response, landing beside Issac with a furious curse. "I'm going to kill him!" she shouted.

"Not in that state, you're not," her brother responded as he appeared in front of her.

She leapt toward him, ready to unleash hell with her fists.

But a ball of sparkling energy formed instead.

And sailed right for his head.

He barely ducked in time, the surprise in his features almost comical.

However, she didn't take a moment to enjoy it. Instead, she threw another one at him. And another. And another. Lighting up the air with flames of fury as she chased him down the beach. "How do you like it?" she yelled at him, her desire to kill him a stamp on her spirit.

But a shimmer of diamonds at her feet gave her pause.

The black sand beach was littered with translucent crystals, all of them glittering in the moonlight in all shades of colors.

Opals, Issac breathed into her mind.

She stopped running, her lips parted at the display of energy.

Stark paused several feet before her, his expression giving nothing away as he observed her.

She swallowed, her hand lifting as though under some sort of spell, and she attempted to draw a *W* once more.

This time, her essence followed, alighting the air with dozens of sparkles that quickly faded into the night. Just like the residual embers on the sand below.

"Holy crap," she whispered, startled and amazed by the power.

"You're welcome," Stark replied, his tone lacking emotion. But she caught a subtle gleam of pride in his gaze. There and gone in a second.

Then he threw another ball at her head.

And the chase began again.

CHAPTER 11

LEELA

A WARM TINGLING SENSATION TICKLED LEELA'S SENSES, drawing her to awareness.

Lips caressed her skin.

Her neck.

Her shoulder.

Her collarbone.

A moan teased the edges of her mind as heat shot down her spine. *When did I fall asleep?* she wondered, noting her revitalized senses. She felt rejuvenated. Alive. *On fire.*

"Shh," a deep voice hushed in her ear. "Just relax."

Balthazar.

Oh, how many times she'd dreamt of having him in her bed again…

Mmm, but now he was here, with one thigh resting on top of hers and a heavy palm claiming her abdomen.

She'd lost her shirt.

And her jeans.

Last night while kissing B, she recalled dreamily. He'd remained true to his word, taking her mouth until she'd fallen asleep.

There had been some light petting. A few knowing touches. But nothing over the top. Just a sensual embrace filled with unspoken memories and wicked intentions.

It'd been exactly what they'd both needed.

And yet it hadn't been nearly enough.

Which had been entirely the point.

"B…" The nickname left her mouth on an unexpected plea. She wanted to taste him. To kiss him. To devour him. To make him reenact every detail.

Part of her realized this weakness stemmed from still being on the cusp of sleep, lost to that pleasant hour where fantasies thrived. She wanted to fall back into a dream. Indulge the cravings of her soul. Revel in Balthazar's talented touch.

"You stole my memories, Lee," he whispered. "I want them back."

"We can re-create them."

"We're going to do more than that," he vowed, his palm a brand against her skin.

Confidence and charisma created an intoxicating combination that was all Balthazar. She lost herself to his aura, his touch, his *existence*, and allowed him to draw her deeper into this dangerous game.

Taking his memories had been more painful than she could ever have anticipated.

But it'd also been the right thing to do.

She'd made a promise to protect Stas, pledged a fealty bond that couldn't be broken, and had put fate before personal desires.

That didn't make Leela a bad person. If anything, it made her a martyr.

Balthazar hummed in response to her thoughts, the Hydraian Elder not even attempting to give her mind a second of privacy.

She supposed he saw it as his due, considering what she'd done to his memories.

Or perhaps he couldn't turn it off.

Mind reading had to be overwhelming.

And useful, she thought.

Particularly in bed.

His lips ghosted across her neck, his tongue pausing to trace her pulse. "I don't need access to your thoughts to understand your desires, Lee. It's your body that tells me what I need to know."

She shivered as his palm skimmed her abdomen to her hip, his thumb gently caressing the bone before finding the pleasure point beside it. Her lips parted on a contented sigh, her veins heating from Balthazar's sensual prowess.

He still wore his black boxer briefs, but nothing else. Her mouth watered with the notion of exploring his fine physique and showing him just what she could do with her tongue.

However, his mouth was already moving downward to her collarbone. Licking, nipping, teasing. So tempting and deliriously perfect.

He avoided the areas most men would go for, choosing the path between her exposed breasts and around to the side to caress her rib cage.

Her nipples hardened in response, the teasing caress lighting a fire deep inside.

She threaded her fingers through his hair, not to guide him but to hold him. Her opposite hand fisted the comforter at her side as he continued his torturous trail downward to where his thumb rested against her hip.

"Mind reading is my oxygen," he whispered against her skin. "It's as natural to me as breathing. And you're right; I can't turn it off."

His nose grazed her lower abdomen, his lips barely

brushing the top of her lace thong. It was all she wore, leaving her almost entirely naked beneath him. However, Balthazar wasn't the type of man to let a little nudity persuade him to act. He would draw this out as long as he desired—a notion he proved via his gaze.

Vivid determination shone in his swirling chocolate depths.

He would wait her out for as long as it took to make his point.

And she'd enjoy every minute of the torturous descent into blissful insanity.

I'll make you work for it, B, she thought at him.

"I wouldn't want it any other way, sweetheart," he murmured, his palms sliding down to grip her thighs and forcing her to spread for him.

But he didn't go for the apex between them.

No, he went to his knees and stared down at her instead. Hotly. Intently. Wickedly.

She didn't move, apart from letting her arm fall after releasing his hair.

If he wanted to admire the view, she wouldn't stop him. Confidence was a trait they shared. She knew her curves were built to entice, just as her flat abdomen merely accentuated the hourglass of her figure.

She was built to fuck.

As was Balthazar.

Over six feet of solid muscle, tanned skin, and a face made for worship. A proper god with devilish eyes, sexy dimples, and a jawline carved from stone.

This was the kind of man that turned heads everywhere he went. He could tempt anyone he desired into joining him in bed.

But what was so innately beautiful about him was the fact that he would never use those traits to convince someone to break a belief or a vow. He respected everyone around him. Ensured satisfaction for all parties involved. Because he actually *cared*.

That was the trait Leela had admired most about him throughout the centuries of observation.

He could use his looks and powers for evil, yet it never even crossed his mind to do so.

Balthazar loved to *live*. And he wanted to share that joy with the world.

His lips curled as he read the thoughts from her mind, fully aware of her admitting that she'd observed him for much longer than a few months.

But what did it matter now? She couldn't fix the rune without Vera's help, and her friend had made it abundantly clear that she didn't want to block Balthazar from her mind.

So why not show him everything?

He already knew about Brazil and what she'd done. She really had nothing else to hide.

And she didn't really want to hide from him.

Something she suspected he knew, which was why he didn't even try to stay out of her thoughts. Of course, he'd just said he couldn't do that even if he attempted to.

Thoughts are his oxygen.

He continued to study her, his fingertips brushing up the sides of her legs as he continued to kneel between her splayed thighs.

"I'm aware that not all thoughts are meant to be heard," he told her softly. "It's why I'm the bearer of many secrets. Some that I never desired to know. Others that are useful in understanding intentions while still being decidedly uncomfortable. But they ground me in a way. Make me feel thankful for this life and the beautiful experiences of the world."

"You've never been the type to use your gifts for nefarious purposes." It was a statement that confirmed what she'd said in her mind about watching him for centuries.

Hell, not centuries.

Millennia.

She'd been aware of his existence for as long as she could remember. Her sensual equal. Or so many would assume.

But her age and experience surpassed his, though she couldn't quite say by how many decades or centuries. Maybe even millennia.

Time was rather irrelevant to her kind. They lived forever, counted their birthdays in decades or sometimes centuries, and a few via millennia.

Osiris was over ten thousand years old. An ancient.

Vera's age rivaled Osiris's, falling short by maybe a few centuries.

While Leela was closer in age to Balthazar, but still older.

"I admire your experience," B said, his lips curling again to reveal those alluring dimples. "Provides another layer to this challenge."

"You can't surprise me." A lie. He'd certainly surprised her in Brazil.

And the glimmer in his brown eyes told her he knew it, too.

Likely from her thoughts.

Or potentially because his confidence told him that just couldn't be true.

His fingers continued to travel up and down her outer thigh from knee to hip and back again. Soft. Tender. Sweet. A tentative stroke to learn her reactions and body.

She understood the intent because she'd done the same to women and men alike.

Although, she wasn't used to it being done to her.

That change suited her nicely. And she particularly enjoyed how he paused at her knee to gently dip beneath and stroke the tender area of her joint. Not many realized just how sensitive that space could be, but he exploited it now, grazing the skin and scattering goose bumps along her flesh.

The urge to close her thighs for friction grew with each tentative stroke, which she suspected was entirely the point.

He touched her so lightly, the purpose clearly being to inspire lust and stoke her need to a flaming inferno.

She didn't fight it, choosing instead to revel in his attentions and allowing her body to react in kind.

His thumbs were magical, his fingers a benediction, his heat an addiction.

She closed her eyes and just melted beneath him.

Lost to the sensations.

To his enchanting existence.

To his knowledgeable touch.

Up and down, around, circling, brushing, teasing. Only the fingertips. Subtle pressure. Light strokes. Warm caresses.

He reached her hips again, this time tracing the bikini area of her thong and then down her inner thighs to the tender space behind her knee once more.

Heat bathed her skin as he bent to press a kiss to her hip, then his mouth began to follow the movement of his fingers. His tongue trailed along the lace between her thighs, tauntingly beautiful in its perfection.

"I can smell your need, Lee," he whispered. "It's a flavor in the air that tells me this is exactly what you want

—to be worshipped by a man who knows how to properly indulge a woman."

His teeth grazed the inner point of her thigh, skimming her femoral artery and nibbling enough to draw focus to that region of her body.

"Your goose bumps and shivers are louder than your thoughts, telling me where to go, how to kiss you, where to touch…" He trailed off as he continued his erotic torment, his mouth eliciting pleasure from her very soul.

True talent.

Beautiful patience.

Stunning seduction.

Leela would never be the same, and she was entirely okay with that fact.

"This is why I don't need your mind, sweetheart." His words resembled a dark promise against her inner thigh. "Your body is an open book, giving me every intimate detail."

She fisted the comforter at her side again, mostly to keep from touching herself. Playing his game would intensify her pleasure. And that meant not giving in to the impulse to stroke her own flesh to completion.

"Your flush is gorgeous," he praised. "A luscious shade of pink. It makes me want to move that lace to the side and see how prettily you glisten."

She swallowed, his words an aphrodisiac to her psyche.

"So beautiful," he added, his lips near her knee. "Your legs are the perfect length for so many intriguing positions. And your athleticism tells me you can handle all of them with a dancer's grace."

He pushed on her thighs, forcing her to spread even more for him.

"Mmm, and your flexibility adds even more ideas to the list, Lee."

"I can fly, too," she told him, her voice a sultry purr that she didn't bother to disguise. "Something I know your former lovers couldn't do."

He paused, his brown irises glittering with excitement. "Can you fuck while ethereal?"

"Yes."

"Good," he replied, his tone deepening with sexual intent. "We'll be exploring that, too."

"We're going to be busy for decades if you keep adding to your list," she warned.

"You'll not hear a complaint from me, little vixen." He lifted her leg to lick the back of her thigh, causing tingles to shoot down her legs to her already throbbing core. "I'm going to taste every inch of you. Fuck you every way. Make you scream my name on repeat. But only after you crawl."

"A few licks won't make me beg."

"I know," he whispered, a smile underscoring his hushed tone. "This is just an introduction to how I prefer to wake a woman up while in my bed."

"My bed," she corrected.

"Is it?" he asked. "Because I think we both know I could easily own you in it."

"A promise you'll have to make good on."

"Yes," he agreed with a tender nibble to her thigh. "After you crawl." He released her leg to switch to the other, his mouth even hotter against her dampening skin.

He was driving her senses wild, taunting her in a manner that forced her focus to remain solely on him. Nowhere else. No one else. Only Balthazar and his beautiful tongue.

Fuck, she wanted him between her thighs.

Licking her slit.

Her clit.

Her insides.

Everything.

She'd experienced it too few times in Brazil and craved so much more now.

These months apart had felt like a dark game of delayed gratification. He'd unknowingly taunted her by bedding others and driving her mad in her dreams.

She'd wanted to join.

To explore.

To indulge.

To *play*.

She'd been dying to mist in and take over, to give him a show he wouldn't soon forget. But she'd been forced to watch from afar, and now that she was beneath him, there wasn't any other place she'd rather—

A buzzing flared across her senses, causing her eyes to widen. *No. That's impossible.* She sat upright, her focus falling to the clock. They'd gone to bed maybe around six or seven in the evening. It was now about the same time in the morning, confirming she'd slept for a while—twelve or so hours, to be precise.

Which meant they'd only been in Melbourne maybe fifteen hours total, sixteen at best.

And it should have taken the Seraphim closer to a week to find them.

"Something isn't right," she said, grabbing Balthazar's shoulders. He'd sat up as well, still on his knees between her thighs. "We need to go."

The alarming sensation had increased, telling her the Seraphim were almost through her barriers already. That implied her first few layers hadn't worked as expected.

Maybe she'd rushed the wards.

But she doubted it.

No, something was definitely wrong. They didn't even

have time to find their clothes. At this rate, the seeking Seraphim would be there in seconds, not minutes.

She wrapped her arms around Balthazar's shoulders and called upon her wings, misting them from the room half a beat later.

Balthazar's hands found her hips midflight, their thighs touching as they both straightened their legs in preparation for landing.

Leela wasn't sure where precisely to go, her instincts firing too fast for her to process her surroundings as their feet touched the ground. She blinked twice, expecting to see the familiar streets of San Francisco—her usual go-to location when fleeing.

But the structures around her were nothing like the hilly California city.

And the signs were definitely not in English.

"Tokyo," Balthazar supplied, his brow furrowing as he took in the bright lights of the city. It was a few hours behind Melbourne and still nighttime here—a realization that was a good thing, considering their mostly naked state. "Where's your flat?"

"I don't have one here," she admitted, her voice barely audible. Tokyo wasn't a place she'd even anticipated going, and yet, standing here felt... familiar. *Too* familiar. Like she and Balthazar had been in this exact place before. But she couldn't find any memory of it within her mind. Not even an inkling.

So why am I experiencing an odd sense of déjà vu? she wondered.

"We can't stay right here," Balthazar said, interrupting her thoughts. "Let's go south. We have a place in Okinawa, right on the water."

A memory taunted Leela's mind, one she couldn't quite define.

Frowning, she followed the trace in her mind before Balthazar could provide directions and took them to southern Japan.

Right to the doorstep of a home she'd never seen before.

Yet recognized as though it were her own.

An Elder home.

Luc's home.

But how do I know that?

And why do I feel like I've been here before?

CHAPTER 12

BALTHAZAR

QUESTIONS ROLLED THROUGH LEELA'S MIND AS SHE glanced around the front yard and back at the door, each inquiring thought rivaling his own queries.

Because she shouldn't know this place existed.

Very few of the Hydraians knew of its existence, and this home wasn't a place Balthazar frequented often. The five-bedroom estate was technically Luc's place, but as with everything else related to the Elders, they shared it for purposes such as this.

Maybe Leela had followed Luc here at one point? Jacque teleported the Hydraian King here when he needed to think, which, lately, was a lot more often than usual because of Aidan's death.

Perhaps that was why Leela knew about it?

But the blocks on the edges of her psyche suggested it wasn't that easy an explanation. Balthazar wanted to prod at them, see if he could move them out of the way. However, their security mattered most at the moment.

"Leela." He kept his voice soft and low in an attempt to coax her from the confusion of her thoughts. "Can you create protective wards here?" They hadn't worked as expected back in Melbourne—yet another issue they needed to address—but Balthazar was determined to take this one step at a time.

Protective barriers first.

Then clothes or maybe food.

Followed by a discussion on their current location and next steps.

I... I... Her mental voice trailed off. She hadn't returned to a corporeal state, leaving her invisible to his senses.

He couldn't feel her arms around his neck, yet he knew they were there because she'd grabbed him like that before leaving Melbourne.

And he could hear her thoughts.

"Leela," he repeated.

Yes, she replied. *Wards. Yes.*

A kiss of wind ruffled his hair, coupled with the distancing of her thoughts, telling him she'd just flown above to work on the wards.

With a nod, he focused on the electronic keypad by the door. It required a passcode for entry—something Jay had installed himself for the sole purpose of not needing a key. They owned too many properties throughout the world for them to carry around keys everywhere they went; thus, this system made it easy to come and go as they pleased.

It also helped with general upkeep.

As this was one of Luc's favorite getaway homes, it was cleaned and stocked regularly.

Which meant there would be food in the fridge and fresh linen on the beds.

Balthazar punched in the requisite code to both disarm the alarm and open the door.

He glanced back at the gate situated at the end of the

drive, then up into the sky, curious all over again as to how Leela had known to come here.

Balthazar had been here maybe once in the last decade, and that'd only been to see what upgrades Luc had made to the place—the Hydraian King was constantly adding new gadgets to his favorite home. And women weren't typically invited here on principle, the estate too precious to Luc for casual flings to temporarily visit.

Yet Leela had known exactly where this home was located. However, the thoughts in her mind had confirmed she couldn't say how or why.

Balthazar continued to puzzle over that while listening to her think through the wards above. They were distant, but definitely within a mile or so of him—something he knew since he could still hear her.

She was currently considering where to place each ward, confirming none existed here presently.

Not a surprise, really, but he'd wondered at the possibility since she'd been able to mist them directly here without directions.

He closed the front door, the locks sliding immediately into place. Leela would need to either ring the bell or mist inside. He assumed she would do the latter.

Balthazar passed through the two-story foyer, beyond the white marble staircase, and past the open seating area to his left, heading straight for the kitchen.

Which was fully upgraded, as he'd expected.

A quick glance in the wood-plated fridge confirmed a recent supply of food had been delivered, including a few pre-made meals.

Those would definitely come in handy.

Luc's service typically stopped by every third day, taking any untouched food back with them to feed themselves and replacing upgraded supplies.

It was all part of their ongoing property maintenance throughout the world. Upgrades, cleanliness, and general preparedness were organized by a team of Hydraians that specialized in international laws and financial management. They were the only ones other than the Elders and a handful of Guardians who knew about these properties.

Well, them and Ichorians like Wakefield since he'd helped invest in a few.

Aidan had known about them as well.

They weren't exactly secrets, just investments left to prosper and grow. But many of them required constant attention, like this property and its close proximity to the beach. There were also gardens out back that Luc kept meticulously groomed.

This home resembled peace to the very old Hydraian.

At least it used to prior to Aidan's death.

Balthazar sighed and closed the fridge before venturing through another seating area toward the back of the estate. Luc's den would have the supplies needed to touch base with those at home.

He pushed through the double doors and paused to admire the furniture. It'd changed since his last visit. No more wood and oversized chairs. Instead, there was a glass table, a single executive seat, and a wall of tech.

"Well, you've been busy," Balthazar murmured, admiring the giant touch screen. It was over seven feet tall and took up the entire wall to his left. The surface behind the desk was all tinted glass that overlooked the patio, pool, and beach beyond it.

Meanwhile, the other two walls were boring in comparison—stark white. Luc probably used those to focus while delving through his thousands of years of knowledge.

"Where did you put the phones and cash?" Balthazar wondered out loud, searching the area for signs of a safe. It used to be behind an old Italian oil painting. But now that was a computer screen.

Balthazar considered it for a moment before walking over and pressing his palm to the center.

Nothing happened.

Not surprising. Unlike Luc and Jay, Balthazar didn't really care for fancy technology.

Sighing, he returned to Luc's empty desk. No drawers. No pens. No phones.

"All right." He left the office to head toward the back staircase and took the steps two at a time upward to check out the bedrooms.

Most of them were the same—minimal decorations, beds, dressers of clothes, and fully stocked bathrooms.

However, Luc's door was locked, causing Balthazar to arch a brow.

His oldest friend never locked anyone out, yet it felt oddly appropriate given his recent behavior.

They really did need to have a talk soon.

Which requires a phone, Balthazar thought, heading back to the third bedroom, which belonged to Jay.

If Luc were to move the safe anywhere, it would be to somewhere in here, as Jay was the emergency preparedness expert.

And sure enough, there was a safe lodged into the back of the closet.

Balthazar grinned as he keyed in the code he knew his fellow Elder would use—a seven-digit joke of a number that only the Hydraian Elders knew.

A hiss sounded with the unlocking of the door.

"Voilà," Balthazar said, grinning as the safe revealed

an extended section of the closet that was essentially the size of another room.

Unlike Leela's safe, this one had guns, knives, and a myriad of fake passports and falsified visas. There were a few charged tablets as well. And, of course, an array of burner phones.

Right beside the bookshelf of cash in various currencies.

It all looked exactly the same as what he'd anticipated finding in the den downstairs, which suggested Jay had helped Luc move all this up here.

Although, it was odd he hadn't mentioned it to Balthazar. So perhaps Luc had done this on his own. All he'd really done was partition off the walk-in closet by inserting a reinforced wall guarded by a high-tech entry system. That sort of project certainly suited Luc.

However, it left Balthazar wondering about the purpose of the screen downstairs.

Selecting a burner phone, he shot Luc a text in an ancient language his friend would be able to read—one that roughly translated to, *It's B. Call me back at this number.*

He left the safe behind, closing it along the way, and took the phone with him to the bedroom he typically used while staying here.

The phone started ringing almost as soon as he stepped through the threshold.

"Luc," Balthazar said as he walked over to the bed he hadn't slept on in years. It probably wasn't even the same mattress or original frame at this point. But it worked.

"Good to hear your voice," his oldest friend replied.

Balthazar smiled. "I thought you might be worried."

"Me? Never."

A lie, but Balthazar let it slide. The Hydraian King

always worried about his people. It was what made him a good leader.

"When did you turn your den into a computer?" Balthazar asked, the question serving as a good way to convey his current location to Luc without outwardly stating it. Balthazar might be on an encrypted burner phone, but that didn't mean it was entirely safe to speak openly.

Especially since their resident tech genius, Mateo, was likely working for Osiris.

Unless it's only been Vera all along, Balthazar thought, recalling his suspicions about her behavior. The distrust likely stemmed from what she'd done to his mind.

But his instincts rarely failed him, and right now they told him that Vera was hiding something. Something important.

And not just the detail about her working with Osiris.

"My regular screen only allows so many research tabs to be open at one time. So I improved the process by expanding the size to encompass the wall, but it's still not large enough to keep up with my mental processing. It's a work in progress." Luc sounded a bit frustrated by the project.

Balthazar imagined his face would match the tone if he could see him, but this burner phone wasn't built with that technology. With facial scanner tech being utilized throughout the world, they just couldn't risk using an upgraded platform. It'd actually taken quite some effort for Jay to procure these old devices for this purpose.

"Everything good?" Luc pressed, curiosity lightening his tone.

"Yeah," Balthazar replied. "Just business as usual. We'll be staying here for a few days." It was an important statement because it meant this home wasn't currently safe for Luc to visit and might not be for the foreseeable future.

Leela would need to elaborate more on Seraphim protocols and what they would do upon discovery of this location. Would they monitor it? Forget about it? Destroy it?

"We were found quickly," Balthazar continued. "But the fail-safes in place gave us enough notice."

"There are certain countermeasures in place surrounding my *computer* that should help you there as well," Luc replied, his emphasis on *computer* meaning *home*.

"Excellent." Balthazar already knew Luc would have some sort of security system installed to guard his estate investment. Every property they owned maintained a similar framework for protection. Not just for the homes themselves, but for the potential occupants inside.

"Things are progressing here," Luc told him, aware of the update Balthazar would want. "The retired Sentinel says it's going to take four or five days to finish the review."

The retired Sentinel being Gabriel Stark, Balthazar translated. Because he wouldn't use that term to describe Tom or Stas.

The only other "retired Sentinel" in Hydria right now was Blake, and he definitely wasn't involved. As far as Balthazar knew, the human was still recovering from whatever mindfuck John had done to him. The now-dead CEO of the Catastrophic Relief Foundation (CRF) was a piece of fucking work and had subjected Blake to a form of rehabilitation to punish him for not adhering to an order.

Similar to how the Seraphim apparently subjected their own to reformation when they showed signs of feelings or emotions.

"It would go faster if he had help," Luc added. "But one of his allies is unaccounted for."

Balthazar considered his statement for a moment, wondering if he meant Leela. However, that didn't make sense. Luc wouldn't factor Leela into the equation, as she had another mission—to distract the Seraphim.

Which meant he was referring to those with the power to help Stark reinforce the wards.

It's not Osiris. Luc would never grant him safe passage in Hydria. So it's either Stas, Sethios, Caro, or... "V?" he guessed, using her first initial rather than her name.

If Mateo was listening in and also a mole, then he would already know that Vera's presence had been noticed. He would also be aware of Stark's current task to fortify the wards. Therefore, they risked nothing by mentioning her first initial.

Unless the Seraphim were listening, in which case, they might be able to deduce the meaning eventually.

But that was a risk Balthazar accepted.

"Yes," Luc confirmed. "Hasn't been seen since Iceland."

"I see." Balthazar would need to mention that to Leela. "I'll check in tomorrow to see if that's changed."

"Twelve-hour updates, not twenty-four," Luc countered. "You could use my den if you want."

"That requires turning on your screen."

"So say *hello* to it."

Balthazar frowned. "Hello?"

"Exactly. Your voice is recognized. She'll respond to you." The frustration in his tone had been replaced by pride, suggesting he had a love-hate relationship going with his computer.

"How are things otherwise?" Balthazar hedged,

wondering if his oldest friend would open up about anything useful.

"Safe," he replied. "Certain situations are still under evaluation. Others are settling nicely."

Balthazar assumed Luc referred to Mateo in the former part of that statement, and the *others* part applied to Jay, Lizzie, and Aidyn. It was an estimated guess based on millennia of knowing Luc and how his mind operated.

"Take care of yourself, old friend," Luc murmured in a dead language very few understood.

"I always do," Balthazar replied in the same language. "Make sure you take your own advice."

Luc snorted. "I'm fine."

"Are you?" Balthazar asked seriously, still speaking the ancient dialect.

Silence fell between them.

After several beats, Luc said, "We'll discuss it soon." Then he ended the call.

Balthazar's lips pinched to the side. Forcing Luc to open up would never end well. His oldest friend needed to determine his path on his own. But that didn't mean Balthazar couldn't nudge him a little in the right direction.

With a soft shake of his head, he turned off the burner phone and set it on the dresser. He'd destroy it later. For now, he needed some clothes for himself and his Seraphim.

He pulled on a pair of gray sweatpants and a white T-shirt, then grabbed a pair of boxer shorts and another white T-shirt for Leela. It would be a shame to cover her assets, but he'd committed them to memory.

At least until her best friend decided to erase them again.

Just the thought caused his brow to furrow.

How did that work? Was there a point where Vera

couldn't alter the memories anymore because they were just too ingrained in the other person's psyche?

Questions he would need to ask Leela.

Or perhaps the memory-altering Seraphim herself.

Assuming she ever showed up again.

Where are you? he wondered as he wandered back downstairs. *What are you really up to?* Leela might trust her, but Balthazar didn't. Not after what she'd done to his head, and her obvious alliance with Osiris.

Leela hadn't thought much about Vera or her intentions. His sweet vixen had been too preoccupied with the chase and everything else to question her best friend.

Right now her thoughts were on the wards she'd just finished creating all over the property. He listened as she considered each detail, confirming in her mind that everything was accurate.

Which led to her questioning the wards in Melbourne and their failure to notify them about the arrival of the Seraphim until the last second.

Something isn't right, she kept saying to herself. *They shouldn't have found us that fast. And my wards should have held.*

Balthazar found her standing on the back patio by the pool, her gaze on the still-dark sky above. Frustration radiated off her stance and through her mind.

But a hint of concern underlined it all.

What if he *finds me?* was a dark question whispering in the back of her thoughts, haunting her.

She'd apparently already found an off-white dress shirt, and from the look of the size and cut of the fabric, it was one of *his* dress shirts. Which suggested she'd misted into his room to grab it while he'd been wandering throughout the house.

Interesting that she'd found his closet of all five

available in the house. Almost like she'd known exactly where to look.

Or perhaps it was a coincidence of choice.

However, given that she'd misted them here without directions, he suspected there wasn't anything coincidental about it. Something else was at play here. Something neither of them fully understood.

He set the T-shirt and boxers down on the dining table and opened the sliding glass doors at the back to join her on the patio. She didn't look at him, her focus still on the low moon. It would be morning soon.

But he didn't care about that.

Not with the sight before him.

Leela resembled a goddess with her golden hair pulled over one shoulder and her long, shapely legs on display. The dress shirt—which was definitely his, as he recognized the brand—flirted with her thighs, giving her a sexy appeal that spoke directly to his soul.

She's perfect, he thought, moving to stand behind her.

It wasn't just her beauty, but *her*, the female. His literal equal in so many ways.

Her only flaw had been her decision to alter his memories, but hearing the justifications in her mind had calmed his ire. She'd sacrificed their connection for a superior fate. At least, that was her perspective on it.

It had been a mistake.

She shouldn't have done it.

But she'd had no way of knowing how Balthazar would react to her purpose. He would have helped her had she just given him the chance.

Which was what bothered him most—she hadn't trusted him enough to support her quest.

He would prove to her now that he was worthy of her faith.

And, in time, he would hopefully restore his faith in her, too.

He wrapped his arms around her waist and pressed his lips to her throat. She sighed, relaxing into him, but her mind continued to race.

How did they find us?

Does he *know it's me they're tracking?*

Is this even working?

How did they find us so quickly?

The questions whirled in sequence, the answers all convoluted in nature. Because she didn't know, and that disturbed her more.

"What will they do when they find us here?" he finally asked, adding his own question to the mix. "Will they destroy Luc's home?"

She merely shook her head. *I don't know* repeated through her mind. Followed by *They shouldn't have even found us that quickly.*

"Maybe they knew about your flat," he suggested.

"That's impossible. Only Vera knew about it."

He rested his chin on her shoulder, his arms still hugging her waist. "How long have you known her?"

"All my life," she whispered. "She's my Jay, B. She would never betray me, just as he would never betray you."

"Yet she's been working with Osiris," he pointed out. "Jay would never do that."

"He would if given the right motivation," Leela stressed. "If Vera really is working with Osiris, she has a reason. Or maybe he's compelling her. Regardless, I know it's not nefarious." She turned in his arms, her hands going to his shoulders. "Vera would never give the trackers my location."

Her mind reaffirmed her statements, telling him how

adamantly she believed in her friend's innocence. Their friendship was old and grounded in trust.

Just like the one between Balthazar and Jay.

And if this were Jay they were talking about, he would feel the same. He'd be adamant about Jay's innocence, too.

"All right," Balthazar murmured, deciding to respect Leela's assertions. Part of him was still wary, but he would reserve his judgment for now. "Is it possible any other Seraphim knew about your flat? Have the trackers followed you there before?"

Leela shook her head. Then she shrugged. Then she shook her head again.

"I don't know. They shouldn't know anything about it. But they shouldn't have found us that fast either." She bit her lip, her attention going to the sky. "I keep wondering if I made a mistake with the outer wards. But I don't think I did."

"How do you feel about the ones you made here?"

Her blue-green irises flared. "They're perfect. I checked them three times."

"Then we can relax for a bit and see if they hold," he murmured.

Balthazar had several ideas for how to help Leela properly relax. Starting with giving her something to concentrate on to help calm her mind.

Because right now, her thoughts were scattered and too chaotic to formulate productive answers. All she needed was a little tenderness and a way to release her nerves. Then the rest would fall into place.

A protest began forming on her lips, but he silenced it by pressing a finger to her mouth while his opposite arm tightened around her waist.

"The wards warned us in time, didn't they?" he asked

softly. "You misted us to a new location. Now we're here. We're safe. And we can continue what we started."

Which had originally just been a game meant to tease her until she begged him to fuck her.

But her mental state now required something a little different.

A break of sorts.

Underlined in sensuality.

To help her regain her confidence and focus.

And Balthazar was absolutely the right man for the task.

"Mist us to my bedroom, Lee," he told her, the demand a test to confirm what he'd suspected—that she already knew where to go.

His vixen didn't disappoint, her arms encircling his neck as she took them upstairs.

Don't ask me how I know this is your room. I just do, she thought at him, her mental voice exhausted.

Which further proved how much she needed an outlet for all that confusion and frustration rioting in her mind.

"The only thing I want from you right now is that lacy thong, Lee," he replied. "Take it off and hand it to me. Then climb up on that bed and spread your legs. The rest can wait."

CHAPTER 13

LEELA

LEELA KNEW WHAT BALTHAZAR WAS TRYING TO DO—ground her. Settle her mind. Sharpen her focus by giving her something else to concentrate on. Distract her from her thoughts.

Devour her.

Indulging in sex might be the worst decision they could make in this situation.

Or it might turn out to be for the best.

Because Balthazar was right—they were safe. *For now.*

She could dwell on how quickly the Seraphim had found them and spend the day worried about when they would show up again. Or she could let Balthazar provide the ultimate form of a distraction and help quiet her mind.

The latter most definitely appealed to her.

Mostly because she knew she functioned better when calm and collected, and right now, she was neither of those things.

She felt disturbed. Lost. Confused. *Scared.*

The last part was why she'd turned in his arms. She'd

wanted to borrow his strength. And now, she wanted to lose herself in his touch.

Which was why she'd misted them upstairs. To his bedroom. Filled with intangible memories she couldn't define. Because every corner of the room was familiar to her, and yet entirely foreign.

"Stop thinking," Balthazar said, his fingers clasping her chin and forcing her to meet his molten-chocolate gaze. "Remove the lace for me, sweetheart. I want to properly taste you, Lee. Every inch. Inside and out."

She shivered, his sensual words infused with a hint of dominance that called to her inner deviant.

Balthazar didn't just know how to touch a woman; he knew how to stroke them with his words alone. Soft platitudes. Wicked promises. Dark intentions. Heartfelt praise. He was a master of them all.

Which was how he knew exactly how to speak to her now.

Part demand. Part coaxing. One hundred percent confident.

"Now, Leela," he added, his tone stern.

She wanted to challenge him, to make him work for it. But she also recognized the gift in his touch, the fact that he was doing this for her more than himself.

And that was the primary reason she complied.

He released her as she moved, his eyes roaming over her torso and down to her legs as she gently took hold of the lace strands decorating her hips. His expression didn't change, the heat in his gaze mild.

That won't do, she thought at him, deciding to make a show of removing the lace.

It was easy to do.

She turned to present her backside, then slowly bent as she slid the undergarment down her thighs, over her knees, along her calves, and all the way to her ankles. His dress shirt rode upward with each movement, giving him a tantalizing glimpse of her ass when the lacy fabric met her calf. And she remained partially exposed while removing the rest of the garment.

It was a demonstration in patience, a show worthy of a stripping queen, and when she glanced back at him, she knew she'd succeeded. That mild heat in his eyes had blossomed into twin pools of fervency.

With the fabric in her palm, she slowly stood, allowing the shirt to slide back down and cover her curvy assets. Then she turned and held out the lace for him.

He smiled, his dimples peeking playfully at her from the sides. Then they disappeared as he bent his head to take the lace from her fingertips... with his teeth.

Her heart skipped a beat, the warmth between them growing hotter by the second.

His irises held a sinful promise that had her thighs clenching with need, the fire within burning her all the way to her soul.

She wanted more.

So. Much. More.

And he was offering her a glimpse of his prowess now. A taste. A distraction. A way to ground herself and feel normal again.

She wasn't about to turn him down. No, she intended to embrace him fully, to see what he had in store for her, and let him be in charge while she settled her mind.

Her bare feet whispered across the carpet as she moved backward toward the bed, her gaze holding his with each step. It was an intimate dance filled with a familiarity she didn't understand. Because she knew exactly where the mattress was without looking.

Yes, she'd already seen it.

But this was somehow more than a visual understanding of the room's layout. This was an intrinsic movement, one her body knew by memory despite the missing pieces in her mind.

Balthazar's hungry gaze told her not to worry about it, to focus on the present, to indulge in this mutual lust and nothing else.

It helped settle her fluttering pulse, gave her one focal point for her attention, and allowed her to *breathe*.

Yes. More of this, she thought as she slid back onto the bed. *More intensity. More heat. More Balthazar.*

He hadn't removed the lace from his mouth, his brown eyes darkening with each passing second until the orbs reminded her of black coffee.

She wanted a drink.

One doused in the sweetness that was all B's tongue.

And spiced by the flavor of his intoxicating touch.

She positioned herself in the middle of the bed, her hair fanning out around her on the pillows. It was a seductive pose she knew well, one she highlighted by drawing her knees upward and spreading her thighs in blatant invitation.

Balthazar's gaze continued to hold hers rather than roam down to the prize waiting for him. He wasn't the kind of man to rush it, which made this all the more enticing. Because he knew when and how to draw out a moment, as he did now by just watching her with her panties in his mouth.

She knew he was tasting her on the lace.

His tongue gently stroking the bits clamped between his teeth, warming up for the meal to come.

And damn if that thought didn't almost make her come.

He was passion personified. A god in the bedroom. *A*

god about to claim his goddess, she mused. Because he wasn't the only one skilled at this game.

Her fingertips brushed her sides as she slowly traced her own form up to her breasts and the buttons of the shirt covering them.

He hadn't said to remove it.

But he hadn't said she couldn't either.

The top button unfastened with a nimble flick, drawing his gaze down to her chest. She undid the second and the third one, his eyes on her the entire time. No comments. No movement aside from the slight shift in his focus. They were both barely even breathing.

Button number four slipped free from the fabric.

Followed by the fifth.

The shirt parted along the way, revealing her creamy skin while continuing to hide the sensual bits from his view.

At least until she reached the final button.

That one, coupled with her splayed thighs, ensured he would see every bit of her arousal.

He admired the view now, his nostrils flaring at the sight. She instinctively knew what he would want next and obliged him by slipping her fingers through the wetness of her folds, tracing the lines she longed for him to lick.

She was very ready for him, and she showed him that with a few soft caresses. A moan parted her lips, the sound another form of an invitation underlined with *need*—which she allowed him to see in her eyes as well.

He took in the sight of her ready form, his irises glittering in the moonlight streaming in through the windows. He resembled an incubus with his thick brown hair perfectly mussed and those gray sweatpants slung low on his muscular hips. She wanted to explore every inch of his sculpted torso with her tongue.

But she knew that wasn't on the menu right now.

Not with the way he was studying her body and watching her fingers stroke her arousal.

He lifted his hand slowly to his lips, capturing the lace and making a show of slowly removing it from his mouth. A peek of his tongue. The clench of his jaw. Those full, masculine lips destined to caress a woman's flesh.

Ohhh... The sight alone had her legs tensing and shot heat through her lower abdomen, because, dear wings, that was hot.

It was such a simple act, but there was something undeniably erotic about it. Like he wasn't holding back from his baser instincts and allowing the feral male beneath the veneer to show. Just for a moment.

It made her feel... *owned.*

Yet she couldn't define the how or the why of it.

Only that she liked it, and she very much wanted him to possess her in every way.

He folded her lace into a neat triangle and set it on the nightstand beside her. Then his eyes roamed over her once more, taking in the parting of the shirt, her partially exposed breasts, her flat abdomen, all the way down to the apex between her thighs.

"So this is what an angel really looks like," he mused as he lifted a knee to the bed beside her. "You've somehow managed to surpass my every expectation."

His opposite knee joined the mattress next, bringing him to a kneeling position beside her.

She allowed her gaze to travel up his long, muscular form, from his thighs to the impressive bulge and up along the valleys and grooves of his abdomen to his strong pecs.

Male perfection, she thought with a sigh. *You could be an angel, too.*

Except he was too sensual for it. He resembled more of a fallen angel, maybe. A tempting devil. *My very own incubus.*

His lips curled. "Does that make you my very own succubus?"

Yes. She drew her finger through her slickness and lifted her hand toward his mouth. "Do I tempt you, B? Worried I might corrupt your soul?"

He caught her wrist, then brought her fingers to his lips. "You can't corrupt me, sweetheart," he murmured, his tongue flashing out to lick the tip. "But tempt me? Mmm, yes, you can certainly do that."

Balthazar took her index finger between his lips, sucking it deep into his mouth.

A quiver skated down her spine, causing her stomach muscles to tighten at the purely seductive touch. *Mmm,* she hummed, loving how hot she was already, thanks to his skill and patience.

This male understood foreplay.

He knew how words impacted a woman.

And he absolutely grasped the concept of delayed gratification.

She loved it.

Wanted more.

Craved his tongue on other areas of her body.

But knew he would take his time.

Revel in the motions. Prolong the inevitable. Memorize every inch of her.

Which he proceeded to do after sucking each of her fingers clean.

He started with her wrist, nibbling the pulse and applying just enough pressure to drive her wild. Then he traveled upward to her elbow, taking the shirtsleeve up along with it before touching erogenous zones very few others knew about.

He skimmed the fabric along her biceps and up to her

shoulder before nuzzling her neck and slipping one of his thighs between her legs.

His fingers went into her hair, his touch commanding yet reassuring as his mouth captured hers in a kiss that was all tongue.

Devouring.

Claiming.

Setting her blood on fire.

It was intoxicating and mind-blowing and utter perfection. She almost came from his kiss alone, her body so primed and ready without truly being touched yet.

His teeth grazed her lower lip, his grasp releasing her hair to palm her cheek. "You're more than tempting, Lee," he said against her mouth. "You're a vixen meant to bring every man around you to his proverbial knees."

"And yet you want me to crawl," she replied breathlessly.

"Yes, and you will," he whispered. "But not today. Today, I'm going to worship you. Make you scream my name and come all over my tongue on repeat until you're properly satisfied." His palm slid down to her shirt, parting the fabric to reveal her breast on one side. "Grab the headboard, baby. I don't want you flying away on me."

She smiled. "The best orgasms make me go ethereal."

His mouth mimicked her own. "Then I'll set that as the bar and see that it's raised." He nipped her bottom lip, then kissed her jaw and started working his way down her throat.

More licking and soft bites. Never harsh, but enough to leave a subtle mark behind to show he'd claimed that part of her skin.

He went down the center of her sternum to her belly button, then over to her side and back up along her rib cage, stroking her thoroughly with his tongue. Her nipples were so damn hard that they almost hurt, the taut peaks craving his mouth so fiercely that goose bumps pebbled along her breasts.

His nose skimmed the underside of her curvy flesh, his hum heating her skin and drawing out the moment to the point of near pain.

She groaned, her fingers curling around the poles of the headboard, just like he'd asked. But if he didn't lick her properly soon, she'd take a fistful of his hair and direct him appropriately.

"Touch me and I'll start over," he whispered, the vow in his voice making her legs tense. He was still straddling her thigh with his knee close to the place she desired him most, but not quite touching.

Another taunt.

Another way to draw out the moment.

She both loved and hated him for it.

Which was exactly the point.

She'd played this game before, but never quite like this. Never with someone so undeniably skilled. Her almost equal. Or maybe her equal. She wasn't particularly sure anymore because this male certainly knew how to indulge her needs in every way.

Because this was exactly the sort of torment she needed to ensure all her focus was on him and nothing else.

Just Balthazar.

His hands. His tongue. His clever fingers.

He'd slid the fabric off her opposite side now, exposing both her breasts, and was tracing her rib cage with his nose. Gentle caresses. Knowing. Intoxicating. *Overwhelming*.

Her body practically vibrated with need, her core weeping with desire and a craving only Balthazar could satisfy.

He was trying to ruin her for other men.

Or master her completely.

She wasn't sure, but she'd absolutely be repaying the favor later.

His lips curled against her skin, hearing that vow. "I welcome it," he told her softly, his teeth grazing her breast. "We'll see which one of us can come the hardest and the longest." His tongue flickered over her nipple, drawing a scream from her throat. "Which one of us will be the *loudest*," he added, then took her stiff peak into his mouth and sucked so hard that she nearly came.

But there wasn't enough friction.

His leg only barely brushed the inside of her thighs, providing a tease without completion.

She wanted to kill him.

She wanted to fuck him.

She wanted to grab him, pull down those sweatpants, and free the rock-hard cock beneath. Because she knew it was there. She had seen the outline of it earlier.

But now she wanted to ride it.

To push him to his back, straddle his hips, and seat him deep inside her.

She could picture it perfectly, remember the way he'd felt, how powerful his thrusts had been, how perfectly they'd *fit*.

His mouth switched breasts, a sense of increasing urgency throbbing between them because he could hear her thoughts, feel her desire, sense the intrinsic need boiling inside her lower abdomen.

All because of him.

And his teasing.

And these months apart.

Oh, how she'd missed him.

He resembled a forbidden yearning, one she shouldn't

indulge yet was helpless to stop. Because he understood her in a way no one else ever had. *My true equal*, she decided. At least in the bedroom. Perhaps out of it. Perhaps in life itself.

Her nails bit into the metal pole, spiking pain down her arms. But she ignored it in favor of his tongue on her flesh.

Then he began to move downward, the teasing giving way to the final act.

This was what so many men failed to grasp. It wasn't just about the clit but also about every other part of a woman's body. The mouth and tongue could elicit so much enjoyment if just the right amount of time were applied.

And Balthazar certainly knew that.

His lips worshipped her, just as he'd promised, drawing out every inkling of sensual gratification before gradually slipping down to the crevice between her thighs.

It was perfectly executed and done with the sole intention of this very moment... where his tongue *finally* stroked her damp skin. Deeply. Thoroughly. Penetrating her entrance before drawing up to that sensitive spot that would send her to the stars.

Her abdomen clenched in anticipation, her thighs straining to contain the blossoming bliss within.

And then he was there, taking her clit between his lips and sucking her so profoundly that she couldn't resist the fall.

Down. Down. Down.

Swirling.

Dying.

Drowning in an oblivion of overwhelming sensation.

She didn't try to breathe. She didn't try to resurface. She let him take her deeper, knowing that pure ecstasy waited for her at the bottom.

His fingers slid inside her, stoking that place few men

could ever properly find, causing her to shoot out of the deep waves and into the heavens above.

It was a rolling climax that she never wanted to end, escalating with each passing second until blackness coated her vision. Her throat was raw from screaming. Her mind utterly vacant apart from the euphoria rocking through her replete form.

But he wasn't done.

He kept licking and nibbling, drawing out more and more and more.

She lost feeling in her hands from holding on to the headboard with such tight fists.

Her lungs ached from her erratic breathing.

Her throat protested each scream.

But her body reveled in Balthazar's tongue, his touch, his hums of contentment as she came all over his face.

He didn't stop and she didn't ask him to, even when it hurt.

Because it also felt too damn good. Months. She'd gone *months* without this. Not because she'd felt the need to be faithful, but because no one else had really compared to what had happened in Brazil. She'd not wanted to waste her time. And she'd much preferred to watch him with others—the pleasure she'd given herself after that had been more than enough.

Yet his touch now told her that was a lie.

Because nothing could compare to Balthazar's brand of hedonism.

Having him inside her mind now made it that much more powerful.

He could hear her approval, knew exactly what she wanted, and introduced her to things she hadn't even realized she desired.

Hours passed.

Orgasms continued.

His tongue and mouth were everywhere again. He didn't let a single inch of her go untouched. It was the perfect variability of rapture and reverence.

Proving B's superiority in the bedroom.

At least in comparison to others.

But next time, it would be her turn to blow his mind.

"I look forward to it," he whispered in her ear as he pulled her against him.

She'd started to doze, her body exhausted from the onslaught of his mouth.

He held her, coaxing her into a dream.

Or maybe it was a reality.

With Balthazar, it was hard to say. Because he was her ultimate fantasy.

A cherished secret.

A life she could truly enjoy.

A future… that was never meant to be hers.

CHAPTER 14

ISSAC

"SHE'S GOING TO FIGURE OUT HOW TO TAKE HIS SWORD soon," Sethios said as he materialized on the beach beside Issac. "And I, for one, cannot wait to see what she does to him with it."

"Hmm," Issac hummed in agreement, very much looking forward to that as well.

Gabriel had been tormenting Aya all night. First with his method of teaching wards—something he'd taken over from Caro since he was more advanced at protective markings—and now with his sparring methods in the sky.

While it certainly worked, it also infuriated Aya to the point where her mind appeared to be solely focused on one task: maiming her older brother.

Sethios and Caro had attended some of the lecture—if it could truly be called that—to learn more about the wards and other ways to defensively use ethereal energy. Issac had remained on the beach below the entire time, observing the lesson through Aya's eyes and hearing her internal comments along the way.

I'm going to fucking kill him was her current chant.

Gabriel had spent the last hour helping Aya learn how to perfect her aim.

Or that was Issac's translation of the events, anyway. Gabriel had kept throwing ethereal energy at her via his sword, which she was now catching with her hands and tossing right back at him.

Her brother responded by increasing his speed and power, pushing Aya to her limits both physically and mentally.

She was clearly exhausted.

Meanwhile, Gabriel appeared to be out for an afternoon jog.

Sethios and Issac continued observing the pair in the sky as the sun began to rise over Hydria. They didn't speak, the roll of the waves the only sound other than Aya's constant cursing in Issac's mind.

She was certainly creative.

And colorful.

He was about to suggest she come down for a break when an image of Tristan mouthing, *Sire*, flashed inside his mind.

Issac's ability to manipulate vision essentially granted him access to a thousand mental images at once inside his mind—something he'd learned to control ages ago—but those who mattered most to him always remained relatively close to his thoughts.

His two progeny qualified.

Luc and Amelia, too.

And, of course, Aya.

It helped those close to him catch his attention easily, typically in a manner such as what Tristan had just done.

He responded by tapping into Tristan's vision and portraying an image of himself arching an inquisitive brow. That was Issac speak for, *Yes?*

Tristan drew up a mental fantasy of Issac walking into the nearby tree line to join Tristan and Mateo.

Hmm, Issac thought, conveying the message to Aya. *It appears my progeny want to have a private word.*

At least, he assumed that was why Tristan had reached out mentally rather than calling for him to join them. Maybe he didn't want Sethios to hear whatever they had to say.

An odd development.

But Issac would entertain the notion for Tristan. They were best friends, after all. And it was the least he could do after temporarily questioning Tristan's loyalty.

Try not to kill Gabriel while I'm gone, love. I would hate to miss the show.

No promises, she hissed back at him.

"I'm going to make Aya something to eat," he said to Sethios. "She'll be hungry when she's done."

Tristan's ability to pick up sound would allow him to overhear the statement. But just in case he didn't receive the message, Issac showed him a vision of Balthazar's home. It wasn't too far from the beach.

The image changed to Tristan giving a nod.

"Keep taking care of my daughter and I'll keep allowing you to live," Sethios drawled.

Issac's lips twitched. "I think we both know Aya would kill me herself if I ever hurt her."

"I'd bring you back just to do it again."

"Noted," Issac murmured, not at all intimidated.

Sethios was sadistic and known for his lethal penchants. Many feared him, but Issac merely respected his power.

He was also thankful the ancient immortal cared about Aya. That only added to her personal security—a measure Issac took very seriously.

It was also the primary reason he felt comfortable

leaving her now to go speak with his progeny. Sethios wouldn't let anyone harm her.

Of course, she could take care of herself, too. But that didn't stop him from worrying. Particularly as this was the beach she'd died on only a few weeks ago.

An event he never wanted to witness again.

Ever.

Pancakes, darling? he asked as he started down the beach. *Since we're still staying at Balthazar's house, it seems—*

Her scream had him spinning on his heel to see her falling from the sky in a spiral that had his heart skipping several beats in his chest. "Aya!" he shouted, running toward her. Only, she disappeared in the next breath and reappeared on her feet beside him.

With her right wing covered in flames.

"Christ!" Issac started to reach for her, but Caro materialized behind Aya, her hands already rising to soothe the simmering feathers.

"That was a bit much, Gabriel," Caro said, her tone lacking emotion.

Her son lowered from above, hands at his sides, expression bored. No apology. Just a glimmer in his light green eyes that suggested mild disappointment—a subtle change from his usually stoic features.

Something had changed with Gabriel.

Something that had to do with Clara.

But neither party was talking about it.

And right now, Issac didn't care enough to ask. His focus was on Aya.

Are you all right, love? He kept the question between them, aware that she wouldn't want to voice a weakness out loud.

I'm going to kill him, she told Issac for the thousandth

time. *I'm going to burn his feathers off his back and stab him in the heart with that fucking sword of his.*

Issac's lips twitched again, amused now that she'd proved he didn't need to be concerned. *A vivid fantasy.* One he could see clearly in her mind. He cupped her face and brushed his thumb along her cheekbone.

"Pancakes?" he prompted, drawing them back to the food discussion.

It was nearly morning, making an American breakfast appropriate. And, as he'd said, they were staying at Balthazar's house, which meant they had access to a myriad of fancy gadgets and high-quality ingredients.

Aya stretched out her wing, her mother's healing energy having already repaired the feathers and smothered the flame. "Yeah," she replied, her pretty eyes meeting his. *But I assume Tristan wants to talk to you alone first, so you go do that while I teach my brother a lesson.*

By killing him? Issac guessed.

Yes.

"A break is a good idea," Caro said, unaware of the conversation happening between Issac and Aya. "We can rest and pick this up in a few hours."

Gabriel snorted, the sound uncharacteristic for him. "Yes. I'm sure Leek and Kital will be more than happy to allow Stas to rest during a fight," he deadpanned.

Aya glowered up at him, then misted up into the sky and lobbed another ethereal ball at his head.

Caro sighed and shook her head. "Stubborn. Just like her father."

"And her mother," Sethios murmured, grinning. "She's tenacious, too. And determined." He glanced up to watch her bolt through the sky toward Gabriel.

He ducked and outmaneuvered her with fluid ease, his sword reappearing as he created more energy to throw

Aya's way. Her brother clearly wasn't averse to hurting her, something that bothered Issac.

But he could admit it was necessary.

As much as he disliked Gabriel's training methods, Issac could acknowledge the fact that they were useful. Very few others, himself included, would be willing to test Aya's limits in that manner. The warrior Seraphim wouldn't go easy on her, which meant she needed this brand of instruction to survive.

Besides, it was better than Osiris taking the lead.

"We did good together, angel," Sethios said softly, his palm cupping Caro's nape. "She's perfect."

Indeed, Issac thought, backing away to allow them their moment.

He'd barely taken three steps when Sethios called, "Pancakes sound great, Wakefield. Count us in."

"Sethios," Caro chastised.

"What?"

"The pancakes were for Stas, not us."

"I'm sure he meant to include us in his preparations, angel." Sethios lifted his green eyes to Issac. "Right, *son-in-law*?"

Issac flinched at the term, not caring for it. What he shared with Aya far surpassed matrimonial contexts. And to think of Sethios as a father-in-law felt... *wrong*.

But he supposed he could make the infamous sadist some breakfast.

"Pancakes for four," Issac replied. "Sounds brilliant."

"Doesn't it?" Sethios smiled, his focus returning to Caro. "See, angel? I can be a good father-in-law."

She just sighed and shook her head again.

"You'd prefer I keep thinking about killing him?" Sethios offered. "Because I'm very okay with that."

"Liar," she accused. "You like him."

Sethios grunted. "I've admitted that he's useful."

"And you *like* him."

Issac smirked and started walking away again, leaving them to their discussion. *Your parents are talking about me like I'm not ten feet away from them,* he told Aya. *They've also invited themselves to breakfast.*

Just so long as Stark isn't invited, Aya gritted out, her mental voice still holding that touch of exhaustion from before.

He gazed up at the stars and caught her opal brilliance flashing around in the still-dark sky. A flare of red followed, indicating her brother's pursuit. *I won't extend the invite to Gabriel. But I have no control over your father.*

Just as he had no control over Issac.

Respecting elders came naturally, but Issac drew the line at being told what to do and how to handle Aya. Fortunately, Sethios didn't appear all that inclined to dictate rules around their relationship. He'd actually been rather understanding, given the circumstances.

Call me if you need me, Aya.

Always, she breathed back to him.

Always, he echoed, their version of exchanging vows.

But not the marriage kind.

Those felt inadequate in comparison to their true bond.

He left Aya with her family and headed up the path from the beach to the cobblestone streets and up the hill toward Balthazar's house. He lived closest to Jayson, their homes of a quaint size, boasting two to three bedrooms, living areas, beautiful kitchens, and private pools out back.

They weren't as large as Issac's usual estates, but they were perfectly in line with the homes on Hydria.

His sister and Tom planned to build one nearby and were currently staying in the home meant for Hydraian fledglings. There were two or three houses built for that purpose—typically used to shelter those who hadn't yet turned into Hydraians.

Fledglings were rare, though. Issac had been shocked when he'd first discovered Aya, but she wasn't a true fledgling because of her Seraphim ties.

However, Hydria's latest addition, Eliza, qualified. Although, last he heard, her powers were still unknown.

But she was definitely a Hydraian now, as she'd been killed on the beach alongside Aidan and the others. Only, unlike them, she'd woken up immortal and very much alive a few short hours later.

She was the first fledgling to grace Hydria shores in over a hundred years, thanks to the Ichorians going out and slaughtering their own children.

Nizari Assassins.

And the leader of them all was temporarily residing in Hydria on a mostly uninhabited part of the island.

Issac doubted the Hydraians were thrilled with that development since Ezekiel had spent most of the last millennium hunting down and slaying fledglings.

However, Luc had granted them safe passage for now, stating Skye's visions were imperative for survival. Some of the Hydraians were questioning the decision, which was keeping the Hydraian King rather busy at the moment.

Fortunately, Jay agreed with the decision as well, which helped cool some of the concern on the island.

But the changing dynamics were definitely being felt by everyone.

Something big was coming, and everyone knew it.

Alas, Issac had his own problems waiting for him in the form of two progeny, one of whom was likely betraying them all to Osiris.

He found Tristan and Mateo standing in Balthazar's living room, having let themselves inside.

Issac shut the door behind him and started toward the kitchen. "We can discuss whatever this is while I cook."

Because Aya needed food, and apparently his "in-laws" were coming over as well.

They'd taken over Jayson's guest room but hadn't slept much. Just like Aya and Issac. Everyone was too preoccupied with preparing for a potential invasion.

Tristan and Mateo took over the barstools of the kitchen island while Issac began pulling ingredients from Balthazar's cupboards and fridge. It served as a good distraction. Otherwise, Issac might be inclined to demand Mateo explain his actions, and he didn't have enough proof yet to properly accuse his progeny.

The pair remained quiet, watching Issac arrange everything he needed on the counter beside Balthazar's six-burner stove. There was a griddle in the middle as well, likely created for the sole purpose of making pancakes.

He and Luc were always bickering over the superior breakfast food and engaging in inane challenges to prove the other wrong.

This was the one case where Issac actually agreed with Balthazar—pancakes were much better than waffles.

"You're the one who wanted to talk," Tristan said quietly, causing Issac's brow to furrow. "So I suggest you start talking, mate."

What? Issac turned around, confused. "I'm not—"

Mateo cleared his throat, interrupting Issac. "Osiris first approached me about a year after you became my Sire."

Now Issac's eyebrows flew up to his hairline. He hadn't expected a confession. His gaze flew to Tristan, noting his resigned expression.

"He knows we're onto him," Tristan said, stating the obvious. "But he's asked for a chance to explain himself."

Explain himself? He has to be bloody joking, Issac thought, his desire for pancakes flying right out the bloody window.

"And why the fuck should I give you that chance?" Issac demanded, his focus on Mateo again. "You betrayed us. You betrayed *me*. Fuck, Aidan is dead because of you. And you have the audacity to admit it so casually? As though I don't want to rip your fucking throat out?"

Issac's ire increased by the second, all the pent-up rage he'd held inside flaring out of him in a breath.

Because now there was no chance at Mateo being innocent.

He'd just bloody admitted his guilt.

And so fucking casually, too.

The nerve of that man to speak as though he were worth the chance of an explanation!

Issac? Aya whispered.

Mateo is confessing, he replied, unable to hold back the note of anger in his mental tone. *He's come here to explain himself*. Which wasn't bloody happening. "Why would I give a damn about your explanation?"

Mateo flinched. And rightly so. He'd given key information to Jonathan that had allowed him to attack the island. "*Aya* died. *Because of you*." It was a fucking miracle she'd come back. "I don't—"

"Because of Jonathan," Mateo interjected. "The update I sent through was for Osiris, but Jonathan used it to exact his own revenge. I could never have anticipated that."

"You should never have been informing on us to begin with," Issac countered, furious. "I *trusted* you, my own progeny, and you—"

"I've been protecting you!" he shouted.

Tristan's jaw clenched in response, his expression otherwise giving nothing away.

"Osiris has always known about your ties to Luc, how you and Aidan were secretly meeting with the Hydraians, how your relationships were the same as they'd always been. He was concerned that technological advancements would make your connections obvious. He ordered me to ensure that didn't happen."

Issac gaped at him.

"Now you see why I agreed to let him explain himself to you," Tristan muttered.

"The communication about the wedding was meant as an update on Elizabeth," Mateo continued, ignoring Tristan's side commentary. "Osiris and Jonathan had an alliance primarily founded in research. Elizabeth was the first successful lab creation and Osiris wanted updates, but he had me sending them through Jonathan since they mattered to him, too. I had no idea he would... he would..." He trailed off, swallowing.

Issac's fists clenched, the beach massacre playing out behind his eyes.

Not from Mateo's mind, but from his own.

Aya's dead body.

Aidan's last breath.

The screams.

Issac's grief.

The agony of losing Aya...

His gaze misted over, the memory too fresh, too new, too *real.*

"Osiris compelled me not to tell you," Mateo continued in a whisper. "But I assisted him of my own accord. I was... I was protecting all of you. All of *us.* Which was how I justified it. And for decades, that's all it was. Until Jonathan..."

"You framed Clara," Issac whispered.

"Osiris did," Mateo clarified. "But yes, I helped. Because he told me it was a test for Stas. A way to teach her about her gifts." He swallowed again, his face pale. "He lifted my compulsion last night. Otherwise, I would have come forward sooner."

Issac's forearms were beginning to ache from clenching his fists so hard. He was torn between punching his progeny in the face and throttling him.

But a logical part of him also wanted more answers.

Anything to help him understand Mateo's decisions.

He was still his progeny. That made him family.

Except betrayal... betrayal destroyed everything. Even blood.

Still, he wanted to understand how much Osiris knew and why Osiris had lifted the compulsion now.

"Start from the beginning," he said. "And don't leave out a single detail."

CHAPTER 15

LEELA

MMM, BLISS. SO. BEAUTIFUL. BLISS.

Leela ran her fingers through the hot water of the bath Balthazar had poured for her, indulging in the minty fresh scents and relaxing salts.

She'd been in here for at least an hour while he worked on dinner downstairs.

This was an experience she could certainly repeat over and over again.

Too bad the lingering threat of tracking Seraphim hung over their heads. But Balthazar's attentions had calmed her mind enough for her to live in the moment and enjoy—a gift she would need to repay at some point.

Perhaps she would crawl after all.

He'd earned it.

And she really did feel bad about having his memories erased.

Of course, she didn't mind having to re-create those memories now.

Her lips curled as she considered all the sensual reenactments they could indulge in during this chase around the globe. They played out in her mind, some of them based on what had happened in Brazil, others crafted from her own fantasies.

They all felt so real.

So enticing and fresh.

It was almost difficult to decipher reality from fiction, her mind having drawn up several intricately intimate situations that certainly seemed factual.

Maybe in another life she'd done those things with him.

Who knew anymore?

She sank down beneath the water and blew out a breath, content and alive. Then she misted herself to the rug beside the tub and grabbed a towel. Her skin was beginning to prune, suggesting she'd been in the bath too long.

And the scents wafting up from downstairs were beginning to make her stomach growl. It'd been a day since her last meal. Maybe more. It was hard to say with the various time zones.

She dried herself off, then found the clothes Balthazar had set out for her—another button-down shirt and a pair of his boxers. He'd also found her a brush and a few other hygienic items. She used them, brushed her teeth, dressed, and misted down to the living room instead of taking the stairs.

"…confessed to Issac," a deep voice was saying in the kitchen.

Luc, Leela recognized.

"He's been helping Osiris for decades," he continued. "Says he was ensuring technology didn't out our connections to the wrong people and that Osiris put him up to it."

Leela walked around the corner into the dining area to

find Balthazar shirtless by the stove. He glanced at her and then back to the speaker in the wall.

"What else did he put him up to?" Balthazar asked, his tone and expression giving nothing away.

"Not much else. According to Mateo, Osiris occasionally requested an update, but it wasn't often. And Mateo never gave him information unless directly requested. He says he never told him about Stas, or Issac's relationship with her."

"So he was sharing details with John instead," Balthazar muttered.

"Not exactly," Luc replied. "Mateo said that John requested an update on Lizzie on behalf of Osiris. Their working relationship wasn't a secret to Mateo; he knew that Osiris had outsourced his lab experiments to John, so he thought nothing of it and provided the update, saying she was about to marry Jay."

Balthazar fell silent, his brow furrowing. "You believe this?"

"He was able to provide proof via the original recording he left for John," Luc said. "Of course, it could have been doctored, just like he did with the evidence surrounding Clara. Which, by the way, he says was Osiris's idea and a way to test Stas—something that Sethios has already confirmed sounds like a lesson his father would orchestrate."

"And the CRF explosion?"

"Was all John. Mateo didn't warn him but says John must have expected the retaliation, or perhaps had a fail-safe built in around Mateo's hacking. He's not sure, but he swears he didn't give him that information."

Balthazar considered that for a moment. "It's plausible, I guess. Especially if the records Mateo pulled originally were all fake. We have no way of truly knowing."

"He said Osiris will confirm everything he's said, that Osiris wanted Jonathan dead for what he'd done. He didn't condone the attack on Hydria. Actually, from what Mateo has claimed, it sounds like he let us kill John."

"Have you tried confirming with Osiris?" Balthazar's tone held a note of unease, probably because the idea of asking Osiris to confirm anything seemed outlandish. He'd been enemy number one for... millennia. Not just for Seraphim, but for Hydraians, too.

"Not yet." Luc cleared his throat, the sound reverberating through the kitchen. "Unfortunately, it sounds like he might be the only one who can confirm any of this, including Mateo's sworn statement that he didn't know John was going to attack us on the beach."

"I suppose the question is, why now? What does Osiris have to gain from telling us the truth now?" Balthazar wondered out loud.

A very good question, one Leela shared as well. *Why did he come forward now?*

"Mateo already knew we were onto him," Luc replied, not to Leela's thought but to Balthazar's question. "He's apparently known all along. So Osiris let him off his leash. Supposedly, he'd been compelled not to say anything. A compulsion Osiris removed last night."

"I see." Balthazar glanced at Leela, perhaps wanting her thoughts on Osiris's actions.

Sounds like something he would do, she admitted. Because compelling Mateo to safeguard the secret absolutely fit Osiris's typical methods. And he wouldn't release him from that compulsion without good cause.

"I have Lacy talking to Mateo now," Luc added, the name not ringing a bell with Leela. "We'll see if she senses any lies in his statements, but she's nowhere near as powerful a lie detector as John was."

"Her power is based more on feelings than on actual statements," Balthazar murmured. "She may be able to pick something up, but I don't think it'll matter. You already suspect Mateo's telling the truth."

"I don't see how lying would help him," Luc replied. "Which makes me inclined to believe him."

"And potentially reach out to Osiris for confirmation," Balthazar pressed, his expression hardening.

"I'm seriously considering it."

"Don't do it alone." Balthazar's voice held a sternness to it that seemed to be more common in his tones lately.

Luc didn't reply.

"Luc…" Caution underlined Balthazar's tone. "You—"

"There's more," Luc interjected, ignoring Balthazar's commentary entirely. "Mateo also confirmed Vera is working with Osiris but told us it's fairly recent. She started helping them after freeing Sethios."

Leela's eyes widened. Balthazar had mentioned that possibility before, and she'd disregarded it. Vera did everything for a reason. But to have it confirmed…

"Did he say why Vera's working with Osiris?" she asked, making her presence known.

If Balthazar didn't want her to hear this conversation, he wouldn't have put it on speakerphone. Or he would have told Luc to hold on when she'd misted down. Either way, he clearly wanted her to hear it.

Luc didn't reply, perhaps taken aback by her sudden voice.

"It's okay, Luc. I trust her," Balthazar said.

Luc grunted. "We trusted Vera and Mateo, too."

"Leela's not working for Osiris. I can hear her thoughts, Luc. She's on our side. There's a fealty bond between her and Stas, too," Balthazar informed him. "She's safe."

"Fealty bond?" Luc repeated, sounding intrigued.

"Ask Caro about it," Balthazar suggested, clearly having seen that link in Leela's mind. Caro had been present for the fealty bond between Stas and Leela, which meant she could explain it. "Tell us more about Vera and her allegiances. We need to know before we have to jump again."

Luc was silent for another beat before saying, "From what Mateo said, it has something to do with a memory she saw in Osiris's mind. He doesn't know the details but claims she'll tell us when she's back."

"And where is she now?"

"He doesn't know."

"Convenient," Balthazar murmured, making Leela frown.

She's an ally, she promised.

He didn't look at her this time, instead focusing on the speaker. "Has he said anything else useful?"

"No, just asked that Clara be taken out of the cells, which has already been done. She and Gabriel are staying near Ezekiel and Skye on the quieter part of the island. "

Which meant they were closer to the rockier beaches. Most of the Hydraians lived together near the port, but some were spaced out over the hills. And some chose to live in the dense part of the island, surrounded by trees. Then there were the beaches with more rocks than sand—that was the *quiet* part. At least in her experience of misting around the island, anyway.

Balthazar nodded, not that Luc could see him. "That's likely better for Clara. I can't imagine she wants to be around others right now."

"No, and she said as much when we released her

again." Luc sounded a bit more tired than usual. "The island is growing restless. I need to prepare everyone for the inevitable."

A Seraphim attack, Leela translated, causing B to nod again, this time at her in confirmation.

"I'll be back to help soon," he promised. "Just as soon as we know the baby is safe."

Which meant the wards had to be in place.

How long? Leela asked him.

Three days, he mouthed at her. *Maybe more*.

Hydria wasn't that big, but the wards would have to be intense to protect it. So the timeline made sense.

"Check in again in a few hours," Luc said. "I'll need your input on how to handle Mateo. The others want his blood."

Balthazar's eyebrow inched upward, something in Luc's voice catching his interest. "And you? What do you want?"

Luc remained quiet for a beat. "I want the right man to pay for the crime. And that man is already dead." His words were soft, almost barely existent.

Then the line went dead.

Balthazar stared at the speaker for another moment, clearly lost to his thoughts. Then he returned his focus to the stove and started stirring whatever soup he'd crafted. "We need to eat," he told her. "We've been here almost as long as we were in Melbourne."

Leela swallowed, her gaze automatically lifting up to the wards. Part of her wanted to check them, just to be sure. But she knew they were right. She'd already reviewed them several times.

Yet she couldn't shake this feeling that they weren't enough.

"Eat first," Balthazar said, grabbing a bowl from the

cupboard and filling it with fresh ramen. "Then you can check again." He started adding items to her soup, including a hard-boiled egg, and some sort of vegetables from another skillet. It was an intricate meal that was definitely heavier than just some broth and noodles.

He set the bowl in front of her with a proper spoon before walking across the kitchen to the counter beside the fridge. Her eyes widened as he brought back a board of freshly prepared sushi.

"How...?" She trailed off, unable to finish because her stomach was demanding that she start eating. *Now.*

"Luc keeps this home prepared for his frequent visits," Balthazar explained. "Since I don't know what your Seraphim will do when they find this location, I thought we might as well ensure most of the fresh food doesn't go to waste."

She nodded. She wasn't sure what they would do either. Likely ignore it and move on, but it really depended on what the Fates had seen regarding this home and any directives from the High Council of Seraph.

He poured her a glass of water to go with the meal, then went about preparing his own bowl while she started eating. He was still wearing those gray sweatpants. She really hoped the Seraphim didn't interrupt, because she had plans for those pants.

His chocolate eyes grinned at her as he faced her, the alluring depths filled with knowledge. But she wasn't ashamed in the slightest. He'd probably heard all her fantasies upstairs, too.

"I did," he confirmed, not bothering to pretend. "I look forward to re-creating them later."

Her lips curled. "Likewise."

He finished assembling his food and took the chair beside her. They ate in comfortable silence with him occasionally using the chopsticks on the sushi tray to feed Leela a bite before taking one for himself. It was companionable bliss, aided by his ability to read her every desire.

Maybe having him in her head wasn't such a bad thing.

He winked at her thought, then stole some of her water since he hadn't filled a glass for himself. She stood to fix the problem and felt his eyes on her as she moved around the kitchen.

He fed her another piece of sushi upon her return, then accepted the glass from her and took a grateful sip.

Their silent game continued until they finished, then Balthazar started cleaning up. "I should do that," she pointed out.

"You check the wards again now that you're feeling refreshed. I'll do the dishes."

"I know they're right."

"Prove it," he dared. But she knew it wasn't about proving it to him so much as herself.

She nibbled her lip for a second, then misted up into the clouds to check her handiwork. The setting sun made it easy to see the ethereal glow, allowing her to review every ward in a handful of minutes. They were all correct.

So why do I feel uneasy? she wondered, unable to shake the feeling of uncertainty as she returned to the kitchen. Balthazar was mostly done with the dishes by that point, having put the leftover soup in a container off to the side of the fridge. It was probably too hot to put inside.

"Is it Vera making you uneasy?" he asked conversationally. "The fact that she's been working with Osiris without saying anything. And then you trusted her with your blood, yet the trackers found us faster than expected. It might not be related, but our minds piece suspicions together for a reason."

"I trust her," Leela stressed. However, she couldn't argue his logic. It did make Vera appear quite suspicious. But… "She's family to me, B. She… she's essentially my sister. Or the one I wanted, anyway. Instead, we share Melanythos."

Leela shuddered with the dreaded name. *Mel* for short. She very much took after her maternal line, which happened to be the one she shared with Vera. It was the paternal line that Leela shared with her.

"We're essentially blood without the blood," Leela continued, refocusing on Vera, not the horrid half sister she and Vera shared. "Anything she does, she does with a reason. Whatever she saw in Osiris's past must have convinced her to help him. I'm sure she'll explain it when she can."

"Then where is she?"

"I have no idea. She disappears all the time." Leela couldn't help the frustration in her tone. "I've known her my entire life, B. Please trust me. She's one of us. I know she is. She would never betray us, even when it seems like she could or did. Our best interests are in mind. Always."

"Perhaps like Mateo," B murmured, his gaze narrowing as he set the dish towel on a rack to dry. "He's young and impressionable, but I don't see him betraying us without good intentions. And what Luc has said implies Mateo did those things to protect us. Which could all be another lie, perhaps contrived by Osiris this time, but it's hard to say."

"Will, uh, Lacy, be able to tell if it's the truth?" Leela asked. "I assume she's a lie detector of a sort."

"Of a sort," Balthazar echoed. "If Mateo's been

compelled to believe the truth, then she might not be able to help."

"Was she able to read Clara?"

"We didn't ask her to try." Balthazar's expression turned grim. "We took Clara's claims at face value, believing her duplicity without vetting it."

Leela suspected that Balthazar would blame himself for that oversight for quite some time.

"I couldn't sense her frustration," he continued, his brow furrowing. "I should have delved deeper. And her thoughts were too superficial. I should have recognized the wrongness. But I was too angry to evaluate the situation properly. And my focus had been more on Luc and keeping him calm."

He ran his fingers through his hair and leaned his hip against the counter as he faced her.

"I don't want to make the same mistake with Mateo," he confided in her. "We know he's guilty. But I want to believe he did it for the right reasons. At least in his own mind."

"According to Luc, it sounds like he wasn't trying to hurt anyone."

"Yet good people died because of him."

"Not directly," she said softly. "He couldn't have known the information would be used nefariously. From what Luc said, it sounds like Mateo was just providing a general update. He wasn't giving specs or helping the Sentinels plan an attack."

"No, but he lied to us afterward and framed Clara."

"Because Osiris told him to."

"I'm not sure that excuses any of it." Balthazar's abdomen clenched as he pushed off the counter. "Betrayal destroys trust. It's hard to come back from that."

There was a hint of something else in those words.

A statement that went beyond Mateo and applied directly to her.

Because she'd altered his memories, thereby betraying him to an extent. Yet he'd just told Luc that he trusted her.

"As I said, sometimes things are done with the right intentions in mind. That doesn't mean they're correct. It just means the reasoning behind the actions weren't nefarious or cruel in nature." His quiet tone hit her right in the heart.

"I had to protect Stas."

"At my expense. At the expense of us. At the expense of a future that may never be the same." He shook his head, his disappointment palpable as he started toward her. "You could have tried to trust me instead. But you chose the path for us without even attempting to confide in me."

"Balthazar…"

"Shh," he hushed, his fingertip brushing her lips. "I'm not saying I don't trust you, Lee. I'm saying it takes time to recover from a betrayal. It can be a difficult path to navigate. But not an impossible one."

He leaned forward to gently press his mouth to hers.

An apology threatened her thoughts, her heart panging uncomfortably in her chest.

Because he was right.

She could have tried to talk to him.

Instead, she'd chosen to suffer on her own and remove herself from his mind. He was never supposed to know. It was her burden to bear, not his.

Yet now he knew.

And she could feel the disappointment radiating off him in waves of punishing regret.

"It's not my intent to truly punish you, Lee," he whispered. "I understand why you did it. But now we both have to live with the consequences of that decision."

"I didn't want to hurt you."

"I know."

"I… You weren't supposed to know."

"That almost makes it worse," he murmured, his palm cupping her cheek. "Those memories were for us to enjoy, not for you to remember alone."

He kissed her again, more intently this time, with his tongue leading the way. It wasn't forgiveness. Nor was it an apology. Just something in between. An intangible sensation. A new path forward, one created by mutual desire and a yearning to learn more.

Leela's soul rejoiced deep inside, spreading foreign warmth to her veins and reminding her of something important. Something she should remember. A moment in the past. An impossible connection that she didn't understand.

It was there and gone in a flash, the recollection disappearing into the abyss and leaving her chasing after the ghost of a sensation.

What was that? she marveled, breathless. It left alarm bells ringing in her head, cascading goose bumps down her arms and legs. It had felt so real. So improbable. So—

Her eyes flew open.

Alarms.

Real alarms.

But not from her wards. The house had sprung to life around them, blaring out a warning she didn't understand.

"Leela. We need to go!" The urgency in Balthazar's tone suggested he was repeating himself, but she'd missed it the first time around.

His hands were no longer cupping her face but grasping her hips.

"*Leela.*"

Bullets fired outside from some sort of defensive mechanism tied to the house.

She didn't have time to ask how or where it came from because she could feel the Seraphim outside now. Not from her wards, but from her own sense of self-preservation.

She'd been in this position before.

Yet couldn't say when.

A strange realization, one she ignored as she threw her arms around Balthazar's neck and misted them to the first place she could think of—a random doorstep in…

She frowned as she returned to her corporeal state.

Italy? she guessed, taking in the canal behind her and the long boat drifting along it. The gothic architecture with the touch of Byzantine influences and famous waterways quickly confirmed their current location. *Venice.*

But she didn't own a place here.

Strange.

However, as she glanced up to meet Balthazar's startled gaze, she realized it might not be that strange after all.

A fact he proved as he reached around her.

To key in the code to the door at her back.

CHAPTER 16

BALTHAZAR

THIS LOCATION ALMOST FELT APPROPRIATE, GIVEN IT WAS Jay's main house off the island. Like all the other Elder locations, it came equipped with upgraded security, a door code, and enough bedrooms to give each male his space when needed.

Balthazar guided Leela into the double-story foyer, then closed and locked the door behind her. An Oriental rug decorated the marble floor, leading them to the seating room with windows overlooking the front terrace and canal beyond.

I've been here before, she whispered to herself. *But when?*

He followed her gaze to a painting on the wall between the oversized windows.

Her feet whispered over the floor with a dancer's grace, her focus consumed by the painting. Was that the location she'd recognized? Or was it the residence around them?

Jay had renovated the home to match current times in regard to plumbing and general electricity, but he'd kept much of the ambience the same as when he'd purchased the home several centuries ago. It was one of those residences that continued to be passed down through generations.

All the paperwork and legalities were handled by the estate team in Hydria. Balthazar understood most of what they did, but not all, as it varied by country and often changed over the decades.

"How often do you visit this house?" Leela asked, her voice sounding a bit far away as her mind continued spinning into a memory she couldn't quite grasp. *Have I followed him here before? No. Maybe. I've been here. When?*

"More often than the others, but not often enough for it to be notable," he replied. "This is Jay's home."

"Yes," she whispered. *I know. But how do I know?* She started toward the dining area and the massive kitchen beyond it. *Stone ovens. Pizza.* She glanced at the table meant for eight. *Pepperoni and Italian sausage.*

Leela wandered to a door, opening it to confirm what she already knew. *A wine cellar.* She started thinking about the brands, how she'd picked a red wine—one of Balthazar's favorites.

He frowned, not understanding how she knew all this. It was as though their minds had melded in some way, sharing memories that were his, not hers.

But as she continued her exploration, leading him to the staircase at the back, up to the second and then the third floor, he started to wonder if they were *their* memories. Because she knew every room, recognized them before seeing them, and took him directly to the space he considered his own. To the bed she was sure she'd slept in.

"Impossible," he told her. "We don't bring women here."

It wasn't a rule so much as a courtesy. Balthazar would never have brought Leela to this room, even if for a fun week of sex.

Lizzie would be an exception for Jay now.

Just as Jenika had been one for Alik.

But Balthazar and Luc had never taken an exception.

Yet some part of his mind recognized this moment. *Leela laughing. Her hair flowing freely. That come-hither smile on her lips. So much life. So much love.*

She spun around to face him as though experiencing the same thoughts, except hers were about him. *His chocolate eyes, grinning with wicked intent. His dimples flashing enticingly. His fingers removing his tie.*

Only, he wasn't wearing one.

Just gray sweatpants.

But his fingers brushed the column of his throat anyway, entranced by the description in her thoughts.

He removed his tie. Black. And hung it... She went to his closet, finding it exactly where she remembered against the wall. Her fingers ran over the silk before glancing at the midnight shirt he would typically pair with it. *He wore this...*

"What memory is this?" he asked.

"It's a fantasy," she whispered. "But it feels... it feels so real..." Her blue-green eyes sparkled as she turned toward him, the sun outside hanging at a midday position in the sky that hit his windows just right.

Leela strode toward them, her nimble fingers moving over the locks to open them wide. Winter in Venice was usually cool, and today was no exception. But the chilly afternoon air barely brushed his overly hot skin. His mind was lost to Leela's memory, her knowing movements throughout the room unnerving and yet hypnotically beautiful.

She stepped out onto his balcony terrace, her thoughts confirming every detail.

Then she turned and paused, her silhouette in the daylight almost too much. Her blonde hair hung in slightly damp waves over her shoulders, where his white dress shirt clung to her feminine curves.

Perfection.

But in another life, she was wearing a white summer dress that caressed her hourglass figure and showcased those rosebud nipples.

He pictured it for the briefest of seconds, then shook his head, confused. "What are you doing to me?"

"I don't know," she said softly, biting her lip. "I don't understand any of this. Just that… that I've… we've…"

"Yes," he replied, stepping toward her, his bare feet barely feeling the plush carpet beneath his soles. "Yes," he repeated, his palm encircling the back of her neck and tugging her to him. "*Yes.*" He couldn't say anything else.

Because there was nothing else to say.

He had to know if this was true. If this was right. If this was *real.* Because he felt lost to a dream that shouldn't exist. A fantasy that wasn't his own.

And yet, it was happening.

To him.

To *them.*

"Kiss me," she breathed, the words taunting a foreign memory he couldn't fully grasp. "Take me, B. Make me fly."

She was reciting something from her mind that neither of them understood.

However, he was eager to comply.

I have to know, he thought, his opposite hand going to her hip as he used the palm around her neck to pull her into a kiss.

Heat sizzled between them, firing off nerves he'd never touched before. Nerves he'd never realized he owned. *Who are you to me?* he wondered, his arm encircling Leela's waist as he pulled her flush against him.

Consume me. The plea hummed through her mind.

He obliged, his tongue parting her lips and delving inside to dance intimately with her own. It was so familiar. So right. *A dream riddled in fantasy.*

Balthazar struggled for air, uncertain of how to stop, where to go, which way was up or down.

But then he was falling to the mattress with Leela beneath him.

His hands were on her skin, her breasts, his shirt lying in tatters on the floor. *A memory or reality?* He wasn't sure. But he had to *feel.*

"Balthazar," Leela moaned, her body arching into his.

Real, he decided, her body hot and sinful beneath his own.

He pulled his mouth away from hers and found the shirt he'd just torn from her body. Except it shifted between shades of white and black. *Real and memory. Life and fantasy. Now and a dream.*

Her fingernails bit into his shoulders, drawing his focus back to her.

Blonde hair spilling over his black satin sheets. An angel. *His* angel. Lost to the throes of passion, except not quite.

Because she still had on his boxers.

And he was still wearing pants.

This dream required more.

"You were wearing a dress," he whispered. "White and thin. Silk meant to tempt even the devil himself to fall."

She'd been beautiful that night, walking through the streets of Venice, laughing, seducing, taunting every man and woman in her wake.

A stunning goddess.

His goddess.

He'd worn a suit of black to counter her white.

A game of sensuality and grace.

They were gods together, wandering the streets… How long ago? Was it real? A dream?

Her lips brushed his, pulling him back into the kiss, his mind melting to the blissful contentment of their embrace.

Fuck, her tits are perfect.

Firm and just the right size.

He kissed a path down her neck to her nipple, taking it into his mouth just like he'd done that night. She moaned, her fingers sliding into his hair to hold him in place, guiding him in that way she favored.

Not that he needed it.

He knew what she desired. Just as she knew his every need.

But how? he marveled. *Did we do this in Brazil?*

"More," she begged, her mind completely lost to whatever dream they'd once created here.

Or a fantasy, perhaps of her own conception.

Whatever it was, it tugged him under, drowning him in sensory memory and forcing him on a path down her abdomen to the boxers at her hips.

"You didn't wear any panties that night, vixen." He could picture it perfectly, the way her arousal had glistened freely for him to lick when he'd lifted the skirts of her dress.

He removed the boxers now, needing to see her, to *remember* that night.

Her thighs spread for him, her pretty pink flesh just as beautiful as…

As earlier, he thought. *Not that night. That didn't happen.*

Except this bed… her hair… her thighs spread just like this… he'd experienced it.

Once upon a time.

In some other life.

She sat up, her fingers going to his sweatpants. But in

her mind, she was thinking about dress pants. Black to match his shirt and tie. The same color as his boxers beneath.

She pulled the fabric down, exposing him to her hungry gaze.

He couldn't stop her.

He didn't even try.

It just felt too right to demand they cease this madness now.

They both had to know. They had to *re-create* whatever this was between them.

He sat down on the bed with his back against the headboard, aware of what came next as she straddled his thighs.

They'd made love just like this. To take the edge off. To begin their long weekend of fucking.

Hours. Days. Sometimes weeks.

His head throbbed with the onslaught of memories that weren't his. Of thoughts that couldn't be real.

And then he was inside her.

Deep. Wet. *Tight*.

Fuck, it was better than a fantasy. Their bodies fit in a harmony that shouldn't be real. Moving sensuously in blissful passion.

She dictated the pace, but he met her thrust for thrust with his hips moving up off the bed to slam deeper inside her.

She cried out, his name a benediction in the air as he moved forward to let her wrap her legs around his lower back.

An intimate position.

Their chests pressed together.

Her arms encircling his neck.

Her lips tasting his.

His hand on her hip and the other fisting her hair.

Pants. Raging pulses. Blistering heat.

It's always like this. A flawless union. Intense. Rapturous. Madness. Leela's thoughts rivaled his own, only she had the complete understanding of Brazil to compare to this experience.

And that made this all the more powerful.

Because he could hear her comparison, noting the rightness of both unions and the dark passion underlying this one.

He grabbed the back of her neck again and kissed her as though his life depended on it while her thighs shook around his own. His opposite hand went to the small of her back to urge her onward, taking control of her pace and adding a few deviations of his own.

Then he spun her onto the bed, slamming her back against the mattress, and drove home inside her again. She screamed, the sound one he'd heard before.

So many times.

On repeat.

Yes, just like that.

His palm went to her throat, holding her beneath him as he gave her everything he owned, guiding her to an oblivion only his body seemed capable of doing.

They both knew it, understood that this coupling surpassed all others, their souls rejoicing at the reconnection of fate.

He shook, his veins pulsating from their passionate inferno, as he fucked her into a euphoric state he could taste on his tongue.

She cried, tears streaming down her cheeks—then and now—as she moaned his name. "Balthazar…"

Not B.

But the full name.

Over and over again.

He kept his punishing pace, reveling in the way her tight channel squeezed his shaft.

Then he paused to stare down at her, his beautiful vixen, spent in the sheets, with her golden hair resembling a halo around her head.

The visual alone sent him over the edge, causing his abdomen to clench as his climax thundered through his being.

"*Leela*," he groaned, his world spinning off its axis as reality and fantasy combined.

He'd never been here before.

And yet he had.

Inside her. Just like this. Hearing her scream, feeling her throb, watching her come undone beneath him.

He grabbed the pillow beside her head, fisting the feathers inside as he gave a final thrust, his pleasure so intense that he could hardly breathe.

Just like before.

And every other time…

"I don't understand what's happening," he whispered against her ear, his fingers stroking her hip while his other hand rested on the pillow beside her head. "We've done that before."

"We definitely have," she agreed, her voice a rasp of sound.

He managed to pull back just enough to meet her gaze. "When?"

"I don't know," she admitted.

"I don't either." His gaze dropped to her mouth before returning to her sparkling eyes. "But I want to do it again."

"Yes," she replied. "Very much yes."

Another echo from a dream.

Another fantasy to repeat.

Another life… forgotten.

But his soul remembered. That life source beat deep inside, urging him to continue. To explore. To relive the moments.

So he kissed Leela.

And their fantasy began again.

CHAPTER 17

BALTHAZAR

LEELA DIDN'T BOTHER MAKING ANY WARDS. THEY HADN'T worked in Japan, so she assumed they wouldn't here.

Balthazar didn't press the issue.

This property had a security system similar to the one at Luc's place. If that had worked against the Seraphim, so would this.

Although, he wasn't quite sure *how* it had worked against them. They were ethereal beings. Perhaps they'd gone corporeal outside and that was what had triggered the alarms? If that was the case, they wouldn't make the mistake again, which left Leela and Balthazar a bit more vulnerable here.

But Leela wondered if her wards were what the Seraphim were tracking, not her blood.

Which was another reason not to create them.

They were close enough to Hydria here for him to feel somewhat safe. If they needed to mist, they could fly there in a few seconds flat. Then deal with the consequences.

His latest update from Luc—which he'd just finished

receiving—said they were on schedule and needed two more days, maybe less.

Vera was still nowhere to be found.

And Luc also hadn't decided what to do with Mateo.

Given that only about five hours had passed since their last conversation, Balthazar wasn't surprised.

He'd briefly considered telling Luc about the strange mind-meld happening between him and Leela but decided the Hydraian King had enough on his plate right now. Balthazar and Leela would figure this out on their own.

After he took her to dinner.

It was a risk, but surrounding themselves with humans might actually work as a better alarm system than the one in the house. According to Leela, the Seraphim wanted to remain hidden. It was why they'd warded the shit out of their home islands—to stay off mortal maps.

Which meant they would be less inclined to attack Leela and Balthazar while out in public.

Of course, they might not even know where to find them yet. It seemed they showed up in twelve-to-thirteen-hour intervals, and they'd only been in Venice for less than six.

This gave them plenty of time to explore this mind-meld and determine truth from fiction. If they'd truly walked these streets together before, then more memories might surface. And they could follow those strands for more information.

He suspected Vera had something to do with this. She'd manipulated his memories of Brazil, but who was to say that had been the first time? Maybe she'd done it to Leela, too.

So why were they remembering now? Because he could link to her mind as a result of Vera's rune? Or was this an entirely different mindfuck, one meant for them to think they'd been together before when, in reality, they hadn't?

What would be the purpose of such a thing?

To distract them, perhaps?

He wasn't sure, but he intended to find out.

As did Leela.

He could hear the determination in her thoughts as she finished putting on the dress he'd had delivered for her. It wasn't white like the one from the memory, but a long-sleeved navy ensemble that would flirt with her calves. A pair of black knee-high boots would complete the outfit.

No panties.

No bra.

Because they both knew she wouldn't wear them anyway.

Just as he wore nothing beneath his black trousers. He'd paired them with an off-white button-down that he'd left unfastened at the neck and intended to add a dark sports jacket.

It was just after eight in Venice, making it the perfect time to find dinner.

They hadn't made a reservation, as the whole point of this venture was to see where their minds took them.

He waited at the bottom of the back stairs for Leela, her boot heels clicking softly against the wood as she descended.

His lips curled as she came into view. Her perky breasts were beautifully on display with the tight fabric, giving him a tantalizing view of nipple. It was still modest enough for them to venture out, but the perfect tease to distract him and anyone else who looked her way tonight.

Truly a goddess, he marveled, the sense of déjà vu settling over him once again. Because he'd thought that about her countless times before, and not just today.

Not just yesterday.

Not just in Brazil.

But *before*.

The question was *when?*

Leela's thoughts mimicked his as she recognized the heat in his gaze. She'd seen it before. *Long, long ago*, she whispered to herself.

He held out his hand for hers. She accepted, sending another shock wave of familiarity through him. He didn't comment on it, because she felt the same electricity throbbing through her veins, provoking a memory she couldn't fully grasp.

Balthazar brought her hand to his lips, brushing a kiss over the knuckles, then tucked her arm beneath his as he led her through the house and toward the front door.

They wouldn't go far.

However, it also might be for the best. He'd hate to compromise another of the Elder homes to the Seraphim.

Although, if they saw Leela and Balthazar together, they'd realize they weren't Jay and Lizzie. Which could ruin the whole chase.

Fortunately, they had at least seven hours before that would happen, thus giving them time to decide how to proceed.

"You'll sense them if they arrive sooner, right?" Balthazar asked before opening the front door.

"I should," she replied. "But honestly, nothing feels certain anymore. Did you warn Luc?"

"I told him we had to move earlier than expected again and that his security system saved us. But this place is a bit different. We're much closer to humans here, with mortals living all around us. The place in Japan is a lot more secluded."

She nodded. "Venice is going to make it harder for them to track us. Except, it's similar to Melbourne."

"True."

He leaned against the door, facing her. "Should we stay here? I don't want to risk Jay, Lizzie, and little LJ." He desperately wanted to know what was happening between him and Leela, but not at his best friend's expense.

"It's only been a few hours, and I didn't even know where we were going when I misted us here. There's no way they followed us. I really don't think they'll find us this quickly. But on the off chance that they do, they'll try to capture us when we're alone and away from the humans."

"They won't realize it's a false chase and mist to Hydria?"

"They'll realize it was a false chase and demand answers for it. From me. Which means they'll focus first on taking me in for questioning, then continue their pursuit of Lizzie and her child."

He considered that for a moment. It meant if the Seraphim caught them, they'd have time to warn the others, and it might still prolong the inevitable because the warrior and tracker Seraphim would pursue Leela for answers before continuing their hunting mission.

"Can they keep you from misting?" he wondered out loud, considering the possibility of stretching this chase another day or two, if caught.

"Only if they're able to temporarily subdue me," she replied. "Like by shooting me in the head or something."

He frowned. Well, there went that suggestion, then. "We should stay here."

Balthazar wasn't going to risk her getting shot in the head again. And not just because she was his escape route, but because he cared about her well-being.

"No, we should go out," she countered. "And find out

what's happening between us. Enjoy ourselves a little. I'll sense them if they're near, and I'll mist us out of Venice."

"Your wards failed in Japan, and we only sensed them because of Luc's alarms."

"True." She nibbled her lip. "But I don't want to just hide here. I'm… I need to understand this. To follow the lead in my mind. It's… There's something here, B. And I hate that I can't define it."

"It's like someone messed with your head, yeah?" he asked.

"Yes."

"And you hate it, right?"

"Of course I do," she said, sounding frustrated. "I feel violated."

"Hmm." He arched a brow, waiting for her to realize what she'd just admitted.

It didn't take her long, her eyes widening. "Shit. Okay, I know. Yes, I should have at least tried to talk to you. It was wrong. I… I put Stas first. I shouldn't have told Vera to remove your memories. But I never expected it to lead to this."

"You never expected me to find out."

"Exactly."

"So whoever did this to us expected the same," he pointed out. "Yet we can sense it now, whatever this is, and it's frustrating as hell."

Her jaw clenched. "Yes. It is. Do you need me to crawl now? Beg for forgiveness?"

His lips curled. "Maybe after dinner." He needed to feed her after the day they'd experienced. Taking care of a lover was one of his favorite parts of the experience. And he very much wanted to take care of Leela.

She blew out a breath and shook her head sadly. "I'm sorry, B. I'm sorry I—"

He pulled her into a kiss, silencing the apology he could hear echoing in her mind. She continued voicing it in her thoughts, causing his hand to clamp tightly around her nape.

This had never been about holding a grudge or seeking revenge, or really even about having her crawl. He'd merely wanted a way to move forward, a path to navigate toward a mutually beneficial future.

Because there was no question in his mind that he and Leela were destined for something. They were too much alike for there to be any other alternative.

His tongue skated along her lower lip, dampening it before he grabbed hold with his teeth. She startled as he bit down, leaving his mark for all to see.

At least until she healed.

It wouldn't take long, as he hadn't drawn any blood. But it added a sexual glint to her gaze that she'd wear most of the evening.

Because she would want to do the same to him.

Except he moved his mouth away before she had the chance.

The dark desire turned her irises into a siren shade of blue, intensifying her features that much more and making her utterly exquisite in that pretty dress.

"Mmm, I'd take you back upstairs to sate that craving, but there are other parts of you that need to be fed first, sweet vixen," he whispered.

"Maybe I'll hook up with our waiter instead. Take the edge off."

"Only if I can watch," he replied, his arm sliding around her waist as his opposite hand went to her chin. "If you need an appetizer, you're more than welcome to slide under our table for a taste. Unless it's indulging others that suits you more."

"You'd approve of me fucking another man in front of you?"

"I'd approve of anything that fulfills your fantasies, sweetheart," he murmured, meaning it. "So long as you understood that I'd be the one taking you home afterward. Because we both know you'd need my brand of sex to truly satisfy you."

"And you? What do you need, B?"

He stared down into her eyes, his touch shifting from her chin to her cheek and down to brush his knuckles along the column of her neck. "Right now?" he asked, his voice softening as he seriously considered her query. "Right now, all I need is you." And he meant it, too.

Not every occasion required group involvement.

Sometimes it was nice to play one-on-one.

Especially with a partner as gifted as Leela.

"Then I suppose you'll have to give me that appetizer," she whispered, her fingers trailing up the buttons of his shirt. "Take me to dinner, B. Please. I'm tired of hiding. I want to see if we can trigger any more memories by walking around. And I promise to mist us out of here at the first sign of trouble."

He wanted to see if anything sparked more memories, too. And there was only one way to find out—by exploring.

Fortunately, Leela had more than proved her ability to mist quickly.

While conscious, he thought, gazing down at her pleading expression.

"I'll stay extra vigilant," she said. "I can sense ethereal presences. I just have to be paying attention. And I wasn't in Japan, because I was relying on my wards. I won't make that mistake again, B. I promise I can protect us."

That was the second time in a span of a minute that she'd used the phrase *I promise.*

He couldn't help responding to it.

"I do trust you," he told her, the words a gift that meant more than their face value.

Because he was essentially saying that he accepted her apology.

Which she'd understand, as he'd just told her earlier that it took time to recover from a betrayal, that trust didn't always come naturally as a result.

Sometimes, there was no coming back from a broken vow.

But he and Leela were walking the road to recovery, each step pointing them in the right direction, every confession solidifying the bond between them.

Each kiss whispering a chance to experience something *more.*

His lips brushed hers now, a sinful promise burning between them. "Lead the way, vixen. Tonight, I'm yours to do with as you please."

Chapter 18

Stas

Issac's hands were magical. His thumbs found pressure points Stas had never even known existed as he massaged the knots from her shoulders.

I'm supposed to be immortal. How am I sore? she wondered.

Maybe because you've not let yourself properly rest, Issac suggested. *Our bodies heal quickly, but that doesn't mean we don't still hurt.*

She sighed, knowing he was right.

She'd paused her training today only long enough to learn about Mateo's reasoning and to console Issac on his impossible decision—one he hadn't yet made.

He could no longer trust Mateo, but he was still his progeny. Did he exile him? Kill him? Allow him a chance to redeem himself?

Those were the questions rolling through Issac's mind, his thoughts open to Stas through their mental link. She couldn't help him other than to offer her own perspective.

Osiris had his claws in all of them in some way. But Mateo had made it clear he'd monitored the tech willingly. Except it'd been done to keep them all safe.

Which added a strange layer to this whole mess.

Because it implied Osiris had been trying to protect Issac's and Aidan's connections with the Hydraians by keeping it a secret.

"Why create a Conclave with rules about Hydraian and Ichorian interactions, just to allow some of his constituents to break those rules and, moreover, to also aid them in doing so?" Issac had asked Luc earlier.

The Hydraian King hadn't replied, his emerald eyes taking on that faraway gleam they did whenever he engaged his omniscience ability.

However, Stas's father had arrived right at that point in the conversation and had added his two cents. "My father plays every potential angle available to him. He's cultivated power throughout several millennia for a reason. If he felt your alliance was a strong one, he'd seek to use it, not destroy it."

"Yet he created rules and punished Ichorians for seeking similar alliances," Issac had pointed out.

Which had prompted Stas to mutter, "He skinned Sierra alive before forcing her maker to light her on fire, just for knowing Owen was in the city without reporting his presence to Osiris."

"Because that showed a lack of loyalty to the cause," her dad had replied. "My father would not take that behavior lightly."

"Yet we've spent the last three hundred years maintaining this alliance in secret." Issac had frowned. "Unless…"

"Unless Aidan had already told him," Luc had finished for him, his expression giving nothing away. "As head of the line, it would have been his duty to do so. And he never promised to stop seeing me. Actually, he told Osiris long ago that he would not choose politics over his own son."

Everyone had fallen silent after that.

Then Luc had left, saying he wanted to talk to Mateo alone.

That'd been three hours ago.

No one knew what he was going to do. Typically, he conferred with the others, especially the Elders, but neither Jay nor Alik had heard from him since taking Mateo to his house. Not to the dungeon like he'd done with Clara. But to his own home.

Concern radiated from Issac, but he continued to massage Stas's shoulders rather than voice his worries aloud. He trusted Luc to do what was right. And he wasn't ready to make his own decision yet anyway.

All thoughts she could hear clearly because he didn't shy away from her, not even for a moment. His streaming consciousness remained open to her through their link, allowing her to hear every word.

It almost made her smile, as their relationship definitely hadn't always been like this. He used to adore his secrets.

She sighed, leaning back into him, loving their closeness and the momentary reprieve he provided her with.

Their moments alone seemed to be few and far between, but he'd held her back at Balthazar's home for just a few extra minutes. Then he'd begun working magic on her shoulders, and, well, she'd already forgotten where she needed to be.

Well, not really.

Her mother and Stark were working on the wards again now that night had fallen. And Stas planned to join them.

Except... She yawned. *Except I'm probably too exhausted to be useful.* She didn't know enough about the wards or ethereal energy to truly help. It was more of a learning exercise, which would be poorly retained in her current state.

She hadn't slept in over twenty-four hours now, having spent all her time learning about wards and ethereal energy. She felt so behind in her studies, but her mother assured her this was normal. Most Seraphim couldn't truly begin their lessons until they found their wings.

You're magnificent, Issac murmured into her mind. *But it's okay to rest a bit.*

We don't know when the Seraphim are going to attack. I need to be ready.

You won't be ready if you're exhausted, love, he whispered back to her, his nose running along the column of her neck to her ear. "Come to bed with me, Aya. I can send an image of you sleeping to Caro. She'll understand."

"Yeah, except immortals don't have to sleep." Her body absolutely disagreed with that statement. However, it should be true. Immortality meant she could survive without food or sleep. In theory, anyway.

"You're right, love. We don't. But it's not sleeping that I actually have in mind. However, as I suspect your mother won't appreciate the imagery of what I intend to do to you, I'll send her a visual of you sleeping instead."

His hands slid down her shoulders to her arms as he pulled her back to his chest.

"Come to bed with me, Aya," he repeated, his hands finding her hips as he started walking them backward out of the living room. "I'll take care of your every need, and you'll feel so much better afterward. I promise."

"Issac..."

"You're taking a break," he told her, a hint of steel underling his tone. Just enough for her to know that wasn't a request but a demand. "Your parents took one. Gabriel took one. You have not. It's time to listen to the soreness of your body and let me take care of you."

"I took a break," she argued half-heartedly. "I haven't flown in a few hours."

His lips brushed her pulse. "Not all exhaustion is of the body, Aya. Sometimes it's of the mind, too."

Hmm, she hummed, reading between the lines of his proclamation.

This wasn't just for her but for him, too. Because he needed her for emotional support, something he wouldn't admit out loud yet did with his statement. She wasn't mentally exhausted, but Issac certainly was. He'd spent all afternoon and evening thinking about Mateo and what his confession implied.

His progeny had indirectly helped murder Issac's equivalent of a father figure. Aidan wasn't just his maker but also the one who had more or less adopted him as a young boy and essentially raised him as his own. He'd been in love with Issac's mother, had created Amelia with her, and had been Issac's true family.

While Mateo was his responsibility.

His progeny.

The one he'd made into an Ichorian.

And his actions had cost Issac his father's life.

Issac was right.

She couldn't continue training right now. Her soul mate needed her, and this was his subtle way of begging her to stay, under the guise of wanting to take care of her. Because that would help him feel better.

And honestly, it would help her feel better, too.

She turned in his arms, and he pushed her up against the hallway wall, his sapphire gaze burning with quiet passion. "Astasiya—"

"Kiss me, Issac," she demanded, compulsion emboldening her words.

His irises darkened to a shade of midnight blue, telling her it was the right thing to say and exactly what he needed. Her lips tingled with expectation, her tongue thrumming with heated intent.

Only, he didn't kiss her on the mouth.

He went for her throat instead, his lips sealing around her pulse in an open-mouthed embrace that set her veins on fire.

You didn't say where to kiss you, love, he whispered into her mind, his incisors pricking her flesh.

She gasped as he bit her deeply, his throat working as he pulled her essence into his mouth to swallow.

Euphoria hummed through her veins in response, stirring a fire deep within her that begged for more.

His hands remained on her hips, holding her against the wall as he pressed his groin into hers. They were both wearing jeans, which heightened the anticipation by delaying the inevitable connection.

Because Issac Wakefield never rushed.

No, he devoured.

Slowly. Thoroughly. *Purposefully*.

And tonight would be no exception.

Stas's thighs clenched as he slowly released her neck to kiss a path up to her ear. "I want you naked and waiting for me on that bed, Aya. You have thirty seconds."

She didn't bother asking what she would be given for complying. Instead, she misted to the bedroom and ripped her shirt over her head. Her fingers traced the strap of her bra, her teeth snagging her lower lip as she pondered her options.

He'd said naked.

But defiance was often rewarded.

She left the bra alone and focused on her jeans instead, then slipped off her socks and crawled up onto the bed they'd temporarily claimed as their own.

With Balthazar gone, it sort of felt like they were house-sitting for him.

Stas relaxed into the pillows, her gaze on the door.

Then she began to count.

When thirty seconds came and went, she began to frown.

Then thirty seconds became a minute.

And a minute grew into two minutes.

Issac?

No reply.

She started to sit up as the door opened with her demon on the other side holding a glass of red wine.

Her brow furrowed as she fell back to her elbows. *You went to grab a drink?*

He didn't respond, instead walking inside and quietly shutting the door behind him. The lock snapped with a click that reverberated down her spine. "That's not naked, Aya," he said casually, his alluring gaze taking in the black lace decorating her flesh.

"It's much more fun when you remove my clothes," she told him.

"Mmm," he hummed noncommittally as he sauntered over to the nightstand beside her. He set the wine glass down, his eyes still roaming over her body.

She loved when he looked at her like that. It made her feel powerful, as though she could convince him to do anything in that moment without even trying.

But she also knew he valued control. He very rarely relinquished it in the bedroom, and his expression told her tonight would be no exception.

This was how he found emotional balance, how he

took charge of his own feelings and gave his mind a break from the decision he inevitably needed to make.

"I sent a visual note to Caro, and I locked all the external doors. We shouldn't be bothered for a bit."

"Is this the part where you tell me no one will hear me scream?" she taunted.

"Oh, the entire island is going to hear you scream, love. Assuming I do my job right."

"My parents might not like that." A statement she'd never thought she'd say.

"Your parents are not a factor in my thoughts right now, love. Not with you defying me by wearing that sexy-as-fuck lace."

She shivered at the dangerous note in his tone, the one that said he was about to take back the control of the situation and bring her to her proverbial knees. "I'm not sorry."

"I know you're not," he murmured, leaning over to capture her nipple through the thin fabric of her bra. *With his teeth.*

She arched off the bed, but his palm on her stomach immediately pushed her down, his opposite hand going to her shoulder to press her into the pillows.

"Issac," she hissed, the pleasure-pain causing her muscles to tighten along her limbs. She grabbed the comforter, her nails digging into the soft cotton as his tongue laved her bruised peak.

"Press your palms to the headboard for me," he ordered, straightening once more.

She swallowed but did as he demanded, the flat wood surface cool beneath her hands.

"Don't move from that position until I say otherwise."

Goose bumps pebbled down her arms. It would be so easy to disobey and see what he would do, but she knew he needed this to find balance. Besides, she would absolutely benefit from his current mood, something the devious twinkle in his gaze confirmed for her.

If she wanted slow and sensual, he'd immediately oblige.

But she found herself more often craving this side of Issac. His dominance. The alpha male part of him that possessed her like no one else could.

Afterward, he would massage her again. Bathe her. Cherish her.

However, right now, he wanted passion.

And he was going to evoke it from her by any means necessary.

His lips curled, her demon taking on the role he was destined to play in their life—the role of sin personified.

"Brilliant," he said, sensuality caressing each syllable. "You're ready." Not a question, but a statement.

Still, she felt inclined to reply, "I am."

"Then let's begin."

Chapter 19

Issac

AYA'S LIPS PARTED, HER EXHALE A KISS OF A PROMISE ON the air. He could read her without words, could understand her needs without touching her mind.

She was his.

And she trusted him implicitly, just as he did her.

She was his other half. His heart. His source of calm and contentment after a shit day. And while he was doing this partly for her, it was also very much for himself.

Which she knew, of course.

Because she knew him better than anyone else.

Their connection ran deeper than blood, marrying them on the soul plane, their spirits intertwined for eternity, allowing him to keep this female for the rest of his very long life.

It was a gift he didn't deserve, but one he vowed to cherish. Just as he intended to do right now.

Her hands remained flattened against the dark wood of the headboard, leaving her body on exquisite display.

She'd kept on her panties and bra, knowing full well it would drive him to madness. Because he absolutely adored her fetish for matching lingerie. It was almost innocent, yet sexy as hell. Her penchant for lace and silk was all her own, something she'd indulged in prior to him meeting her.

But it was a quirk he absolutely enjoyed about her, from the very first time he'd fondled her in that black thong at the Conclave.

Fuck, she'd been stunning in that sinfully short dress.

Just thinking of it made his lips curl.

She'd needed his help to remove it.

Then he'd turned around like a proper gentleman while she'd undressed.

But there was nothing proper about him now.

"Hmm," he hummed, drawing a finger from her collarbone down the center of her chest to her belly button. "I'm positively parched, Astasiya. I need more blood."

A lie, of course.

He no longer required the essence of others to survive. His bond to Aya was turning him into a Seraphim, thereby curing him of his former Ichorian needs.

However, that didn't mean he'd stopped enjoying the flavor.

Blood was the staple of Seraphim kind, what created the bonds between them, and the element that acted as a vessel of power. So it was only natural that he still enjoyed biting Aya, and from the flare of her nostrils, he wasn't the only one who enjoyed it, either.

"Open your mouth, love," he murmured.

She complied beautifully, her full lips parting to allow him to do whatever he desired.

He picked up the glass of wine and took a sip before bending to give her a taste. It was a drier red from Argentina that could use some sweetening.

His tongue fed her the wine, allowing her to familiarize herself with the flavor. She moaned, not because of the wine but because of the erotic sensuality of sharing the drink.

Issac kissed her, drawing out the moment while carefully holding the wine beside her head on the pillow. "You're going to sweeten that for me, Aya," he told her, his voice hushed and low and filled with dark promises.

He drew his nose along her cheekbone, loving the way her blush chased his touch. So decadent and beautiful.

His mouth skimmed her throat, pausing to kiss the place he'd bitten her in the hall before skating down to her shoulder.

He took her bra strap between his teeth along the way, taking it with him down the athletic curve to her arm, all the way to her elbow. It left the fleshier part of her breast exposed, the lace having caught on her stiff nipple.

Issac could see it easily through the fabric, the gauzy material merely masking the rosy color and giving it a slightly darker quality.

"You should have removed this, love. I could have moved a little quicker."

"I prefer drawing it out," she replied. "As do you."

"Indeed," he agreed, loving that she knew exactly how to play his games. She represented a conundrum for him that he'd never experienced. Because she knew his preferences yet made every embrace feel new at the same time.

It was intoxicating.

Addicting.

And so damn exciting.

He loved that she could keep up with him yet also make each encounter fresh.

Or maybe that was just his interpretation.

He would never tire of her. If anything, he felt like eternity would never be enough.

His lips feathered across the top of her breast to the fabric covering her nipple. He caught it in his teeth and tugged it down to expose her tit.

But rather than indulge himself, he went to her opposite strap and began the process all over again. By the time her curves were fully exposed, gooseflesh had pebbled all over her chest, drawing her pretty peaks to tight little points.

"Stunning," he marveled, taking another sip of his wine.

He didn't indulge in her breasts, instead focusing on the scrap of lace between her thighs.

That would be harder to remove.

However, he wasn't one to shy away from a challenge.

He kissed a path down her flat abdomen to the edge of the panties covering her shaved mound. Then he dipped his head between her legs to taste her sweetness through the fabric, the scent drawing out the predator within him.

"Mmm." She tasted absolutely divine. He paired it with another sip of wine and groaned. "Yes. That's what the wine needs." More than her blood.

Or maybe… a mix of both.

His mouth left her sweet heat, traveling down her thigh to his favorite artery. Her legs tensed as he kissed her throbbing pulse.

She knew what he desired.

And the flush painting her face and breasts told him she more than approved.

But before he could bite, he needed that lace removed.

His gaze slid up to hers as he slowly straightened, still holding the wine in one hand. He'd been standing the whole time, leaning over her alluring form on the bed and using his free hand for balance against the mattress.

He set the glass down to focus on those panties again, his patience slowly slipping away.

It'd been a long fucking day.

And he wanted to drink his fill. To hear her scream. To fuck her into oblivion and forget all their worries for just one beautiful moment.

Decided, he grabbed her panties by their thin straps along her hips and ripped them from her skin.

She gasped in shock, her brow immediately furrowing. *You owe me a new pair of underwear, Mister Wakefield.*

I'll buy you a fucking lingerie line, he replied as he tore his shirt over his head.

Her eyes immediately went to his physique, as they always did. He hadn't been as regularly active lately, his swimming routine utterly fucked from current events. But the way she looked at him said it hadn't made much difference.

The perks of immortality, he supposed.

Which meant she was forever frozen in her current form—a fact he would thank destiny for every damn day.

Because she redefined the meaning of beauty with her gorgeous blonde hair, glittering green eyes, elven chin, perfect tits, slender waist, and long fuck-me legs.

Every part of her was perfect, as though destiny had made her just for him.

And the way Aya looked at him said she felt the exact same way about him.

He popped the button on his jeans, sighing in relief as he drew the zipper down. His cock was so damn hard for her—*always so damn hard for her*—that it hurt to breathe.

Delayed gratification had its perks.

But sometimes, he just wanted to be inside his female and never let the pleasure end instead.

"Still planning to sweeten your wine?" Aya taunted, her gaze knowing.

"Maybe after I fuck you," he said, kicking off his jeans and boxer shorts along the way.

Her gaze ran down his body to the part of him that desired her most. "I'm okay with that."

His lips curled. "Are you?" he asked, lifting his knee up to the bed to begin crawling toward her.

"Yes," she whispered, her irises flaring with approval.

He paused near her thighs, his mouth begging him for a taste of her first.

Issac held her gaze as he dipped his head to trace his tongue along her slick folds. Her fingers flexed against the wood, her desire to grab him showing in the strain of her arms.

He deepened the taunt by applying more pressure and sliding his tongue inside her.

Fuck, she whispered, the thought likely meant for herself more than him. *Fuck. Fuck. Fuck.*

That is the general idea, darling, he teased as he drew his touch up to circle her clit.

A moan parted her full lips, her pupils flaring as she fought to maintain eye contact with him.

He gave her another lick, testing her resolve.

She didn't move, her gaze remaining locked on his as her breathing grew labored. He took her nub into his mouth for a long, sensuous pull that had her hips attempting to buck beneath him. But his hands on her hips held her down, his elbows pinning her thighs to the mattress as he forced her to take more of his sensual assault.

The cursing in her thoughts grew more colorful, his name adding to the mix.

Her eyelashes began to flutter, her ability to hold his gaze faltering with each passing second. *Issac... I'm... I'm going to...*

He removed his mouth, drawing another expletive from her, this time from her mouth and not just within her mind. "Asshole."

"I'll make it up to you, love," he promised as he kissed a path up to her breasts. He slipped his hand beneath her to unsnap the bra, then finished removing it while sucking one of her nipples deep into his mouth.

She cried out in response, her legs wrapping around his torso in an attempt to urge him upward. He caught her gaze once more, telling her with a look to be patient as he switched to her other breast.

Her palms remained against the headboard the whole time, her obedience making him that much harder. Because she could so easily top him with a few choice commands. Yet she chose to submit. She chose to defer to him. She chose to let him lead.

And that was a beautiful gift, one he would never take for granted.

He continued his path upward, licking and nipping along the way, then paused at her neck to gently lick the blood that had trickled out from the wound before naturally closing.

Her flavor went straight to his groin, readying him that much more for her as he slid his shaft through her welcoming heat.

"You're always so perfect, Aya," he whispered reverently against her ear as he slowly began to enter her. "So beautiful. So tempting. So warm and *tight*." He thrust all the way inside, eliciting a gasp from her lips. "I'll never tire of this, the way it feels to be inside you."

"Let me touch you," she begged. "Please."

He went to his elbows on either side of her head, then reached up to take hold of one wrist and bring her palm to his cheek. She shuddered at the contact, her eyes almost rolling back into her head. He grinned, loving that he had that effect on her.

"You can move now, Aya," he told her softly. "Just so long as you let me worship you."

She wrapped her legs more tightly around his waist, her opposite hand going to the back of his neck as she pulled him down into a kiss.

And then their bodies began to dance.

It wasn't a gentle rhythm, but they rarely ever moved tenderly with one another. It was always intense, passionate heat between them, and now was no different.

He thrust deep.

She lifted her hips to meet him.

Her calves tightened against his ass.

Her nails bit into the back of his neck.

And the hand on his face slid back into his hair to hold him against her.

Their tongues were languid, their kiss one born of sensuality and grace while their hips married each other. Her excitement coated every inch of him, gripping him with a passion that tightened his groin.

He rolled to his back, taking her with him, needing more, needing *her*.

She sat up and he followed, his arms wrapping around her as he devoured her mouth. Her legs slipped around his waist, seating her in his lap as they continued their embrace.

Every part of them was touching.

Her breasts to his chest.

Her arousal to his.

Her arms encircling his neck.

Her fingers in his hair.

Her tongue in his mouth.

Fuck, he was done for, but he needed her to come. He'd promised to take care of her, not just tonight, but for always, and he'd meant it.

He could feel her teetering on the edge, her body needing his touch to push her over, and maybe his words, too.

"You're going to come for me, Aya," he whispered, his hand slipping between them to find the place that would force her over the edge. "You're going to come for me right *now*." He thrust up into the spot that would send her to the stars while pressing down on her clit at the exact same time.

"*Issac*," she gasped, her grip around him tightening as her body began to shake.

His lips found her neck, his instincts demanding he mark her again.

She screamed as he bit her, the endorphins of his bite tripling the ecstasy she felt inside and forcing her right into another orgasm before the first had come to an end. He hoped those endorphines remained with him always and weren't just an Ichorian trait. But if they did eventually leave him, he would find other pleasurable ways to bite his Aya.

Because *fuck*, he loved her reaction to his mouth.

Her tight sheath squeezed him to the point of near pain, forcing him to follow her into oblivion. There was no choice. Not that he wanted one.

He chased after her, longing to fly at her side, dreaming of the day where he grew his own wings.

But for now, he would settle for these shared moments of bliss, these rapturous kisses between their souls that drugged them both in inexplicable euphoria.

His heart hammered in his chest as he erupted, claiming her from the inside out as she clawed his back in response, her own pleasure still unraveling.

He captured her mouth once more, kissing her through their union and whispering vows of more against her tongue.

She moaned, her muscles slowly unclenching as he gently coaxed her down from her high.

Her blonde hair fanned out across the pillow as he laid her down, his cock still deep inside her as he hovered over her, their bodies moving in slow, subtle strokes to draw out the residual quakes of their pleasure.

Then his forehead met hers, his lips curling in an exhausted yet gratified grin. "How do you feel, Aya?"

"Alive," she whispered.

"Me, too." He kissed her again, his tongue lazily stroking hers as he waited for their bodies to recover.

It wouldn't take long, their immortal souls quick to rejuvenate and replenish their reserves.

Her fingers slid up and down his spine, her happiness warming their bond. *You were right*, she marveled. *I definitely needed rest.*

He chuckled, his lips leaving hers to kiss a path to her ear. "It's good for the body and…"

A vision of Balthazar's living room had him trailing off with a frown. He'd locked the door, which meant whoever was currently in the house had either misted in or purposely ignored the clear *do not enter* sign.

"What is it?" she asked.

"Someone's here," he muttered, sliding out of her. "I'll go handle it. You stay here." He opened up a nearby drawer to pull on a pair of flannel pants and didn't bother with a shirt. "This won't take long."

Famous last words.

Because the moment he stepped into the hallway, he knew this wasn't going to be quick.

Vera stood leaning against the wall, her navy wings flared around her. "We should talk."

He arched a brow. "Who's with you?" Because it was that person's vision he was seeing inside his mind, not hers.

Osiris stepped into view, his expression giving nothing away. "So compelling you to see an image does work. Good to know."

Issac frowned, not liking that development at all. *Aya. You're going to want to find your clothes.*

Already on it, she told him.

"Why are you here?" he demanded.

"I only followed Vera in for an update, which she's just provided. Has Stas given any more thought to her training?"

"No," Aya answered as she stepped into the hallway behind Issac. She'd pulled on a pair of sleep shorts and a tank top. "I'm still working with Stark and my mom. And it's only been a few days."

"Has it?" Osiris considered that for a moment. "Well." He shrugged, glancing at Vera. "Until our next update, then." He disappeared in a breath, leaving the three of them in the hallway.

"You're providing updates to him now?" Aya sounded as incredulous as Issac felt.

"There's a lot you don't know," Vera said, sounding tired.

"Yeah, I'm getting that," Stas replied. "And you disappearing after Iceland doesn't help matters."

Vera pinched her lips to the side. "I was following a strand of a memory that I found in Patreel's mind."

"Patreel?" Aya repeated.

"One of the tracker Seraphim pursuing Leela and Balthazar. I had to alter his remembrance of what happened in Iceland, and while doing that, I... I found something." Vera palmed the back of her neck, her stance and expression the most uncomfortable Issac had seen in her.

Not that he knew her well, but she certainly appeared to be exhausted and perhaps a bit overwhelmed.

"What did you find?" he wondered out loud.

Vera's wings disappeared as she turned fully corporeal, her irises shifting from blue-green to silver.

She blinked once. Twice. Yet her gaze remained unfocused as though she couldn't seem to find her current reality.

"Brazil wasn't the first time Balthazar and Leela met," she whispered, more to herself than to them. "They've... they've known each other for a very long time." She cleared her throat, her gaze locking on his. "Issac, they've known each other for over three thousand years."

Chapter 20

Leela

THE SAVORY AROMA OF GARLIC GRACED THE NIGHT AIR, leaving a palpable hunger in its wake.

Mmm. This was heaven.

Fresh ingredients, a Mediterranean flair, and a little off-the-beaten-path ristorante.

Leela sipped her wine, loving the way the sweet white paired with the tomato dish she'd selected. It tasted exactly as she'd expected.

No.

Exactly as she *remembered*.

Same with the ambience.

But the people were all new.

Balthazar casually asked their waiter about the history of the place, which led to them meeting the owner himself.

He was an average-height, middle-aged male with beautiful brown eyes and a lovely accent. When he'd realized Leela and Balthazar spoke Italian, he had happily told them all about his great-great-grandfather who'd originally opened the restaurant.

Which meant Balthazar and Leela could have visited

this establishment anytime in the last hundred or two hundred years.

It definitely hadn't been recently, given that the current owner wasn't familiar at all.

And other than being clearly attracted to B and Leela, he hadn't shown a single flare of recognition when looking at them.

Balthazar had thanked him heartily for the details.

Now he kept checking in every ten minutes to see how they liked their meal.

He was adorable, so they didn't mind. And the food truly was divine.

"Definitely a family recipe," she decided out loud. "Because I've experienced this exact dish."

Some might think Italian foods were all the same, but Leela knew better. Proper Italian cooking varied by family, down to the precise spice.

And this dish could never be replicated.

Not exactly, anyway.

Her taste buds confirmed it all. She'd eaten this dish before and in this exact same restaurant.

With Balthazar.

"I fed it to you last time," he said softly. "We sat next to each other, and I fed you because your hand was otherwise occupied."

"You remember?"

"Only flashes of detail." His brown eyes lifted to hers. "Like you swallowing me for dessert."

She narrowed her gaze. "How do I know you're not just saying that because you're craving my mouth on you?"

"Because I'll always crave those beautiful lips, Lee," he murmured. "And I don't need to fabricate a story to seduce you."

"True, you don't require an approach at all, do you?"

245

she mused, thinking back on Brazil and how he'd said that right before kissing the hell out of her on that beach. He'd demonstrated the right amount of control and tenderness to sweep her right off her feet. It'd been impressive and incredibly suave.

"What else did I do in Brazil?" he asked, a grin in his voice.

"I thought you knew it all," she murmured, recalling his statement... When was that? A few days ago? Weeks ago? Time was moving strangely between them. Regardless, he'd said at one point that he knew everything.

But his eyes told her now that he didn't.

Not at all.

His teasing mood disappeared behind a frown, his brow furrowing. "I remember your hand on my cock, stroking me while I fed you that pasta. It's more sensory memory than a vivid visual, but it absolutely happened. Yet I can't recall anything about Brazil."

"Maybe it's because we're here and not there," Leela suggested.

He considered that for a moment. "Perhaps." His tone implied he didn't believe that at all.

She took another bite of her food while he continued to think.

He'd ordered a dish with wine sauce as the base. After she finished swallowing, she reached across to steal one of his penne noodles. His irises swirled with admiration as he observed her. Then he mimed her actions by taking some of her pasta for himself as well.

It was warmly intimate.

Just like that night.

And all the others, her soul whispered. She tried to chase the memories, to define them, to determine if they were

246

truly real or some sort of figment spell meant to distract her from something obvious.

"The events of Brazil are rather dull in my head," Balthazar said, interrupting her inner musings. "They hold no real importance, meaning there's nothing about those memories that would make me even think of them at all. It was just another experience, one I'd probably never consider again because nothing about it calls to me."

His words struck her right in the heart, immediately killing her appetite.

Because that weekend… that weekend had been one of the most memorable weekends of her life.

And he'd just called it *dull*.

Which wasn't his fault. She'd asked Vera to remove his memories. She'd known the consequences and had agreed to pay the price for them.

But to hear him speak about their profound connection as though it didn't matter at all truly put the pain into proper perspective.

That weekend meant nothing to him at all. He'd never considered it again afterward—and would never think of it again—while she'd spent the last few months constantly reminiscing about their intimate connection.

He reached across the table to take control of her fork, his strong fingers twirling it around some pasta before bringing it to her lips. "We'll make new memories, Lee," he promised her. "Now open that pretty mouth and swallow for me. I want to see how much you can take."

If he remembered Brazil, he'd already know.

His eyes narrowed. "Stop punishing yourself and swallow."

"Some might argue that's an ideal punishment for the crime," she replied, infusing a double meaning to her words.

He grinned. "An idea for after you crawl, perhaps." He pressed the fork to her lips. "Open for me, baby."

She did, only because she wanted to obey, and she appreciated what he was doing—distracting her with sexual puns and lighter thoughts.

But that didn't erase the guilt consuming her inside for what she'd done.

Maybe not guilt so much as sadness.

She wanted him to remember, to understand the beauty of that weekend. Just as she wanted to remember whatever this was in Venice, whatever memory they were chasing.

"That's the interesting part," Balthazar murmured as he prepared another bite for her. "I have this deep sense of understanding and familiarity of our time together here. Yet I feel nothing about Brazil. We know Vera took my memories there. But whoever stole my recollection of our time in Venice clearly wasn't as thorough."

She frowned as she chewed the pasta he'd just slid into her mouth.

"It feels too different to be the same person," he continued. "So either someone else tampered with my memories here, or it's someone weaving a very powerful enchantment between us for an unknown benefit."

Leela swallowed as he took a bite for himself out of her meal. "I don't know of a power that can weave an enchantment like this. Some sort of Cupid type, maybe? But that's my line of existence—fertility—and none of us have powers that facilitate this sort of hallucination trip."

He set her fork back down and took a sip of his wine. "Then it's more likely the former, that someone other than Vera altered our memories."

She enjoyed her own healthy gulp of alcohol while she considered that possibility. "There's a whole line of memory manipulators, but aside from Vera's mother, she's the best."

"Which only firms up my theory that much more because whoever did this wasn't Vera."

"Because you don't remember anything about Brazil, but you're picking up pieces of memories here," she said, repeating what he'd already stated. "Why now? Why here? Why not before?" She'd been following him for months and hadn't picked up on the slightest inkling of familiarity other than her time with him in Brazil.

His gaze went to her arm. "Your rune granted me access to your mind. Maybe it unlocked some sort of door to the past as an unexpected side effect." He relaxed into his chair with his wine glass in his hand. "Yet another marker that suggests Vera's innocence."

"She is innocent," Leela stressed. "I've told you that."

He nodded as he swirled the contents of his drink, his gaze holding hers. "You mentioned a half sister before. She and Vera share a mother?"

"Mel," Leela muttered. She couldn't remember if she'd mentioned the lineage out loud to him or not, but she'd probably at least thought about it. "She can manipulate memories, yes."

"Would she have any cause to fuck with our minds?" he asked conversationally.

"I guess that would depend on what happened in those memories," Leela said slowly, not appreciating the notion in the slightest.

Because if Mel had had cause to alter Leela's memories, it was because Leela and Balthazar had broken a rule of some kind. Or the High Council of Seraph had demanded it.

Except, no. They would have sent Vera for the job, not Mel. Vera was the second in line, her power extraordinary and far more fitting than Mel's mediocre grasp on the bloodline.

Leela continued thinking while she finished her wine.

Then the owner returned to ask if she required more. She politely declined, which led them to dessert conversations.

Balthazar ordered a tiramisu for them to share and two after-dinner espressos.

They indulged in the dessert in comfortable silence, both of them considering everything they'd discussed while Balthazar managed the fork. She rather enjoyed him feeding her. And the glint in his chocolate gaze said he liked it, too.

"What did we do after dinner?" Leela asked softly, her gaze holding his as he offered her the final bite on the fork. "After I swallowed you for dessert," she clarified before taking the piece from the fork between her teeth.

"Mmm," he hummed, reaching forward to drag his thumb along her bottom lip, catching a crumb she'd left behind. He brought it to his mouth to lick clean, then set the fork down. "We went for a walk."

"And?" she prompted, her pulse kicking up a notch.

"And I think we need to go on that walk to find out what happened next." Balthazar winked before catching the owner's eye once more. It wasn't hard to do. The male was watching both of them expectantly.

The three of them exchanged pleasantries, with Leela and Balthazar complimenting the chef and the whole ambience of dinner. They'd stayed rather late, but the owner didn't seem to mind.

Balthazar handled the bill, promising to return again, then took Leela by the arm and guided her down the mostly empty footpath between the colorful buildings.

"I love the lack of cars in this city," Leela admitted,

inhaling the air and blowing out a carefree breath. "The boats are much more romantic."

"Maybe you should buy a place here," Balthazar suggested.

"I might." She'd considered it before but had bought her flat in Melbourne instead. Maybe this would be her next investment. "Where do you own property?"

"Hydria." His lips quirked up at the sides, flashing his sexy dimples at her. "The Elders have homes all over, but none of them are primarily mine. I helped invest in all of them, but that's because we share our money in Hydria."

"There isn't a place you consider yours, similar to how Venice belongs to Jay?" Hadn't he mentioned Stockholm before?

He lifted a shoulder. "I've always favored group activities more than solo ones. So apart from my place in Hydria, I don't really own another. And yes, I do have a place I enjoy staying in Stockholm." The devious twinkle in his gaze said he'd heard that thought from her. "But I don't own it. Wakefield does."

"Does he mind you staying at his place?"

"Yes." Balthazar's amusement was palpable. "That's exactly why I do it."

She laughed and shook her head. "I wonder what he's doing at your place right now," she mused. "Since you both clearly have rivalry and all."

"Oh, he's absolutely fucking Stas right now," he replied without missing a beat. "Assuming Sethios hasn't castrated him yet."

Leela laughed even louder. "As though Sethios has any room to talk. He and Caro play with knives."

"Wakefield's more into subtle dominance play," Balthazar said thoughtfully. "A knife might be a limit for him."

"You've clearly thought about this."

"Many times." There wasn't an ounce of shame in that admission. "But I respect his preferences, and…" He trailed off, his gaze lifting to the night above. "And I like seeing him happy." Soft words and spoken with a hint of adoration.

"You love him."

"Like a brother," he murmured. "We have our differences, but we're family."

"That's Vera to me." Leela didn't really have anyone else. Seraphim weren't the family-oriented types. They considered love and familial ties to be weaknesses. Wastes of time. Unimportant frivolities meant for mortals, not higher beings. "I haven't spoken to either of my parents in over a thousand years. And I never talk to Mel."

"Many Hydraians are the same since our fathers have always tried to kill us. So we created our own families among each other."

"That's the best way." Leela leaned into his side as he slid his arm around her lower back. "I chose my family, too."

"Vera."

"Vera," she repeated, confirming it. "Gabriel, too. But he's more like a surly older brother. And Ezekiel is trouble personified. However, we're all family in a way. Bonded by a cause."

He hummed in agreement, his steps slowing as they reached a crossing section of walking paths. One way led back to the water and up to Jay's house. The other took them into another area of the city.

Balthazar went in the latter direction.

She didn't ask why, just let him lead. He was following a memory, one that tickled the edges of her thoughts now. *A smile. Warm touches. Laughter in the air.*

Her heart warmed just thinking about it.

"I really should invest in this city," she mused aloud. "It's beautiful." And peaceful despite being populated. She loved the overall ambience, the water, the beautifully colored buildings.

A sigh trickled from her mouth, her eyes almost shutting in exquisite bliss.

"Need me to carry you, sweetheart?" Balthazar whispered against her ear.

Her lips turned upward. "I can always just float along beside you."

"In your angelic form?"

"Mmm," she hummed, lost to the romantic moment of walking the street with an essential god of a man. It felt so right and perfect.

"So memorable," he echoed, steering them along another turn again. She moved with him, not paying attention at all until he shifted to push her up against the wall of a building. Her lashes fluttered all the way open, her gaze darting up to his.

That sense of déjà vu slammed into her senses, stealing her breath.

We've fucked here. Against this wall.

He didn't answer her verbally, instead choosing to kiss her.

Soft and sensual.

Slow and thorough.

Seductive and taunting.

All wrapped up into a single embrace underlined by his skilled tongue.

He explored her mouth as though it was their first time, memorizing and mapping every reaction. She moaned, loving his attention to detail.

His palms were on her hips, then her sides, his thumb

tracing the undersides of her braless breasts. *Ohhh.* It was a hot tease of a touch, stiffening her nipples to sharp beacons of *need*.

He played her body perfectly.

And she longed to repay the favor, her hands sliding up his chest to wrap around his neck. She angled him for a deeper kiss, showing him her own skill as he continued the subtle gliding caress along her ribs.

People could see them here.

Which was entirely the point.

They'd drawn an audience last time, too.

Why not do it aga—

A subtle prickle against her neck yanked her out of the moment, her heart skipping a beat. *Seraphim.*

She pulled her mouth away from Balthazar, her eyes flying toward the source of magic stroking her senses.

Patreel.

Fuck!

She didn't think; she reacted, wrapping her arms around Balthazar's neck and misting them out of Venice. The world shifted around the familiar buildings giving way to another city. This one with smaller buildings. White textures. Domed roofs. Mountains.

Her brow furrowed, this location not one she recognized. And yet, like with everything else, she knew it.

Another Elder home? she wondered, glancing at the trees nearby adding privacy to the buildings behind it.

A few splashes of color down the street caught her eye, but the architecture here definitely wasn't gothic Italian anymore.

And this wasn't somewhere she would typically choose to mist herself.

"Balthazar?" she asked, glancing up into his wide eyes. "Where are we?"

"Bulgaria," he whispered. "I grew up near here. Not in one of these current buildings, or anything at all like it. But… near this place." He took in the building in front of them before looking around with memories darkening his gaze. Not bad ones, just… old ones.

"Do you have another place near here?"

"No."

She frowned. "Then why did I…?" She trailed off as that prickle returned to her senses, her gaze flying around to search for the source as Patreel appeared again in Seraphim form, his golden wings fluttering soundlessly as his long white hair floated on a heavenly breeze.

"Impossible," she breathed. He shouldn't have been able to follow her so quickly. *Unless… unless he somehow imbibed more of my blood, enabling him to…*

Her eyes widened, unable to finish the thought. *You need to run,* she told Balthazar as she released him. *Run now!*

She didn't give him a chance to argue, misting toward Patreel with a sphere of ethereal energy forming on her palm.

Seraphim didn't fight with standard weapons.

They used energy.

And she'd learned quite a bit about defending herself over the years.

"Leela!" Balthazar shouted.

He's tracking me too easily, B! You have to ru—

A rope of energy flew through the air, the net barely missing her left wing as she shot upward into the sky. Patreel followed, allowing her to unleash the sphere she'd been creating.

He dodged, the energy dissipating into mist at having missed its target.

"Leela," he said, his tone lacking emotion. "Let's—"

She threw another creation at him, this one sharper and shaped like a blade.

He ducked, his golden-brown irises flashing with something that looked a lot like emotion. She blinked, certain she'd made it up. But his lips were curled down.

Seraphim do not feel.

So why is he frowning at me?

He shot upward to become level with her, his hands out in front of him. "I just want to talk."

"Is that why you threw a net at me?"

"Well, yes. I didn't want to fight, just subdue you long enough to say what I need to say." He spoke directly, just as all Seraphim did.

However, his voice held a note of exasperation to it.

One that was not very Seraphim-like at all.

"Vera sent me to talk to you," he continued. "Both of you."

Vera sent him? How? When? And what did he mean by... "Both of us?"

He nodded. "You and the abomination."

"Balthazar," she corrected him immediately. The term *abomination* had never appealed to her.

"Yes. Balthazar. Your bonded half."

"Bonded half?" she repeated, starting to feel like an echoing channel.

He blinked at her, the mannerism a bit more Seraphim-like in his obvious confusion. "Vera said you would want him involved in this conversation."

Leela straightened, allowing the ethereal energy crawling over her arms to subside. Was this a trap of some kind?

She didn't sense anyone else.

But that didn't mean they wouldn't appear in the next few seconds.

She narrowed her gaze. "Why should I believe you?"

"Because I'm the reason they haven't found you yet," he replied without missing a beat. "I recognized your blood on the cloth immediately, as I've been assigned to you since your first reformation. But Vera convinced me not to say anything. And now it's time for me to tell you why I agreed."

CHAPTER 21

LEELA

"RE-REFORMATION?" LEELA STUTTERED. *FIRST reformation? What... what does he mean... b-by "first"?* Her wings faltered around her, sending her down a few feet in the air before Patreel caught her by the elbow.

She jerked out of his hold, his touch burning her senses with all sorts of wrongness.

"Part of your reformation requires mandatory memory cleansing," he said, his voice featherlike soft. "You don't remember the process as a result."

She swallowed, her heart beating a mile a minute in her chest. "That's... that's impossible." She would remember undergoing reformation.

More than once.

That's what first *means, right?*

More. Than. Once.

The world began to swirl around her. She ignored it. She followed the strands of memory, desperately searching for the truth of his words.

But nothing came to mind.

I... I don't...

Black spots decorated Patreel's angelic features, his pale skin darkening.

This doesn't… It can't be true.

"I've been assigned to you since your first reformation."

Patreel's statement reverberated through her mind. *First reformation. First reformation. First reformation.*

No. No. NO.

This was a trick. A way to subdue her. To make her falter. To allow her to be captured. To be ensnared!

No. No. No!

She wouldn't believe it. Wouldn't let him capture her so easily. Because that would lead to her true *first reformation.*

Feathers flew around her.

They're coming. The warrior Seraphim are coming. I have to fight. To… to…

Everything went dark for too long of a blink, air whooshing in her ears, her wings struggling to find strength.

It's too late. They're here! I'm trapped!

Strong bands of muscle caught her. Wrapped around her. Strangled her. Destroying her life. Her purpose. *Drowning me in… in… nothingness.*

She fought, clawing at the air, her lungs burning as she tried to scream without access to oxygen. A dark night. A black swathe of intense energy. Forcing her deeper. Taking hold of her and stilling her breath.

There's no oxygen here.

No way to inhale.

I'm going to die here.

Alone.

In a glass cage.

A tear tracked down her cheek, but she couldn't feel it. There was nothing here but the rumble of a machine and those harsh steel bands.

Her name whispered into the abyss. A croak of sadness echoing in its wake.

This is death, she mused. *No, this is worse than death.*

She blinked into the starless night, her brow furrowing along the way.

Why am I giving in to this? She should fight. Scream. *Mist.*

But that required air.

Life.

Breathing.

So breathe, she told herself. *Breathe!*

Leela didn't give up. She didn't let others dictate her life. She was independent. In charge. *Alive.*

I refuse this fate.

No more.

No reformation.

No isolation.

No to this bullshit!

Leela's lips parted on a denial, but an influx of warm air shoved itself inside and down her throat to her aching lungs. She coughed and choked on the unexpected intrusion.

It burned!

She gasped, her chest screaming in agony as oxygen revitalized her senses. Every part of her shook as tingles swept up and down her arms and legs.

Feeling.

Oh, glorious feeling…

A hard slab of concrete prickled against her back, the surface almost making her weep. Because she could sense it. Understand it. *I'm alive. I'm free.*

But her vision was still dark.

Yet a warm caress against her cheek had her leaning into the much-needed touch. *More,* she begged. *Help me feel more.*

Heat swept along her jaw to her neck, the gentle brush of fingers relaxing her inside and helping her breathe. Each inhale lessened the ache inside her, allowing her to feel grounded and more aware.

Lips softly whispered across her own, the kiss going straight to her heart. "You're safe, Lee," a deep voice promised. "I've got you."

She shuddered, that voice a drug she'd hadn't realized she craved.

"Just breathe," he continued, his lips against her ear now. "That's it, Lee. Come back to me, sweet vixen."

If this was a part of reformation, some sort of dark trick, she'd scream.

"Not reformation, sweetheart," he promised. "We're still in Bulgaria."

Her brow furrowed. *We are?*

"You fell," he told her, his mouth moving from her ear to her lips again. Another kiss. So tender. So perfect. So *B.* "I caught you."

She tried to process how that was possible.

Seraphim didn't really fall.

Not unless they were knocked out by something.

Her eyes flashed open. *Patreel! They're here!*

"Shh," Balthazar hushed, pulling her from the concrete and into his arms. "You're safe, Lee. Just keep breathing with me, okay?"

Was he out of his mind? *They're here! We have to mist!*

But she couldn't seem to find her wings.

Her ethereal energy was… was… *gone.*

Her heart began to race, her body trembling all over again as she fought to find her—

Balthazar kissed her, his mouth sealing over hers as he cradled her face between his palms. She grabbed him, trying to push him away, to tell him this wasn't the time, but his grip was too strong.

"You're safe," he repeated once more. "I have you, Lee. It's okay."

None of this felt safe or real.

A reformation trick. It has to be.

"Touch me, Lee," he said. "Feel my hair. The stubble along my jaw. My shoulders. I'm very real. And we are very much here. In Bulgaria. Sitting on a random sidewalk less than a mile from where I was born."

She swallowed, her pulse still raging. *I don't understand. This… reformation…*

"You had a panic attack," he whispered, his hands still holding her face hostage. "You're still on the vestiges of one. Just look into my eyes and try to breathe with me, all right?"

Leela continued to shake, uncertain. This could all be a horrible trick. *But… but on the off chance it isn't…*

She lifted her gaze to his, allowing herself to dive into the chocolate swirls of his beautiful irises. He truly was a work of art.

So handsome. She lifted her hand to his cheek to trace the solid bone with her thumb, all the way along to the side and down to his chiseled jaw. *Perfection.*

"Inhale, Lee."

She obeyed the soft command from his alluring mouth, her thumb moving to trace the bottom lip.

"Good girl," he praised. "Now exhale."

The breath left her slowly, her heartbeat gradually returning to normal, soothing the rhythmic beating in her ears.

"Very good," he continued, coaxing more breaths from her. Each time she complied, he gave her a kiss. Either on her lips or her cheek, and also on her thumb and then her wrist.

She felt so young and vulnerable. So shattered and broken. But the way he looked at her with that appraising gleam in his pretty eyes made her feel alive and womanly.

"You're the most beautiful woman I've ever met," he told her.

That wasn't a line.

Because Balthazar never lied.

He only spoke the truth. It was part of what made him so charming. A person could always trust his words. He didn't hold back, he didn't hide, and he never seduced anyone with false platitudes.

Which meant he truly found her to be the most beautiful woman he'd ever met.

Normally, she'd just smile and say it was her Seraphim genetics.

But the moment felt too tender to spoil with an offhanded remark.

She craved his heat, his touch, his soothing nature. And therefore, she indulged it now, allowing him to fully calm the nerves firing within her.

His fingers brushed her hair away from her face, his opposite hand going to her neck.

"You fell from the sky after turning corporeal," he told her softly. "Because you were having a panic attack. I caught you with Patreel's help."

Her shoulders stiffened at the name. *They're*—

"Shh," Balthazar hushed again, his fingertip tracing her jaw once more. "We're safe, Lee. Patreel only wants to talk. And he's very much alone."

But he couldn't know that for sure because he couldn't see the Seraphim.

She tried to rip her gaze from his, to search the night

for any others, but his fingers caught her chin and forced her to remain focused on him. "We're safe, Lee," he repeated for the thousandth time.

"Stop telling me that. If Patreel is here, we're not safe."

"If I wanted to take you back to your reformation chamber, I would have done so already," a dark voice said, infiltrating her calm.

She immediately froze.

But Balthazar's touch warmed her in the next breath, his arms encircling her protectively as he pressed his lips to her ear again. "I'm here, Lee. I have you. Trust me."

This could be a trap.

"It's not," he replied. "Patreel wants to tell us the truth about these memories. He drew a rune on his arm to grant me temporary access to his mind. Just like I can read yours. He's telling the truth."

She startled, her eyes rounding. *You can read his mind?*

He nodded. "He's been assigned to you for over three thousand years. Since we first met. Here. In Bulgaria."

What? She blinked at him. *I… I don't…*

"Tell her," Balthazar said, his gaze not leaving hers. "Tell her what you've told me."

"You were only about five hundred years old when your mother sent you to live among humans to perfect your fertility powers. She sent you here. To Bulgaria. To the very brothel Balthazar had been born in. It's how you met."

She tried to glance at him, but Balthazar kept hold of her chin. She swallowed, her heart starting to beat a little faster again.

"He was in his early twenties. You… fornicated."

Balthazar snorted at the term but didn't otherwise interrupt.

"Your mother sent Melanythos to monitor the

situation, as she knew the impact mortals could have on your abilities," he continued. "She didn't want to risk anything jeopardizing your procreation appointment with Dian."

Ice drizzled through Leela's veins.

Dian.

Seraphim of Death and Destruction.

Procreation.

A violent shiver trekked down her spine, but she was too cold to truly feel it.

Reformation. Reformation. Reformation.

"Leela," Balthazar said, interrupting Patreel. He'd still been talking, but his words had resembled a buzz around her ears. She couldn't hear them. Didn't *want* to hear them. "I have you. I'm right here." Balthazar cupped her cheek again, his thumb tracing her cheekbone.

Feathers, she felt so *childlike.*

Alone.

Frozen.

Reformation.

Fragile...

His lips brushed hers, drawing her back to the moment, giving her mind a temporary reprieve from the chilling kiss of her past.

Or was it her present?

Dian haunted her past, present, and future.

The Fates had predicted a child. It was only a matter of *when.*

"It already happened," Balthazar whispered. "That's what Patreel is trying to tell you."

She blinked. "Wh-what?"

"You denied Dian," he told her. "You denied the council."

"For him," Patreel added before she could speak. "You

bit Balthazar to ignite the bond, thereby soiling your bloodline. Dian ordered your reformation. I was the one who tracked you down and took you in."

Her heart stopped beating. "No…"

"They altered your memories and removed Balthazar from your mind entirely." Patreel spoke as though she hadn't denied his statement. "It was Dian's suggestion. He told the council it was the only way to ensure your reformation succeeded. Except it didn't. You've returned to Balthazar multiple times since then, undergone two more rounds of reformation, had countless memories altered, and still, you find him."

Her vision blurred as the veracity of his statement vibrated through her soul.

Balthazar continued to hold her, his eyes holding a touch of understanding, as though his soul felt the same shift of knowledge, that reverberation of truth telling them this wasn't a lie, but very real.

All their moments.

The visceral sense of déjà vu.

"This was the first time you had his memory of you altered of your own volition, which showed promise. At least in the eyes of the council," Patreel went on. "But when I caught your blood on that cloth, I knew it went deeper than that. However, Vera stopped me before I could do something about it."

"How?" Balthazar asked, the question rolling through Leela's mind as well. "What did she do that made you stop?"

"She told me the truth about reformation," Patreel replied. "The origin story. How it came to be. And… and that truth has me questioning everything I know. Including this. Including everything I've done. I've tracked Leela so many times. And if I catch her now, she'll go through reformation again. But what will it change? She's proven to be utterly broken."

"She's not broken," Balthazar retorted, a hint of darkness in his tone. "If anything is shattered in her, it's a result of that torture you call *reformation*. There is nothing wrong with emotions. They make us superior, not inferior."

Patreel didn't reply.

He probably didn't see much point in arguing about emotions. He would consider it a frivolous discussion unworthy of his time.

"She always goes back to you," Patreel said as though thoughtful. "Yet your memories were altered, too."

By Mel, Leela thought, frowning. "And Vera didn't know?"

"Very few people know about this," Patreel replied. "That's the case with all reformation assignments. Key members of the High Council of Seraph are aware of the details, but the general population has no idea. It's how they re-assimilate members back into society. Otherwise, they would be outcasts."

"And they wipe the memories of those closest to them," Balthazar said.

"From what little I know, yes," Patreel admitted. "Leela is my primary case. But I'm not the only tracker."

No. There was an army of them. *Are they all assigned to cases like mine?* she wondered. *Is that why the Fates often suggest procreation within that line?*

"Did they alter Vera's memories?" Balthazar asked. "Of Leela, I mean."

"Her mother manipulated some, yes. Just enough to keep the truth of Leela's reformation from her."

"Yet she discovered it from you," Balthazar replied.

"She discovered the truth after trying to contort my recollection of what happened in the Bahamas," Patreel confirmed. "The cloth she used with your blood immediately conflicted with my sensory memory, and my mind rejected the manipulation."

"And she sent you to me," Leela whispered.

"Not quite. She took me to Osiris first, to learn the truth about reformation. To prove to me that everything I've ever been told about the purpose and source of it has been a lie."

Balthazar released her chin as she glanced up at Patreel. He stood beside them in corporeal form wearing jeans and a sweater. The picture of angelic innocence. Except for the ancient flare of knowledge in his eyes.

"What did he tell you?" she asked, her voice low.

"Osiris created reformation." Patreel's jaw hardened. "That's why the council exiled him. Not for making it, but to remove his ability to control it. Because they wanted the power for themselves. To control *us* by removing emotion and feeling from the world, thereby forcing us to fall in line."

"They've turned you into powerful puppets," Balthazar replied.

"Essentially, yes. With only a handful of Seraphim in true control." Patreel's golden-brown irises darkened. "And Dian is one of them."

CHAPTER 22

VERA

"LEELA FIRST MET BALTHAZAR IN CURRENT-DAY BULGARIA at the brothel he'd grown up in." Vera paced the length of Balthazar's living room while Stas, Issac, and Luc listened.

She'd intended to tell Gabriel this first, but Osiris had caught her upon entering and suggested she go to Stas and Issac. She'd been too exhausted to question his directions.

Then Issac had insisted on Luc joining them for this history discussion.

She'd expected the Hydraian King to want his fellow Elders present, but he'd merely sat down and waved for her to start talking.

So she had.

First telling them about Patreel and how he'd been assigned to Leela for her first reformation—a fact she'd learned when her memory manipulation had failed.

She'd continued into a discussion on how she'd subdued him and taken him to Osiris. Which led to Luc asking why.

"Let me tell you about Balthazar and Leela first. Then

I'll explain everything you want to know about Osiris," she'd said. "Well, everything I can, anyway."

Luc had agreed with a nod.

And so her tale began at the brothel.

She didn't know much about what had happened, at least not the full details, but she knew enough to explain the events at a high level.

"Leela had been assigned there to learn more about her fertility gifts," she explained. "It was meant to empower her and help coax her into her own cycle. The Fates had predicted a procreation match between Leela and Dian."

Vera swallowed, the name not one she wanted to mention in conversation. The lethal Seraphim's intimidating aura was well known among her kind.

"He's the Seraphim of Death and Destruction," she added. "His powers are essentially the opposite of Osiris. Where Osiris resurrects, Dian kills."

"Even Seraphim?" Stas asked.

"As far as I know, that theory has never been tested." That wasn't to say it hadn't been. And that thought scared her even more. "He's as old as Osiris. Sits on the High Council of Seraph. And he has no progeny or any other members within his line. Because Leela denied him."

No. It was worse than that.

"She also tainted her bloodline," Vera continued. "Which served as an even larger rejection, not just to Dian but to the entire council. She defied a direct edict and broke decorum."

Luc stared at her. "How exactly did she taint her bloodline?"

"Leela bit Balthazar." Vera gave them a moment to absorb the shock, as it'd certainly been a huge surprise to her.

"She bonded him," Luc translated. "When?"

"She partially bonded him," she corrected him. "He never bit her back." Had he bitten her, reformation would have been that much worse.

Or maybe he would have provided her with a mental anchor.

It was hard to say, and Vera didn't want to waste time pondering what-ifs when the damage was already done.

"As to when it happened, it took place at some point after he left the brothel and shortly before he met you for the first time."

"How do you know when we met?" He didn't sound suspicious so much as genuinely curious.

"Because your mind was altered to an extent as a result of all this," she told him. And now that she knew what to look for, she could confirm the truth of Patreel's claims.

Not that she'd really doubted it.

The story had rung too true to be fake.

"My half sister, Melanythos, has been in your head," she went on, her gaze on Luc. "She established an elaborate affair with Balthazar to sink her mental claws deep into his psyche to alter all his memories of Leela. Including their partial bond."

All while Leela underwent reformation.

"Melanythos?" Luc repeated, his gaze sharpening. "As in, *Nythos*?"

"It's the name she assumed while seducing Balthazar, yes," she replied. "She inherited her memory-altering abilities from my maternal side of the family. Meaning we share a mother. And she shares her desirability with Leela's paternal bloodline, as they both share a father."

Not the Seraphim line of fertility.

But a different one.

"Their father is Adonis. And there's a reason his

271

name has become popular in human myths. He's the Seraphim of Beauty and Desire." Leela often attributed her sensuality to her mother's side of the family. But Vera knew better. It was an intoxicating mix of both bloodlines that made her irresistible to everyone in her path.

Including Dian.

"Patreel said Dian required Leela to remember the council's decision regarding their intended procreation, but to weave it in a way that the date for said event had not yet been determined. He claimed it would be a good way to test her reformation. When she goes to him during a fertility cycle to see the edict through, she'll be considered cured."

Instead, she was terrified of him and what he represented.

"She's undergone three different reformations and has had countless memories altered over the last three thousand years. Balthazar, too." Just thinking about it made Vera want to kill everyone involved in this harsh fate.

Melanythos and Dian being at the top of that list.

Because the reformation and memory altering had been Dian's idea. And her half sister had willingly allowed it.

Not to mention the involvement of Vera's own mother. "The council had some of my memories altered as well. By my own mother. And I never noticed because I don't make it a habit to fuck around in my best friend's head."

She hadn't noticed the alterations in Balthazar's mind either because she'd been hyper-focused on Brazil and altering his memories in a way that he would subtly remember Leela.

Vera had thought she was helping out her best friend—Balthazar and Leela were clearly meant for each other.

The irony was, had Vera pried just a little more, she might have discovered how right she was about their fate.

And the only reason she'd noticed any of this in Patreel's mind was because of his link to Leela's blood. Had she not followed that strand, she wouldn't have learned any of this.

"The council mandated everything in an effort to reform Leela," she continued. "Which brings me to Osiris."

This was the part she'd been able to use to recruit Patreel to their side.

It was also the reason she'd aligned herself with Osiris lately.

Because now she knew the truth about his exile.

"My kind has been led to believe that Osiris was exiled for killing a Seraphim," she started, getting straight to the point. "And he did. To an extent. He created a form of rebirth that wiped the Seraphim's psyche entirely and helped the being to find appropriate purpose again. Meaning he reprogrammed the Seraphim's mind to a practical state, driving out any and all forms of emotion."

He'd explained some of this to her, saying the being hadn't been one of his choosing. But one from the council.

Adriel.

Which was why Vera had been heading toward Gabriel in Hydria, not Stas and Issac. But she'd go there next since Osiris had suggested she start here.

"Reformation," Luc translated, his emerald gaze gleaming with his power of omniscience. He pieced together puzzles faster than anyone she'd ever met. Which, she supposed, made it almost relieving to have him here because he removed all the guesswork from her explanation.

"Yes, Osiris created reformation," she confirmed.

"Under the direction of the High Council of Seraph—or those in power at the time." It was an important distinction that she would return to in a moment. "The council rewarded his efforts by exiling him."

Luc considered her for a moment. "There can only be two reasons for that. Either he used the technique on someone without their approval, or they decided reformation was too powerful a tool to be left in his hands."

"They provided him with the subject for his first and only reformation, so that should tell you the answer," she replied.

"They exiled him for power. And now they use his tool to keep all the Seraphim in line."

He fell into a contemplative silence.

She glanced at Stas and Issac to see if they had any questions, but they were both watching Luc.

Vera returned her focus to him as he began to nod as though he approved.

"It's a brilliant tactic, actually. Seraphim are not supposed to feel—at least, that's the standard as prescribed by your council," he mused. "However, those who do experience emotion would also be prone to fear reformation. Thus, the procedure serves as an enforcement mechanism to ensure everyone behaves as the council declares."

"They're using reformation to control the Seraphim," Issac added.

"Precisely," Luc murmured. "Similar to how Osiris created the Conclave to manage his Ichorians. He's always used fear as a motivator."

"The Conclave is actually a replica of the council," Vera informed them. "Well, the concept of it, anyway. He created his own version, but it's strongly inspired by the

High Council of Seraph. Except he invites all Ichorians to attend, not just the highest ranked in each bloodline."

Most of the time, the highest-ranked Seraphim was the original or first of the line.

But not always.

Gabriel was a great example of someone with the potential to overthrow Adriel as the head of the line as a result of power, not age.

Luc nodded again, suggesting he already knew the information about the Conclave, or had at least suspected it. "So how many of your council members know the truth about reformation?" he asked.

"According to Osiris, only five Seraphim know the truth. And of them, only one is currently on the council. Dian. Which is why he was able to orchestrate the parameters of Leela's reformation." A statement that made her blood boil all over again.

He deserved a fate worse than death for what he'd done to Leela.

"Subjecting Leela to reformation and a memory wipe, in addition to having Balthazar's memories erased by her own half sister, certainly feels a bit *vengeful* to me," Issac commented conversationally. "And last I checked, a desire for revenge is often characterized as an emotional state."

"Suggesting the five who now control reformation are not fully embracing the Seraphim way of being unfeeling and stoic," Luc replied. "Instead, they force those requirements on the masses because it makes them easier to control. I can't imagine the Seraphim populace and current council would be too enthused by this information."

"Patreel certainly wasn't," Vera admitted. "He's actually on his way to meet with Leela and Balthazar now to tell them the whole truth. Or he may already be with them. I'm not sure."

She was exhausted from the past however many days or weeks. Seraphim might not require sleep, but that didn't keep her kind from experiencing fatigue.

Both of the mental and physical variety.

"You said only one of them is currently on the council. Where are the other four?" Luc asked.

"They're resting, as most ancients do. Dian is the only one who is currently awake and knows the truth. However, Osiris speculated that the others may actually be awake and just assumed to be asleep." As much as Vera didn't really care for Osiris, she believed him.

Maybe because he'd allowed her to witness the memory of his exile without interference.

Or, more likely, because she'd spent the last thousand or so years questioning the council's verdicts and the destinies prescribed by the Fates. They felt a bit too convenient.

"Regardless, it's clear there is some sort of corruption inside the Seraphim Council. And the truth of reformation may expand beyond the original five now. But most definitely believe Osiris is evil, which wouldn't be the case if they knew the history."

"Others had to have seen the events of his exile or, at a minimum, have been aware of it." Issac uttered the words slowly, his brow furrowing. "Did they alter everyone's memories?"

Vera shook her head. "From what I saw in Osiris's mind, the original High Council of Seraph was much smaller. And it predated most of our existence. The expansion happened as new lines formed." Which was a mystery in terms of *how* they came to be. They just appeared, the ethereal energies combining to create corporeal entities that grew into Seraphim.

She explained some of that out loud since Luc immediately asked what she meant by "formed." He absorbed the information with a nod, then shifted back to the political part of the discussion. "How do the Seraphim think reformation came to be?"

"We've all been led to believe that it's a tool created through superior intellect," Vera explained. "The actual presentation of it is quite scientific in nature. But only those who have gone through it know the full scope of what it feels like. However, they don't fully understand the mechanisms."

"Or their memories are altered to forget it," Stas muttered. "As is Leela's case, apparently. But my mom remembers parts of her experience."

"Has she described it at all?" Luc inquired.

Stas shook her head. "Not really. But she's interested in talking with Blake. Clara mentioned his presence in the dungeon, and my mom asked what he'd done. Issac explained that he can't be trusted yet because of what John did to him. She said the rehabilitation process sounded similar to reformation."

Luc rubbed his jaw, his eyes gleaming. "Considering Osiris's alliance with John and the experiments at the CRF in general, it wouldn't be a stretch to assume they created some sort of reformation to keep the Sentinels in line. Or to brainwash them entirely."

"I'd suggest Mateo look into it, but…" Issac trailed off.

"I'll talk to him," Luc replied. "See what he knows."

"Or ask Osiris," Vera suggested. "His methods may not be all that agreeable, but his intentions are mostly in line with our own here."

Stas snorted. "Tell that to my parents."

"I intend to. And Gabriel as well." Assuming she had any energy left after this conversation.

Luc's expression told her she might not, as he clearly had more questions for her. At least he would retain all the answers. Maybe she could ask him to tell the others.

"Who are the other four Seraphim that know the truth about reformation?" he asked.

These details truly wouldn't appeal to anyone else, as the names she was about to give wouldn't reveal anything.

But Luc would remember them.

And perhaps run them through his catalog of intellect to find any potential links.

Which was why she answered him in full, giving him the names of each member from the old council and their lineage designations.

Dian, the original and only Seraphim of Death and Destruction—the one he already knew.

Cassia, the original Seraphim of Destiny. She was the first Fate.

Pakhet, the original Seraphim of the Hunt. The tracker abilities stemmed from his line.

Veles, the original Seraphim of Elements. Several lines had formed after hers, representing each element individually. However, she retained the ability to collectively control all the elements.

Marduk, the original Seraphim of Judgment, which differed from the Seraphim of Justice. Silvia, a current member of the council, was the latter. Her powers were all about balance. Whereas Marduk's were all about punishment and castigation.

"They're some of the oldest of our kind," Vera concluded. "Just like Osiris."

"Were other Seraphim in existence at that point in history?" Luc asked.

"A few. It was the dawn of our creation. Or that's when Osiris began working on reformation, anyway. Cassia had predicted there would come a time when it would be needed. He spent millennia perfecting the process." From what Vera knew, Osiris was well over ten thousand years old. Just like the others of his era.

But Seraphim lines had continued to develop well into his exile. It was like they'd grown off from the original roots of life, creating massive trees with various branches. Some of which had intertwined, while others had grown in opposite directions.

The result was a forest of power with some trees being much larger and more robust than the rest.

"And once he perfected the process, they exiled him," Luc said.

"Yes. And they use him as an example of what not to do for all Seraphim kind."

"Clever." Luc sounded impressed, probably because he could understand that strategy on an intelligent level. "Makes him a villain while also being used as yet another control mechanism for the general populace."

She nodded in agreement. "The story we've been told is that reformation didn't work on him, which is one of the many reasons he's known as the Poisoned One among my kind. It's also because he's seen as poisoning the blood of humans by creating Ichorians and Hydraians."

"And to vilify us, they call us abominations."

Her chin dipped again. "Yes, because part of Osiris's punishment was a provision that forbade him from continuing his bloodline. The Seraphim see Hydraians and Ichorians as a blatant disrespect of a council edict."

"My father and I are direct descendants of the line," Stas pointed out. "Yet the council wants to meet with me."

"Because the Fates have prophesied that you'll destroy

Osiris and his creations. Or that's the council's interpretation of the prophecy, anyway," Vera replied. "Whether it's true or not remains to be seen."

"I won't be destroying anyone," Stas vowed.

Don't make promises you can't keep, young one, Vera thought. But that was a discussion for another day. She didn't have the energy to debate fate tonight.

"They forbade Osiris from procreating to ensure no one else could take control of reformation," Luc said thoughtfully. "Or I imagine that was the reason, anyway. Yet Stas is prophesied to destroy his creations. Do you think the Fates mean *reformation*? That Stas is destined to destroy it?"

That wasn't something Vera had considered yet.

And from the silence of the others, neither had they.

"My parents mentioned that they think the Fates are actually trying to work against the council, as it's clear they've been enslaved by them." Stas spoke slowly, as though half her mind was still reeling from Luc's suggestion.

Vera noted that Stas didn't immediately deny that possibility. Very unlike how she'd reacted to Vera commenting on her destroying Osiris's creations.

Which meant that perhaps this path seemed more agreeable to her.

Could that be what the prophecy truly means, then? Or is it just the surprise of the suggestion giving her pause?

Issac stretched his arm along the back of the couch behind Stas, offering comfort in the way a bonded mate should. "It's quite possible that the Fates see Aya as some sort of salvation that will destroy the mechanism currently holding Seraphim kind hostage."

"An unknown power is surfacing. She will possess the strength and will to destroy us all unless certain measures are put in place to

curb her inclinations." Luc recited Skye's original prophecy without so much as blinking, each word verbatim. "Do we know if that's the same prophecy the Fates delivered to the council?"

Vera shook her head. "Only the council hears the prophecies."

Luc leaned forward to balance his forearms on his splayed thighs. "Recordings of them? Or in person?"

"Echoes," Vera confirmed. "Similar to recordings, but not." They were captured by scribe Seraphim that played them back for the council in visual form.

"Which means they could be manipulated," Luc pointed out.

"Yes," Vera agreed. "But Seraphim would never think of that. They're too practical."

"As a result of their council making them value practicality over emotion." Luc relaxed back into his chair. "Your council has perfected the art of a beautiful dictatorship filled with obedient sheep."

"Not all of us are obedient." It might not have come naturally to her or Leela or Gabriel or Caro, but they were all here now. And they could recruit more to their side with the right strategy.

Which led her to her next point.

"I've seen Osiris's memories. I don't know all of his intentions outside of what he's told me, but it involves showing the Seraphim the truth. Which was a good enough reason for me to willingly talk to him. Everything he's done for Lizzie and Jayson was his way of proving himself to us as a worthy source."

Stas snorted again. "Right. Except he kidnapped my best friend because he intended to use her as an incubator for his own child. Or did he fail to mention that?"

"To him, it was a practical recourse, as he saw her as a

vessel to deliver a powerful being that he could use in his struggle against the Seraphim." Vera held up a hand, silencing Stas before she could bite back at that statement. "I didn't say I agree with him. In fact, I don't. But that'll be his explanation. He's true to Seraphim form in that he lacks emotion. Whether his actions are right or wrong is irrelevant to him. He only sees success as a positive motivator."

"So you started working for him after you saw his memories for the first time," Luc said, cutting off whatever Stas had been about to say in response.

"I went back to him after we freed Sethios and asked if I could see the full memory of what happened. I never agreed to work *for* him, only *with* him, when it came to keeping everyone safe. That's when I found out about Mateo also assisting him, at least partially." She met Luc's gaze. "I assume you've put him in the dungeon?"

The question served two purposes.

First, to tell her what he'd done with Mateo.

Second, to find out what he intended to do to her. Because if he thought to imprison her, he'd soon realize the impossibility of ensnaring her.

"He's at my house in the guest room," he replied, surprising her.

"Yet you imprisoned Clara without remorse?" The comment slipped from her mouth before she could think to retract it. Mostly because he'd shocked her with his admission.

"Clara's explanation for her actions was superficial and shallow at best. Which I now realize should have been a red flag, but at the time, I wasn't in the frame of mind to properly evaluate her." Luc's voice wasn't defensive, just flat and matter of fact. Similar to a Seraphim's. "Mateo's situation is unique and still unfolding."

"You'll confer with me before you decide what to do with him," Issac interjected, his tone clearly indicating this wasn't a request but a mandate.

Luc glanced at him and nodded before refocusing on Vera. "I want to know more about your sister and the mindfuck she's done on B. He's not going to be pleased."

"No, I imagine he won't be," Vera agreed, sighing.

She'd been pacing this entire time while the others sat.

Rather than continuing to wear down Balthazar's floors, she chose the only other chair in the room.

"It might be easier if I untwist the memories in your mind to show you what really happened," Vera said, accepting the fact that sleep was not in her near future.

Besides, it would help her regain some trust with Luc and the others.

Which was very much needed after everything with Osiris.

She'd meant well. And she wouldn't apologize.

But she would show loyalty where it was due.

"Close your eyes," she instructed. "It'll hurt less."

At least for him.

For her, it would hurt a hell of a lot.

Because it further drove home the knife of betrayal.

Melanythos had destroyed Leela's life. Shattered her heart. And fucked with a bond that should never have been touched.

And this memory in Luc's head was only the tip of the proverbial iceberg.

CHAPTER 23

BALTHAZAR

BALTHAZAR LISTENED AS PATREEL EXPLAINED WHAT HE'D learned about the council's corruption.

Osiris created reformation. That statement continued to reverberate in Balthazar's thoughts, mostly because Leela kept repeating it.

Patreel told them the names of the original council members, how they'd tasked Osiris with developing a protocol that could revert a Seraphim soul to its intended stoic state, and how they'd vilified him afterward.

All to obtain control.

Everything the Seraphim had been told was essentially founded on a lie. At least where Osiris was concerned. Which left Patreel wondering what else they'd lied about.

Balthazar still had access to his thoughts, allowing him to hear the chaos unfolding in the other man's mind.

We're not supposed to feel, yet I... I feel... overly warm.

Buzzing with energy.

Violent.

Like I want to... to punch Dian.

Why? What is this? Anger?

Will I be subjected to reformation now? Is that the point of all this? To fear the mechanism? To turn on each other at the first sign of emotion?

Who am I?

What will happen to me now?

The things I've done…

This is… this is overwhelming.

Shut it off.

How do I make it stop?

Balthazar had sent a soothing shimmer through Patreel's psyche, comforting him enough to ensure he maintained a peaceful facade while speaking.

The emotional assistance wasn't provided as a favor to the other man; it was done to ensure he remained calm because Leela required serenity right now.

Her mind reeled from the influx of information, that dark sense of panic still lingering on the cusp of her thoughts. But she'd relaxed enough to process the information without falling back into a spiraling state.

He kept his arms around her, his palm gently cradling the back of her neck to demonstrate physical support as she rested her head against his shoulder.

She seemed oblivious to the fact that she sat in his lap on the sidewalk, her entire focus on Patreel and his words.

Fortunately, the late hour meant fewer people were outside.

Not that Balthazar minded being seen with a gorgeous woman in his arms.

But he suspected Leela would mind.

Her panic attack had been a sign of weakness, one she hadn't even known she possessed until tonight.

Because her past had been riddled with false memories.

As has mine, he thought.

She'd bitten him. Had established a partial bond.

And he possessed no inkling of the memory.

Yet it'd happened here. In Bulgaria. Just a few blocks away.

Patreel's mind had provided some of the details, but Balthazar wanted to know more.

He needed his memories back.

He wanted to know what had happened between him and Leela. Why she'd bitten him. Because he refused to believe Patreel's mental review of events.

She bit him to soil her bloodline, Patreel thought.

If that were true, then why did she keep finding Balthazar? Because of the link? Or was it something more?

Balthazar had witnessed the intensity between Issac and Stas. That hadn't just been because of Issac biting her first. They were meant for each other. Everyone who had seen them together knew that.

So what did that mean for Leela and Balthazar?

He understood the blood bond. Once fully established —whereby both parties bit each other—they would remain together for eternity.

Utterly faithful.

That'd been the reason for Stark's annoyance with Issac. He'd warned him not to complete the bond with Stas because of the resulting fidelity clause.

It was automatic and very real.

However, Issac hadn't cared in the slightest.

Stas was it for him.

Balthazar had heard the vows in his thoughts soon after meeting Stas.

Had Leela bitten Balthazar, knowing full well he'd never bite her back? Was that the point? Had they made an agreement where it would always be a partial bond?

Or had he once considered engaging in monogamy?

If there was any woman in the world that would give him cause to desire such a state... it just might be her.

She fit him.

She understood him.

The passion between them was undeniable, probably one of the most potent of his existence.

A connection thrived between them as well. Because of the bond? Or something more?

He needed to understand. To see more. To *remember*.

Patreel had fallen silent, his explanation of Osiris's involvement with reformation complete. Now he observed Leela with a semblance of sadness, one his mind was struggling to comprehend.

This male of however many thousand years had never allowed himself to feel.

But every rule inside him had fractured upon learning the truth about Osiris.

He no longer knew whom to trust, what to think, how to *feel*.

Leela felt similarly, the name *Dian* revolving in her thoughts. A childlike part of her was terrified—likely the part that remembered some semblance of reformation.

But as the seconds grew, a strong part of her surfaced.

A fighting spirit that called to Balthazar on every level.

And that spirit was fury incarnate.

She wanted to paint the council chambers red in the blood of those who had wronged her. She wanted to scream for everyone to hear the truth. And she wanted her memories back.

Melanythos did this. She stole my memories. She was inside Balthazar's mind, too.

Her desire for murder drowned beneath the stark need

to know the truth. Her blue-green irises met his, the fire blossoming in the depths of her pupils.

This was partly an escape from the agony spearing her inside. Yet it also held an antidote of a sort, the knowledge the balm they both needed to soothe the pain.

"We need to go to the brothel," he told her. It didn't exist anymore. But maybe being on the same ground would spark something between them, just like in Venice.

"I know." She wrapped her arms around his neck and misted them without another word.

Patreel could track her, which he did, following along the way.

Balthazar's feet met pavement as Leela guided them to a vacant street. She stood as well with her arms still around him. He couldn't see her in this form, but he felt her presence in his mind.

Too bad the partial bond didn't grant him access to ethereal sight.

Stas had told him about Leela's purple wings. *What shade are they?* he wondered. *Violet? Lavender? Are there any other hues to match the marble effect of her blue-green eyes?*

She slowly turned corporeal, those stunning irises of hers locked on him. But the memory of their past remained a mystery to both their minds. Perhaps it had been too long ago or too much had changed.

"I tracked you here over three thousand years ago," Patreel said softly, his brow furrowing as he recalled the day. "I hadn't been given your blood yet. And we didn't know each other at all. But you were my mission. One I accomplished."

"Clearly," she replied flatly.

"If you imbibed her blood, then are you partially bonded as well?" Balthazar asked, feeling an odd sense of annoyance at the thought. Sharing had never bothered him, but the idea of Patreel being linked to Leela so intimately…

No. That does not appeal to me.

In fact, he didn't like the idea of Patreel and Leela together at all.

Which was also strange because the concept of watching another couple fuck always turned him on.

Just like he enjoyed joining parties of two or more.

However, Patreel… he didn't deserve Leela.

Very few ever would.

"The bond requires biting. So no. We are not bonded." Patreel sounded disgusted by the prospect. Whether by the idea of bonding Leela or the notion of biting her, Balthazar wasn't sure. But it irritated him just enough to pull away some of his soothing energy.

Emotional assistance had to be earned.

And Patreel most certainly had not earned a damn thing from Balthazar. If anything, he should be worsening the Seraphim's emotional turbulence, not calming it.

However, he kept a loose thread between them, just to ensure he didn't go entirely off the rails.

There were still questions that required answers.

"Tell us about that day," Balthazar said without averting his gaze from Leela.

Patreel appeared in his peripheral vision, taking on a corporeal state once more.

"There's not much to tell. I tracked Leela here and took her directly to Dian." He cleared his throat. "Dian took the matter to the council. I don't know who was involved, as I wasn't privy to the discussion. But Dian confirmed her reformation assignment and told me you would be dealt with. I didn't ask any questions."

Balthazar tracked the statements in the Seraphim's mind, searching for any hint of a lie.

"Go on," he said when he found the lingering strand of information at the forefront of Patreel's thoughts. He hadn't known what had happened at the time. But he'd learned some key details later.

"Leela spent a century in reformation." His statement matched the one in his mind.

Balthazar swept his thumb along the column of Leela's throat, his palm still around her nape just like it'd been when they were sitting.

But she didn't react to the news with panic this time.

No, her fighting spirit had taken over entirely now.

She wanted blood.

"I was given a vial of her blood about a week into her sentence. The purpose was to link me to her in case she somehow escaped the process. Then it turned into a monitoring assignment once she completed reformation."

"Meaning you stalked me," Leela muttered.

"I was assigned to *track* you, yes. Which is why I knew about the memory manipulation. Dian told me Melanythos had taken care of both of your memories. I asked why Balthazar wasn't just killed. Dian stated it was to protect you, as it could harm your soul to fracture a partial blood bond."

Leela snorted. "His ego was wounded, and he wanted Balthazar and me to suffer." Her gaze left Balthazar to narrow at Patreel. "I've feared him for eternity. Because he wanted me to fear him. To fear our procreation prophecy. That wasn't done to aid reformation. That was done to torture me."

Balthazar agreed. That was absolutely the response of a male who didn't appreciate being denied. He'd made Leela's life hell for thousands of years.

"He was the one who ordered that part, right?" Leela stressed. "The part where I didn't remember denying him and kept waiting for the dreaded day when the Fates called me up to breed with him?"

"He said it was part of your reformation, that you would be considered cured when you finally went to him willingly." Patreel's tone lacked emotion, but his mind processed those words through a new filter. One he'd just recently allowed himself to access.

Emotion.

"It was never about curing me," Leela spat. "It was about torturing me. That's why he allowed Balthazar to live. He knew the memories would haunt me and probably intends to take them all away again now. You're just here as a ruse to waste time until he shows himself. With Melanythos, no doubt."

Patreel frowned, his practical senses reviewing her comments and finding them darkly true.

Because it would be just like the council to make him a puppet. They'd essentially turned all of Seraphim society into a theater production with each being playing whatever role the council had given them.

An easy task to accomplish when the entire populace was brainwashed to believe emotions were a weakness that should be destroyed.

No chance for mutiny when the citizens couldn't feel anger or passion.

Just a practical world driven by logic.

How boring and dull.

That wasn't a life. It was a glorified prison sentence for an eternity of solitude and meaningless existence.

The Seraphim didn't even have proper families.

"Not a ruse," Patreel said slowly. "Vera checked my

memories for tampering and found none. I've never learned the truth before. Not until now."

Leela evaluated him, her lips pursing. She moved to Balthazar's side, her arm sliding around his waist to keep him close. While she inferred Patreel spoke the truth, she didn't trust the situation.

Balthazar felt similarly. Dian or Melanythos could appear at any moment.

Assuming they were keeping the tracker under surveillance.

They might not realize yet what Patreel had learned. And if that was the case, they likely wouldn't even consider following him. Suspicion was an emotion, after all. They'd need concrete evidence to find any sort of logic in trailing the tracker Seraphim. Until then, they had no reason to believe he wouldn't do his job. Especially since he'd been doing it for millennia.

Leela's thoughts rivaled Balthazar's assessment, but that didn't relax her at all.

She wanted to know more about their history, how this had happened, and when Melanythos had infiltrated Balthazar's head.

He desired the same information.

"My memories of growing up here are tied to lighthearted moments of experimentation once I came of age. I also don't remember much about my immortality, just that it involved a jealous lover. He killed me after a night in bed with him and his wife. And I woke up immortal."

It wasn't a grand story.

Balthazar hadn't been all that pleased with the man, but he'd been more intrigued by his own immortality and had chosen to embrace the second chance at life rather than seek revenge.

Of course, it hadn't been the last time a pride-wounded male had killed him for a bedroom performance. Fortunately, Balthazar's ability to control emotions helped him perfect the art of reading his lovers better and knowing what to expect from them.

He no longer bedded aggressive types.

Unless the need truly called for it.

"I don't have a single memory here of Leela," he continued, frowning. "Which is strange. Because I sensed moments in Venice. And even in Japan."

"Those are more recent," Patreel replied. "The memories here are much older. And from what I understand, Melanythos spent several years with you afterward to fully manipulate your memories and plant a strand for her to tug on in the future as needed. It was intricately done."

"Several years?" Balthazar repeated.

"Yes. While Leela was in reformation." Patreel glanced at her. "Your mind was altered after his, but just as thoroughly impacted."

"Clearly," she deadpanned.

But Balthazar was still mulling over the *several years* comment. "Are you saying I *know* Melanythos?"

Patreel considered him for a moment. "Yes, I believe so. Unless she altered the memories of herself as well, but I doubt it. Ingraining herself in your history would give her immediate access to your mind for any needed manipulations in the future—which, as I've said, has been required several times since the first instance."

Balthazar's brow furrowed.

He didn't like *anyone* in his mind.

And to have known her, too?

That just added insult to injury.

But who was she? he wondered, repeating her name and thinking back on that period of—

His eyebrows flew upward. "Melanythos." The name rolled off his tongue… the name… so similar to another… "*Nythos.*"

No. Impossible. That couldn't be…

But the timeline…

He swallowed, his gaze finding Leela. "Describe your half sister to me." But he already knew it was her. It had to be. Because it made too much damn sense.

"Um. Auburn hair. Black eyes. Pale. A bit shorter than me. Curvier, too. And she has more of our father's sensual touch than I do…" She trailed off, her expression hardening as she caught the glimmer of understanding in Balthazar's eyes. "What is it? What did she do?"

Balthazar's jaw clenched, a curse threatening his tongue.

He'd watched her die. He'd mourned her death. He'd *killed* for her.

And all of it… had been a ruse? A way to manipulate his mind into forgetting Leela?

How much of it was true? Had he fucked her like he had in his memories? Did Aidan and Luc truly bed her, too?

His fists clenched.

He'd been tricked before, but never like this. Never by someone he'd *loved.*

Unless those emotions had never existed either.

Or had they been for Leela?

"She manipulated me," he bit out, trying to respond to Leela's question. "She faked her own death, too. Taught us the difference between Ichorians and Hydraians." Which he now realized had been done with a purpose.

One that made him release a humorless laugh.

Because it truly was a brilliant play.

"She taught us how to kill Ichorians." Probably with the hope that he and Luc would use the information to take down some of Osiris's *abominations*. "She timed it perfectly, too. She *demonstrated* the difference by biting me during sex as a newly turned Ichorian and dying in my fucking arms. Of course, it may just be an implanted memory since she couldn't have actually died from that. And biting me would create a bond…" He trailed off, glancing at Leela. "Unless that memory was you, just replaced by her image…"

Fuck, this made his head hurt just to think about.

But it made too much fucking sense.

"We met the other Hydraians soon after that because Osiris had begun collecting them from all his Ichorian creations." And Nythos—*Melanythos*—had armed him, Luc, and Aidan with the information on how to kill an Ichorian right before that happened.

Maybe because the Fates had warned her or Dian about the impending event.

Regardless, it was beautifully executed.

And could have led to mass slaughter.

Except Aidan and Luc had been too strategic for such a simplistic plan. *Did the Fates project that, too? Have they been playing the long game this whole time?*

He shook his head. "I need to call Luc and tell him about this."

"Vera is already in Hydria," Patreel said. "She went there when I came here."

That wasn't good enough. Vera might not know to tell him these details. And she might not even be talking to him. "I know a place nearby. An inn." They would have a phone for him to use. And he had a standing arrangement with the owner.

LEXI C. FOSS

She wasn't a direct descendant of his line, just a woman with ancestors he once knew. Not from his early years, either. He'd met the family a few centuries ago and kept coming back to pay his respects as he was able.

"We might not be safe here," Leela pointed out.

"Then it's a good thing you have wings," he replied, drawing his finger down her spine as he released her shoulders. "This won't take long."

Her blue-green irises swirled with uncertainty, but the urgency she read from his expression had her nodding. *Okay*, she thought, the message clearly for him.

He bent to brush his lips across hers. "We're not done discussing the past, vixen."

"I know."

"We're going to figure this out." Because he was determined to retrieve his memories. Every last one of them.

She swallowed and dipped her chin once in agreement. But whispers of uncertainty taunted her psyche, her concern about reformation beginning to press down on her thoughts once more.

"I'm not going to let them catch you this time," Balthazar vowed. It was a dangerous promise to make, considering what they were up against, but he was determined to end this game.

The Seraphim had fucked with his mind.

Nythos had destroyed his trust.

And Leela's history with reformation broke his damn heart.

Never again, he pledged. *I'm never going to let them touch you again.*

He sealed the unspoken vow with another kiss, this time adding a passionate stroke of his tongue against hers.

He didn't care that Patreel was watching.

Maybe he'd learn something.

Maybe he'd fuck off.

All that mattered was Leela and the buzzing connection between her and Balthazar.

And the past he longed to remember.

CHAPTER 24

BALTHAZAR

LUC KNEW EXACTLY WHAT B WANTED TO DISCUSS. Something he proved by answering the phone with, "Did Patreel tell you about Nythos?"

Their discussion spiraled from there, taking a long visit down memory lane.

Only, Vera had apparently fixed Luc's remembrance, allowing him to tell B his version of realistic events.

The sensual relationship between Nythos and Balthazar had been real.

But the blood sharing hadn't been.

That'd been Nythos's escape plan—a diversion to give her an opportunity to return to the Seraphim.

She'd never drunk from Aidan.

She'd never died and come back.

And Balthazar had never killed her.

His jaw clenched several times throughout their conversation, making his teeth ache. Luc explained that Leela and Nythos shared Adonis for a father. Both females had inherited his gift of sensuality, allowing Nythos to rival Leela's grace in bed.

From what Luc guessed, Nythos had likely pulled memories that Balthazar possessed of Leela and either re-created them or bent his memories to see Nythos instead of Leela for several of the interactions.

So while he'd slept with Nythos, it might not have been as many times as he remembered.

Or it was exactly that many times, but the actions were all based on his prior relationship with Leela.

Both possibilities had him wanting to kill Nythos.

And everyone else involved in this mental mindfuck.

"How's Leela?" Luc asked after a beat of silence from Balthazar.

He glanced at the female in question. She sat in the middle of the family area of the inn with a pair of dogs on either side of her. They'd all but mauled her upon arrival, their excitement palpable. Leela had fallen to the floor to greet them, her concerns vanishing beneath the fluffy weight of paws and sloppy tongues.

Apparently, they'd given her the emotional therapy she'd needed to pull the rest of her psyche from the grips of her earlier panic.

"She's all right," Balthazar said, standing closer to the back exit of the home. Patreel had chosen to remain outside. Or maybe he'd misted somewhere else. It was partly why Balthazar had kept Leela in his sights, just in case they needed to escape quickly.

Her lips curled as the dog with the shorter snout attempted to sit in her lap. The full-grown boxer mix—or maybe it was a Staffordshire terrier mix with that black-and-white fur—had to weigh sixty or so pounds. It most certainly was not a lapdog, but it seemed hell-bent on trying to claim Leela.

Balthazar understood the desire.

She had beautiful legs.

And she smelled divine, too.

"She's currently being love-attacked by two dogs," Balthazar added.

"On the street?" Luc sounded confused.

"At an inn. The Spriggs family adopted some cute mutts."

"Ah," Luc replied, immediately deciphering Balthazar and Leela's current location. Because *Spriggs* was a name all the Elders knew. It wasn't the real surname for the family that owned this inn, but a nickname for one of the ancestors.

The black-and-tan mix on her opposite side lay down and put a paw on her thigh while staring up at Leela with pretty caramel-brown irises.

Puppy eyes, he mused, his lips twitching despite the anger still thundering through his veins.

Maybe a little fluffy love would help calm him down, too.

"I should go," he said to Luc. "We won't be here long."

"That's wise. Touch base in six. I'll give you an update on everything here." Luc ended the call before Balthazar could agree to the timetable.

Twelve-hour check-ins were easier to manage.

If Luc wanted to chat in six hours, then it meant they were close to finalizing the wards.

A weight slipped from Balthazar's shoulders. He missed Hydria. His home. His *bed*.

Mmm, he wanted Leela in that bed. Tied up. Wet. Begging him to fuck her.

Would it bring back more memories, or merely make new ones?

A laugh left her luscious mouth, drawing him for his erotic musings. The boxer mix was still trying to climb into her lap. Much to the chagrin of the floppy-eared one using her thigh as a pillow for its long snout.

Balthazar sauntered toward them, the phone still in his hand. Leela's eyes danced with a delight that matched her thoughts, causing his lips to curl.

Happiness made her shine even more. This was a female who deserved to smile. To laugh. To enjoy life. Her existence had been darkened by a lifetime of cruel tampering.

And that darkness had bled into him as well, taunting his memories and mind and removing this delightful creature from his thoughts.

Who would they be today had the council not separated them?

Bonded mates?

Still partially bonded?

Not bonded at all?

Had Leela only bitten him to taint her bloodline? Or had they been in love?

She laughed again as the floppy-eared German shepherd mix sat up to give her an unexpected lick on the chin.

Balthazar's grin grew at the sight and sound of her joy.

Stunning, he marveled, almost hypnotized by her beauty. But he wanted his own kiss, too.

On her lips.

He closed the distance between them and bent to claim her mouth with his own, telling her with his tongue that he didn't blame her for anything that had happened and only wanted her happiness going forward.

She clung to his shirt as though she needed him for balance when he pulled back. Her smile had disappeared into a content expression mingled with lust.

"Who are your new friends?" he asked softly, feeling the nose of one of them against his cheek.

Sniffing sounds had replaced the happy panting as the two dogs evaluated Balthazar's character and intentions.

Leela's irises brightened as her lips ticked upward into another of those breathtaking grins.

"This is Bella," she said, her palm gently caressing the velvety coat of the black-and-white boxer mix. "And this is Lola." Her opposite hand went to the head of the fluffy, floppy-eared one.

"Bella and Lola," he repeated, going into a crouch before Leela and placing himself slightly lower than the dogs.

Standing would be a little more intimidating, as his over-six-foot height certainly towered over their much shorter frames—even with the couch boosting their position.

Lola gave him a hesitant glance, uncertainty radiating from her light brown eyes. But Bella immediately lunged for him, her shorter snout armed and ready to lay claim to his face via licks of excitement.

He caught the beast—she was larger than he thought, maybe closer to eighty pounds of solid muscle—and let her love on him for a bit.

Lola was less eager but gave him a little nudge of permission to scratch the soft, feathery fur behind her ears.

"Ah, there you are," a female voice said in Bulgarian. "Stop attacking my guests."

"These are the types of attacks I enjoy," he replied in the same language. "Licks full of love and devotion."

And yes, that held an obvious double meaning, which he conveyed with a glance at Leela. But her focus remained on the fluffy creature at her side.

However, she'd heard him because she translated part

of his statement in her thoughts, suggesting she knew at least a little bit of Bulgarian, or maybe another similar Slavic language.

"Mr. B," Mrs. Spriggs said, her smile reaching her dark eyes. "Your room is ready. The little monsters stay here."

"I'm not sure your little monsters are going to let Leela leave," he mused as Lola gave his little vixen a big kiss on the nose. Leela laughed in response and ruffled up the pretty animal's ears. Bella bumped Balthazar's hand, telling him to pet her more. He obliged her while telling Mrs. Spriggs they would be up in a few minutes. She left the key with them instead, saying she was too tired to stay up and to make themselves at home.

Balthazar thanked her again, then indulged Leela in her version of fluffy heaven. "Do you have a pet?" he asked her after several minutes of cuddling Bella and Lola.

Leela shook her head. "I'm never in one place long enough to have one. You?"

"No. But several of the Hydraians have dogs and cats. Lara helps prolong their longevity. She has a cat, Pouncer, who is close to forty years old now." The tigerlike house cat was notorious on the island for laying claim to various beds throughout the residential area, many of which were not meant to be cat beds. But everyone knew better than to move her.

"Lara, the healer?" Leela asked.

"The very one." She was a younger Hydraian, but very useful. As Leela knew since she'd recently been healed by the Hydraian.

"I wasn't sure if there was more than one. Lara's a popular name."

"In current times," he agreed. "But we don't have many current Hydraians."

"True." She leaned down to kiss Lola between the ears.

"You're a very good girl," she cooed. Then she looked at Bella and said, "And you're very good, too." Both animals ate up the attention but eventually went to their respective beds in the living area to curl up together for a nap.

Balthazar took that as a sign to steal Leela away, even though she seemed perfectly content to just watch them.

"I arranged a room for the night," he told her quietly. "But we're not staying in it." It was too risky for them to stay here. But he'd wanted to compensate Mrs. Spriggs for giving him access to her phone.

Unfortunately, that was also why they had to leave. Because the landline could be tracked far too easily.

And Patreel was still outside, something Balthazar knew since he could still hear the other man's thoughts. He'd been flying around in ethereal form, mulling over everything he'd learned about Osiris and emotions and reformation.

Leela gave the pups one more wistful look before quietly standing and meeting his gaze. Her dreamy expression melted into firmer lines as a resolve clicked in her thoughts.

The snuggle session had given her clarity, a moment to think and process everything they'd learned. Which had allowed her to come to a conclusion.

"I want our memories back." She spoke softly but with a conviction that reverberated through her mind. "I know that'll likely involve remembering the horrors of reformation, too. But it's a price I'm willing to pay to remember you."

Part of him wanted to argue against that decision because he worried about how her mind would react to the trauma of her past.

But it wasn't his choice. It was hers. And he would always respect that, no matter the cost.

"All right. We need Vera," he said. Because he wanted their memories back, too. Leela wouldn't be going through the past alone. He'd be right there with her, every step of the way.

"Or you could bite her," Patreel informed them as he appeared in his corporeal form beside them. The dogs immediately perked up, their ears swiveling as they tried to find the source of the voice. Lola spotted the angel first, her head coming up quickly, followed by her body as she took on a defensive pose.

Balthazar learned a long time ago to listen to the instincts of animals. They typically read situations accurately and effectively.

"If I've learned anything, it's that a blood bond is the most powerful magic of all. Use it to free your minds," Patreel suggested, causing Lola to growl.

Bella went on high alert as well, noticing the angel's location now beside Leela.

"I think that's my cue to leave," Patreel continued. "I'll do what I can to distract the others, but I don't suggest remaining here for long." He vanished in the next second, just as the dogs started toward him.

They both froze, looking around, and Leela quickly soothed them.

But Balthazar remained frozen as he processed what Patreel had just said. He'd spoken so casually, as though his suggestion wouldn't alter both Leela's and Balthazar's lives forever.

Or you could bite her.

A blood bond is the most powerful magic of all. Use it to free your minds.

It was extremely powerful. But it would also bind them together for eternity. Something Leela had clearly known when she'd bitten him the first time.

But had Balthazar wanted that? Was it something they both desired? A monogamous relationship for… forever?

The blood bond could conceivably show them the truth.

A risk.

A huge leap of faith.

A potentially catastrophic decision.

What if we bond just to discover that she only bit me to hide from Dian?

Balthazar frowned. That didn't feel right. Leela wasn't self-serving. She wouldn't use him to conceal herself or disguise her bloodline. She would fight her battles head-on.

"B?" Leela asked, her tone suggesting she'd said his name more than once.

He blinked, her aura radiating concern as her mind confirmed she'd been trying to talk to him about what Patreel had said. Uncertainty echoed in her thoughts, similar questions rolling through her psyche about the risk of a bond.

Is it worth our memories?

Would forced monogamy lead to bitterness?

Are we even capable of being with only each other?

A softer part of her mind whispered, *Yes*, in response.

And Balthazar felt a shimmer of understanding humming through his being, radiating from an intangible place deep inside him.

He rubbed his chest, uncertain if he appreciated the sensation or disliked it.

"B?" Leela repeated.

"I want my memories back," he said, echoing her statement from only minutes ago. "But we can't return to Hydria yet."

Which meant they had to wait to talk to Vera. As her presence and expertise were needed there more than here.

Once Hydria finished fortifying their wards, they could return. He would always put the protection of others over his own wants and needs.

"Our memories will need to wait," he concluded.

"Not all of them," Leela replied, her fingers trailing down his arm to his hand. "There are a few in my head that I could share…" She trailed off, but the rest of her statement thrummed between them.

Brazil. Because she possessed those memories in full.

Or we could re-create them, she added in a mental whisper meant only for him.

He laced his fingers through hers, his opposite arm encircling her waist. He'd already prepaid for the room. Mrs. Spriggs would notice he hadn't touched it, but she wouldn't ask any questions. Which meant they had nothing else left to explore here.

And everything to explore in Brazil.

"I want to know every detail, Lee," he murmured, his lips going to her ear. "Intimately."

If they were going to distract themselves, they were going to do it properly.

"Mist us, vixen." He tightened his grip. "Show me everything."

CHAPTER 25

LEELA

THE MOON REFLECTED OFF THE WATER, CREATING AN almost mystical gleam as the waves rolled up onto the sand.

Leela laced her fingers through Balthazar's, telling him about how he'd approached her on this beach. They'd shared a drink—some fruity concoction he'd ordered—before engaging in a verbal sparring match layered in innuendos.

"You were very confident," she told him, leading him to the place he'd kissed her. "I asked if your approach was to ask a few innocent questions, feign interest, and use the information later to turn up the charm."

"And I told you I don't have an approach," he replied, stepping around her to take hold of her hip and pause their walk as he faced her.

"You remember?"

He shook his head, his thick, dark hair falling over his forehead in an artful manner. "No, I don't remember. I just know what I'd say." His opposite hand curled around the back of her neck, his thumb brushing her pulse. "I would tell you that I don't need an approach."

"Yeah?" she asked, repeating her words from that day on purpose, curious to see if he'd respond similarly. "And why is that?"

The palm on her hip slid to her ass as he pulled her tight against him. "Because I don't need an approach, sweetheart," he murmured, replying with almost the exact same phrase as that day.

His gaze smoldered knowingly, telling her he already knew what had come next.

And he didn't disappoint, his mouth taking hers with a boldness that rivaled that day, shooting fresh sparks of heat through her veins.

She moaned against him, unabashedly returning the embrace as his tongue slowly took control of her mouth.

Not rushed.

Not overindulgent.

But the kiss of a patient man ensuring his lover enjoyed every second of the embrace.

He took his time memorizing her every reaction, his thumb resting against her neck to read the thrum of her pulse.

She positively melted against him, just like she had that day.

Then she told him in her mind what had happened next, how he'd taken her to another part of the beach where Luc had been playing with maple body shots.

Leela had taken one off a female—the name one she no longer remembered, as it hadn't been important—before telling Balthazar to find her later.

He'd fulfilled her request, capturing her attention inside the hotel at the bar. *You asked if I wanted to invite the other man to play with us later, then proceeded to devour me in front of him.*

Balthazar smiled against her mouth. "Like this?" he

asked before deepening their kiss to a searing level of madness that left her dizzy in his arms.

Not as intense as this, she admitted. *But don't you dare stop.*

Of course, he didn't heed the warning, choosing instead to pull back just enough to grin down at her. "Then what happened?"

She almost didn't want to tell him.

Except it would lead to exactly what she craved.

"We went dancing," she whispered. It'd been one of the most erotic evenings of her existence.

Perhaps even the most erotic.

And she'd dreamt of it in detail several times since that night.

"Show me, Lee." The words were a soft seduction in the night air, sending a ripple of excitement down her spine.

Because it was exactly what she wanted to do—to forget everything. The past. The future. Just enjoy a few blissful moments in the present with the male who made her feel things no one else ever had.

A brief kiss of life.

An experience underlined in heat and passion.

An escape into dark oblivion.

She pressed her lips to the edge of his mouth, then grabbed the hand on her ass and spun out of his arms. He allowed her fluid movement, his amusement a palpable warmth in her wake as she guided him toward one of the hotel's outside bars.

To the very dance floor they'd played on months ago.

A new crowd greeted them this time, their lust an intoxicating cloud that stirred hot memories and excited her every nerve. *There are more people here tonight*, she informed him. *It's hotter, too.* They'd been here in this hemisphere's winter last time. Now the summer heat had caressed the air, leaving behind a balmy kiss against her skin.

She regretted wearing a long-sleeved dress in this environment. The short black one she'd worn the original night would be so much more appropriate.

Leela described the outfit to him at length, telling him about his jeans and button-down shirt combination as well.

Balthazar wrapped his arm around her waist, tugging her away from the dance floor and into a darker area beneath a palm tree. The music wasn't as loud here, but the seductive beat hummed in the air, calling to her dancing heart.

"Don't move," he said against her ear, his chest to her back.

Then his heat disappeared, his hand leaving hers.

Her brow furrowed. *What—*

A rip sounded below as he tore the hem of her dress on one side all the way up to her hip. She glanced back to find him kneeling behind her, his focus going to her opposite seam.

Another tear followed.

And the warm air touched her bare thighs. "Better?" he asked, still squatting behind her.

Yes. The fabric danced around her bare calves and tantalizingly parted as she wiggled her hips.

She'd lost her boots on the beach somewhere, as she'd wanted to feel the sand between her toes. Just as Balthazar had discarded his sports jacket, leaving him in slacks and his button-down shirt. He'd rolled the sleeves to the elbows, exposing his toned forearms.

They were both ready to dance.

I wore stilettos that night, she told him. *But I can move just as well on bare feet.*

Assuming there wasn't anything sharp or slippery on the floor, anyway.

Balthazar caught her hips before she could move off the sand, his body pressing against hers as he stood again.

"Let's dance on the beach instead," he suggested, kicking off his own shoes and socks. "Unless you can't keep up in the sand."

The taunt lit a fire within her soul. "You have no idea what I can do, B."

"Then show me, vixen." He nipped her earlobe. Not sharply, just enough to tease. "Do your best."

Her lips curled. Balthazar had said that exact line to her that night. Right before she'd fucked him on a barstool.

"Mmm, is that what comes next?" he asked, his mouth still against her ear. "Where did we fuck?"

"We danced first." And he'd made her come in front of the crowd. "Then we went to the abandoned bar over there. Several people watched."

It'd been such an intense sensation with all their envious eyes on them.

The air had hummed with sex and need, calling to her Seraphim soul.

Similar to how it did now.

Except it felt so much more intimate than it had before. Because Balthazar was in her head, hearing the want from deep within her spirit. He could anticipate her every move, knew all her desires, and read her body almost as well as her mind.

"You enjoy being watched." He spoke the words as a statement, not a question. His palms grasped her hips, whirling her around before she could respond.

Not that she needed to.

He already knew the truth.

Exhibitionism always appealed to her. Voyeurism, too. It just depended on the situation. She lived for the moment, indulging in whatever atmosphere the universe had created for that precise minute of time.

His lips brushed hers, his gaze holding a thousand promises underlined in sin. He didn't ask if she was ready to dance. He just started to move.

And she met him step for step, twirl for twirl, dip for dip.

The sensual beat from the dance floor bar echoed around them, the music softer than their original dance, yet equally as powerful.

Their movements matched the song's intent, sensuality thickening the warm air. Balthazar twisted Leela into a position that caused the tips of her long blonde hair to skim the sand. Then he whirled her back upright, catching her deftly by the hips.

"Dancing," he murmured, his lips grazing hers, "is my favorite kind of foreplay."

His hips pressed into hers, the impressive bulge touching her lower belly. Then they were flying across the beach again, their feet carrying them as expertly as her wings.

She told him how he'd slid his hand up her skirt last time, stroking her to climax in front of the crowd. But rather than repeat the act, he continued to dance with her, drawing out the moment, prolonging the expectation, and leaving her to wonder what he would do next.

She'd shared the memory.

Would he repeat it?

Or create a new one?

His gaze sparkled in the night, the secrets in his head a seductive glimmer she wanted to explore. But he gave nothing away as he whirled her into oblivion, his firm body pressing enticingly against hers with an erotic grace that set her veins on fire.

She indulged in the game, using some of her own moves to increase the connection. A shift of her hips. A brush against his groin. Her lips ghosting along the smooth skin of his neck or his hand, depending on whatever position he put her in.

A crowd had begun to gather at the edges, everyone intrigued by the godlike beings dancing in the night.

Balthazar lifted her into a throw, caught her with ease, and sent her hair down to the sand again. Only, when he righted her, she wrapped her thighs around his waist in a grip that begged for sex.

He let her head fall back once more, his palms skimming her sides, then he whipped her upward to press her chest against his own. "You're a goddess, Lee," he praised. "And fucking perfect."

Her ripped skirt gave their audience a clear view of her legs, making it very apparent that she wore nothing else beneath her dress.

Nudity had never fazed her.

Public sex excited her.

And being in Balthazar's arms... completed her.

His mouth found hers, his tongue dipping inside to duel hers for the whole world to see. She returned the embrace in kind, adding her own twists that would bring a regular man to his knees.

But not B.

She moaned as he pressed his arousal into her own, his trousers a thin barrier she longed to remove.

"So do it," he said against her mouth. "Reach down and unzip me, Lee."

A shiver traversed her spine, causing warmth to pool inside her, readying her for what came next. They were both breathing hard, their dancing almost as exhilarating as the current moment.

There were so many eyes on them, everyone curious to see what would come next.

And Balthazar had just agreed to provide them with the ultimate show.

She slipped her hand between them, her thumb flicking open the button of his pants with a dexterous ease before lowering the zipper along his length.

Smooth, hot skin met her fingertips. She gave it a teasing caress before freeing him completely from the confines of his slacks.

His muscles flexed as he continued to hold her in the air, her thighs still wrapped around his hips and leaving her utterly exposed beneath her skirts.

She rubbed his head along her slick folds, leading him to her entrance.

Then he thrust inside, filling her to completion and drawing a sharp moan from her mouth.

A heady rush of desire followed, the crowd fully aware of what they were witnessing. Balthazar ignored them, his focus entirely on her, yet she knew he could feel their lust through his emotional connections to others.

Just as she could pick up on their intrigue and interest.

One twist of a thought and they would all fall to their knees on a series of orgasms that would blow their minds. That was one of Leela's gifts, her ability to evoke pleasure without touching another person.

She'd used that talent on Balthazar in Brazil, but only after making him come the old-fashioned way.

It'd been a lesson in who she was, a way of showing him without telling him.

Yet every other climax between them had been natural.

LEXI C. FOSS

Because he hadn't needed her psychic talents, just as she hadn't required his.

They'd been dynamite together without the mystical energy.

Rather than fuck her now, he merely stayed connected to her, his tongue sliding sensuously against hers, worshipping her in a manner few others would ever understand.

He always took his time, being thorough to the very end. So much restraint. Confidence. Prolonged enticement.

She lost herself to him, the subtle touches along her sides, the way his cock pulsed deep inside her, the tender strokes of his tongue, the hum of approval radiating between them.

It was just them on this beach.

The bystanders no longer mattered, their collective desires merely an atmospheric addition that heightened the intensity and blended into the overall sensual environment.

Balthazar's palms slid to her back, one going to her ass and the other traveling up to wrap around her nape. Then he deepened their kiss, his movements still slow and measured, complete and concise, and oh-so perfect.

He was a man who devoured and conquered through unexpected touches and patient embraces. He understood that sex wasn't just about power but about understanding what the other person needed. He added emotion to create an intoxicating mix of tenderness and sexiness that took her breath away.

Because he knew she needed this tonight.

He knew she wanted him to make love to her, not fuck her.

And he was doing exactly that with his body and mind.

His knees bent as he lowered them to the beach, his

strength and power radiating around them as he executed the move with flawless grace. Her skirts formed a blanket beneath her as he settled between her thighs, his palm sliding from her nape to her cheek.

She stared up into his dark eyes, saw the emotion radiating back at her.

The connection between them throbbed, the moon painting them in a romantic embrace destined for the heavens.

His hips shifted slowly, gliding his thick arousal through her tight sheath, penetrating her deep before slipping back to the tip to begin all over again.

She arched into him, a soft cry of need parting her lips. But he didn't increase his pace, instead ensuring she felt every inch of him gliding in and out of her with each measured movement.

Her legs wrapped around his waist, squeezing him as he filled her once more.

He kissed her again, this time with intent, his tongue coaxing and urging her to give in to him, to focus solely on him, to be one with him.

It wasn't hard to obey, her body already his to command. She'd never felt more at home, more comfortable, more in tune with another, in her entire existence.

This was Balthazar. *Her* Balthazar. And he knew exactly what she craved.

His thumb grazed her cheekbone before tracing downward to her neck and all the way to her breast. He rolled her stiff nipple between his fingertips, shooting vibrations through every inch of her body. Such a simple touch and yet so undeniably erotic.

She sighed, her hips meeting his, her body melting into the sand beneath him.

He gave a sudden thrust, hitting that spot deep within her and eliciting a sharp sound from her throat. One he swallowed with his tongue before coaxing her back into a delirious state of dark sensuality.

She drew her nails up his back, her fingertips reveling in the muscles beneath his shirt and longing to pet the silken skin beneath. But there was something undeniably sexy about fucking in their clothes.

On a public beach.

With spectators nearby.

It was the perfect moment. An even better memory than before. And she basked in the beauty of it all.

"You're perfect," Balthazar whispered, the praise going straight to her heart. "Everything about you is perfect."

His kiss turned molten, the passion thrumming between them in full force as the pace between their hips subtly increased.

Some of the bystanders had joined in, the electricity in the air intensifying as they indulged in the hedonistic display on the beach. Leela groaned, their open sensuality an aphrodisiac to her senses.

Maybe Balthazar had given them a little push with his power.

Or perhaps it was the energy radiating from them that had enticed the others to play.

She didn't overthink it, didn't analyze how it had happened, just savored the sexual charisma of the night. "Harder," she told him.

He obliged, his body exuding power and grace as he drove into her.

The others were following suit, the wake of heat a palpable enticement.

She had no idea how many had joined them on the beach. She didn't care. The scents and sounds rolled with the waves, drugging her senses and drowning her in a sea of blissful ignorance with Balthazar as her guide.

He kissed her through the sensations, his control resolute.

And she fell headfirst into his every whim, her body acutely his to play with and please.

His hand left her breast, sliding between them to thrum her clit, his intentions clear.

Not that she needed his permission or his gentle coaxing.

Her body was nearly there without it, her thighs tensing from the onslaught of the orgasmic oblivion surrounding them and the power of his hips riding her own.

A deep tremble grew inside her, spreading to her limbs and touching her nerve endings, taunting her with electrifying zaps that made her body jolt with excitement.

"I want to hear you scream my name, Lee." His teeth grazed her lower lip. "I want to watch you come, over and over and over again, and feel you squeeze my shaft. Then I'm going to empty myself inside you and begin again. All night. Here on the beach. Up in a room. Wherever you want to go. But I'm not stopping until you pass out on my cock."

Her heart skipped a beat, his words the aphrodisiac she craved.

"Balthazar…" The name left her on a soft plea, her lungs burning as she forgot how to breathe.

The world began to shift around her, blinking in shades of black and white as a rapturous kiss skated down her spine to the space between her thighs.

Her mind blanked.

Her vision ceased to be.

And ecstasy swallowed her whole, turning her into a being of sensation and feeling and nothing else.

It rolled through her, capturing every neuron and invigorating her spirit.

Just to shoot her into the sky, to reach the stars, in a cataclysmic moment of complete and utter euphoria.

Every part of her shook, down to her very soul.

Hot. Intense. Explosive. *Peace*.

It rocked her senses, knocking her out of the world for a brief moment of time as Balthazar continued to pump into her, driving her onward and upward and prolonging her orgasm to impossible lengths.

But with him, anything was possible.

And he proved that by sending her cascading into a second orgasm that was almost as intense as the first and slaying her ability to concentrate on anything other than the sensations he evoked from her core.

He filled her so completely. So perfectly. So intensely.

This memory put the ones from Brazil to shame, setting the bar even higher and giving them a new level of fulfillment to reach.

Which Balthazar surely would strive to do.

And she'd welcome each and every challenge that followed.

His mouth covered hers, his tongue a demand that yanked her back to him as he began to pulsate inside her, his seed a hot brand she would own for eternity.

Because he belonged to her in a way no one else ever would.

Her half mate.

She sensed the bond now, that powerful pull that drew her to him as though tethered by an ethereal string. It was a deeply ingrained part of her that she'd never explored. But now that she knew it existed, she couldn't let it go.

His groan of completion vibrated against her chest, his intensity radiating through every part of her being as he kissed her through his own climax.

Pleasure echoed around them, others coming undone at the same time as though compelled to follow Leela and Balthazar into erotic oblivion.

"Mist us," he said, his voice a deeply sensual sound against her ear. "Mist us to a room so we can finish this properly."

Alone, she interpreted.

He enjoyed playing around others, evoking orgies, and indulging in group sex. But he was done sharing her tonight. She could sense it in the way his body covered hers, the protective energy radiating from his spirit as he laid claim to her very soul.

She understood because he was just as much hers.

They'd shared enough with the world. Given them the gift of pleasure and excitement.

Now they would continue this dance in private.

In the very room he'd taken her to months ago.

Right here in Brazil.

CHAPTER 26

BALTHAZAR

LEELA'S LIPS AND TONGUE WERE A DIVINE CREATION THAT deserved to be worshipped. The way she stroked Balthazar's shaft in long, languorous movements had his abdomen clenching in dark anticipation of his release.

And those eyes.

Fuck.

He loved that sinful sparkle in her pretty irises. She was driving him to madness, and the grin in her gaze said she knew it, too.

Slow, languid pulls.

Beautiful suction.

A twirl of that talented tongue.

He groaned, his fingers fisting in her hair as he gave in to her pace and let her lead the way to ecstasy.

They'd lost their clothes hours ago, reveling in the feel of skin on skin, their mouths tracing every inch of each other.

Time had ceased around them.

Their worries had fled.

Because all that mattered was their intimate connection and the chasing of memories from their past.

Balthazar still couldn't remember a single thing about Brazil, but he trusted Leela to guide him, to share the moments he longed to know.

She showed him now what she'd done with her mouth then. Except she didn't coax him to orgasm the way he now knew she could. Instead, she brought him pleasure through sensual skill alone.

He'd experiment with her powers later, learn more about what line of her family tree they came from. Likely the Adonis side—a detail about Leela that he'd learned from Patreel.

Or maybe her powers were a mixture of both bloodlines.

"Leela," Balthazar bit out as the head of his cock nudged the back of her throat. She demanded his attention, her mouth requiring his devoted focus to the ministrations of her tongue.

This female lived up to her vixen-like persona, taking him to the edge with the skill of a superior being. His grip tightened in her hair, his abdomen clenching as her cheeks hollowed around him, demanding he come hard inside her.

He wasn't one to disappoint a lover, and he certainly wasn't going to hold back with this one.

Her nails dug into his thighs, her own legs clenching with a need he could taste in the air. Sucking him off turned her on.

And now she wanted him to explode down her pretty little throat.

"Swallow, Lee," he told her, his voice gruff and deepened with sex. "Swallow and I'll reward you."

Her gaze danced with challenge, her excitement an

erotic kiss in the air that sent him tumbling over the edge into decadent oblivion.

His dick pulsed inside her mouth, the orgasm rolling through his veins like liquid fire. It was intense and stunning and so fucking hot.

Leela took him beautifully, her tongue stroking the underside of his shaft as her throat clenched around his head, swallowing each drop as he spent himself inside her.

She'd perfected the art of oral sex, setting a bar so incredibly high that he doubted anyone else in his lifetime would ever reach it.

And he fully intended to return the favor.

"I'm going to devour you," he vowed, his voice a low growl of approval.

She responded with another suck that had him seeing stars, her power igniting as she coerced even more from his groin.

He cursed, his head falling back into the pillows on a cry of pleasure mingled with pain. It was too soon to come again and yet… "*Fuck…*"

She forced it from him, the rapture spiraling through his being and leaving him depleted beneath her. His grip in her hair was all that kept him sane, the world a myriad of sensual colors and prickles of hot coals.

His breath stilled, his heart racing in his chest as he fought for control of his mind.

Her mouth was magic against his skin.

Sucking. Nipping. Swallowing.

Drawing out the intensity and leaving him senseless beneath her.

But a small flicker of light snagged his focus, and he latched onto it, his fingers clenching as he pulled her lips from his shaft and yanked her upward to his mouth.

She hummed in approval, confirming what he already

knew about his Seraphim—she liked a dominant man in the bedroom.

"Hands above your head," he demanded, flipping her to her back as he rolled on top of her. "And don't move."

"I told you that on the stool," she murmured, obliging his command by lifting her arms to rest in the pillows cradling her head. "Right before I straddled you."

"Did you give me a good ride?" he asked, already aware of the answer. He'd taken control then, too, dictating the pace even while she'd been on top. Chants of approval whispered through her consciousness at the memory, telling him he'd more than lived up to her expectations even without access to her thoughts.

"It's always an amazing ride with you," she replied, her blue-green irises glittering with promise.

"Mmm," he hummed, the feeling very much mutual.

His little vixen created a whole new playground of opportunity, providing him with a breath of newness and a challenge unlike any other. There were no limits here, anything and everything possible, and just the thought of it drugged his senses with warmth and expectation.

He could fuck her however he desired.

Test her in a manner impossible for so many others.

And she would indulge every minute of it. Enjoy it, too.

He didn't do pain. No blood or physical injury. But sometimes pleasure could hurt.

As she'd just demonstrated with her mouth.

He kissed a path to her breasts, adoring them with his mouth and hands and taunting the sweet little rosy peaks. Her eyes remained on him, blue flames dancing around the edges as she admired the view.

His teeth skimmed her nipple, testing her reaction.

Her nostrils flared, her legs tensing around his.

So he bit down just enough to pinch.

She moaned, her body writhing in wanton need.

He repeated the action on her other breast, his tongue soothing the ache before he continued downward along her ribs to her hip. His tongue traced the bone there, causing goose bumps to scatter along her skin.

"I love how your body talks to me, Lee," he told her, his nose skimming her lower belly as his lips neared the smooth skin of her mound. "Do you always shave?" he asked, a memory of groomed hairs taunting the vestiges of his mind. "Or do you change your grooming habits?"

"I do whatever matches my mood," she murmured, her voice a throaty purr. "Lately, I've preferred hairless. But I do whatever is in fashion. Why? Do you have a preference?"

"Whatever makes you comfortable," he replied, meaning it. He didn't shave, just kept himself groomed because he preferred it that way. "Comfort inspires confidence."

And confidence was sexy on a woman.

As Leela demonstrated beautifully before him with her seductive smile and knowing gaze. She resembled a goddess in this bed, her sensual charisma a beacon that called to his inner deviant.

Everything about her enchanted him.

Her mind.

Her prowess.

Her long legs.

Her flawless skin, as pale as porcelain and so incredibly soft.

Her full lips.

That sinful tongue.

That come-hither gleam in her multicolored irises.

The sweet aroma of her arousal.

He wanted to devour her. Worship her. Re-create all their lost memories. Make new ones. Explore every potential position and fuck all over the world while evoking erotic scenes in their wake.

A perfect life. A whirlwind romance. An exotic journey around the globe.

"Where's my reward?" she asked huskily. "I swallowed, didn't I?"

"Vixen," he murmured, amused by her attempt to top from the bottom. They both knew she preferred his domination. Not rough or sadistic kink. Just a hint of power and strength.

Which he gave her now as he palmed her thighs and forced her to spread wider.

So flexible and limber. Something he already knew but the knowledge of it intrigued him all over again. Because it added even more position ideas for them to try.

His list would last a century.

Likely more.

Some of the activities required more players. But most of his ideas were just for Leela.

A new train of thought, as he didn't usually indulge the notion of limiting his experiences to just him and one other person.

However, he rather liked the notion of keeping Leela to himself, because it served as a challenge. Being her only lover meant he had to be good enough for a goddess.

Which meant he had to sexually satisfy her at every turn to maintain her interest.

No mistakes. No laziness. No distractions.

A stimulating situation meant to test Balthazar's sensual prowess.

Would he be enough for her?

Yes. Yes, I will, he decided as he bent to draw his tongue through her slick folds. "You taste like sex, Leela," he said softly, loving the flavor of their mixed arousals. "Decadent. Delicious. Perfect."

Her thighs clenched beneath his palms, her breath shuddering out on a sigh.

He laved her with his tongue, adoring her the way a man should with thorough strokes and subtle pressure. It was a dance that required patience and the ability to read cues from the body.

A bit of tension and prolonged teasing went a very long way to properly please a woman. And Leela was a masterpiece worth his effort and dedication.

She squirmed and moaned, her fingers gliding through his hair to hold him right where she needed him. He granted her the director role just long enough to nearly drive her over the edge before pulling back to begin once more.

"Balthazar," she growled when he did it a second time.

"Trust me," he replied against her damp flesh.

And proceeded to draw out her pleasure a third time.

Her huff of frustration when he stopped again was a beautiful sound that told him they were reaching the final destination of this session.

Two more times.

He circled her clit, massaged her channel with his fingers, and smiled when a colorful curse left her mouth.

"Stop teasing me and fuck me," Leela demanded.

"Soon," he promised, his cock still at half-mast from the ecstasy she'd wrung from him with her pretty mouth.

She repeated his name, the protest underlining her tone making his lips curl.

Her mind told him that most of her previous lovers rushed to the finish line. But that wasn't him. And it wasn't her preference, either. Something he knew from her body more than her thoughts.

She really is my equal, he marveled, listening as she analyzed his every move, appreciating his patience and ability to draw out the moment.

Leela knew what was coming.

She might be protesting the process, but she would absolutely appreciate the end result.

The truth rested in her thoughts, lounging around for him to overhear. However, it was the goose bumps and shivers across her skin that told him he was close to the point of no return now.

She would come this time.

And she would come hard.

He drew his tongue along her seam, reveling in the sweet flavor of hedonism between her thighs. She tasted like hours of fucking gone right, her body a temple that had been properly worshipped by his cock, and was in deep need of *more*.

Which he gave her now as he curled his fingers inside her, caressing that place that made all women melt. Leela was no different, her lips parting on a groan that vibrated all the way down to her core. He felt it against his tongue, the reverberation one that had him humming in response.

This display of eroticism was one he wouldn't mind seeing on repeat for days or years on end.

Maybe even for forever, he thought, thinking about their half bond. *Have I loved her all my life without knowing it?* She certainly felt perfect in his hands, her pleasure an aphrodisiac that drew out the moment and had him nearly ready to go again.

And again.

And again.

He'd never experienced such sensual grace with another being.

Except that wasn't true. He had experienced it before, just couldn't remember doing so. And then there was Nythos...

How many of those memories were actually between him and Leela?

If he bit her now, would he find out? Would he begin to remember? Would it dismantle all the mental blocks in his mind?

But a blood bond required faithfulness. He would never desire another.

Was that worth the cost of his memories? Would it matter if he had Leela?

Do I love her? He felt as though he could. She was his equal in every way. What wasn't there to love? But only her? Did he have that in him?

"Balthazar," she moaned, her grip tightening in his hair as she demanded he let her fall into oblivion. "Please..."

His lips curled against her flesh. "You would absolutely crawl for me right now, wouldn't you?"

"Yes," she admitted on a hiss, her mind rioting at the thought of having to move. But her legs started to shift as though she wanted to demonstrate her willingness to do whatever he asked.

He pressed his palm to her belly, holding her to the bed. "I don't want you on your knees, Lee. I want your pleasure in my mouth instead." Which he proceeded to demonstrate as he sealed his lips around her clit again.

His tongue circled the tender nub, his fingers working her into oblivion as his gaze lifted to hold hers.

Pools of green and blue stared back at him, her irises constantly shifting colors. Sometimes green while lost to passion. Sometimes blue. Or a mixture of both, as they were right now. He wondered what it all meant, if she had a preferred color or if that changing blend of blue green was just her.

"I want you inside me," Leela whispered. "I want you to feel me coming around you. Please, B. I need—"

He nipped her sensitive flesh, drawing a scream from her that distracted her long enough for him to move and settle between her thighs. Then he slid home in a single thrust that had her arching up into him on a hiss of pleasure-induced pain.

And their bodies began to move in a frantic dance.

He didn't hold back, giving her everything he had with the pistoning of his hips, his movements ensuring he rubbed her clit with each thrust.

She mewled in response, her core tightening around him as she teetered on the rapturous cliff between orgasm and anticipation. Her nails dug into his nape, her opposite hand against his back as their mouths fused together on a kiss that would slay a normal person.

All heat and need and erotic grace.

Balthazar grabbed her hip, angling her just right, his other palm against her cheek as their tongues whispered secrets to one another about their shared past.

It was intense, beautiful, and intoxicating. He nearly forgot everything else in that moment, Leela being the sole focus of his thoughts.

Her power hummed through him, that sensual energy pulling on his essence to demand they fall into oblivion together. Joined. Their souls bonding in a manner unlike any other.

Their kiss slowed, the tenderness radiating between them as his hips matched the pace of their mouths.

Not gentle, just thorough. Powerful. Languid. *Making love*.

A tremor skated down his spine, leaving him bewildered above her, yet he felt *full*. Overwhelmed. Drunk. *Pleased*.

Her nails scraped up into his hair, drawing him back to her as she wrapped her legs around his waist and lifted her lower body up to meet his in a slow-motion roll that sent a quiver through his entire being.

The climax built so slowly, so impactfully, that he forgot how to breathe.

She became his lifeline, her mouth his only connection to air and oxygen in this world as they both came undone in tandem with each other.

Pure, unadulterated bliss pulsed through them, marrying their bodies in an ageless passion that surpassed time and existence.

It stole his vision, cascading him in a sea of dark rapture that quaked through his limbs and torso, draining his essence into her body, into the slick crevice between her thighs, into her very soul.

Her tongue stroked his, serving as a lifeline that kept him bound to reality. Or maybe it was the other way around because he could sense the same experience in her mind, that loss of all concept of existence within her thoughts.

They kissed through the passionate cloud, their bodies connected below and moving at a gradual pace that prolonged this insanity.

Until the world finally began to form around them once more.

Slowly, with just the sights and sounds of the room and the sensation of kissing and being saturated in sex.

A hedonistic wet dream.

Erotic art.

A perfect existence.

This is a life worth living, he marveled, his eyes opening to meet Leela's gaze. *And she's a creature worth loving.*

He kissed her with all the emotion building inside him, the realization of what they might have missed out on for all these millennia blossoming in his mind.

Perhaps this was why he'd chosen a "love all" approach over monogamy.

Because the one woman he was meant to be with had been stolen from him three thousand years ago.

He couldn't say for sure.

So he devoured her mouth instead.

And their game began anew, their bodies making up for lost time as they reacquainted themselves in the most intimate of ways.

Through sex.

Animalistic passion.

Ignoring all the rest.

Just existing in this blissful moment of sensual harmony.

Creating new memories meant to last a lifetime.

CHAPTER 27

ISSAC

ASTASIYA HAD SPENT A GOOD PORTION OF THE NIGHT AND early morning working on the wards while Issac had observed through her mind. Most of the ethereal charms were done; only the exterior was left.

Vera had helped them—after restoring Lucian's memories, a task that had clearly exhausted her. However, Gabriel had soon arrived afterward, saying, "You can fill me in on where you've been while we work."

The memory-manipulating Seraphim had sighed, clearly exhausted, but then she'd followed him up into the sky to explain everything about Osiris and Patreel.

Lucian had brought Alik and Jayson up to speed on Balthazar and Leela, as well as Osiris, leaving Issac to talk to Tristan. Which he'd done while keeping an eye on Astasiya in the sky.

"What do you intend to do about Mateo?" his progeny asked softly in the living area of Balthazar's home. Issac had just finished brewing coffee for Aya but poured some into a cup for himself and one for Tristan.

He handed the latter to his progeny before settling into a chair beside the couch. "Lucian is still talking to him."

"Yes, but after that?"

"I don't know," Issac admitted. "He betrayed all of us. But his intentions…"

"Were mostly in our favor," Tristan finished for him. "Yes."

They lapsed into thoughtful silence, sipping their coffee while thousands of unspoken words flowed between them. Their friendship spanned two centuries, allowing them to truly know each other, thus making conversation unnecessary.

Tristan would know Issac's internal battle regarding how to respond to this situation because Mateo was part of their family. And not just by blood, but by choice. Issac *had chosen* Mateo.

And he'd betrayed them all.

Which meant Issac was partially liable for bringing him into the fold.

Tristan wouldn't blame him. And neither would anyone else, really. But Issac held himself accountable. He would be in charge of delivering punishment to his progeny.

The question remained as to what the punishment would actually require.

Lucian not placing Mateo in the dungeon was an interesting tell. Perhaps he felt that Osiris had compelled his progeny. Issac wondered the same, but Mateo had been rather clear that his involvement in the matter was voluntary.

To protect them.

"Do you believe him?" Issac wondered out loud. "That he worked with Osiris to keep us safe?"

Tristan sipped his coffee, his expression giving nothing

away. "I think Mateo would never hurt us. Either he was compelled, or his voluntary actions helped us in some way, thus justifying his participation."

Issac agreed with a nod. Because that summarized his thoughts as well.

"I don't think he knew about Amelia," Tristan continued. "Jonathan keeping her, I mean. I don't think he knew she was at the CRF all that time."

A chill skated down Issac's spine. "Did you ask him about it?"

"I didn't," Tristan replied. "Did you?"

"No." And he should have. But he'd been more focused on Mateo's involvement in Aidan's death. "I'll ask him." Or he'd check with Lucian, as he'd likely inquired about it already. "Mateo said he primarily spoke to Osiris and only occasionally went through Jonathan. So it's doubtful he knew about Amelia."

"Did Osiris?" Tristan asked.

Issac's jaw ticked. "Likely, yes."

"Have you told her all this?"

"Not yet." He'd prioritized Tristan, while Lucian had prioritized the Elders. "I should do." His English accent always came out more when speaking to his best friend. A habit of their long history.

"Or I could do it," Tristan offered. "Stas needs you right now. You can focus on her while I speak with Tom and Amelia."

Issac considered him for a moment. "Did you just suggest a way to help me prioritize taking care of Aya?"

Tristan's green eyes gave nothing away. "She's your bonded mate and therefore a primary responsibility."

Issac arched a brow. "Is that the only reason?"

His best friend's gaze narrowed. "What are you playing at?"

"Just wondering if you've had a change of heart, is all."

Tristan snorted. "She's learning how to be useful. I can respect that."

"Hmm," Issac hummed, amused by the response. "I think you like her."

"And I think you're away with the fairies again, mate," Tristan drawled, his Irish accent shining through his choice of phrasing. But a glimmer of humor colored his features, his lips quirking a bit at the sides.

He'd notoriously disapproved of Aya because of what her relationship with Issac had represented—death.

But now she wasn't a threat.

If anything, she made Issac stronger.

"Hmm," Issac repeated, setting his coffee to the side. "Well, she'll be here any second now. So try to be nice."

"I'm always nice," Tristan drawled, adding his own mug to the same table as Issac's. He ran his fingers through his dark hair, making a show of relaxing into the chair rather than sprinting for the door.

Issac just shook his head, aware of his best friend's penchant for mischief. He was lucky Aya hadn't put him in his place yet. She was too consumed with anger toward her brother to give Tristan much attention, but that'd likely change some—

"I've never seen you this happy," his best friend said quietly, interrupting his musings. "She's good for you, Issac. I worried before, but now…" He trailed off, clearing his throat. "I'm glad you found each other."

Issac's eyes widened at the admission. "Are you trying to make me feel better about Mateo?" It was an honest question, as his best friend *never* spoke fondly of Aya or his relationship with her.

Tristan grunted. "Am I not allowed to say something kind?"

"Of course you are, but you never do."

"That's not true," Tristan argued. "I say kind things to Amelia all the time."

Issac scoffed at that. "My sister is an entirely different situation."

Tristan merely smiled in response.

Aya appeared in the next blink, her blonde hair flowing in the wind of her arrival as her wings settled at her back. She glanced at Tristan and huffed a breath, clearly not thrilled to see him in the living area, but shifted into her corporeal state anyway so he would know she'd arrived.

Otherwise, he wouldn't have been able to see or hear her.

"Hello, Stas," Tristan greeted with false cheer. "How was training this morning? Good?"

Issac rolled his eyes at his best friend's forced attempt at being "nice."

Aya blinked at him, her brow furrowing. "Are you feeling okay?"

"I'm fine," Tristan drawled. "Perfect, really. You?"

What the hell is wrong with him? Aya asked.

He's trying to be nice.

Well, tell him to stop. It's freaking me out.

Issac chuckled and just shook his head again. "There's fresh coffee waiting for you in the kitchen. I already added a teaspoon of brown sugar, too."

That immediately grabbed Aya's attention, taking her away from Tristan's odd behavior. "Thank you." She misted from the room in an array of beautiful opal shades.

Stunning, he whispered to her. *Absolutely stunning.*

You're just trying to make me feel better about the pink plumes.

Hardly, love. I've never been one for false platitudes.

Unless giving a woman a line to entice her into bed, she tossed back at him.

I believe we've already had this discussion once, he reminded her. *And it ended in your pretty blush being displayed all over the tabloids.*

She snorted, appearing again with the coffee in her hand and at her lips. *You're a demon.*

I'm your demon, he returned.

"Right," Tristan said, pushing up from his chair. "This is my cue to leave, then."

Aya started to smile, her green eyes glittering with warmth and humor as she lifted the mug to her mouth again for another sip. Only, she paused midway, her brow furrowing.

"What is it?" Issac asked, causing Tristan to pause right beside him on his way to the door.

"You know bloody well what it is," he returned. "All that mental jabbering is going to lead to a snogging session that I have no…" He trailed off, his voice disappearing into the room as Issac maintained his focus on Aya. His best friend must have realized the question hadn't been for him but for Aya.

She'd fallen utterly still, her attention having lifted to the ceiling. *Something's coming,* she whispered, her shiver visible even from across the room. *Something powerful.*

Issac cast his power out across the island, searching everyone's visions for any clue of what she might be sensing.

Lucian was speaking with Jayson and Alik in his house. Mateo stood with them. The visual gave him a momentary pause as he wondered what they were discussing.

But Aya's unease trickled through his mind, shoving him back on track as he searched for Elizabeth's mind. *Dreaming,* he confirmed before moving on to his sister and Thomas.

Which was a huge mistake that had him gasping for air

because he never wanted to see *that* ever again. He mentally growled, shaking his head violently to rid himself of that particular image of his sister on the bed.

Fuck, he thought, attempting to build a mental wall between him and Thomas.

But a gasp from his Aya yanked him right back to the room with her and to the couple that had just appeared in the center of the room.

"Skye's just had a vision," Sethios said quickly. "She keeps saying, 'They know,' on repeat, but she won't tell us more. So we don't know if she means the Fates, the council, or the warrior Seraphim. Can you tap into her vision?"

The question was for Issac. However, he was already doing just that before Sethios ceased speaking.

And the visual that awaited him stole the air from his lungs.

Death. Destruction. Blood and violence.

Littering the grounds of Hydria.

Lifeless eyes.

A flurry of wings and swords and ethereal energy.

A screaming child.

A bright light at the center of it all.

Aya's furious expression.

Aya's vacant expression.

Aya's agonized scream.

Aya's blank stare.

He frowned. "She's seeing several different fates at once," he said, translating the image out loud. "Aya is at the center of it all. Here in Hydria. And she's surrounded by death."

"Of course I am," she muttered. "Because I'm destined to kill us all."

"We choose our destinies," her mother said as she

appeared in a flurry of light blue feathers before turning corporeal. "Gabriel and Vera are trying to finish the outer wards now, as it's clear we don't have much time."

"The warriors are definitely coming," Issac agreed, still watching the images flash through Skye's mind. "I think she's saying the council knows, but it could also be a shared projection from the Fates. It's hard to say for sure, as it's all quite chaotic." And giving him a bloody headache, too.

He tried to discern any kind of order to the visions, but they appeared to be coming to her in a random sequence, depicting events that might happen in a few minutes or a few centuries.

Issac pulled out of her head, unable to bear another minute.

Then he blinked at finding Lucian in the doorway.

Time had apparently slipped by him while he'd been dancing through the intricacies of Skye's mind.

"It's time for B to come home," Lucian declared. "We need him. He's the key to Hydraian morale."

Issac agreed with a nod.

Because he was right.

All the Elders maintained a certain role as leaders of their kind. Lucian served as the strategic mastermind. Jayson demonstrated strength through action. Alik took on the tasks no one else had the courage to conquer.

And Balthazar was Hydria's heart.

Issac might not always see eye to eye with the mind reader, but he could acknowledge his purpose and power on this island.

Balthazar was the emotional glue that secured the Hydraians together, the leader they all followed willingly because they trusted him implicitly.

If they were about to be attacked by an army of

Seraphim, they needed the Elder who resembled hope and love.

They needed Balthazar.

"The next time he rings in for an update, I'll tell him it's time," Lucian said, reading the agreement in Issac's nod and likely through his expression as well. "Until then, we need to prepare the island for an attack unlike any we've ever seen."

Issac inclined his head. "Tell me what you need, and I'll see that it's done."

Chapter 28

Balthazar

Leela stretched, her curves rubbing against Balthazar's torso and groin with the beautifully executed movement.

This woman oozed sex.

It poured out of her, demanding he devour her to completion, encouraging him to indulge in every inch of her flawless form and bow to her in worship.

"You're a succubus," he mused, his lips skating along her throat as he pulled her body back into his to press his chest to her back. "Sucking all the energy from my veins."

"From your cock," she corrected.

He grinned against her pulse, nibbling the sweet flesh and wondering what her blood would taste like on his tongue. It was a bizarre craving, one he'd never experienced with another female.

Because of the bond, he realized.

What had possessed her to bite him? A mutual agreement? A desire to be together? She'd still been able to seduce other people since, which meant they weren't secured by a monogamous link. He'd even asked her about it last night, curious as to how it worked.

She'd told him the partial bond left them both free to play with others. Or perhaps it was her sensual spirit that required it. She wasn't quite sure.

Would that change if he bit her? Or would it remain the same between them?

They were both passionate creatures.

Although, the idea of sharing her didn't necessarily appeal to him. He'd probably enjoy the show on a sexual level, mostly because no one else could please her better than he could.

And if, by chance, she did find someone, then that person was worthy of worshipping her body because it would bring her pleasure.

A normal man or woman just wouldn't do.

And they were too potent together to really invite a third into their bed.

So how many of the memories with Nythos were truly Leela? Because Nythos had enjoyed playing around with others. Were those recollections infused by moments he'd shared with Leela? Had he watched her bed other men and women? Or had all that been Nythos?

The only way to truly know was to bite her.

Even then, it wasn't guaranteed. Patreel had just guessed it would help them break the chains on their minds.

Like Caro and Sethios.

But Caro had only undergone reformation for less than two decades, while Leela had experienced a century of it.

What if they caught her again? Would they wipe him from her mind? Dismantle his memories of her as well?

How long would it be before they found each other again?

Is my history with her why I've never craved monogamy with anyone else?

So many questions. Not enough answers.

But with her ass grinding against his groin, he found himself otherwise distracted by the new experiences they'd just shared in this bed and the fresh memory of taking her from behind mere hours ago.

He'd indulged her in every way imaginable, the limits between them nonexistent.

Because his vixen enjoyed all manner of sex, just as he did. And they both knew how to play in bed for hours or days or weeks.

It was equally possible that his own sexuality had been influenced by his link to Leela—a notion he'd realized somewhere in the middle of the night when Leela had commented on his insatiability.

"Most men can't keep up with my pace," she'd confided to him on a pant as he'd taken her ass for the first time. "But you're actually making me work for it." She'd moaned after that, then collapsed into the pillows when he'd reached around to fondle her clit and sent her cascading over the edge into oblivion.

She'd clenched so hard around him that he'd followed her into the blissful climax.

Then they'd showered before starting all over again.

Which had led to a nap as the sun was rising in Brazil.

Balthazar owed Luc another check-in call, but he hadn't been able to stop worshipping his siren. She tasted amazing, and her moans were utterly addictive.

Leela rotated in his arms, the green in her irises having chased away the blue this morning. She pressed her lips to his, engaging him in a lazy kiss as she hooked her leg around his hip.

He indulged her, his hand finding her cheek before gliding back into her silky hair.

Mmm, she resembled ambrosia, all sweet and flavorful and intoxicating.

Her mind hummed in approval, her thoughts filled with a mixture of wonder and contentment.

"I've dreamt of this so many times," she whispered against his mouth. "Waking up in Brazil and our time together never ending."

"Who says you're not dreaming now?" he teased softly.

"Maybe I am." She licked his bottom lip. "Maybe all of this is a dream."

"A good one, I hope," he replied, his groin pressing into the slick heat between her thighs. The head of his arousal nudged her flesh without entering her, just enough to taunt and seduce.

She arched into him, her full breasts perfect against the flat planes of his chest. "Every dream with you is a good one, B."

He smiled. "And how is reality measuring up to the fantasies?"

"Reality is better," she admitted, her lips finding his once again.

Their embrace turned sensual, a hint of warm emotion underlying every touch. He could absolutely become accustomed to this act of waking up with Leela daily. She fit him so beautifully, her body a divine entity worthy of constant prayer. But it was more than just her physical appearance and her prowess in the bedroom.

It was *her*.

His sweet Seraphim.

His flirtatious siren.

His witty vixen.

She oozed confidence and sensuality and possessed a positive outlook on life that suited his own perspective.

Happiness radiated from her eyes, a happiness that called to his very soul.

Those stunning irises grinned up at him now, her lips curling against his as she maneuvered him to his back and straddled his hips. Their bodies connected automatically, his cock sliding into her hot, wet channel.

Her nails bit into his pecs as she began to move, her breasts swaying with each beautiful shift of her lower half. He lifted himself to meet her, matching her pace without provocation.

It was slow, not rushed.

Patient. Engaging. Sensual.

He pushed himself upright to kiss her, then wrapped his palm around the back of her neck to drag her over him to maintain the connection between their torsos and their hips.

She allowed it, the little vixen preferring his control.

So he flipped her and drove deep inside her, drawing a sweet gasp from her mouth.

"Harder," she breathed.

"No." He wanted to keep the tender pace between them, to coax out the passion lurking deep within her soul.

And afterward, he would take her to breakfast somewhere.

Her teeth sank into his bottom lip in protest.

He caught her wrists and pulled her arms over her head to secure her hands beneath one of his. Then he palmed and squeezed her breast in subtle reprimand, tweaking the nipple as he continued to slowly fill her to the hilt and draw out again.

She growled.

He grinned.

LEXI C. FOSS

Then her power wrapped around him, exciting his pulse and tightening his balls. "Fuck, Lee."

"That's the idea," she said, her ankles hooking behind his ass. "Now move."

He chuckled, unable to help it. This demanding little siren proved powerful at every turn.

So he gave in to her command and took control through sheer power alone, showing her what his body could do and bringing them both to climax on a series of scream-filled moans that ended in pants of pleasure.

He kissed her afterward, long and hard, then carried her to the walk-in shower nearby and continued their passionate embrace against the stone wall.

She came again, her body shaking beneath the onslaught of rapture, her eyes drooping as though preparing to sleep once more. But he wouldn't allow it, choosing to wash her instead, massaging her muscles and cleaning her hair before focusing on himself. Then he wrapped her in a fluffy robe and took her to the kitchen inside their suite.

The fridge was empty since they hadn't actually reserved this room, just misted into it, leaving them with no choice but to go out to eat.

Leela misted them to a store to find some clothes. It wasn't open yet, so Balthazar left some money on the counter. Not that the owners would have any idea what had happened or why. They'd also have to convert the cash into their local currency, but they'd come out ahead in the end.

Balthazar chose jeans and a fitted T-shirt, with a pair of socks and new boots.

Leela went with a cute dress meant for summer, selected a pair of sandals that wrapped up her calves in a fashionable manner meant for ancient Greece more than current-day Brazil, and found a brush for her hair.

With a grin, she told him she knew just the place for them to enjoy brunch.

Buenos Aires.

At a little cafe that served a mixture of international cuisine.

Balthazar ordered pancakes, the superior breakfast food. Leela followed suit, and they lounged on the patio seating outside while awaiting their meal.

"This place really is a little Europe," Leela mused, glancing around at the colorful architecture and lack of skyscrapers. "It reminds me of Rome, but also the coast of France, with a splash of Barcelona and Madrid sprinkled on top."

His lips curled. "It's not my first choice for pancakes, but we'll see how they do."

"Your first choice would be in your own kitchen. Naked. With me lathered in syrup on the counter."

"Is that a fantasy or something that's happened?"

"A fantasy inspired by what happened in Brazil after making me pancakes one morning," she replied, her gaze sparkling with devious intent. "One we can absolutely do once we're back in Hydria."

"Which reminds me, I need to call Luc."

She nodded her chin toward the restaurant. "I'm sure you can borrow a phone from someone inside."

He grinned. "Are you asking me to seduce a phone off a patron?"

She considered him for a moment, then looked inside at the waiters before taking in the various patrons. "Hmm, only if I'm allowed to choose."

"What happens when I win?"

"I'll let you decide if he or she can join us for dessert."

He already knew he wouldn't be inviting anyone here to bed other than Leela. "How about I win my choice of positions for dessert instead."

Her lips curled. "Not in the mood for a third?"

"You're the only one I'm craving for dessert, vixen." The admission rolled off his tongue, the statement one he'd never said to another person before.

Her expression softened, her eyes losing some of the teasing glint. "Keep saying things like that and you won't need to win a game to pick a position."

He reached for her hand and brought it to his lips. "But games are how we thrive."

"Sensual ones."

"Sensual ones," he echoed, holding her gaze as he turned her hand over to place a kiss on her palm. "Did you pick a patron?" he asked against her skin.

"No," she whispered. "Because the only appetizing item on the menu is you."

He grinned at her twisting his words right back at him. "Hmm." His lips parted around her finger, pulling the digit into his mouth for a little swirl with his tongue. Her pupils dilated in response, a soft shudder of breath infiltrating the air.

"You're making me want to skip right to…" She trailed off, her brow furrowing as a hum of electricity teased the atmosphere around them. "*Shit.*"

She reached for him, but the vibration knocked her back into the chair. He leapt forward, his hands finding her shoulders. "Mist."

"I can't," she gritted out, her mind telling him some sort of ethereal net had bound her ability to sprout wings.

"How do I remove it?" His hands ran over her arms, feeling nothing but soft skin. "How do I free you?"

"You can't," a familiar voice said to his left as an

auburn-haired woman with ebony eyes approached. She was the spitting image of a dream. A memory he once reminisced about with a mixture of nostalgia and melancholy.

He'd blamed himself for her death.

Because it'd been his blood that she'd imbibed.

Yet here she stood, fucking smiling at him as though they were long-lost lovers.

He slowly straightened his spine and placed himself behind Leela, his back to her while he faced the approaching woman.

"Balthazar," Nythos purred, her voice exactly as he remembered it. All sultry sensuality, which he now knew came from her father's lineage.

Just like Leela.

Except there was nothing else alike between the pair.

One was an angel with creamy skin, honest eyes, and a mind he admired more and more with each passing second.

The other was a temptress with pouty lips, a devious smile, and auburn hair that resembled an ominous cloud around her slender shoulders.

"It's been a few centuries," she continued in that low voice that beckoned sex. "I've missed you."

"A few centuries?" he repeated as he tracked her every move. She was only a few feet away from them now with Leela still unable to move because of whatever net her half sister had ensnared her with. His hands hung loosely at his sides, his back nearly touching Leela's chair. He wanted to be able to grab her if he needed to.

Which was likely, given the situation.

However, that invisible net around her certainly posed a problem.

She'd not mentioned the possibility of something like

this, and her thoughts told him she'd not anticipated it either.

Have they used this on me before? she was wondering. *Can I somehow escape it?*

Memories crept along the edges of her mind, ones that told her she'd been in a situation very much like this before. Perhaps more than once.

With Balthazar right at her side.

He followed the strands of thought while continuing to monitor Nythos.

A sense of déjà vu hit him square in the chest as Nythos flipped her long hair over her shoulder, the triumph in her gaze one he'd seen before. Not just in bed, but in an event similar to this.

With Leela trapped by a magic she didn't understand.

Because they'd wiped it from her mind.

His hands curled into fists, a lash of heat assaulting his veins.

Leela's mind had been so thoroughly raped by her own kind that she didn't even know how to properly protect herself. She'd tried in her own way by investing in properties and learning defensive wards, but the Seraphim had been one step ahead by ensuring she had no memory of how they'd taken her down.

And worse, they'd done the same to him.

Because they'd absolutely been in a similar situation to this, something Nythos proved as she cooed, "Well, I suppose it's been more like three millennia or so in your mind, hmm?"

She cocked her head to the side, evaluating him in a manner that made his skin crawl. It was the look of an interested woman, something he always adored seeing on a female's face.

But not this one.

He wanted nothing to do with this bitch.

"I've missed you," she repeated, that voice acidly sweet.

"The feeling isn't mutual," he replied flatly.

Her eyebrows rose, some of that sultry glow disappearing into an expression of shock. "What?"

"You heard me. The feeling is not mutual." He folded his arms. She'd fucked with his head. He would never forgive her for that, or for all the memories she'd stolen from him. And he certainly would not forgive her for the pain radiating inside Leela now, the abject terror at being caught again and the realization of what was to come.

Because once she'd realized this net felt too eerily familiar, thus confirming it'd happened before, her mind had entered a panicked swirl of dire expectation.

They're going to make me forget him again.

Forget us.

Forget all that we've just learned. Everything we've just been through together.

He won't remember me at all. I'll lose what little memories I have of Brazil. And I won't be able to help protect Lizzie or baby Aidyn.

I've failed everyone.

I've… I've failed him.

He nearly shifted backward to grab her neck, to comfort her once more, but he couldn't risk the distraction.

We need a plan, he thought. Because Melanythos likely wasn't here alone.

"You're usually quite shocked to see me," she said, taking a step forward, that look of confusion still marring her features. "Sometimes you're even happy about it. You've even kissed me before, something that always kills poor Leela." She canted her head again. "What's different this time? You're not even surprised I'm here."

A spike of hurt drilled at his heart, the comment about

kissing pulling Leela from her thoughts long enough to react to the painful notion of him embracing another woman.

And not just any woman, but her half sister.

Anger soon followed, the emotion seeming to ground Leela in the present and help pull her from the worrying spiral in her mind.

Her thoughts changed from failure to fury.

She wanted to kill her half sister, which wasn't possible since she was a Seraphim, but that didn't stop Leela from fantasizing about it.

So many lies.

So much trickery.

All to control a Seraphim and to keep her from her bonded mate.

Is Dian nearby? Balthazar wondered. *Is he watching to ensure the sanctity of his millennia-old vendetta?*

Because clearly the Seraphim was obsessed with Leela and fed off her pain.

All because she'd denied him a child?

How very un-Seraphim-like of him.

But Balthazar suspected there was a lot more to it than just this one bout of desired revenge. The Seraphim were being controlled by a select few, their society founded on the values of stoicism when, in reality, those in charge absolutely felt something.

An evil dynamic.

With Dian heavily involved.

And sweet Leela being played as a victim.

Perhaps she'd known about the dynamic early on but had chosen a life with Balthazar over her purpose on the council?

Had Nythos replaced her as a pet of some kind? The

sadistic bitch certainly didn't seem all that stoic now as she continued to study him through narrowed eyes.

Stark was the model of unfeeling, at least until recently.

Nythos, however, embodied emotion in every way.

"Are you starting to remember?" Nythos guessed when he didn't immediately reply. She frowned. "No, that's impossible. Unless you…?"

Unless I've bitten her, Balthazar finished for her, aware of what she'd intended to say.

It was a telling statement that indicated Patreel was likely right—if Balthazar finished the bond, he and Leela might be able to unravel everything else.

Nythos took another step forward, placing herself within arm's reach.

"Don't touch me," Balthazar said, his voice holding a lethal edge he rarely used. But he was not about to let this woman in his head again.

His words merely made her smile. "Sweetheart, I will absolutely be touching you. With or without your consent."

The statement sent another wave of liquid fire through his veins, the lack of compliance in this whole situation infuriating him.

Balthazar tolerated many things in life.

Forcing intent on an unwilling person was not one of those things.

Nythos reached for him, causing him to take a step around Leela.

Run, B! she screamed mentally. *Run now! There's more*—

A crack in the air grabbed his attention for a split second as two Seraphim appeared nearby. One of them lifted a hand toward the patrons at the restaurant—all of whom had been listening and watching the events unfold around them with dropped jaws—freezing them in place. Literally.

"Dian is not going to be pleased about this, Melanythos," the male said, his voice emotionless and very Seraphim-like. "These mortals will need to be dealt with."

"I'll wipe their memories," she replied flippantly. "Once I'm done with Balthazar."

His eyebrows rose. "You sound rather confident about something I have no intention of allowing."

She smiled. "You won't have a choice, baby."

Two more Seraphim appeared, bringing the playing field up to five against two.

Well, technically one since Leela couldn't move.

She couldn't seem to speak either, her body frozen beneath whatever spell that net had woven over her. Her mind wept, the sensation reminding her of reformation, where she'd go to die and forget everything she cared about in life.

Including him.

Caro had been able to fight it because of Sethios, her mind rebelling at every turn.

But Leela had only established half of their bond.

Without Balthazar's bite, she would be lost to the madness of reformation. And his own mind would be altered in kind.

Perhaps even worse since Nythos would have to erase all his knowledge of her, too.

Would Vera tell him the truth?

Or would she be hunted next?

Nythos would see all their links, learn about Stark's and Vera's true connections to Osiris.

She'd also hear the truth about Osiris's past.

Would she react to it like Patreel had? Or did she already know?

Every secret in his head would be at risk. Every relationship he'd ever created or craved, potentially destroyed. And his link to Leela would be dismantled once more.

Because what they had wasn't permanent. Not yet.

But it could be.

With a bite.

A way to protect them both. A way to secure this connection. A way to ensure they both remembered.

Maybe she'd bitten him once to establish an anchor, a person she could always come back to for the truth.

Maybe she'd bitten him because they were in love.

Maybe she'd bitten him because she knew he was the one for her.

Maybe she'd bitten him because he'd wanted her to.

Or maybe she'd bitten him to save herself.

Whatever the cause, it no longer mattered.

Because his soul already knew the truth. Her past motivation served the sole purpose of bringing them together today, to this very moment, to this current reality.

For him to make a decision.

To either solidify this connection and cement them together for eternity.

Or to give her up forever.

Because there would be no coming back this time, not with everything they both knew now. A war was coming. It was time to pick a side.

And Balthazar chose Leela.

He chose them.

He chose their future, their world, the existence where they faced her kind as a unit with the full force of Hydria behind them.

He chose *fate*.

His lips curled, giving Nythos pause. For a brief moment, she appeared relieved, as though she'd expected that expression from him the moment she'd appeared.

But this smile wasn't for her.

It was for Leela.

"As it turns out, I do have a choice," he told Nythos, his palm wrapping around Leela's nape as his gaze met hers. "And I choose *this*."

She blinked up at him, the only part of her seeming to be able to move. *You'll be tied to me forever*, she whispered, understanding what he was saying via his choice.

I choose this. I choose us. I choose our bond. Because it was the only way to secure their future.

It was also the only thing that felt *right*.

You'll be tied to me forever echoed through her mind, ensuring he heard it.

She was telling him he might not be able to be intimate with another soul ever again, which was a huge sacrifice for him to make. Her, too, because she liked to play just as much as he did.

But it didn't matter that he'd be tied to her forever because…

"Sweetheart, I already am," he replied, bending to sink his teeth into her neck.

She gasped in response, her mind rioting with surprise and elation.

Then the sweet ambrosia of her blood touched his tongue.

And he swallowed.

CHAPTER 29

LEELA

ELECTRICITY HUMMED THROUGH LEELA'S VEINS, HER HEART hammering rapidly inside her chest.

Her vision blurred as though lost to a dream, reality spiraling into a sea of insanity where time ceased to exist.

She could hear Balthazar's mind, his thoughts, his assurance that this was what he wanted, what they needed, what would save them both.

But it went deeper than that.

He'd bitten her for the memories. For the sensation of rightness. For the realization that they were fated to be together.

They were two halves of the same being.

A pair destined to rule together, their combined sensuality a threat to all of mankind. Or perhaps a gift.

Oh, the fun we'll have, she heard him musing.

Which sent them over the edge into a world of experiences that proved his thought to already be true.

They'd provoked sexual experiences all over the globe, just like last night on the beach.

They were dynamite together, a duo destined to seduce everyone in their path.

But those weren't the memories Leela sought. She wanted the ones defining how they'd first met, to understand why she'd bitten him, to confirm what her heart already knew.

I love him.

Not past tense.

Because her feelings for Balthazar had only deepened throughout the millennia, each meeting further defining the link between their souls.

A sharp slap to her cheek drew her from the mental playground for a moment to see Mel standing before her with a furious expression. Her mouth was moving, but Leela couldn't hear anything she said, choosing instead to fall back into her mind with Balthazar as her guide.

They were connected now, their psyches traversing the same wavelength and intertwining in a way that secured them together for eternity.

She wished they were alone to indulge in the moment in private. However, Mel was already privy to every memory in Leela's mind, so one more wouldn't hurt.

Because Mel no longer mattered.

Only Balthazar.

Only their connection.

Only this warm existence securing their souls together in an irrevocable bond.

Reformation could drown Leela in a sea of nothingness, but that link to Balthazar would always remain. Even if they forced her to forget him, she'd find him and remember all over again.

Not just because of the bond, but because of the power between them.

She could feel him in her mind, dismantling the blocks

with his mind-reading ability, destroying the obstacles to find the memories he craved.

Or maybe that was within his own mind.

She couldn't tell, their psyches so intertwined that everything felt intimately connected.

His frustration was her frustration.

His need was her need.

His determination was her determination.

He wanted to unlock their memories, undo Nythos's tampering, and free them both from this cruel spell. To find a way to stop them from doing it again. To work together to escape their cruelty.

They raped our minds and tampered with destiny, he seethed.

Another slap to her cheek almost drew her out of the connection, but Balthazar yanked her right back into his psyche, their souls melding as they fought an invisible enemy inside their minds.

Blocks.

Curves.

Roads that led to endless spirals and false walls.

Leela was dizzy as she tried to find her way out, to understand the path forward, to decipher truth from fiction.

Her throat worked.

Her heart beat.

Her lungs screamed.

No, *she* screamed.

It hurt. But it was so freeing, so liberating to *feel*.

The net around her burned. She could feel it trapping her in her corporeal form, refusing to allow any ethereal energy to slip from her being.

Wingless.

Emotionless.

Captured.

Darkness crept over her, a cold, hard bed at her back, the soundless, windowless, *soulless* existence surrounding her.

A pod.

Clinical.

Reformation.

Every part of her revolted, begging someone to free her.

But she was trapped, drowning in this cold metal container, her soul forever bound... forever lost...

Except a warmth tugged at her psyche, a familiar masculine presence that yanked her back to an existing state of being, forcing her to feel, to breathe, to *remember*.

This was a memory.

A wicked, dark, nightmarish reality that she'd once endured.

But she wasn't there now.

No, she was still in Buenos Aires, trapped beneath an intrusive net of someone else's energy.

She wanted to claw at the strands. To shout at the Seraphim around them to free her. To demand a real trial.

I was never given one before, she realized, the memory of that fated day coming back to her.

She and Balthazar had been walking through the woods, hand in hand, enjoying the day. He'd intended to fuck her up against a tree. They were always playing. Always laughing. Always *living*.

A tear escaped her eye at the beautiful nature of their existence.

So carefree and *happy*.

Love, she thought, sighing. *We were in love*.

And their souls still were today.

They'd been chasing each other for an eternity, trying

to reach this very moment of matrimony between their spirits, to finally exist as one.

But the Seraphim had stolen everything from her.

Patreel had arrived that day, taking her from Balthazar and directly to Dian.

He'd been furious at her partial bond—something that had just happened only days before whilst making love. Balthazar hadn't returned the bite because they'd still been discovering what it all meant. She'd bitten him because it had felt right. Not for any other reason at all, just a moment of bliss.

Leela had learned the importance of that inclination after being taken into custody.

"You initiated an illegal link," Dian had roared. "With an *abomination*."

She'd stood frozen, ensnared by his magic and confused by his words. The notion of a blood bond had made no sense to her. Because no one had explained the possibility to her.

Seraphim rarely spoke about blood bonds and how they were created. The links were ancient and forbidden because emotions always followed, or were what led them to the arrangement.

And Seraphim were not meant to feel.

Blood bonds also required monogamy, the souls refusing to dance with another, thereby making pregnancy impossible.

Dian could have used her with a partial bond in place, but he'd chosen not to. He'd chosen to subject her to this torment, to erase the events from her mind during reformation.

However, he'd made her watch Balthazar lose his memories first.

Her heart clenched at the remembrance, her breath stilling in her lungs.

Balthazar being forced to forget by having his experiences replaced by visions of Melanythos.

Which had required the two of them to actually meet and her half sister to seduce him—an act Leela had been forced to observe.

A sob caught in her throat at the horrible memory, the pain that had followed, the absolute agony of having her soul shredded before her.

"He'll live a life of debauchery, never finding his true mate and indulging in everyone else except you," Dian had said. "He'll crave touch, sex, carnality, and eroticism, all because of his ties to you and your treacherous sensuality. Thereby defiling your bond every day for the rest of your pathetic existence."

Leela hadn't been able to reply, her body immobilized by the damn net.

The same one I'm wearing now.

Oh, how he'd ensnared her.

So many times over the millennia.

Because she'd kept going back to Balthazar, always finding him, sleeping with him, indulging in a bond neither of them understood.

Just to be caught and sent back to Dian.

Memories erased each and every time.

Reformation occurred twice more in her history, the causes of both tied to Balthazar and her feelings overriding the alterations in her mind. She'd found him too quickly, causing the second round of reformation. And the third, which had taken place only three centuries ago, had been a result of Dian's impatience with her refusing to heel.

He'd been waiting for her to grovel, to go to him and

beg him to copulate. To fulfill the wish of the Fates. To be the mother of his future child.

Now that would never happen. Balthazar's soul was tied to hers, his immortality complete. Dian could never separate them through death.

Her body no longer belonged to the predictions of fate.

Her body belonged to Balthazar, to herself, to their shared destiny of *choice*.

A sharp crack drew her back to reality, ethereal energy sizzling through the air.

Gabe, she thought, catching sight of his red plumes.

A flash of navy wings danced near him, making Leela's heart soar. *Vera*.

They were in the air, battling warrior Seraphim.

Is this a dream? she wondered, blinking up at the magical lines tracking across the bright blue sky. *Where did they come from?*

Patreel, Balthazar answered, startling her. *He arrived with them.*

She searched for the source of that soothing tone and found Balthazar kneeling before her, his brown eyes full of life.

Leela tried to reach for him, but the netting burned, holding her against the chair.

You're in my head, she marveled, loving the way his voice sounded inside her. But something still felt incomplete. Like they were missing a key detail of their bond.

She searched for a cause, the memories fleeting and coming to her in an obscure order that she couldn't fully organize.

Balthazar wrapped his palm around the back of her neck, his lips near hers as he whispered, "Bite me."

Real or a memory? She couldn't say because it reminded her of the night she'd first bitten him. They'd been joined intimately, his mouth an obsession she'd been worshipping with her tongue. He'd been on top of her, slowly penetrating her with his thick arousal and driving her to oblivion.

She'd wanted to bite him.

She'd admitted it out loud.

And he'd given her permission with those two sweet words.

"Bite me," he repeated now, drawing her back to him.

Was she dreaming this? Everything felt so fuzzy, the air sizzling around them with static electricity from the fight above.

Vera and Gabe.

Melanythos.

Warrior Seraphim.

Her head spun, the dizzying sensation threatening to swallow her whole.

She needed her anchor. Her Balthazar. Her reality. Her *choice*.

He guided her lips to his neck, her body held captive by the net. She fought to part her lips, to force her face to move.

It hurt.

It burned.

The nets sank into her skin like razor wire, cutting through the fiber of her being, but Balthazar mattered more.

Love is worth the sacrifice, she thought, the words an echo of something she'd said to Dian long ago. He'd asked her to choose her memories over Balthazar's life.

She'd sacrificed her mind for him.

Leela strove to capture the scene in whole, to remember how she'd been brought to that point, but the manufactured walls in her head blocked her entry.

She clawed at them, trying to dismantle them brick by brick.

And failed.

Too much.

Too hard.

Bite me, Leela, Balthazar echoed into her mind.

She followed his desire, searching for the purpose, and realized the reason less than a second later, having discovered the cause via her own logic.

To hasten the bond, she thought. Her original bite had happened over three thousand years ago. He'd finally returned the sentiment, sealing their bond, but time had deteriorated her initial bite.

Blood bonds never died.

But they could be constantly reinforced through the sharing of blood.

Because everything in her world revolved around the seraphic essence—the soul—and the soul was connected to the corporeal form by *blood*.

The realization sent a fresh surge of determination through her, forcing her to fight through the pain of the net to finish opening her mouth. Tears stung her eyes, the sharp sensation of blades cutting into her skin almost enough to send her spiraling into the land of unconsciousness.

I'm stronger than this, she told herself. *I can defeat this. Them. This fate.*

I choose my own destiny.

I choose Balthazar.

Her teeth met his skin, the net digging into her gums now, slicing her apart inside.

You. She started to clamp down.

Will. The skin began to give beneath her incision.

Not. Balthazar's fingers dug into her neck, lending her his strength to finish it.

Defeat. Agony ripped through her mouth, her face, her entire being, as she finally broke through his skin and the net around her jaw.

Me. Blood touched her tongue, shooting euphoria through her veins and chasing away the sharp pangs around her mouth.

Mine, she thought, sighing as she swallowed. *Balthazar is mine.*

CHAPTER 30

ISSAC

"BALTHAZAR SHOULD HAVE CHECKED IN BY NOW," LUCIAN said, his feet carrying him swiftly over the black sand beach to Issac. "Something's wrong."

Issac glanced at the setting sun and up to where Aya flew around with Gabriel and Vera above. That sense of dread had continued to darken, her mind shifting through thoughts of concern and preparation all at once.

I'm not ready, she kept saying.

None of us are, Issac echoed back at her.

At least the wards were pretty much done now. Vera, Gabriel, Caro, Sethios, and Aya had all worked through the day to prepare, ensuring the outer protective spells were in place.

But Aya felt it wouldn't be enough.

Issac agreed.

Something was coming; even he could feel the ominous presence building with each passing second.

And now Balthazar couldn't be found.

Issac relayed the message up to Aya, telling her that Balthazar had missed his check-in protocol.

She misted down to them in the next second, landing easily beside Issac, her wings tucking up at her back as she turned corporeal for Lucian to see her.

"The wards are done, but they won't be enough." Aya spoke plainly, knowing Lucian would appreciate the directness. "They'll only buy us time to evaluate the attack and determine a strategy."

Lucian nodded. "I'll handle that part once I see what we're up against."

"Seraphim don't die," Aya stressed.

"Perhaps not, but they can be incapacitated," he replied.

"Temporarily."

Lucian studied her for a moment before shifting his focus to Issac. "Balthazar's last known location was Bulgaria. I doubt he's still there, but I'm sending Jacque in to see if he can gather any intel on where B and Leela misted to afterward."

"They likely didn't leave any clues behind since they're trying to hide," Issac pointed out.

"I agree, but it's the only lead we have, and we need him," Lucian replied.

"Have you considered any evacuation protocols?" Sethios asked as he appeared beside them, his tone and expression missing that usual arrogant flair. He felt the threat approaching, too. And, like other Seraphim, he doubted their ability to win the upcoming fight.

"We have protocols in place, but we're not going to need them." Lucian's confident tone made Issac frown.

"How can you be so certain?" he wondered out loud, curious as to what Lucian seemed to know that the rest of them didn't.

"Because I trust the process," he replied vaguely. "But the protocols are in place should our protective measures fail." His attention went to Vera as she materialized beside Sethios. "Balthazar missed his check-in. Something's wrong."

She started to reply when something captured her focus in the sky.

Issac sensed it in the next breath, the subtle shimmer of energy cascading electricity across his skin. Aya's thoughts rivaled his, only she voiced their mutual question out loud. "What is that?"

"A Seraphim's version of a knock," Vera answered, her eyes narrowing. She vanished again, leaving the rest of them staring after her.

He attempted to see whatever visual awaited her in the sky, but he couldn't latch onto her mind or anyone else in the sky.

Which meant whoever was "knocking" had a rune like hers that prevented him from accessing the mind.

His ability to manipulate vision seemed to be hit or miss when it came to Seraphim, the gift still developing. Caro had already explained that Seraphim were naturally immune to Hydraian and Ichorian gifts. Runes were used to block seraphic powers as well, but they had to be constantly rewritten to continue to work.

But Issac suspected it was more than just runes and also involved the establishment of power as a new Seraphim because Sethios remained inaccessible to Issac. A good thing, really. Perhaps even a gift from fate to ensure both men survived their first year together as "family."

Caro joined them on the beach, her blue wings disappearing as she turned corporeal. "Patreel is here," she said. "He's talking to Gabriel and Vera."

"The tracker?" Sethios asked.

She nodded. "The one Vera learned the truth from about Balthazar and Leela."

"What's he saying?" Lucian demanded, his calm facade slipping marginally. Issac could understand the concern, given everything the Hydraian King had just endured with the loss of Aidan. It had left them all on edge, Lucian even more so.

"I don't know. I wasn't close enough to hear." Caro's blue eyes lifted to the sky. "But the lack of energy in the clouds tells me he came alone and he's not here to fight."

They all fell silent as they waited for Vera or Gabriel to return.

Aya shivered again, another wave of that dark energy seeming to swirl around them.

I don't like this, she told Issac. *Something isn't right.*

I know. He attempted to see beyond the island again, but nothing caught his attention. Just the usual minds.

Skye's continued to whirl with visions of the future, her visuals spinning rapidly and changing every few seconds.

Blood.

Aya.

Bright light.

Aya.

Broken feathers.

Aya.

Elizabeth screaming.

Aya.

Issac swallowed, not liking the changing expressions in Aya's eyes. She went from murderous rage to gleeful to loving to furious again. But the worst one was the one with a dead expression, as though she didn't care at all about life or meaning anymore.

He hoped that vision never came to fruition.

Pushing the haunting images from his mind, he searched the rest of the island for anything out of the ordinary. He found nothing other than a sense of preparedness and unwavering determination, the Hydraians ready for battle.

"Balthazar's in Buenos Aires." Vera's voice preceded her appearance, her navy wings disappearing in a flash. "Melanythos found them. Several warrior Seraphim, too. They need us."

Gabriel misted down, his red feathers vanishing as he returned to his corporeal state. "It's a risk," he told her. "We do this, and they'll know our allegiance."

"They'll know as soon as Melanythos attempts to alter their memories again," Lucian interjected, folding his arms. "Balthazar and Leela are worth more than any risk. Take whatever resources you need. Any Hydraians that you think can help. Whatever it takes. We need them here. And we need them here now."

"Your resources won't help us," Gabriel returned, his focus going to Vera. "We go. Leave Sethios, Caro, and Stas here to protect the boundaries. That'll buy us maybe thirty minutes."

Vera nodded. "Looks like that nap I wanted isn't going to happen."

He blinked at her. "You're immortal. Sleep isn't a requirement."

She sighed, long and loud. "Just when I thought Clara might be impacting your sensibilities, you go and say something like *that*." She shook her head.

He studied her for a moment. "You're wasting time." He vanished with the words, causing Vera to mutter a curse.

"Thirty minutes," she echoed, looking at Sethios. "If we're not back by then, assume the worst."

She disappeared before anyone could reply, leaving them all staring at the place she'd just occupied.

"Failure isn't an option," Lucian said into the silence. "I need to go prepare the others. Notify me of—"

"Wakefield," Ezekiel snapped, appearing on the beach in a black cloak of air. "I need you to subdue Skye. She's screaming, 'They're coming!' and I can't make her calm down enough to tell me what we need to know."

Issac shared a look with Lucian and then Aya.

But the latter was short-lived as her green orbs darted up into the sky in the next moment. "Shit," she breathed as a crack sounded through the atmosphere.

Her opal feathers appeared in the next breath as she shot upward into the sky.

"Thirty minutes starts now," Sethios announced, taking off after his daughter.

Caro's expression turned grim, her lips flattening. "Well, fuzz."

CHAPTER 31

BALTHAZAR

ANGELS DANCED IN THE SKY ABOVE, SHOWERING ELECTRIC sparks over the humans below.

A startling sight, one that Balthazar could finally *see*.

And yet it was the female before him that captivated all his attention.

Energy sizzled around her, the net a barrier that separated them physically. But their minds were fully linked, as were their souls.

She'd bitten him through the magical bindings, her pain a scream inside her mind that had quickly morphed into a moan as she swallowed.

Balthazar kept his hand around the back of her neck, absorbing the spasm shooting up his arm—the source of it coming from the ethereal energy ensnaring his vixen.

It burned.

But he endured it for her, his need to be touching her, holding her, surpassing the pain evoked by her binds.

Leela, he breathed, his power fully engaged as he shoved the remaining blocks from their minds, needing to know every detail of their past.

Love.

Life.

Laughter.

Oh, how intertwined they'd once been, his Leela, the female who'd first introduced him to true pleasure. She'd taught him everything he knew. Just as he'd returned the favor.

There'd been a few before her.

Just as she'd indulged before him.

But they hadn't found true chemistry until they'd met each other.

So much passion and heat, a whirlwind romance underlined in a flutter of fate.

They were made for each other, their bodies fitting together so beautifully and perfectly that it was no wonder they kept circumventing the memory manipulation.

Leela's soul belonged to him.

And his soul belonged to her.

The bond had been partially complete only because neither of them had understood the ramifications of her bite. But neither of them would have cared, either.

Because they'd only had eyes for each other, a sensation Balthazar had never thought possible but remembered every second of now.

She'd tempted him so completely that he hadn't wanted to look at another soul.

Until he'd been forced to forget her. Yet their spirits had been connected, his desire to find her overwhelming and intoxicating and driving his actions throughout the millennia.

She's always been meant for me, he marveled, his forehead touching hers. The resulting zing reminded him of the netting, but he ignored it, needing his vixen and the memories inside them both.

They spiraled together through a history of sex and intrigue, their lives constantly crossing as they found each other time and again.

Only to have the memories ripped from their psyches.

Melanythos had screwed with his head. She'd always shown up, confused his understanding of the past, seduced him, and mindfucked him.

His heart ached at the onslaught of stolen experiences, twisted recollections, and harmful deeds that Leela had been forced to watch before having her own memories erased.

Dian had forced her to choose—Balthazar's life or the moments they'd shared.

She'd chosen Balthazar, begging for him to be allowed to live.

Without the bond in place, he could be killed.

But now they were forever linked, their spirits thriving together as one.

War raged around them, the Seraphim battling in the sky while Balthazar clung to Leela, reliving a dozen memories at once.

They'd found each other throughout the centuries, playing and fornicating and often coming close to the truth. But this was the first time they'd actually learned about their history, had actually been able to experience it together, because it was the first time Balthazar had linked to her thoughts.

The rules had been redefined.

The tables turned.

And now their futures would intertwine indefinitely.

Leela could suffer reform, but it wouldn't dismantle her ties to Balthazar.

He could undergo a similar treatment, but his soul would forever be hers.

His lips curled in triumph, the emotions of his youth caressing his heart to deepen how he already felt about Leela.

His sweet Seraphim.

His vivacious vixen.

His daring deviant.

Fuck, he wanted to kiss her. To devour her. To consummate this bond in the truest of manners.

But the damn net held her captive.

The sky opened up with more ethereal energy, Stark's sword a flash of light that caught Balthazar's attention. It clashed against another warrior, the rage a rope of fire lassoing Balthazar's senses and urging his power to come out to play.

Because he could now affect the Seraphim. Sense them. *Feel* them.

Yet his gift stopped short at being able to manipulate their essence.

The protective runes, he realized. Vera remained entirely mute to him, while Stark's mind boasted fragmented thoughts.

How do the protective runes work? he asked Leela. *The ones that block Seraphim from using their powers on each other, I mean.*

Leela hummed something in response, her mind blissed out on memories as she recalled an incident in Scandinavia about three hundred years ago. They'd run into each other on the street, quite literally, and ended up spending a weekend in bed.

That had been the last time Melanythos had altered their minds.

Leela had gone into reformation again soon after, starting the process over entirely.

Balthazar hadn't known, his grasp on reality utterly altered by Nythos's arrival. She'd played him so perfectly, appearing as a ghost from his past and destroying the moment he'd shared with Leela.

A part of him had felt the wrongness of it, something that radiated now within his gut, but he'd been lost to her manipulation.

His link to Leela's psyche this time had thwarted any and all attempts to dismantle his memories.

Not via the blood bond they'd just formed, but per the fact that he now knew her mind.

A fascinating development because it'd always been his inability to hear Leela's thoughts that had drawn him to her each time they'd "met" over the millennia. When what he'd really needed was that mental connection to break their tormented cycle.

Perhaps he'd suspected that on some level, thus prompting him to pursue her.

Or maybe it had just been fate.

Another sharp crack pulled his focus upward to where a Seraphim fell lifelessly through the sky. The bulky mass crashed into one of the tables, causing the mortals to scream as the angel turned corporeal.

Stark wasted no time in the sky, slamming another Seraphim with a similar bolt of light that sent him spiraling downward as well.

However, a hint of concern clouded Stark's aura. There and gone in a flash. Balthazar sought the cause of it, as the warrior seemed to be slaying his brethren with fluid ease.

Distraction, Stark thought. *This… distraction.*

Balthazar frowned and took in the scene again.

Melanythos had Vera wrapped up in a battle of mystical energy while Stark handled the warriors. It'd been four against one, with only two Seraphim left to subdue. One of whom didn't have a sword like the others.

He was the one who initially froze the humans, Balthazar recalled, studying the male's lengthy physique. He appeared more clinical and thoughtful in his approach, creating some kind of rune he clearly intended to release on Stark.

But the warrior Seraphim caught it with his sword, crumbling the energy to dust before volleying a fiery sphere of magic at the male. He dodged it. However, the ball rotated and exploded at his back, ensnaring his pale feathers and sending him soaring toward the earth.

He landed among the mortals he'd originally frozen, their bodies long since freed from whatever mystic hold he'd cast over them.

Many of them were taking pictures and videos rather than running for their lives.

The definition of humanity today, Balthazar thought, disgusted. No one wanted to help. No one wanted to protect others. They were too busy being bystanders through their damn phones to do much else.

Distraction. The word caught Balthazar's attention again, only this time it came from Leela.

He met her alert gaze, her journey down memory lane temporarily subsiding in favor of their current surroundings.

Leek and Kital are missing, she continued, her eyes darting to the three incapacitated Seraphim before flicking upward into the sky. *Something's very wrong, B. These warriors are too young for this mission. Which means the elite members... are somewhere else.*

He glanced upward at Vera and Stark once more and noted the missing Seraphim in the sky.

Patreel's gone. Yet he'd seen the tracker arrive with the other two.

Which could really mean only one thing.

The council knows about Vera and Stark, he said on a low growl. Either Patreel had told them, or they'd found out another way. But the rest was clear. *The council lured Vera and Stark here in order to leave Hydria unprotected.*

Because they were Hydria's primary allies, apart from Leela, who knew how the council and warriors functioned.

Caro knew a bit, but her recent reformation left her out of the loop.

So the council had set up a situation they knew would attract Vera's and Stark's attention—by putting Balthazar's and Leela's lives in jeopardy.

Had Patreel led them here?

Or had they misted right into a trap?

Balthazar shook his head—what was done was done. Stark and Vera were here.

And the warrior Seraphim were likely taking advantage of their absence in Hydria. Right now. At this minute.

Shit, Leela muttered.

Balthazar echoed the sentiment, but he wasn't about to let the setback deter him. His Hydraians needed him, and fuck if he was going to fall into this trap set by the Seraphim.

This was where family mattered.

Where emotions excelled.

He would never give up fighting for those he loved, something these stoic Seraphim assholes were about to learn.

"We need to remove this net," he said to Leela, determination darkening his resolve. "Sorry, sweetheart, but this is going to hurt."

Chapter 32

Stas

A Seraphim with ruby feathers hovered just beyond the wards, his light green eyes and chiseled features similar to Stark's.

"You must be Adriel," Stas guessed, noting his muscular shoulders and thick golden hair. The color wasn't as light blond as Stark's but was a similar enough shade to match the overall resemblance to his son. *Yeah, definitely Stark's dad.*

Be careful, Aya, Issac cautioned, concern radiating through their blood bond.

"And you must be Astasiya," the Seraphim of Warriors responded flatly. "The council would like a word."

"Yes, I've heard," she replied.

"Gabriel was supposed to bring you in for a discussion. I fear his intentions have… changed."

"Hmm, yeah, he's been busy kicking my ass," she answered honestly. "But we'll see what next week looks like on the calendar and get back to you."

His brow furrowed, the only sign that he might

somewhat feel anything. *Confusion*. "You can't ignore a summons, child. Edicts exist for a reason."

"To control all of Seraphim kind," her father answered, appearing beside her. "Yes, I find the whole High Council of Seraph quite fascinating. You sit around in a dome, reiterating the fates you wish to discuss and assigning edicts that everyone just magically obeys. How boring that must be for you."

Adriel blinked at him before returning his focus to Stas. "Your upbringing has been flawed by the influence of abominations. We will correct that for you."

"I bet you will," her father drawled. "Didn't work so well on Caro, though, did it?"

"We can help you understand the purpose of our kind and how we thrive." Adriel continued speaking as though her father hadn't said a word.

"The purpose being to blindly follow council orders without any regard to personal choice or desire," her father interjected again. "I think we'll pass."

While Stas agreed that she wanted nothing to do with these beings, she was also willing to negotiate if it meant allowing Lizzie and Aidyn to live. "If I agreed to go with you to meet the council, would you spare Lizzie and her daughter?"

Adriel stared at her. "The abominations?"

Stas folded her arms, her wings beating softly at her back to keep her aloft. "They're not abominations. They have names. Lizzie and Aidyn."

He blinked again, his expression otherwise giving nothing away. "The abominations cannot live."

"Then I guess I won't be going to see your council."

His head canted a bit to the side, reminding her of a perplexed bird. "You choose them over your own kind?"

"I choose my family over a council that kills without

mercy or just cause," she returned, arching a brow. "If they're willing to negotiate, I'd be willing to meet with them." She let that sentence hang between them for him to consider, but his green eyes stared blankly at her.

A beat passed.

Followed by another.

And a third.

When he finally said, "If you will not come willingly, then we will escort you after we finish our task here." He lifted a hand up, causing six more Seraphim to appear in the clouds. "Unless you wish to hand over the abominations now? Then we will leave the island with them, and you, to return to the council. They would live in that situation. At least until we finish studying them."

"Subject my best friend and her daughter to experimentation and eventual death, and meet with the council that mandated it," she reiterated, her voice sarcastically thoughtful.

Something that was clearly lost on Adriel because he replied, "Yes."

"Hmm," she hummed, tilting her head. "Yeah, I think I'll pass."

"Then you subject this island to a consequence of destruction," Adriel replied.

"On what grounds?" her mother interjected, appearing on her opposite side.

Her presence gave Adriel momentary pause, his green eyes flickering with an emotion that disappeared in a flash. "Caro."

"Adriel."

Stas's father snorted. "What a touching reunion."

"Has the council mandated extermination of the abominations?" her mother pressed, her focus on Adriel.

"We are here for the lab-created Seraphim and the

illegitimate child," he replied. "We will exterminate all those who stand in our way."

"Including me?" her mother asked.

"You will return to reform."

"That's not happening," her father said, his tone ice cold. "*Ever.*"

"Her programming is flawed," Adriel replied, finally addressing her father. "As is yours."

"So you want to put me in a box, too?" Her father grunted. "My father recently forced me to drown myself in a block of cement. So, to echo my daughter, I think I'm going to *pass* on your claustrophobic opportunity. Thanks, anyway, though."

Adriel glanced at Stas. "Your fate can be saved if you allow the council to help guide you. You're a child in our eyes. Your sins are not your own."

"My fate is directly tied to a destruction prophecy," Stas deadpanned. "I think I'll take my chances with those I love."

"Love," Adriel repeated, his eyebrows lifting. "That's impractical."

She studied him. "Love is far more powerful than any of you realize."

"Adriel," her mother interjected again. "There's so much you don't understand here. So much you don't *know.*"

"You dare speak such things to an elder?" he asked, his tone not exactly offended but borderline shocked.

Emotion, Stas thought. *Adriel shows signs of emotion.*

He was Osiris's first candidate for reformation, Issac replied. *Perhaps this is why.*

"Osiris—"

"We are done with this conversation, Caro," Adriel replied. "You will be sent back to reformation and joined by your mate and daughter. Gabriel will go as well, since we now have proof of his intentions. He's betrayed us. And I have no doubt you are the cause of that betrayal."

He pulled out his sword, the six behind him following suit.

"Last chance to come willingly," he threatened.

"Is that what my father said when he invited you into the reformation chamber?" her father asked conversationally.

Adriel's brow furrowed. "I've not undergone reformation."

"Osiris—"

"Sir, they're wasting time," one of the warrior Seraphim interjected. "We need to strike now before Gabriel returns."

Stas frowned. *They know Stark isn't here.*

How? Issac asked. *Can they sense it?*

No. They know he left and will be back. A sense of unease trickled through her veins, causing a shiver to traverse her spine. *They must have set up a distraction.*

With Balthazar and Leela as bait, Issac translated. *Shit.*

Tell Luc.

Already on it, he replied.

That meant Patreel must have betrayed them, but he wasn't here now. She only vaguely recognized the angel who had spoken. He was either Leek or Kital. Both males were present now. She recognized them from Iceland, but not which name went with which appearance.

The other tracker was here as well. *Arvane.*

But not Patreel.

We have at least three warrior Seraphim, one of which is the eldest and strongest, and a tracker. The other three are unknown, but all have swords. So I'm guessing they're warriors or something similar.

Conveying details to Lucian, Issac replied.

Adriel doesn't seem to know about his own reform, and the warrior beside him isn't letting him ask. Her mother had tried to explain twice while Stas had been talking to Isaac. But the warrior had kept interrupting, stating they were stalling.

The blankness in Adriel's features suggested he agreed with the warrior beside him.

It's something we should use, Issac murmured, the words sounding more like Luc's than his, but perhaps he was conveying the sentiment.

I don't think he's in a listening mood, Stas said as Adriel's sword slammed into one of the wards.

Energy sizzled through the air, reminding her of a lightning bolt as the magic behind the marking crumbled to dust.

Uh, incoming... she whispered as the others started slamming their swords into the wards before them. "Shit."

She ducked down to the second security layer, her parents following suit.

"We're not going to last thirty minutes," her father said.

No, we'll be lucky to last five, Stas thought as the Seraphim finished smashing through their first line of defense.

"He brought the three highest members of his line after Gabriel," Stas's mother replied. "A tracker, a telepath, and a cryptographer."

"A cryptographer?" Stas repeated. "Like, someone who specializes in patterns?"

"In this case, they specialize in runes," her mom replied grimly. "They knew about the wards."

"Patreel?" Stas's father guessed.

"Or they've always known," her mother said, flinching as the Seraphim began on the second line of defense. "We need to go to the ground."

What's happening, love? Issac asked.

Stas updated him on their descent, landing beside him as she finished.

Luc stood among them, his gaze on the sky. Alik was beside him with a horde of Hydraians around them, most of them Guardians, some of them stronger immortals with defensive abilities.

"Adriel is the key," Luc announced without preamble. "We need him to understand reformation and what we know. He's the leader; therefore, his confusion will trickle into the others."

"Leek wouldn't let me finish," her mother said, referring to the dark-haired warrior who'd kept interrupting her.

"Does he know the truth?" Luc asked.

"It's impossible to say, but he easily convinced Adriel that we're trying to stall," she replied. "It's a practical strategy, so I can see why he jumped to that conclusion."

"Or it was a clever ruse to keep you from telling Adriel the truth," Stas's father murmured, his focus on the sky. "We need a new strategy."

"Our strategy is convincing Adriel of the truth," Luc reiterated.

"How do you propose we do that?" Issac's tone held a note of seriousness to it, not ridicule, his curiosity genuine. His mind echoed the sentiment, agreeing with Luc's idea but wanting to know how to achieve it.

"We need Osiris," Luc said, silencing everyone. "Without Vera's memory manipulation talent and Stark's ability to potentially appeal to Adriel's paternal instincts—if he even has any at all—we're out of options. Osiris is the only one who can convince him of the truth."

"There has to be a better way," her father immediately argued. "Besides, it's not like we can just call up my father.

He's spent a lifetime appearing on his own terms, not on anyone else's."

"Mateo can call him," Luc pointed out.

"Do it," Issac interjected before Stas's father could speak.

"Have you lost your fucking mind?" her father demanded, obviously not on board with the idea. Stas wasn't sure she agreed with it either.

Her mother reached for him as he attempted to step into Issac's space. "Sethios—"

"I may not like the plan, or the fact that we're about to rely on the very person we've been trying to hide our ties from for hundreds of years, but we need his expertise," Issac said, meeting her father's lethal glare with an icy look of his own. "He isn't going to want to lose his Hydraian assets to a handful of Seraphim in the sky. He'll help us."

"At what cost?" her father asked. "An agreement from Stas to work with him?"

"If that's what it'll take to keep everyone safe, I'll pay that price," Stas inserted before Issac could speak for her. Not that he would, but he knew her mind and her determination. He would know her intention before she even voiced it, and the look he gave her proved it.

"We don't have time to keep debating this," she continued. "Luc, try Osiris. Until then, we need a secondary plan on how to convince Adriel of the truth." Because she agreed that was their best plan. If they could convince him of his history, he might falter enough to cause the other Seraphim to pause with him.

Of course, Patreel had faltered.

And now he was nowhere to be seen after clearly having lured Vera and Stark into a trap.

Unless he'd been somehow persuaded to do it.

Osiris's familial line could compel because of the

control over resurrection and life, but was there another bloodline that could do the same?

A question she'd have to voice *after* they dealt with the chaos in the sky.

"Blake," her mother said suddenly.

"What?" several of them voiced at once, including Stas.

"Yes," Luc replied with a nod. "His present condition may be enough to pique their curiosity."

Her mother nodded. "I will mist and grab him." She disappeared, leaving Stas's father to frown in her wake. He didn't speak out loud, suggesting he was speaking to her mother via their bond.

Which didn't exactly help Stas understand the point. "Why Blake?"

"Because he's a human who has undergone a version of reformation, something that proves Osiris at least has a working knowledge of the process. The impractical use of applying such a thing to a human may be the distraction we need to keep the Seraphim at bay."

"And if it isn't?" Issac pressed as another surge of power thundered through the air.

Only one barrier left, Stas thought grimly.

"Then we hope our fight lasts long enough for Osiris or the others to arrive," Luc replied, holding his hand out to Jacque. "Teleport me to Mateo. We have a plan to discuss. This is your show now, Alik."

The telepath smiled. "About fucking time."

"Where are Jay and Lizzie?" Stas asked.

"Safe," Alik answered vaguely, his focus above. "All right, here's what we're going to do." He began issuing orders to the Hydraians, causing them to jump into action with an efficiency that said they'd prepared for a moment like this for the last few centuries.

Except they had anticipated fighting Ichorians.

Not Seraphim.

Something that became evident almost immediately as the angels reached the beach. They appeared almost bored, their swords having been put away in a show of arrogance that made Stas's insides twist.

"Last chance to comply, child," Adriel said, his gaze on Stas.

Shit. They were not going to have time for a distraction. Because even if her mother was able to bring Blake up for a chat, these Seraphim were in the mood to kill. Stas could sense it in their stances, see the need for blood in their eyes.

They despised abominations.

They were here to mercilessly kill those they felt weren't meant for this world.

Which left them only one choice.

We fight.

We fight, Issac echoed. *Always.*

Always, she agreed, her lips curling at the confidence in his tone and the way the word worked as a caress to her senses.

"I choose life," she admitted honestly. "I choose love. I choose family."

She started drawing a rune that Gabriel had taught her, aware that it would do hardly anything to a being of Adriel's power. But it served as a message.

I will not bend.

She threw the ward.

Adriel deflected it.

And the battle began.

Chapter 33

Leela

A tug at Leela's consciousness made her wince. It was directly tied to the rune on her lower back, the fealty bond alerting her to Stas's discomfort.

She conveyed the sensation to Balthazar, telling him what it meant.

They were right about this being a distraction, a way to lure Vera and Gabe away from Hydria.

They'll hold the island, Balthazar assured her.

Your Hydraians are not prepared to fight Seraphim.

We're more capable than you realize.

They're fighting an invisible enemy that uses ethereal power in battle, not standard weapons, she pointed out.

They'll find a way. His confidence helped counter her apprehension, but that niggling sensation crawling along her lower back continued.

He yanked apart a strand of the net along her throat, drawing a hiss from her lips.

You know, I've always been a fan of bondage, he said conversationally. *But this takes it to a whole new level.*

Only a sadist would enjoy this level of torment in the bedroom, she gritted out, flinching as he broke another cord wrapped around her shoulder. *Sethios would love this.*

Balthazar grunted. *I can think of a few Hydraians that would as well.*

Alik? she guessed.

In a past life, Balthazar replied, sounding sad. *With Jenika.*

Leela recalled the blonde female. *We met once.* She remembered a party and the female dancing with fire licking along her fingertips. *What happened to her?*

Lucinda killed her, he replied, his tone sour. *On Osiris's order.*

Leela frowned. *That seems counterintuitive to his goal to kill one as powerful as Jenika.* She could recall how easily she'd manipulated the flames, causing them to trail along in her wake as she moved down the beach.

Balthazar fell silent, but his mind confirmed that he agreed.

He continued pulling apart the ethereal bands, the pain an echo in his mind. But he endured it for her, his resolve to free her his number one priority and thought.

The final rope around her neck fell, leaving her head completely free.

Balthazar wasted no time, his lips finding hers in a passionate kiss as he continued to move his hands over her body. They were in the middle of chaos with angels dancing above, humans screaming below, her body bound by fiery strands, yet she'd never desired a kiss more in her entire life.

She needed him.

Them.

Their bond.

Everything they had to offer, their bodies aching for

each other as their souls frolicked on a plane neither of them could see, just feel.

His tongue met hers, his kiss powerful and potent and intoxicatingly perfect.

She no longer felt the fire burning around her, the net having dissolved into the background of her thoughts as she indulged in this necessary embrace.

Balthazar's focus remained resolute, his fingers brushing her skin as he continued breaking the ensnaring material.

Until finally she was free and able to launch herself at him.

She wrapped her arms around his neck, her body melting into his strength, the sensation of *home* hitting her senses and overwhelming her entirely.

Mine, she breathed, losing herself for just a moment. *You're mine.*

He grinned against her mouth. *Mmm, I think I like the sound of that.*

Do you? she wondered honestly. *Because I know how you feel about monogamy.* She'd often felt the same. But Balthazar was different. He made her want for nothing. When she was with him, he fulfilled her every desire. No one else compared.

I've not favored monogamy because my soul was never satisfied with anyone else, he whispered back to her, his eyes opening to capture her gaze as he caught her face between his palms. "I've been waiting for you."

To complete our bond, she realized.

He nodded, his palm slipping to the back of her neck to hold her to him as he pressed his palm to her heart. "You're mine, too."

His lips claimed hers before she could reply.

Not that she had much to say.

They were finally complete, two souls married in a ceremony that surpassed time and space.

With hell dancing above them and around them.

Mel had taken this from her. Dian, too. They'd subjected her to three thousand years of loneliness, experimentation, and unending *reformation*.

No wonder she'd felt so strongly throughout her life. She'd been fighting a punishment she didn't deserve. Seeking the love of her life. Her heart. The other half of her soul.

All those lovers meant nothing to her now. Only Balthazar. Only the feelings and sensations he could awaken. And she knew he felt the same.

Those previous encounters paled in comparison to this. To their love. Their *destiny*.

Yet it'd been hidden from her.

By her very own flesh and blood.

Her focus shifted upward to where the bitch battled in the sky with Vera, the two of them radiating power as they fought with their abilities more than anything else.

They would have used a rune to dismantle the blocks against one another.

Then dove into each other's minds in an attempt to ruin the other.

Leela narrowed her gaze. She was sex personified with her fertility and sensuality lines, creating the perfect Aphrodite—a goddess Mel had attempted to embody regularly in the olden times.

But Leela was the true goddess of beauty and love and all things sex. Which meant her psychic abilities weren't all that powerful in battle.

However, she'd taught herself a few tricks.

And she could throw a mean left hook.

The final warrior fell beneath Gabe's sword, the head landing on a table.

Leela didn't even hear the screams, her focus entirely on Mel.

Gabe was already headed toward her to handle her in his own way, causing Leela to react on instinct. She misted up to Vera's side, leaving Balthazar to observe from below, and punched Mel right in the fucking face.

"You *bitch*," she seethed, grabbing her by the hair and yanking so hard that she pulled several strands out. Then she hit her again before creating her own rune to wrap the female in a strand of fiery embers.

It sent her spiraling down to the earth in corporeal form, where she landed on her head in the middle of the street with a satisfying *crunch*.

Blood splattered everywhere.

Her body broken.

It would heal itself back together in a few minutes.

Or not, Leela thought as Gabe appeared beside Mel and severed her neck. *Okay, a few days, then.*

She wouldn't heal like the warriors. They possessed regenerating powers that expedited the process. Some Seraphim could take up to a month to heal from a beheading. Her half sister would probably be more like a few days. Maybe even a week.

Perhaps the humans would put her in the ground by then.

That would trap Mel indefinitely.

A thought that very much appealed to Leela in her current state.

Actually... She swooped down to pick up the remains and misted out to the ocean, about a hundred miles offshore, and dropped her head.

Then she went in the opposite direction another hundred miles to deposit the body.

That would slow her down quite a bit.

Especially if her body or head ended up sinking to the bottom or being eaten by a sea creature.

"Good luck healing from *that*," she said, aware her sister's soul would be nearby. Of course, she couldn't hear her. The spirits didn't lurk in the plane of existence like a ghost so much as disappear to another state temporarily before attempting to piece their corporeal form back together.

Satisfied, Leela returned to Balthazar, Gabe, and Vera. They were taking in the humans with grim expressions, phones snapping photos and videos everywhere.

"There isn't time, Vera," Gabe said. "Their memories will just have to remain."

Balthazar appeared grim. "The videos have already made it online. Even if you altered their minds…" He trailed off, the rest mutually understood.

"Too many have seen it now," Leela voiced out loud.

"This has happened before and been contained," Vera started, her eyes taking on a haunted gleam.

"Not like this," Balthazar replied. "The technology age allows news to spread instantly all around the world."

"They'll come up with some sort of excuse for it," Gabe pressed. "We don't have time to worry about them. The wards have fallen in Hydria. I can *feel* the battle energy in my veins."

"This was a distraction," Vera said, her expression darkening. "My memory manipulation on Leek was too hasty because of his warrior genetics healing him faster than I could work. From what Melanythos told me in the sky, Leek knew something wasn't right and went to the council. They restored his memories and now know our true allegiance."

Gabe fell silent for a moment before nodding. "Then we have nothing to hide."

"Agreed." Vera didn't sound surprised or saddened by it, just accepting.

"We need to go." A hint of urgency underlined Gabe's tone, his pale green irises flickering with concern.

He'd bonded Clara, which meant she'd just said something to him.

Leela almost asked, but a shimmer of dread danced along her spine, the fealty rune throbbing with power and *agony*. *Something is very wrong*.

"We need to go right now," Gabe reiterated, disappearing.

Vera followed without a word.

Gasps echoed through the crowd, causing Balthazar to noticeably flinch. He could hear all their thoughts and feel the confusion radiating from their auras.

Leela wrapped her arms around him. "I have you," she whispered into his ear, engaging her misting ability.

She took them straight to Hydria, landing on the beach beneath the moon.

But it wasn't romantic or sweet.

It was nightmarish and cruel.

With the acrid stench of burnt flesh littering the air.

Soft moans.

Weeping.

A dark sense of power.

And utter devastation.

Hydria…

Hydria resembled *death*.

Chapter 34

Stas

A Half Hour Earlier

Seven against a hundred weren't fair odds.

However, the Seraphim were completely immune to Hydraian gifts.

And invisible in their ethereal states.

The only ones capable of even seeing them were Stas, Issac, and her father.

Her mother hadn't returned yet.

But Eliza had arrived with Amelia, Tom, Tristan, and Nadia.

A whoosh of sound echoed through the beach, Tristan's gaze focused on the Seraphim as they formed a protective V shape with Adriel at the head.

He took a step forward, and the earth thundered in protest, the vibration giving his steps away.

"Brilliant," Issac said, grinning as a second reverberation gave away Leek's position.

How is Tristan doing that? she wondered. He shouldn't be

399

able to… Her eyes widened. *You're showing him where the Seraphim are.*

I'm showing everyone where the Seraphim are, Issac corrected. *Tristan is just amplifying the visual with sound.*

A team of Hydraians sprang forward on Alik's orders, firing guns and throwing knives at the Seraphim.

But the weapons went right through their ethereal forms.

Then Leek sent a rune back at the Hydraians—a rune her father caught and redirected at the ocean. An inferno blasted over the waves, the ethereal energy some sort of grenade-like bomb.

The warrior Seraphim fired several more, two of which she managed to catch and toss away like her father had. But the third struck the Hydraian forces, stirring up a fire that left several of them screaming.

The flames died in the next breath, one of the Hydraians using a gift for controlling water to smother the inferno.

But more wards came, too fast for Stas to catch them all. Sethios tried as well, the two of them the only ones capable of flying fast enough to counter the ethereal firepower.

She suddenly had a new appreciation for Stark's games in the air.

And he really had gone easy on her.

Fuck.

The V formation fractured, Adriel shooting up into the sky with Arvane and Kital on either side of him, leaving Leek to lead the raid on the beach.

"I've got Adriel," her father announced. "Caro will find me once she finishes rousing Blake."

Rousing Blake? Stas thought.

But she didn't have a minute to ask what that meant

because Leek had fired off a series of those grenade-like wards again.

Stas soared through the air, catching the majority and throwing them into the ocean. A few escaped her, causing another fiery explosion, but the Hydraians handled the aftermath.

We need a way to bring them down, Stas gritted out as she continued playing a game of interference. *The Hydraian gifts are useless against them.*

Fire would work on them if they were corporeal, Issac replied.

How do we make them—

A net came soaring toward her, the strands humming with power. She ducked, the edge of the ethereal fabric stroking her wing and drawing a gasp from her throat.

Stark had never shown her *that* trick.

And the scream of a Hydraian on the beach told her it worked on everything that moved, not just a Seraphim in an angelic state.

I'll handle it, Issac said as Stas began to turn toward the poor immortal trapped beneath the energy. It probably resembled an invisible fire to him.

London, Stas recalled, the Hydraian only a few hundred years old with the ability to control air. *Can you show him the strands?*

Already working on it, love, Issac replied, his mental voice exhausted. *Focus on the orbs.*

Stas glanced back at Leek, noting the incoming firepower, and leapt for the sky again to catch his spheres.

Only, these were different.

They didn't wait to explode, they fired the second she touched one, slamming her into the ground. She misted to the ocean before another could touch her, Issac's concerned shout in her mind.

I'm okay, she wheezed, the impact of the initial orb having set her body on fire.

But the water cooled her immediately, dispelling the burn as her immortality kicked into overdrive to heal her.

Stark went way too easy on me, she muttered to herself, attempting to ruffle out her feathers as another glowing ball sailed toward her.

Her eyes widened, and she misted just in time for it to miss.

Leek flew above her, his expression bored. "You should have taken Adriel's offer." A flat statement, followed by another energy net that she barely escaped.

At least he was focused on her and not the Hydraians on the beach. That left three for them to handle via Issac's visual assistance, and one very skilled warrior for her to play a game of hide-and-seek with.

She misted above him into the clouds. Then disappeared to reappear at his right.

Where an orb was already waiting for her.

It hit her square in the abdomen, sending her crashing into the ocean on a gasp of pain. The energy ball morphed into a boulder, shoving her down to the sand below the surface and trapping her beneath the water.

On her back.

Her heart fluttered, nightmares crashing through her mind of being chained beneath the waves.

Screaming in agony.

Dying over and over again.

Unable to escape.

To move.

To *breathe*.

Issac's voice reverberated through her mind, but she couldn't hear him over the rush of water in her ears. She clamped her jaw shut, not wanting to inhale.

But she couldn't mist.

She couldn't *move*.

The magic held her captive, reminding her of being buried beneath the earth.

Oh God…

She shoved with all her strength, unable to move.

Screams sounded in her head. Maybe her own. Maybe Issac's. Maybe Hydraians' from the beach. *Maybe Lizzie's.*

Stas gritted her teeth. *I am not dying here. I am not being subdued this easily. I do not accept this bullshit!*

But the boulder wouldn't fucking move! It resembled chains now, wrapping around her, holding her beneath the water, ensuring she'd drown… just like her mother… just like the nightmares… just like the fate she'd always truly feared.

Her arms shook.

Her legs ceased to work.

Her lungs burned.

Her eyes stung.

No, no, no!

Think!

There had to be a way out of this. A way to counter the ethereal energy.

The fact that it held her captive meant she wasn't truly below sea level yet… right? Seraphim couldn't mist while under the ground.

Except… didn't Stark draw a rune in Osiris's dungeon?

Which meant she could draw one, too. *Maybe.*

She released the boulder of chain-like energy and closed her eyes, focusing on the magic around her, trying to sense a way to counter the enchantment.

Stark had shown her several wards these last few days, most of them defensive in manner. He'd stated there wasn't time for her to learn offensive runes. She needed to know how to defend herself first and foremost.

Hence the lessons on catching and throwing magical balls around.

But she couldn't catch this one.

It'd already hit her.

Now what? Stark's voice echoed in her head, reminding her of when he'd trapped her on a sparring mat during her Sentinel training.

She'd been furious. He'd been such an ass. But now that lesson possessed new meaning.

Move the obstacle. Move me, he'd said.

She'd flipped him off her then.

But she couldn't apply that to the boulder.

However, she could try to make it explode.

Focus, focus, focus, she told herself as her insides begged her to inhale.

Issac's voice was in her head again, his frantic tone grabbing her mind.

Help the others, she told him.

Aya…

I'll figure this out, she promised. *Just… just help the others.*

Fuck, she needed to breathe.

She'd been under too long.

She was going to drown.

To die.

But I'll come back, she thought deliriously. *I'll come back… and I'll have another two or three minutes…*

She'd done this before. She could do it again.

Only, this time, she knew what was happening, she knew she could escape, knew there was a way *out*.

The nightmares threatened her mind again, taking her under, deep into the waves, into the blackness of the sea, to a deteriorated form… her mother dying endlessly… over and over again…

Stas shivered, the coolness of the water drowning her lungs and burning her inside.

She welcomed the pain. It made her feel alive despite the truth of it.

I'll be right back, she told Issac. *Just keep fighting.*

His anger lashed at her senses, following her to the depths of death.

And renewing her with a vengeance as she came awake again.

Aya! he shouted.

Her lips parted, her instinct to inhale hitting her hard in the chest. But she swallowed it, whispered to Issac that she was back, and began thinking through the runes Stark had taught her.

Issac threatened to come to her, to pull her out himself.

Don't, she said. *You're the only one who can help those on the beach.*

It's a fucking slaughter, Aya, he growled, his frustration and fear palpable.

I'm coming, she promised.

But her mouth made her inhale again, taking in more water, and sending her to the darkness once again.

She returned, her mind more focused than ever as she started weaving ethereal energy above the surface, only five or six feet above her head.

Not underground.

I can still see the moon.

I can do this.

But there wasn't enough time. Two minutes came and went, dragging her under, drowning her… burning her lungs.

She returned with a fury, cursing Leek and his fucking boulder. *I'm going to destroy it. Then I'm going to destroy you.*

Except a piercing scream rent the air above, loud enough to reach her beneath the waves.

Hydraians were dying.

The island was losing the battle.

It only took seven, she thought numbly. *Fuck, fuck, fuck!*

She started clawing at the energy, whirling it as fast as she could, sharpening it into one of those fucking grenades, her mind recalling the magic she'd caught over and over again.

Two minutes passed.

Down she went.

Back with a renewed purpose.

Issac's panic continued to filter through her thoughts.

I can't die, she kept reminding him. *Neither can you.*

And she would conquer this.

Almost there.

Triumph hummed in her veins, the ward complete. Now she just needed to coax it toward her. It took focus, restraint, tapping into a power she didn't fully understand as she pulled the strand beneath the waves.

Too late, she thought numbly, her mouth opening again.

Drowning. Drowning. Drowning.

Darkness.

Floating. Floating. Floating.

Hmm? she thought groggily, opening her eyes and mouth to the fresh air above. She sputtered and coughed, realizing her ward had worked, the explosion having occurred while she'd been unconscious.

Yes. She sprung up into the night, her lips parting at the sight of flames crawling along the beach, illuminating the dark blood stained into the black sand. *Issac!*

She bolted forward, misting to where she'd last seen him.

It was a fucking massacre of bodies. Some were fully dead. Some were incapacitated, but in a way that they would heal.

Just like when the Sentinels had stormed the reception after Lizzie and Jayson's wedding.

Lizzie, she thought, her mind reeling. How much time had she lost in the waves? Enough for the Seraphim to have moved inward.

We're holding them, Issac told her, his voice strained. *Barely. But we're holding.*

Where are you? But the answer came to her within a second of asking, a spark flying in the sky as London used his ability to manipulate air to create some sort of whirling shield against the wards.

They're invisible but need a steady stream of airflow to hit us, Issac explained.

Water joined London's air wall, creating an elemental shield of sorts that seemed to be deflecting the Seraphim for now.

It wouldn't last.

They'd find a way around it soon.

Stas started toward them, her mind working in overdrive as she tried to think of an alternative, some way to take them down.

She didn't have a sword.

Her own knowledge of wards clearly wasn't a match.

Leek had subdued her far too easily when he'd put his mind to it and would no doubt do it again. But he was nowhere to be seen. Only two Seraphim appeared to be battling the Hydraians.

Where's Leek? Did he go inland with one of the others? There'd been four on the beach, with the other three having gone to the sky with her father on their tail.

Ezekiel and Eliza drew them down toward the tree line somehow. Something Skye said, a message Ezekiel relayed. I didn't catch it all.

She started to nod, but the Seraphim threw another spiral of energy at the shield, creating a resounding crash that had several Hydraians jumping back.

Their runes were growing stronger.

There has to be a way—

A sharp scream hit her mind again. No. Not her mind. Her *ears*.

She glanced upward, searching for the source. It'd been the same one she'd heard underwater.

Lizzie, she realized. *It's Lizzie.*

Issac—

Go! he told her before she could finish. *I'm fine.*

Stas bolted into the air, misting toward her best friend and the chaos surrounding Luc's home.

Bodies littered the ground.

Including her father and Blake… motionless… dead.

She fell to the field beside them, her eyes rounding at the sight of her father's lifeless stare. "Dad?" she whispered, memories assaulting her of losing him so many years ago.

But he'd lived.

He hadn't died that day. He'd just been taken. She'd *saved* him.

He's a Seraphim. Immortal. He'll come back.

Blake… Blake wouldn't. He was still human. A mortal. His chest completely carved out from the blade of a Seraphim.

Another shriek bit into the air, drawing her focus to her mother… on her knees… a blade at her throat.

Kital held the hilt of the dagger.

Adriel spoke without emotion, his words lost to the wind. Or perhaps just not computing in Stas's mind. Because he held a sword at her best friend's neck. Jayson was on the ground beside her, not breathing.

Not beheaded. Not dead, she thought automatically, her mental voice taking on a strange sort of assessing tone. Stoic in nature. Practical. *Seraphic*.

Aidyn was in Lizzie's arms, clinging to her mother's red hair with tiny little fists.

Both were shaking.

Both were terrified.

Still, Adriel spoke.

Stas couldn't hear him, could only see that blade at Lizzie's creamy throat.

The metal began to move.

Lifting.

Arcing.

Forming an angle that could only mean one thing.

"If that is your choice," Adriel said, his words finally piercing Stas's mind. "Then I'll deliver your fate."

Stas blinked.

Her lips parted.

The sword began to slice through the air.

And a scream escaped Stas's throat. So loud. So commanding. So… *furious*.

These Seraphim had attacked her family. Her loved ones. And this Seraphim of Warriors had the fucking audacity to try to *behead* her best friend *in front of her?*

Power rippled through her veins, unleashing into the wind as she reached for Adriel as though she intended to strangle him.

But he was too far away for her to reach.

Too close to her best friend.

With that fucking sword in the air.

409

About to behead a woman *holding a baby*.

"Stop!" Stas shouted, her voice more commanding than she'd ever heard it. Loud. Reverberating through the earth, heightening the energy sprouting from her fingertips, and singeing the air around them.

She bellowed, screaming to the heavens, demanding retribution for the injustice of it all.

They'd attacked the Hydraians.

Drowned her.

Incapacitated her father. Jayson.

Had her mother at knifepoint.

Had killed Blake.

Grace and Ash, her mind added, taking in their headless forms. *Dead.*

More anger flourished inside her, pouring out through her fingertips in the form of electric arcs that hit Adriel, Kital, and Arvane directly in the chest.

Then they went to the ground, kneeling as she unleashed more. So. Much. More.

They will not hurt anyone else.

They will not take Lizzie.

They will not take Aidyn.

Issac's mental voice radiated concern in her mind again, asking what she was doing, but she couldn't answer. She was *raging*.

These monsters had attacked her family.

They wanted her compliance? Fuck. That.

They could feel the wrath of her noncompliance instead.

Another bellow built in her throat, vibrating the air as more power spiked and left her fingertips, causing the ground to shake beneath her fury.

Hatred unlike anything she'd ever experienced set her veins on fire as images of the beach flashed in her head, the blood, the lives lost, the gruesome battle in this field before Luc's home. She didn't even know if he was still alive. Had Jacque teleported him out in time? Mateo? What about the other Guardians?

The only heads she'd seen belonged to Grace and Ash, but there had to be others. Jay had an entire guard, as did Luc. Were they all dead? Or just incapacitated? Would they wake again?

Tears streamed down her face, the sense of failure hitting her square in the gut and stirring more energy.

Heat.

Lava.

Electricity.

Her nails hurt, the rocky ground below biting into her skin, but she ignored it, her pain and anguish and anger flooding the atmosphere.

Those fucking Seraphim needed to *feel*, to *understand*. They were tools. Weapons. Meaningless shells without emotion. They didn't comprehend the meaning of life. They didn't comprehend the meaning of family. They didn't comprehend the meaning of *love*.

She shoved it at them, forcing them to experience every ounce of existence, demanding they *comply* with the purpose of *living*.

Why exist without emotion?

Why exist without relationships?

Why exist without *feeling*?

Her heart broke at their futile existence, her soul screaming at the injustice done to them.

Everyone around her wept, too.

Lizzie. Aidyn. Stas's mom.

She felt their sorrow and channeled it into the web of existence she'd woven around the island.

Why live? Why exist? Why breathe at all?

These beings were cruel. They lacked purpose. They lived a life for nothing at all.

But she would make them *feel*.

She would force them to comprehend the point of existence.

She would coerce their souls into experiencing sensation, into *existing*.

You. Will. Feel. Pain.

The pain of her loss. Of Issac's loss. Of Luc's loss. Of general loss. Of the potential loss of more lives, friends, loved ones, beings who *mattered*.

Electricity hummed around her, drawing the hairs up along her arms and legs. She was no longer cold. No longer wet from the waves. No longer a corporeal being at all.

But a Seraphim of great power.

An ethereal essence that demanded these angels *bow* to a new purpose.

Sensation.

Life.

Feeling.

Emotion.

Fire lashed at her being, pouring through her veins in an invisible stroke of power that traveled down her arms into the earth once more. She was a spirit possessed by grief and anger and determination.

Tears clouded her vision.

The night caressed her senses.

Everything was beauty personified, the souls dancing around her at her command, bowing beneath her energy.

The intensity *hurt*.

She couldn't breathe. Couldn't move. A slave to the sensation of this purge.

Until finally the quiet met her ears.

Glorified silence.

A whisper of acceptance.

A glimmer of *light*.

She swallowed, her head bowed as she studied her hands. They appeared normal, still pale, her nails dirtied with the grime of the rocks but otherwise exactly as they'd always been. Yet she could feel a buzz of static energy brushing her skin and emboldening her spirit.

So much power, she marveled, staring at her palms as though they held all the answers.

Aya, Issac breathed into her mind. *Are you all right?*

I don't know, she admitted. *I… I feel like I… imploded?*

You brought all the Seraphim to their knees, he told her. *They're… weeping.*

Her brow furrowed, her focus going to Adriel, Kital, and Arvane and finding that they were indeed crying.

H-how? She swallowed again, her stomach clenching at the sight of these powerful beings kneeling and looking at her with reverence and awe in their gazes.

Her mother's expression resembled the same worship, as did Lizzie's.

Stas shook her head. "I… I don't…"

A slow clap started from her left, the sound disturbing the silence around them.

She blinked, her heart thudding rapidly in her chest. Then she slowly followed the sound.

And found Osiris leaning against a tree, his suit-clad legs crossed at the ankles as though there hadn't been an eruption of power only seconds ago.

"Well done, granddaughter," he praised. "Now, can you re-create that power and use it on an entire island of Seraphim?"

CHAPTER 35

BALTHAZAR

FUCKING FINALLY, ALIK SAID, ENGAGING HIS TELEPATHY TO talk to Balthazar directly. *Wakefield is helping us see the Seraphim. But we can't hurt…*

He trailed off.

Balthazar frowned as a static hum danced along his skin.

Power rippled around them, chilling the air with an ominous kiss of death.

Leela shuddered, her grip around his neck tightening.

Balthazar's mind quickly touched those closest to him, searching for an explanation, an update, *anything* to tell him what was happening.

Jay's mental voice didn't exist, causing his heart to skip a beat.

But Lizzie's thoughts confirmed his best friend still lived.

And Luc was observing the source of the energy, his strategic gift analyzing the display before him.

Stas, Balthazar breathed. *That's what we're feeling.*

I know, Leela whispered. *I… I can sense it through the fealty bond.*

What's she doing? he asked.

But in the next second, he had his answer as the minds of the Seraphim blossomed throughout the island, allowing him to not only hear their reactions but also *feel* their emotions.

Balthazar's jaw dropped at the onslaught of confusion, abject terror, and sadness that hit him at once. He nearly lost his footing, but Leela's presence grounded him, giving him a root to hold on to while he absorbed the chaos unraveling in Hydria.

The attacking Seraphim had all fallen to their knees, their minds utterly under Stas's command.

But Leela appeared to be fine.

Had Stark or Vera been impacted? What about Sethios and Caro?

Issac's mind—full of thoughts Balthazar could officially hear again—told him he was fine but mildly concerned about Stas because she wasn't responding to him.

And she'd just drowned several times before taking off toward Luc's house.

Now it appeared she was fully embracing her power, making everyone on this island aware of her strength and power.

By compelling the Seraphim to… to…

She's forcing them to feel? Balthazar wasn't sure how to explain the sensation he was experiencing but wanted to share the assessment with Leela. *It's like she's making them understand the purpose of life.*

She's from Osiris's line. He's the original Seraphim of Life and Resurrection. She's engaging something… a power… from his line, Leela replied, her expression matching her awestruck tone. *I've never seen or felt anything like it.*

You can sense it?

Only through you, she admitted. *And the chill in the air. Otherwise, I don't feel anything. She's not compelling me at all.*

He nodded, his mind searching for Stark. Other than mild surprise, he appeared to be mostly fine. At least from the small glimpses Balthazar picked up from his thoughts.

Clara stood beside him, the warrior Seraphim having gone straight to her upon arrival—something he picked up in Clara's thoughts.

Because he could hear her as he did before, thanks to his bond to Leela.

And Clara had definitely bonded with Stark.

Something he discovered not by prying into her mind but from the feelings emanating from her.

Relief.

Confusion.

A hint of fear.

And a healthy dose of trust.

The emotions on the island had been overwhelming her, but it seemed Stark's appearance helped calm her mind.

For that alone, he approved. But he'd revisit the how and why of that bond later.

Balthazar moved on to search for Sethios or Caro, finding Sethios as quiet as Jayson, but Caro loud and clear. Pride radiated from her, tainted with a hint of fear. *What does this mean?* she wondered. *What will the council do to her when they find out?*

An excellent query.

Balthazar returned to his oldest friend, curious to hear his final assessment, and frowning when he heard a lack of surprise in his thoughts.

We need to go to Luc, Balthazar said slowly. *Can you mist us to his house?*

Leela didn't ask why, just engaged her ability to fly and took them to Luc's living room.

His old friend stood at the window, observing Stas and the three kneeling Seraphim in the grass. Mateo and Jacque flanked him on either side, their gazes on the events outside.

From the mental chatter of the other Hydraians, there were two more Seraphim kneeling on the beach in a similar pose, utterly captivated by whatever trance Stas had woven through the air.

But Mateo and Luc didn't appear all that concerned, their stances relaxed. Jacque was the more vigilant among the group, his silver eyes finding Balthazar as soon as he arrived. His lips curled, relief shining in his features.

Balthazar winked at him, pleased to see him well, too. Owen's thoughts were nearby, suggesting he was also in the house.

Not surprising.

The two had clearly taken their friendship to a new level. It was still in the early stages, so he wouldn't press. But he absolutely approved. Those two Hydraians had been dancing around each other for decades. And that was before Owen's supposed death.

While Jacque clearly didn't appreciate being kept in the dark, he wasn't going to let the opportunity slip by him again.

Although, some residual anger remained in his aura, suggesting the two men were still working out a few details.

"Good to have you home, B," Luc said without turning around. "And just in time, too."

"Some would say I'm late," Balthazar replied.

Luc nodded. "Yes. But you're safe and alive. That's what matters."

"I'm surprised you're still here," Balthazar hedged,

aware that his old friend had a few secrets in that head of his.

One being the fact that he'd anticipated this response from Stas.

Because Osiris had mentioned the capability of it.

A fact that startled Balthazar more than he cared to admit.

Since when are you openly conversing with Osiris? he wanted to demand. But he'd spent over three thousand years trusting Luc. If he was speaking with Osiris, he had a very good reason for it.

"I wouldn't leave Hydria in these conditions," Luc replied, turning to face him. "They needed a leader."

"A king," Balthazar corrected.

His old friend sighed, shaking his blond head. "We both know I'm not in a good place to rule right now, B." His emerald eyes swirled with truth. "I'm in too dark a place to make appropriate and logical decisions right now."

"You may be in a dark place," Balthazar agreed, feeling the fury in his aura. "But your logic is always sound."

Luc considered him for a moment. "Yes, perhaps. However, I keep second-guessing myself and my decisions. I need… a clear head."

Balthazar fell quiet, aware of what his friend desired. It was right there on the cusp of his thoughts, the request for a reprieve. However, he knew that now was quite possibly the worst time to escape for a moment to recharge.

Hence, he'd remained.

But each moment, his psyche worsened, his anger overcoming his ability to be patient.

Luc needed a temporary break from making decisions. A moment to himself to grieve. To rage. To hate the world.

A mental refresh.

And he needed Balthazar to lead in his absence.

Jay was too busy with fatherhood to take the throne.

Alik was too bitter for it.

Leaving Balthazar as the only true option.

For how long? he wanted to ask. But he knew his old friend wouldn't be able to reply with a timeline. He would leave for as long as it took to regain control of his emotions and logical mind.

B, Leela whispered, her focus still on the windows. *Osiris just misted in.*

Balthazar immediately followed her gaze, noting the clapping Seraphim by the tree. Luc's attention shifted as well, but he didn't seem surprised by the arrival.

Because he'd called him—a fact Balthazar learned from his and Mateo's minds.

They'd reached out to him, wanting him to explain reformation to Adriel. A sound plan, except the original Seraphim of Life and Resurrection hadn't shown up in time to be of much help. Instead, his granddaughter had done the job for him.

Which he appeared to be quite proud of now.

The olive tones of his bald head glimmered in the moonlight, the gleam creating a false halo around his scalp.

A fitting ornament for a Seraphim.

But there was nothing angelic about this male or his soul.

Balthazar went to the door, wanting to hear their conversation.

The others followed, joining him outside as Osiris said, "Now, can you re-create that power and use it on an entire island of Seraphim?"

Stas blinked at him, too stunned by his appearance, or perhaps what she'd just accomplished, to speak. Her mind whirred with confusion, her power indescribable. But she knew she'd brought the Seraphim to heel through a form of rebirth, by forcing them to feel. She just had no idea how she'd done it.

In anger.

In desperation.

In exhaustion.

All were possible causes in her mind, but Balthazar suspected it was a combination of all three, underlined by love.

She'd tapped into her true abilities to save her best friend. An admirable feat that definitely deserved praise, but Balthazar doubted she wanted that praise from Osiris.

"Hmm, I thought not," the ancient Seraphim continued, referring to his question about Stas's ability to re-create the power to use against an entire island of Seraphim. "I'm ready to begin your training whenever you desire, Astasiya."

Her brow furrowed, some of her confusion melting beneath a hot wave of intense emotion.

Fury.

It thickened the air around them, drowning out all the other emotions in the clearing.

Leela pressed her palm to Balthazar's lower back, clearly feeling the sensation through their bond.

It resembled a deep red flame, glaring angrily and burning hotter than everything else. Except it was invisible, and no one really seemed to notice it except Balthazar.

Because he could sense Stas's volatile emotions.

Just as he could hear the rage pouring through her thoughts.

She'd pieced together something the rest of them had yet to realize. But the moment she thought it, Balthazar knew she was right.

"You watched it all happen," she said, the words deceptively quiet. "We called you for help, and rather than come to our aid, you stood by and let it all happen."

Osiris stared at her, his green eyes—the same color as his granddaughter's—giving nothing away. "You needed a training field. I provided one."

Her eyebrows lifted.

But it was Caro who spoke next, her ire rivaling her daughter's fury. "You orchestrated this?"

Osiris glanced at her. "Not directly. Leek already knew the truth as a result of Vera's rushed memory manipulation. I merely moved the inevitable along by giving them an agent to manipulate."

"Patreel," Leela said, surprising Balthazar. Not with the answer—he suspected the same—but with her vocalization.

"He'd served his purpose and was no longer of use to any of us," Osiris replied, the words an indirect confirmation of his involvement in tonight's events. "He also deserved his fate, something I imagine you can appreciate, given the part he played in your reformations."

Leela's jaw clenched, her mind echoing an agreement to his words, with an immediate rebuttal following. *Patreel didn't know,* she thought. *He was just a puppet.*

Balthazar leaned into her, telling her without words that she wasn't alone in that mental conflict. Because he agreed that Patreel should be punished for what he'd done, but he also felt that it wasn't truly Patreel's fault, either.

The High Council of Seraph were to blame here more than anyone else. Or the original members of it, anyway.

"Patreel may have earned his fate, whatever it actually ended up being with the council," Stas said. "But Grace didn't deserve to die. Neither did Ash. The Hydraians on the beach didn't deserve to be hurt or killed either. And my father, Jay, Lizzie, and *Baby Aidyn* did not deserve any of this."

Stas stepped forward with each statement until she was only a few feet away from Osiris.

"Sacrifices are often necessary when training one as powerful as yourself," he replied, unfazed by her nearness or the quiet fury pouring off of her.

"*Sacrifices?*" she repeated. "You put everyone in jeopardy. You let innocent people die. Just to *train* me?!" Her fist connected with his jaw, causing everyone around her to gape in shock.

Caro stepped forward, but Osiris lifted his hand, halting her midstep. Either the action had done it, or he'd released some sort of compulsion. Balthazar couldn't read anything off the ancient immortal, his emotions and mind were completely his own. No doubt from a rune of some kind. Or perhaps a result of power alone.

However, that didn't seem to intimidate Stas.

She was in his face as she said, "I will *never* train with you. Not now. Not after this and what you've done. You're a monster."

"I'm not the one who sent the Seraphim here to destroy Elizabeth and her progeny," he pointed out, his voice lacking emotion. "The High Council of Seraph did that."

"Yet you stood by and watched them almost succeed," she snapped. "That makes you just as complicit."

"It makes me patient," he returned. "It means I have faith in what you can do. And I was right to have that faith, as evidenced by *that*."

He gestured to Adriel, Arvane, and Kital, all on their knees, their expressions filled with wonder as they continued to stare at Stas as though she were a goddess worthy of worship.

"And what if you were wrong?" she demanded. "You would have just let them kill Lizzie? Aidyn? Jayson?"

"I'm rarely, if ever, wrong," Osiris replied.

"I'm not willing to put other people at risk on an assumption," she bit out. "I'm not like you."

"Which is exactly why you *need* me," he informed her. "I was here. Had the situation proved futile, I would have stepped in. Alas, I wasn't needed. *You* were the solution. But you needed that push to trust your own power, to know what you can accomplish without relying on your mentors to do it for you."

Meaning Gabe and Vera, Leela thought, her arms folded. *That's how he's involved. He must have compelled Patreel to tell Mel or Dian where to find us, then persuaded Patreel to go to Vera and Gabe for assistance. He wanted them removed from the situation to test Stas.*

So the council wasn't behind the distraction.

They might have been, she murmured. *But it was a result of Osiris's indirect influence through Patreel. He designed the playing board.*

Luc's thoughts echoed Leela's assessment, his own mind pondering through the strategy and finding it logical, even a tad respectable. But he didn't agree with Osiris's sacrificial approach.

Neither did Balthazar.

They'd lost some good lives tonight. Hydraians they desperately needed for the future fight.

Hydraians like Ash and Grace, he thought, his gaze finding their lifeless forms on the ground. *They didn't deserve this.*

Leela's palm flattened against his spine, her head coming to rest on his shoulder as she offered support. Balthazar would be bearing the brunt of that emotional cost, especially if Luc left him in charge.

Who else have we lost? Balthazar wondered. *How many died tonight?*

"You cost us several important lives tonight," Luc said flatly, his thought process on the same wavelength as Balthazar's.

It was why they were well matched to lead. Luc possessed the strategic upper hand, while Balthazar knew the minds and hearts of their people.

"Ash was our best pyrokinetic," Luc continued. "Grace was young, but very skilled in the art of reading history from objects, in addition to fighting."

"I disagree on the former, and you still have Owen for the latter," Osiris replied.

Luc frowned. "We have no other pyrokinetics on the island."

"Perhaps not. But there are spares. Which is what I factored into tonight's events." He clasped his hands before him. "Hydria's overall power remains as strong as ever. If anything, it proved quite influential against the Seraphim, something I know will shock them, as the council only sent seven because they didn't expect much of a fight."

"So this was a training exercise and a test," Stas translated, her fists clenching at her sides as though she wanted to punch Osiris again.

Balthazar doubted the ancient would allow another hit.

So he hoped, for Stas's sake, that she reined in the temper, even though he absolutely agreed with her anger.

"There is more to life than just power," Balthazar said quietly. "We're a family. Loss impacts morale, which can greatly deteriorate our ability to fight as a cohesive unit."

Luc was proof enough of that, his loss of Aidan having impacted his leadership capabilities.

Osiris considered Balthazar for a moment before looking at Lizzie and Aidyn, then returned his gaze to Stas.

"Perhaps there are things you could teach me as well," he offered. "Humanity is typically regarded as weak, but you've shown me today that it can also have its strengths."

"I will not train with you," Stas repeated, her tone resolute. But the emotions surrounding her suggested she'd spoken out of anger.

Balthazar couldn't blame her.

But Luc's mind held an edge of disappointment to it. Because while he didn't agree with Osiris's methods, he could see the practicality of working together.

Balthazar glanced at his oldest friend, surprised by his thoughts.

Luc ignored him, his gaze on the ancient.

Osiris sighed. "You will, child. You won't have a choice." He stepped away from her. "I'll be around." He glanced at his son on the ground, his lips flattening. "Heal him, Caro. Heal them all."

Rather than mist, he merely walked toward the trees.

And disappeared down a path into the night.

"We're just going to let him wander Hydria now?" Stas demanded as Caro knelt beside Sethios.

Compulsion, Balthazar realized. *He just compelled her to heal.*

Of course he did, Leela muttered.

"I think Osiris has been wandering Hydria for centuries," Luc said quietly, his eyes narrowing at the path Osiris had just taken. "How many casualties did we—"

"Luc?" Eliza's voice came from the dark. A hint of fear preceded her arrival, her aura clouded with a mixture of shock and terror.

Balthazar frowned, his power immediately engaging as he attempted to find out what had caused that reaction in her.

He'd spent the last few months monitoring her emotions, helping her heal from the horrors of her past.

But the moment she stepped into the clearing and saw everyone standing around, she froze.

Or maybe it was the icy look Luc gave her. "I do not have time for you right now," he bit out. "Come back later."

"Luc," Balthazar interjected, stepping forward.

Luc cut him a look. "Not. Now." *If she speaks to me right now, I'm going to say or do something I'll regret.* The admission echoed between them, the serious quality of it giving Balthazar pause.

His old friend had continued to deny his attraction to the young Hydraian over the last few months, stating she was too young for him, too inexperienced. But that didn't stop him from secretly wanting her.

He appeared to be openly admitting the attraction now, at least to Balthazar, and saying he wasn't ready to face it in his current mood.

Because he didn't want to risk destroying the potential there with a few choice words.

An interesting development.

Or perhaps it was merely a tired admission.

Regardless, Balthazar nodded, saying he understood.

"But I really—"

"Eliza, I have more important matters to handle right now, including cleaning up the dead on the island," Luc stated firmly. "Unless your statement involves giving me the number of Hydraian casualties we've just endured, it can wait."

The dark-haired female swallowed, her midnight irises clouding over with resolve. She dipped her chin in understanding, her mind going oddly blank as she stepped back into the shadows without another word.

Balthazar sighed. That wasn't the way to handle the situation at all, but it was better than Luc blowing up at her.

Still, he wondered what she wanted to say. She appeared to be blocking it in her mind, perhaps because she'd noticed Balthazar standing nearby, which only intrigued him more.

He almost made to step toward her, to talk to her alone, but Sethios came back to life with a furious curse that distracted them all.

Caro immediately went to work on Jay, not even giving Sethios a kiss or a hug or a comment regarding his recovery.

Which had him frowning down at her and glancing around.

"*Grandpa* compelled her to heal everyone," Stas explained through her teeth.

Sethios's brow furrowed as he ignored everyone else and knelt beside Caro, pressing his palm to her shoulder. Energy flowed between them, the connection palpable and strong.

He didn't even speak, just went right to work trying to help her via their bond.

Is he trying to break the compulsion? Balthazar wondered.

That, or he's offering her energy to keep her stable, Leela replied. *Her healing gift is new and probably exhausting her.*

Which meant she needed help.

Balthazar sought out the mind of the one Hydraian who could assist and found her on the beach. "Lara's healing London," he said, the words for Luc. "From what I can hear in her thoughts, there are not many permanent deaths, just severe wounds or Hydraians that may take a few days to come back."

Hydraians could only die upon beheading, or complete

exsanguination—which happened when an incendiary bullet entered the bloodstream.

However, the Seraphim hadn't used any weapons apart from their ethereal swords. At least, that was all he picked up on from the minds of his Hydraians.

"Aya," Issac breathed, bursting through the tree line where Eliza had just been standing.

Balthazar frowned, realizing she'd disappeared without a word.

He attempted to find her mind, but Issac's emotions whipped across his senses, drawing his focus to the embracing couple in the field.

Love, adoration, respect, and concern all poured off of Issac as he held Stas with a fierceness Balthazar felt all the way to his soul.

Seeing the pair of them embrace right by Sethios and Caro created an odd sort of reality in the field. A new way of life. A destiny Balthazar never knew he desired yet found himself craving more than air itself now.

Because he had that, too.

He had Leela.

The other half of his spirit.

The female he'd always been meant to claim yet spent three millennia finding and losing and finding again.

He caught her blue-green irises, the understanding flourishing between them.

This is us, he thought at her.

What our past denied us, she whispered.

What our future promises us, he countered, his palm finding her cheek.

She leaned into his touch, her eyes falling closed. *What our present already is,* she hummed softly.

He gently pressed his lips to hers. *I still owe you pancakes.*

You do, she agreed.

I'll make them fresh for you once we're done here. It'd probably be morning by the time he fulfilled that promise anyway.

Her long blonde lashes lifted, a hint of wicked intent glittering in her irises. *Only after you let me lick syrup off your abs.*

Are you saying you prefer me over pancakes?

I'm saying your abs remind me of waffles, and I prefer waffles to pancakes, she murmured.

Liar, he said, narrowing his gaze. *I can read your mind, Lee.*

Indeed you can, she replied, grinning. *So you know I'm telling the truth about preferring you drizzled in syrup for breakfast.*

He kissed her again before grazing her cheek and pressing his mouth to her ear. "The feeling is mutual." Which was pretty much a declaration of love for Balthazar. Because pancakes were his passion in life.

But Leela had surpassed his adoration of the breakfast food.

And had become his favorite meal to indulge in.

He brushed his lips against her cheek, then straightened and focused on the night ahead.

Leela would be his dessert.

Later.

After he finished consoling his Hydraians.

And discussing next steps with his fellow Elders.

CHAPTER 36

BALTHAZAR

"Four deaths, including Blake. Thirteen wounded, but mostly healed immortals. And six emotional Seraphim." Jay folded his arms, his feet spread wide as he braced himself. "The latter have been put in the dungeon for now. Not that it'll hold them."

"Yes, but they don't seem all that interested in leaving," Luc replied.

"It's like they're in a weird type of reformation," Caro commented, her head on Sethios's shoulder. He had his arm around her on the couch, offering more of his strength.

The compulsion had either faded or been removed, allowing her to recover from her healing frenzy.

Both options suggested Osiris still lurked nearby, but he'd remained out of sight on the island. Something Issac had confirmed as well because he couldn't see the ancient in anyone's vision.

Of course, he could be using his powers to compel those into not seeing him.

But that was neither here nor there.

It was clear that if Osiris wanted to wander Hydria, he would. With or without permission.

And Balthazar was just too exhausted to let that concern him on top of everything else going on.

"They're coherent, but compliant," Caro continued. "And instead of feeling nothing, they're feeling everything."

"Adriel's memories appear to be returning to him as well," Stark added, his legs crossed casually at the ankles as he leaned against the wall of Luc's living room. "He keeps mentioning someone named Dapharia."

Caro's brow furrowed. "I don't know anyone by that name."

"Neither do I," Stark replied. "But he keeps asking for her."

"I'm not familiar with the name either," Leela added.

"Perhaps I'll unravel the identity when I search his mind," Vera offered as she collapsed into the chair closest to where Sethios and Caro sat on the couch.

Balthazar and Leela had taken over the other chair in the room with her perched on the arm of it, her arm around his shoulders. He wanted to drag her into his lap, but he restrained himself, focusing on the conversation instead.

"What happened to the seventh Seraphim?" Sethios asked. "Did he escape?"

"I haven't sensed Leek anywhere on the island," Stark replied. "And Stas said she couldn't feel him like she could the others."

"Yes, she established some sort of connection," Caro added. "I imagine it's similar to how Osiris connects to his Ichorians."

Stas and Issac had remained with Lizzie and Aidyn for

the evening, Stas feeling the need to be near her best friend in case the Seraphim decided to return.

Jay had almost stayed with them, but he hadn't wanted to miss the Elder meeting. Particularly as he knew Luc's intentions to announce a necessary change in leadership.

Which meant they all had to be on the same page to provide a united front to the Hydraians.

It would be temporary. Just long enough for Luc to regain confidence in his own mind.

Balthazar respected him for recognizing the need to take control of his emotions but wished his old friend would let him help.

However, that wasn't Luc's way.

He had to own his pain to be able to truly heal from it.

"So it's safe to assume Leek has returned to the council," Luc said, his position at the head of the room near his fireplace. It was purposeful, giving him a view of everyone and the door. "Do you think they'll send more Seraphim to attack us?"

"Not until they understand what happened here," Vera replied. "And that could take them a while."

Stark dipped his chin in agreement. "Time works differently for Seraphim. A few weeks is the same as a few months or even years to them. Which makes it difficult to predict their return."

"Skye will help with that," Caro murmured. "And from what Ezekiel said, she's finally calm now."

"Didn't he say something about death coming, though?" Alik replied. "That she kept chanting it right before Stas imploded?"

"Maybe she meant the Seraphim here were about to die and be reborn?" Sethios suggested. "Or she was predicting the Hydraian deaths."

"Or she meant the literal Seraphim of Death and

Destruction," Alik countered. "Since he's clearly obsessed with B's…" He blinked, glancing at Balthazar. "Do I call her a mate? A girlfriend? A wife? I'm honestly curious as to how I address this new addition of yours, as *conquest* applies to far too many others."

"She's not my anything," Balthazar replied. "She's Leela, a fertility Seraphim and the most sensual woman in existence. She's her own person and will always be her own person."

Her lips curled. "A person who chooses to be mated to Balthazar."

"Exactly." He grinned. "A challenge I have to please and worship for eternity."

"A very difficult job," Leela added.

"I would never desire an easy one," he countered seriously.

Leela leaned in to kiss him, her mind full of warm thoughts as her tongue traced his bottom lip. *I'm looking forward to breakfast, B.*

As am I, sweetheart. He returned her embrace, his tongue touching hers in a soft caress meant to tease for the morning ahead. It was almost dawn, and he highly doubted they'd be sleeping anytime soon.

How fortuitous that we don't require sleep, he thought.

Yes, she agreed. *We can go days without.*

Days, he repeated. *A challenge I—*

"I regret my question," Alik deadpanned, interrupting his thoughts. "My point was that Skye's prophecy might be about the Seraphim obsessed with *Leela*. Which makes your exit poorly timed." The words were for Luc. "But I understand the need."

"I won't be gone long," Luc promised. "I just need… to dismantle my grief."

"You need to accept it," Balthazar countered, pulling

433

LEXI C. FOSS

away from Leela's mouth to pin his old friend with a look. "Pain and grief are meant to be embraced, not pushed away."

Luc blinked at him, his mind not committing to the task and instead shifting focus to the days ahead. "The Hydraians will need to be told the truth about my absence. To lie or cover it up will only inspire distrust and confusion, two emotions we cannot afford right now."

Balthazar nodded, agreeing.

"They don't need the details. Just tell them I've gone to mourn and seek renewed purpose." Luc cleared his throat. "They'll need the three of you for emotional support."

Alik snorted. "Not exactly my forte."

"But he'll work on it," Balthazar added before Luc could reply to that. "They'll have me and Jay as well. And Stas." It was important to include her. She'd defeated the Seraphim. That would grant her a certain status amongst the Hydraians that they could use to help put them at ease.

"We're all family," Jay added. "We'll handle this. And we'll respect your absence, Luc. No one will question your need to find peace." He moved forward, his hand grabbing the other man's shoulder. "If anything, we all respect the hell out of you for recognizing that need."

He pulled Luc into a hug, clapping him on the back as he pressed his temple to the other man's head.

"You're still our king," Jay said softly. "This realignment is only temporary."

"I never wanted to be king," Luc muttered, returning the other man's embrace.

"No, but you're the best one for the job, and this, right here, is why," Jay replied, grabbing him by the back of the neck to press his forehead to Luc's. "Try not to go too far, yeah?"

Luc held his gaze for a moment, neither agreeing nor

434

disagreeing. "Jacque will know how to find me," he offered instead.

"Good enough," Jay agreed, releasing him. "We'll handle the masses and potential impact from the viral online videos. You handle your mind."

"Mateo's trying to erase them all from the internet," Luc said, referring to the online videos. "But I fear the damage is already done."

Jay shrugged. "Not for you to worry about. We'll figure it out." His tone held a nonchalant note to it, his best friend clearly trying to play this off as not a big deal, but they all knew it was a very big deal indeed.

Balthazar's and Leela's faces were everywhere.

As were Gabriel's and Vera's and all the dead Seraphim.

They'd just entered a new phase in life, one that might play out similar to where the Greeks and Romans had thought they were gods.

Or it might go the path of the CRF.

Regardless, they would prepare for it and go from there.

"Meanwhile, Vera and I will work on Adriel, and on the others, too," Stark said, pushing off the wall. "We'll let you know if we learn anything useful."

Luc nodded, agreeing to the terms.

"We'll stay with Ezekiel and Skye on the outskirts of the island." Sethios's words weren't a suggestion or an offering so much as a statement. "Stas and Issac will be with us as well."

Balthazar frowned. "They no longer intend to stay in my guest room?"

"Ezekiel has asked Issac to manage Skye's sleep. She's struggling with nightmares. It's easier if they're nearby," Stas's father explained. "At least for now."

Luc nodded again. "He'll also be able to help decipher her visions, too. A strategic move."

Sethios and Caro stood, both of them echoing their agreement with his comment. "Also gives my father a central focus if he decides to visit again, as I doubt your Hydraians will appreciate him openly roaming the island."

"We can't control him," Luc replied.

"No. But we can direct his attention elsewhere." Sethios smiled. "Trust me, I have a few millennia of experience playing his games. I know how he thinks."

And with that, he and Caro left.

Vera and Stark followed.

Leaving Jay, Alik, Luc, Balthazar, and Leela alone in the room.

A brief silence fell, the Elders embracing the defining moment of their future and the necessities that came with this decision.

"We'll tell the Hydraians later today," Balthazar finally said. "After the burial ceremony."

Luc nodded. "I'll be there in spirit." He'd already said goodbye in his own way, blessing their souls in his ancient manner. Not through outward sadness or loss, but by wishing them peace and happiness in the afterlife.

Part of his healing would be in accepting their deaths, in addition to the others.

But Aidan would be the one he'd mourn the most.

His father. His flesh and blood. The other half of his mind.

"I'm going to be all right," he promised, his gaze on Balthazar.

"I know you are," he replied, standing to pull his oldest friend into a hug. "And we'll be waiting for you with open arms upon your return." The words were low and breathed against his ear.

Then he clapped the man on the back, just like Jay had, and took a step back.

"I'm not hugging you," Alik said. "But I'll be actively restructuring our protective lines in your absence."

"I'll expect a full report on my return," Luc replied.

Alik grinned. "I'll give you a demonstration instead."

The two males shared a moment of understanding, both of them having experienced great loss. However, Alik still allowed his residual anger to drive his will to live, while Luc desired a different path. He didn't want to be motivated by a need for revenge. He wanted strategy and logic to be at the front of his mind again.

And he would succeed.

With time.

The four men shared another powerful silence, then each of them left with their tasks in mind.

Balthazar would address the island this evening after leading the funeral ceremonies.

Then he'd announce Luc's temporary departure.

And he'd join his Hydraians in their mourning, offering his ability to soothe their emotions while embracing their thoughts and comments.

Camaraderie and morale were his specialties.

Which meant his powers would be needed tonight and for the foreseeable future.

Fortunately, he had someone to help him through it.

Leela.

His sensual challenge. His perfect mate. His other half.

She smiled up at him now as he led her away from Luc's house, the home isolated at the top of the hill in the center of the island, and down the path toward his home.

"I suppose it's a good thing Issac and Stas are staying with her parents for now," Leela said conversationally as they walked.

"Oh? And why's that?" he asked, already aware of her answer but wanting his vixen to voice it out loud.

"Because I'm not in the mood to share you today," she replied.

"No group orgies on the beach?"

"Hmm, no," she hummed, her blue-green irises swirling with salacious energy. "I'm too ravenous for that."

He nodded, his arm sliding around her lower back. "I only have enough syrup for two anyway."

She giggled at the pun, the sound one he rather enjoyed. "I never did show you what happened the morning you made me pancakes in Brazil."

His mind recalled the memory with ease now that all the blocks had been lifted between them, but he played along anyway. "I hope it involves you licking syrup off my abdomen."

"And your cock," she replied without missing a beat. "Your balls, too."

"Only if I'm allowed to return the favor," he supplied.

"Oh, no. It'll be me returning the favor, B." She stepped in front of him to start walking backward, a come-hither gleam entering her eyes. "Because you'll be the one devouring me first."

Chapter 37

Leela

The marble felt cold beneath Leela's bare thighs, her warm skin a direct contrast to the kitchen counter beneath her.

But the view distracted her from the goose bumps pebbling along her legs.

Balthazar.

Naked.

Beneath an apron.

He flipped a pancake on the griddle pan, his brown gaze swirling with wicked promises.

They'd already played with the syrup, having licked each other to completion more than once before showering off the sticky sweetness.

Now he was intent on feeding her.

But all she really wanted to do was go to her knees and worship him all over again with her mouth.

This potent sexuality between them left her insatiable. And the tenting of his apron said he felt the same.

"That's a hazard," she said conversationally, her gaze on his impressive arousal. "Please don't burn yourself."

Or do, she thought. *I'll kiss it and make it better.*

His lips curled, displaying those delicious dimples in his cheeks. "Don't worry, sweetheart. I'm a professional in the kitchen."

"And the bedroom," she murmured.

"I excel at sex everywhere, vixen."

She arched a brow. "Even in the clouds?"

He paused mid-flip on his other pancake and glanced at her. "We can fuck in the sky?"

She flashed him a smile. "I have wings."

He considered that for a moment. "A new experience."

"For both of us," she admitted. She'd never danced like that with a Seraphim, or anyone else for that matter.

"After breakfast," he decided out loud as he finished flipping the pancake.

"You don't want to wait until you have your own wings?"

He shook his head. "You won't drop me."

"I may, if you do your job right."

He set the spatula down and sauntered over to where she sat on the kitchen island. His hands found her hips as he yanked her forward to stand between her splayed thighs.

"Sweetheart," he said softly, his lips brushing hers. "*When* I do my job right, you'll be too busy clinging to me to let me go."

She wrapped her arms around his neck. "Like this?"

His palms trailed down her legs to her knees and calves, wrapping them around his waist and pulling her even closer until they were intimately flush with one another. The apron was the only barrier, a tease she desperately wanted to remove.

"Like this," he whispered, his mouth capturing hers.

She moaned, indulging in the kiss and the sweetness in his mouth. He tasted like sex, syrup, and carnality.

Her own perfect brand of chocolate.

A dessert she would forever crave.

His chest vibrated in approval, the low growl coming from deep within his soul and inspiring her own spirit to come out to play.

Yet he pulled away slowly in the next minute, his focus returning to the pancakes.

He'd promised her a meal.

And it seemed he was hell-bent on seeing it through.

She allowed it, enjoying the way his ass flexed as he moved.

So muscular and perfect, it was no wonder several statues had been made in his honor. Although, it was an absolute travesty that they hadn't modeled the front after his groin.

"They were intimidated," he said, grinning as he shamelessly listened to her blunt review of his physique. "They didn't want to risk emasculating anyone, so they chose to go small on the front."

"And your ego allowed it because you already know you're stunning."

"Exactly that," he murmured, his grin growing into a smile. "Just as you know you're stunning."

It was true. She knew her appeal and her ability to perform in bed. It was what made them perfect for each other—their shared confidence in all things sensual.

And their shared need to live life to the fullest.

"And our love of pancakes," Balthazar added, still listening to her thoughts.

"I told you, I prefer waffles."

"Keep lying to me and I won't fuck you for dessert."

"What will you do instead?" she inquired, wondering

what devious kink he might explore as an alternative. "Spanking? Flogging? Caning?"

He snorted. "I'm not a sadist, vixen."

"Doesn't mean you wouldn't take on the role."

"True," he admitted. "But only when the partner prefers it, and you don't want to be mastered."

He flipped a pancake onto a plate. Followed by a second. Then he put two on his own dish and turned toward the fridge.

"What do I want?" she asked, curious as to what he'd say.

He pulled out a bunch of fruit and some cream, setting them beside the plates, before going for the syrup.

It wasn't until he had everything situated that he finally looked at her.

"You enjoy dominance, but only when it makes you feel safe." He picked up the plates of decorated pancakes. "You also like to tease to test boundaries, but you wouldn't enjoy being punished for it."

He set the dishes down beside her, then grabbed her hips to move her toward the middle of the island. Her legs parted automatically for him, but he closed them and set a plate on top of her thighs.

She reached for the fork, but he moved her hand away.

"I'm feeding you," he said. "And you're going to tell me how delicious these pancakes are after every bite."

She considered the game. "What do I win for lying?"

"You win more pancakes for telling the truth," he replied. "And if you're really enthusiastic about it, I'll eat my own pancake off your bare skin before licking you clean for dessert."

"So no flying?"

"It'll be an appetizer to flying," he promised her, the

fork already slicing through the deliciousness on the plate. "Now open your mouth."

She parted her lips while gazing up at him with an expression meant to entice. Not that she needed it. He was already hard beneath the apron.

A mixture of succulent flavors hit her tongue, providing the perfect blend of syrup, fruit, cream, and fluffy pancake. She moaned, the response automatic and not forced, and allowed her senses to experience the sweetness of Balthazar's creation.

He grinned as he fed her another bite, not giving her a chance to speak and only enhancing the sound coming from her throat.

So good, she thought at him. *Almost as good as sex.*

Nothing is as good as sex between us, he replied.

Hence my use of the term "almost."

The next piece came, the flavors somehow intensifying with each additional bite. It reminded her of a mounting orgasm, each step taking her that much higher to a euphoric state that left her begging for more.

More sensation.

More flavor.

More *B.*

Her thighs quivered with excitement, her stomach tightening in approval as her tongue worked over the fork. Balthazar's brown gaze turned into liquid chocolate, his interest a palpable stroke in the air that branded her skin, making her hot all over.

She wanted him to push her down and fuck her on the counter.

But his patience won.

He continued to feed her with one hand while his opposite gently traced the outside of her thigh.

The perfect tease.

A temptation meant to strengthen her arousal and drive her into a frenzy.

He was too damn good at this game. And she absolutely loved him for it.

When the final bite came, it wasn't on her fork, but from his fingers. She sucked them clean, drawing her tongue around the tip and watching as the liquid chocolate in his eyes turned molten.

"Lie down," he whispered as he removed the plate.

She complied, his heat temporarily leaving her as he went to deposit her dish in the sink.

But he returned almost as quickly, his fingers trailing along the tops of her thighs as he separated them to create space for his body. The sensation of skin on skin had her eyes flying toward his naked torso.

He'd removed the apron.

And fuck, he was beautiful.

All sensuous lines and muscular valleys.

She licked her lips, hungry all over again.

"My turn for breakfast," Balthazar murmured, leaning forward to take her nipple in his mouth. She threaded her fingers through his hair, arching into him and loving the way he swirled his tongue against her skin.

But he caught her wrists in his hands in the next moment, pushing them above her head while saying, "No moving."

This was the sort of domination she enjoyed, something he knew and obviously liked, too.

Wickedness danced in his gaze as he pulled away from her to pick up his plate. He set it on her stomach, ensuring she really couldn't move or the breakfast would slide off of her.

His fork sliced through the deliciousness, taking some of the pancake to his mouth. His throat hypnotized her.

She wanted to trace the masculine lines with her mouth, feel him swallow against her tongue.

He distracted her focus by drawing the tip of his fork along her mound and down to skim her damp folds.

The sharp quality of the metallic ends provided just enough of a threat to still her breath, yet her heart hammered with expectation.

Balthazar didn't penetrate her; he barely even stroked her, then he took another bite.

She shivered, the erotic nature of his movements holding her captive beneath him.

More teasing strokes, some harder than others, some more intimate as he ensured her arousal touched the metal, then light pets, followed by dark promises from his mind.

He praised her for staying still.

He thanked her for making his food that much sweeter.

He considered making her orgasm from the fork alone.

All of it together left her panting on the counter, her body still frozen beneath his command and the plate on her abdomen. It drew out the anticipation of the moment, leaving her so damn hot she thought she might melt.

As he finished his final bite, she groaned, her body so primed and ready for whatever came next that she couldn't contain her need for another second.

He gently removed the plate, depositing it in the sink with a soft *tink*.

She didn't move, knowing he wanted her absolute submission.

Time seemed to freeze, her desire reaching a peak so near orgasm that her insides shuddered. Balthazar didn't touch her, but she felt his eyes on her, stroking every inch, evaluating his next move.

Part of her wanted to take him to the sky, to slide his cock inside her and ride him to the heavens.

But a deeper part of her wanted to remain here, slip into his arms, and indulge in the growing emotion between them.

Their bond had fully settled into place, their souls forever intertwined, and that needed to be celebrated. Embraced. Adored. *Worshipped.*

Balthazar's lips caressed the inside of her knee, the rest of him not touching her yet. Just his mouth and tongue, teasing her skin and stirring a series of goose bumps along her flesh.

She moaned, needing more.

But she knew him well.

She knew he would take his time, licking and nipping every part of her until he decided she was ready for more.

Leela allowed it, falling into his knowing touch, his mouth an alluring stroke against her skin, his tongue a familiar caress, and his teeth a teasing bite.

"B," she moaned, her climax so close without him even touching her where she desired. He left her breasts alone, as well as the sensitive space between her thighs.

Instead, he focused on every other point of her body, exploring zones few males knew existed, driving her to the brink of madness.

"Mmm, you're almost ready," he whispered, his tongue tracing the crease of her thigh up to her hip.

"More than ready," she replied, her stomach clenching hard from having to remain still for him.

"No, sweetheart." He nipped her hip bone. "I want to make you fly. Go ethereal. See those beautiful purple wings."

Her heart skipped a beat at the desire in his tone. So dark and sensual. "Do you want to fuck in the sky?"

"Only after I make you come so hard you see stars, vixen. Make you lose your mind and grip on reality. Then I'll take you so hard that you'll have no choice but to fly."

Her nipples hardened to painful points, her body so incredibly primed that she felt as though she could cry.

But he continued his sensual assault, driving her that much farther to the brink of her sanity, threatening to do exactly what he'd declared.

She vibrated, her veins humming with liquid fire. "*Balthazar.*" She'd never felt so teased in her entire existence, not even with their previous embraces.

Their playtime with the syrup paled in comparison to this. They'd been taking the edge off and preparing for the morning ahead.

Now Balthazar was ensuring she knew whom her soul had claimed, who had possessed her in kind, whom she was bound to for eternity.

And she didn't mind in the least.

Her body rejoiced in his presence, her spirit dancing in astounding relief.

Because this male was hers.

And she was his.

They were bonded forever.

By blood.

Bound to live a full life of enjoyment and love.

He kissed her then, his own mind and heart radiating the same excitement, a fact he underlined with a stroke of his tongue against hers.

Her legs spread wide as he pulled her to the edge of the counter and slid inside her.

It wasn't what she'd expected, his mouth against her flesh what she'd anticipated to feel, but it was his cock filling her to completion that he gave her instead while his mouth devoured her own.

She groaned, the sound a vibration through her torso that met the growl growing in his chest.

A combination of passion.

A frenzy of need and resounding pleasure.

Her hips lifted to meet his as she wrapped her legs around him.

Her arms encircled his neck.

And he lifted her until she was upright, their bodies flush against each other as he drove deep into her waiting heat.

"B," she whispered, lost to him.

"Fly for me," he replied, his lower body hitting her in such a way that she had no choice but to comply.

She screamed, coming undone for him as she crossed the brink of insanity, losing her mind just as he'd asked.

He continued to move inside her, drawing out the spasms, ensuring she climbed up to tumble down a second time within minutes.

It was an act of perfection.

A male who knew his mate.

A man who fucked like a king.

Her nails drew up and down his back, biting into the skin as she held on for the ride.

And then they were flying, soaring up into the clouds just like she'd suggested.

He didn't hold on tighter. He didn't tense. He just maintained his pace, driving her into a third orgasm without breaking stride.

Because he trusted her not to let him fall.

He allowed the experience to overwhelm them both, his soul and life entirely in her hands without a single concern.

And it only made her heart soar that much more for him.

Trust was the key to everything, to them, to their relationship, to the very bond they'd finally formed. And he proved that he trusted her irrevocably with his actions.

She returned the embrace and sensation, her limbs holding him tightly as they danced through the sky, their bodies mating in a manner that few had ever experienced.

A new enjoyment for them both.

A way to mark the beginning of eternity together.

A passionate affair destined for the stars.

Her arms tightened around him, her lips whispering over his. *I want to feel your seed inside me, B,* she whispered into his mind. *I need to feel you come.*

He smiled against her mouth. "We both know you could make me."

"I could," she agreed. "But I want it to be just us. Just your pleasure and mine."

He kissed her again, his movements intensifying as he dictated the pace between them, making them fly as one above the clouds.

Her wings spread out at her back, allowing them to soar, providing a proverbial bed of feathers for them to make love on.

His thumb found her clit, circling and pressing, forcing her to join him in oblivion as he thrust upward to empty himself inside her.

She screamed, the sound lost to the blue sky around them.

Her body shook and trembled, her insides spasming as she fought to hold on to her ability to fly.

It prolonged the moment, strengthened the intensity, and put their lives in her hands in a way that made her feel strong and equal to Balthazar's prowess.

*I can't wait until you have wing*s, she thought dizzily. *The things we'll do…*

He chuckled, his lips against her throat as their bodies continued to move. *I look forward to properly tasting you beneath the stars,* he whispered. *Driving my tongue deep inside you while using my wings to ensure neither of us falls.*

She quivered, the image alone nearly undoing her yet again.

But their movements were slowing, their hearts needing something softer now, something more tender than before.

Leela misted them to his bedroom in Hydria, her legs straddling his thighs as he landed on his back. She sat up and began to move, her wings on full display while he observed beneath hooded eyes.

"You're stunning," he told her, his hands roaming her curves and memorizing her beneath his palms.

She splayed her plumes out around her, allowing him to study each feather tip.

Then she took him to oblivion again, her power wrapping around them both and drawing the pleasure from their veins.

They panted afterward, falling into a heap beside one another, their tongues dancing lazily as they kissed through the last vestiges of their joint ecstasy.

"You're right," she whispered, nuzzling his neck as her wing stretched out across his torso, claiming him. "I do prefer pancakes."

His lips curled. "They're the superior breakfast food."

She nodded, her lips brushing his pulse. "You're welcome to make them for me anytime."

"How does every morning for eternity sound?"

"Like a challenge we'd both enjoy," she admitted honestly. Because that would require them to be focused enough to make breakfast every day.

"Good thing I enjoy challenges," he whispered, his palm pressing against her cheek as his thumb traced her jaw. "You'll be my favorite one of them all. To pleasure. To hold. To fuck into eternity." He grinned against her mouth. "I'll never allow you to become bored."

"I don't think such a sensation is possible in your company, B."

"I'll endeavor to ensure you never even consider it, Lee," he murmured, his mouth capturing hers in a searing kiss meant to seal them together forever.

For eternity.

For as long as they both shall live.

Which would be until the end of time.

Because Seraphim couldn't die.

Thus, their souls were destined to dance together.

"Spread your legs, sweet vixen," he hummed against her lips. "I have a vow to make between your thighs, and I intend to secure it with my tongue."

EPILOGUE

ELIZA

A FEW HOURS EARLIER

THE ELDERS LEFT LUC'S HOME ABOUT AN HOUR AGO. Eliza paced, waiting for the right minute to knock on the door.

She knew Luc had a lot on his mind between the attack, the videos of bodies falling from the sky going viral on the internet, and everything that had just happened with Stas, but Eliza *really* needed to talk to him.

He hated her and that was fine.

But he'd want to know this.

Hell, it might even convince him to like her a little. Because it certainly made her useful.

She glanced down at her fingertips, her lips twisting to the side.

Maybe it was a fluke.

Except Ezekiel had seen it, too.

Fuck, he'd *expected* it.

Death is coming, Skye had said. *Death is coming.*

452

It was Eliza she'd been talking about. And the deadly ability that had sprouted to life from her very hands.

That Seraphim had been right on top of her, about to kill her with that deadly sword—something she shouldn't have been able to see but suddenly did.

She shivered, picturing his stoic features, the lack of emotion in his eyes as he'd angled that flaming metal at her.

But she'd *caught* the magic.

Just opened her palm, absorbed it, and threw it back.

A completely instinctual response.

That had set the warrior Seraphim on fire, disintegrating him in an instant.

Skye had walked out of the tree line a moment later, nodding. "It's done," she'd said. "The bonds in your mind are fractured. Your power can finally breathe again, his control obsolete."

Then she'd fallen to the sand on a gasp, losing consciousness half a beat later.

Ezekiel had run to her, scooping her frail form up into his arms. "You have the touch of death," he'd told her before disappearing with Skye.

Eliza had blinked at where he'd just stood, then at the ash in the sand, and back at where Ezekiel had vanished with Skye. "What the fuck?" she'd breathed.

And she'd been repeating it ever since.

She'd killed a Seraphim, something that wasn't supposed to be possible.

But that dark-haired bastard certainly hadn't come back. And she'd overheard the others saying one of the Seraphim had escaped.

Not escaped, no. Dead. As in, I killed him.

She needed to tell Luc, had tried, but he'd more or less told her to fuck off.

Which, fine, she'd needed a few more minutes to gather her wits anyway. Or hours. Maybe days.

She ran her fingers through her hair, terrified and awed by what she'd done.

The power had felt invigorating, emboldening her very soul and allowing her to feel *alive*.

Does that mean I'm evil? she wondered, shivering. *To crave death must make me bad, right?*

She wasn't even sure how she'd done it. That sphere had hummed over her skin, the fiery energy calling to some hidden part of her as she'd infused some of herself into the enchantment before throwing it back.

The Seraphim's eyes had widened in shock.

And then he'd… dissolved into ash.

Maybe he would come back from it; maybe he wouldn't. But she suspected it was the latter. Something about it had felt final.

That finality was what had given her the sensation of life, as though she'd absorbed him into her somehow.

Just the notion of it gave her hives.

Because she did *not* want a Seraphim soul inside her.

I really need to talk to Luc.

She just didn't know how to approach him. Their relationship was pretty much nonexistent. He just yelled at her all the time or told her sternly what to do.

She rebelled.

Eliza had lived a life of compliance before and refused to do it again.

Something Luc failed to understand.

She was torn between wanting to kill him—a thought that held new meaning now—and fucking him. Or fucking him and then killing him.

Because she couldn't deny his sex appeal.

Those thick blond locks and startling green eyes made him a prize worth worshipping.

Something that shocked her because she'd vowed never to have sex again after everything she'd been through previously.

Yet her body burned for his every time he came near, her legs clenching as though desiring to be wrapped around his muscular hips.

A craving she longed to ignore.

He haunted her dreams, taking her repeatedly and waking her with a moan lodged in her throat. Only to realize she was alone and desiring the one man on this island who would never touch her.

She ground her teeth together. This was the last thing she needed to be thinking about.

Because I just killed a Seraphim.

Her jaw hurt from clenching it so hard, but it loosened as the door to Luc's house opened.

She expected it to be Mateo, since he'd been staying here the last few days.

The blond hair matched her expectation.

However, the tall, muscular build was all Luc.

His wide shoulders spanned the width of the door as he stepped through it. Then he closed it with a resounding click.

Eliza swallowed, the sight of him making her mouth go dry.

There was something darkly mysterious about the man, his presence one that constantly made her want to kneel. Which was why she fought him so hard. She refused to bow to anyone ever again. The Hydraian King included.

Right, she thought. *I just need to walk up there and demand a word.*

Except he was already moving and taking the path opposite to where she stood.

Sighing, she started off after him.

She'd just make sure he wasn't off to do something important like console the friends of those mourning the lives lost today—Grace, Ash, and Jordy were all well loved by their fellow Hydraians—making it very likely that he was on his way to someone who needed him more than Eliza did.

That was fine.

She'd continue to wait until he had a spare minute. Maybe he'd respect her for it.

More likely not, though.

He didn't seem to respect her at all.

A fact that grated on her nerves because she'd mostly done everything he'd asked. However, he kept treating her like a damn child, not allowing her to train or learn anything about where she fit on this island. He'd made it very clear he didn't want her here at all.

When you learn about what I did to that Seraphim, you'll feel differently, she thought.

It almost excited her, knowing that she might finally impress him.

But he might also hate her power.

It was dangerous.

And he'd probably say something about how she wasn't worthy of it, how she couldn't handle such a gift, how she was too much of a child for it.

Her eyes narrowed at the thought of all the insults he'd throw her way.

Maybe she could go tell Alik instead.

She hesitated for a breath, then shook her head.

No. Luc needs to know.

He'd probably be angry if she went to anyone else with

this. It was a wonder Ezekiel hadn't said anything yet. He was probably too busy consoling Skye.

Eliza swallowed. *This is my responsibility. I'll own it.*

Luc's steps told her he was on some sort of mission, though, so she stayed back, giving him space as she waited for the right moment to talk to him.

Which turned out to be a good thing because he halted suddenly, and had she been just a little closer, her presence behind him would have become obvious.

She stepped behind a tree, observing him with a frown. *What are you doing?*

He'd frozen midstep on the path.

Did you hear me back here?

Maybe she should announce herself and—

"Hello, Lucian," a deep voice said, the familiarity of it sending a chill down her spine.

Osiris.

A memory assaulted her of the first time they'd met.

Her body dressed in chains.

An auction for who would own her life.

His sadistic amusement at the games ahead.

She'd been so cold. So terrified. So *broken*.

Yet furious at the same time.

She'd wanted to kill every asshole in that room.

And then he used a razor to shave off that woman's skin, she thought, her heart in her stomach at the smell and sight of her being doused in alcohol before being set on fire.

Oh God… She felt sick just thinking about it.

Yet here he stood, several meters away, talking to Luc. She tried to focus on what he was saying, but the pounding in her ears made listening impossible.

What is he doing here? How is he here? What's happening?

Luc had started walking with him.

Her feet moved of their own accord, following them, her panic mounting by the second.

Why are you walking with him?

Where is he taking you?

Oh God, did he compel you?

She debated running to someone for help, but they were nearing the water's edge. No one was nearby. Only Eliza.

And the yacht anchored off the dock ahead.

A yacht Osiris appeared to be casually guiding Luc toward.

Her lips worked, a scream building in her throat. But what could she do? Yell? Would anyone be able to arrive in time?

She could try to use her power, to kill the terrifying being before her. But what if she missed and hit Luc instead?

What if it didn't even work?

What if she'd been wrong about it all along?

Luc stepped on board with Osiris right behind him.

Eliza's eyes rounded.

No. No. No.

She couldn't allow this to happen. She had to do something!

Her lips parted, a scream almost touching the tip of her tongue when the engine started.

Everything around her shifted into slow motion.

There was no time.

Luc had willingly stepped onto that yacht, no doubt compelled by the monster beside him.

I can't let this happen, she decided, darting forward. *I can't let them just disappear.*

However, the ship was already moving.

So she did the only thing she could think to do.

She darted down the dock and jumped toward the back of the yacht.

I'm going to miss—

Everything around her shifted.

The world seemed to float.

No, I'm floating.

Then her feet touched the deck.

The air seemed to shimmer around her.

With feathers.

What the fuck just happened? she thought, bewildered, then lost her footing as the yacht picked up speed.

She swallowed a yelp and jumped toward the back of the yacht, ducking behind a random chair.

Where she hid.

As Hydria disappeared behind her.

Find out what happens next in *Blood King*…

Thank you for reading *Wicked Bonds*!

Phew, Balthazar and Leela's story was a whirlwind. I hope you enjoyed the ride (pun intended ;)).

If you're curious about what happened in Brazil, you can find the story in *Elder Bonds*. It's a compilation of stories set in the Immortal Curse World. All for fun, but filled with bonus tidbits.

If you're wondering what happened between Clara and Gabriel, check out their story in *Blood Burden*—available for free with newsletter subscription.

And if you want to know what's happening between

Ezekiel and Skye, then head on over to my website to learn more about *Assassin Bonds*.

Thank you again for reading Balthazar and Leela's story. This world is my heart. <3 If you're enjoying it, please leave a review, as I love hearing your thoughts on the story and what might happen next ;)

Hugs,
Lexi

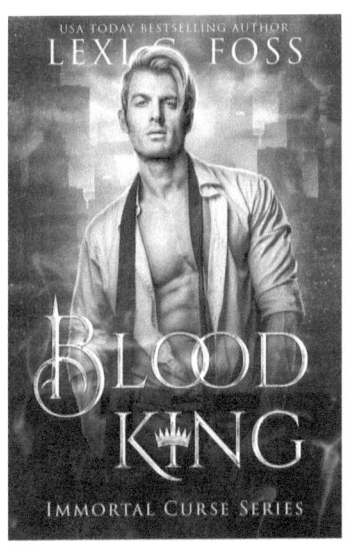

BLOOD KING

Can two broken souls find solace in each other?
Or are they destined to fight for eternity?

A dangerous leap of faith leads to a world of secrets and
truths that threaten to destroy everything Luc holds dear.
He's the Hydraian King. An immortal by birth. The oldest
of his kind. An omniscient soul destined to lead.
With knowledge comes power, but in Luc's case, the power
just might be too much.

His people are in danger.
The stakes have never been higher.
However, the female at his side may be his strongest
weapon of all.
Assuming he can tame her.

Eliza is a stowaway. A woman who followed her heart at the risk of her soul.

She only wanted to protect him. To save him. To prove her worth.

But now she's ensnared in a game of death and magic.

A war she doesn't truly understand.

And her compliance just may be the key to their salvation.

Too bad she refuses to heel.

Submission isn't an option.

Not even to the Blood King.

The High Council of Seraph has issued a new edict.

Join us and rule or remain and serve.

Which side will Eliza choose?

Author's Note: *Blood King* is book eight of the Immortal Curse series. It's strongly recommended that these books be read in order.

WICKED BONDS

MUSIC PLAYLIST

25 - The Pretty Reckless
Black Wedding (feat. Rob Halford) - In This Moment
Breathe - Fleurie & Legends of Runeterra
Can't Help Falling In Love (DARK) (feat. Brooke) - Tommee Profitt
Courtesy Call - Thousand Foot Krutch
Desire - Meg Meyers
Forever Young - Ursine Vulpine
Hallucinations - PVRIS
Hold on for Your Life (Acoustic) - Sam Tinnesz
Legends Never Die (feat. Against The Current) - League of Legends
Man on Fire - Oh The Larceny
Monarch - Fleurie
Parasite Eve - Bring Me The Horizon
Phoenix - League of Legends, Cailin Russo & Chrissy Costanza
The Comedown - Henry Jackman
The Other Side - Mustafa Avşaroğlu
The Wild Card - Really Slow Motion
There's A Hero In You (feat. Fleurie) - Tommee Profitt
Through the Fire (feat. JACSIN & Aurora Olivas) - Chromosomes

Unseelie - CLANN
Vengeance - Zack Hemsey

USA Today Bestselling Author Lexi C. Foss loves to play in dark worlds, especially the ones that bite. She lives in Chapel Hill, North Carolina with her husband and their furry children. When not writing, she's busy crossing items off her travel bucket list, or chasing eclipses around the globe. She's quirky, consumes way too much coffee, and loves to swim.

Want access to the most up-to-date information for all of Lexi's books? Sign-up for her newsletter here.

Lexi also likes to hang out with readers on Facebook in her exclusive readers group - Join Here.

Where To Find Lexi:
www.LexiCFoss.com

Also by Lexi C. Foss

Blood Alliance Series - Dystopian Paranormal

Chastely Bitten

Royally Bitten

Regally Bitten

Rebel Bitten

Kingly Bitten

Cruelly Bitten

Dark Provenance Series - Paranormal Romance

Heiress of Bael (FREE!)

Daughter of Death

Son of Chaos

Paramour of Sin

Princess of Bael

Elemental Fae Academy - Reverse Harem

Book One

Book Two

Book Three

Elemental Fae Queen

Winter Fae Queen

Hell Fae - Reverse Harem

Hell Fae Captive

Immortal Curse Series - Paranormal Romance

Book One: Blood Laws

Book Two: Forbidden Bonds

Book Three: Blood Heart

Book Four: Blood Bonds

Book Five: Angel Bonds

Book Six: Blood Seeker

Book Seven: Wicked Bonds

Book Eight: Blood King

Immortal Curse World - Short Stories & Bonus Fun

Elder Bonds

Blood Burden

Assassin Bonds

Mershano Empire Series - Contemporary Romance

Book One: The Prince's Game

Book Two: The Charmer's Gambit

Book Three: The Rebel's Redemption

Midnight Fae Academy - Reverse Harem

Ella's Masquerade

Book One

Book Two

Book Three

Book Four

Noir Reformatory - Ménage Paranormal Romance

The Beginning

First Offense

Second Offense

Underworld Royals Series - Dark Paranormal Romance

Happily Ever Crowned

Happily Ever Bitten

X-Clan Series - Dystopian Paranormal

Andorra Sector

X-Clan: The Experiment

Winter's Arrow

Bariloche Sector

Hunted

V-Clan Series - Dystopian Paranormal

Blood Sector

Vampire Dynasty - Dark Paranormal

Violet Slays

Crossed Fates

Other Books

Scarlet Mark - Standalone Romantic Suspense

Rotanev - Standalone Poseidon Tale

Carnage Island - Standalone Reverse Harem Romance